Praise for Erin Green:

'A warm, funny, uplifting writer to celebrate!'   Katie Fforde

'A lovely, heart-warming story . . . I was hooked!'
Christina Courtenay

'A delightful tale of friendship, family and love'   Jenni Keer

'Thoroughly entertaining. The characters are warm and well drawn. I thoroughly recommend this book if you are looking for a light-hearted read. 5 stars'   Sue Roberts

'Uplifting'   *Woman & Home*

'Full of humour, poignancy and ultimately uplifting this is an absolutely gorgeous read. We loved it! Highly recommended!'
Hot Brands Cool Places

'Like a scrummy bowl of Devon cream and strawberries, this is a tasty, rich and delicious summer read laced with the warmth of friendships and the possibilities of new beginnings . . . The author has the knack of making her characters spring off the pages so real that you'll care about them'   *Peterborough Telegraph*

'A pleasure to read . . . A summer breezes treat'   *Devon Life*

Erin Green was born and raised in Warwickshire. An avid reader since childhood, her imagination was instinctively drawn to creative writing as she grew older. Erin has two Hons degrees: BA English literature and another BSc Psychology – her previous careers have ranged from part-time waitress, the retail industry, fitness industry and education.

She has an obsession about time, owns several tortoises and an infectious laugh! Erin writes contemporary novels focusing on love, life and laughter. Erin is an active member of the Romantic Novelists' Association and was delighted to be awarded The Katie Fforde Bursary in 2017. An ideal day for Erin involves writing, people watching and drinking copious amounts of tea.

For more information about Erin, visit her website: **www.ErinGreenAuthor.co.uk**, find her on Facebook **www.facebook.com/ErinGreenAuthor** or follow her on Twitter and Instagram **@ErinGreenAuthor**.

By Erin Green

A Christmas Wish
The Single Girl's Calendar
The Magic of Christmas Tree Farm
New Beginnings at Rose Cottage
Taking a Chance on Love
Summer Dreams at the Lakeside Cottage

From Shetland, With Love series
From Shetland, With Love
From Shetland, With Love at Christmas
Sunny Stays at the Shetland Hotel
A Shetland Christmas Carol

Summer Dreams at the Lakeside Cottage

ERIN GREEN

REVIEW

First published in 2023 by
HEADLINE REVIEW
An imprint of HEADLINE PUBLISHING GROUP

2

Cataloguing in Publication Data is available from the British Library

ISBN 978 1 4722 9506 4

Typeset in Sabon by CC Book Production

Printed and bound in Great Britain by
Clays Ltd, Elcograf S.p.A.

Headline's policy is to use papers that are natural, renewable and recyclable
products and made from wood grown in well-managed forests and other
controlled sources. The logging and manufacturing processes are expected
to conform to the environmental regulations of the country of origin.

HEADLINE PUBLISHING GROUP
An Hachette UK Company
Carmelite House
50 Victoria Embankment
London EC4Y 0DZ

www.headline.co.uk
www.hachette.co.uk

Dedicated to those 'moments of truth' within each of our lives – when everything becomes crystal clear.

Nature does not hurry, yet everything is accomplished.

LAO TZU

Prologue

The bridal bouquet lifts high into the air against a backdrop of brilliant blue sky. The bell-shaped petals of lily of the valley tumble amidst an array of emerald foliage, with white satin ribbons fluttering behind, slowly descending towards a sea of outstretched hands – ringless and hopeful – waiting to snatch, grasp and claim this wedding honour as theirs.

A gathering of older relatives and some married friends observe from the sidelines as a group of ten wedding guests – mainly women, with a smattering of men – jostle shoulder to shoulder, hands frantically waving, whilst their undignified scrambling celebrates this age-old tradition.

Despite the designer labels, six-inch heels and perfectly coiffed hair, there are no boundaries – socially, ethically or morally – which can't be breached within this huddle. Each guest is willing the bouquet to divert from its current course, making its way into their outstretched hands. Dreaming that today will be their lucky day, filled with promises of joyful nuptials and a lifetime of happy-ever-after.

It's every woman or man for themselves.

Like a rugby lineout, we jump in unison, reaching for the prize. Though I feel it's pointless; I truly believe that whatever is intended for you won't pass you by!

Chapter One

Bath, Somerset
Sunday 20 August

Beth

A searing pain slashes through my forehead. Before attempting to open my fluttering lids, I vow never to drink again. Ever! And this time, I mean it.

I need paracetamol but lie stock-still, deciding which might prove worse. Lying here for a further ten minutes, hoping the pain will ease. Or the sheer effort and increased agony to my pounding temples, should I attempt to scramble from this bed in search of the half-used blister pack at the bottom of my suitcase. Silently, I praise myself for remembering to pack adequate supplies; I might be methodical in my professional life, caring for museum artefacts, but I'm frequently guilty of frightening lapses regarding my self-care. I'm too lethargic, so remain horizontal, eyes squeezed tightly shut, breathing deeply – ironic, given that I always sneak out of yoga class early to escape the meditation practice, hoping that no one notices.

I have no idea how much I drank, or even what I consumed, though I suspect I flouted the cardinal rule of mixing grape and grain. My plan had been to stick with the bubbly, knowing that copious amounts accelerate the onset of drunkenness; a state deemed necessary in order to survive one's hen-do. I just didn't give much consideration to this, the resulting hangover.

After five minutes, neither my patience nor controlled breathing are helping to ease my throbbing head. This is the morning after the 'big' night before – I need to face reality and take action. I definitely need paracetamol, toothpaste and hot coffee before I contemplate my next move. At least the hen-do is over and done with, which is one less thing for me to think about.

Slowly I prise my eyes open – not a pleasant task. Last night's claggy mascara is firmly welding my eyelids shut, so I blindly pinch and pluck at the dried chunks, freeing my lashes. Trampy teenage tendencies obviously haven't left me, despite my thirty-four years. Sadly, my skin will pay the price for this little misdemeanour, undoing weeks of expensive facials and detox drinks; I mourn my teenage bloom, which always bounced back to a youthful healthy flush within a day. Thankfully, I have seven days' grace in which to fully recover and bring a hint of radiance back to my cheeks. Instinctively, my thumb sweeps the inner base of my ring finger, checking my engagement ring remains in place; the gold band confirms so, which is comforting. A central garnet and diamond cluster – his birthstone romantically encircling mine – custom-made and unique to us. It isn't the ring I'd imagined receiving, but I wouldn't swap it for a solitaire – not now. Or would I?

In the mellow morning light, muted by the room's drawn curtains, I squint beneath the billowing duvet to view my silver-sequinned front. A blurry reminder of the Charleston-style dress I'd insisted on purchasing, while the rest of my bridal party sensibly hired theirs for a fraction of the price. Great! Last night's outfit accompanying last night's make-up! It seemed a 'classier' option than the proverbial net tutu and raunchy basque ensemble that so many brides-to-be choose. But on waking, I resemble a grubbier version of Party Me – like a cheaper version of a Barbie doll for the modern era.

I wiggle my toes: barefoot. At least I had the drunken sense to remove my party heels before sliding between the sheets.

I'd opted for a single room, despite the inflated price – though my ten girlfriends have doubled up, to halve their B&B costs. I didn't fancy topping and tailing on my final night of freedom. And boy, what a celebration! Bubbles, shots, cocktails, the obligatory 'truth or dare' tasks with handsome strangers, and some slightly lewd behaviour involving a five-piece inflatable boy band, who we named The Studs, amidst much squealing and crude laughter. I might have even forgiven them for ruining my Janeite joy earlier in the day. And dancing. Yes, plenty of dancing . . . and singing . . . and . . . my memory stalls, becoming somewhat hazy. I can't remember the night ending, but from past experience – be it big birthdays, graduations or Friday night catch-ups – it would have been fairly late when we staggered back here, to complete an endless round of 'goodnight, love yous' in our usual drunken fashion before retiring to our rooms. I bet no one else fell into bed fully dressed!

Seriously, my head is pounding – I need tablets. Which means moving and starting the actual day, rather than lying here and recalling blurred scenes. The very thought ignites a wave of nausea, causing me to shudder and my mouth to go all watery. No doubt I'll be fine after a fry-up, a few slices of toast and marmalade, and a pot of tea. After which, we'll all bid a hasty retreat back to our rooms to pack our overnight suitcases before our midday check-out. Boy, this dreadful hangover makes me glad we opted for a late check-out. We'll scurry back and forth, cramming our baggage into tiny car boots, overloading back seats with bodies and booty, before trundling home in a three-car procession for a hundred miles along the M3. Bath, with its beautiful Roman Spa, creamy stonemasonry and Austen vibe, will be consigned to my memory box as part of my one-night hen party, to be recalled during girlie catch-ups, just as we reminisce over other occasion.

Something brushes my bare foot! Worse still, it remains

touching; skin on skin. My eyes snap wide open. Hell's bells, no! I'm supposed to be the sole occupant of a single room.

I flip over on to my right side ... to view a body lying beside me.

A woman. And she's fast asleep. Her bare pale shoulders poke from beneath my duvet.

I draw my head back, trying to focus whilst peering through my cobwebbed vision in an attempt to name her. She's older than me. Her wavy hair is attractively coloured, in a marbled effect of marl grey and soft lilac, surrounding a cleansed, but mature complexion. My mind runs through the names in my party: Tara? Abbie? Jules? Nope, no joy. I've never met this woman before in my life – yet here I am, lying beside her in a double bed. What the hell, I'm in a double bed! My gaze lifts to inspect my surroundings. This is not the single room I left last night; mine was a budget room, complete with emulsioned anaglypta and a paper lightshade, not a palatial suite with luxuriously swagged curtains, a fancy chaise longue, a dining table with matching chairs, a marbled fireplace encircled by moss-green couches ... and this, a huge but modern four-poster bed.

Her bare arm lifts and flops over my contorted frame as I fight the instinct to holler.

'Morning,' she slurs, her eyes firmly closed.

'Who are you?' I ask rudely, having taken in my surroundings.

Her eyelids snap open, her arm retracts as if burnt, and her startled expression matches mine.

'What the hell!' she exclaims, pulling the duvet up around her neck. 'Who are you?'

I incline my head, expecting her to answer me.

'This isn't my room!' she cries, sitting upright and taking in the surroundings as I had seconds beforehand.

We both jump apart, snatching the duvet and yanking it taut between us.

'Beth,' I say, not offering my hand in the circumstances.

'I don't know a Beth.'

'And you are?' I ask, preparing for a similar response.

'Koo. Koo Bournebury.'

I shake my head, not a flicker of recognition to explain her existence in my life.

'What are you doing on my hen weekend?' I ask, deeply perturbed.

'What are you doing on mine?'

Lulu

The crick in my neck ignites an excruciating pain along my left shoulder, causing me to wince. Raising my hand, in an attempt to slowly roll my shoulder and ease the stiffness, I view my left arm swathed in black cloth. My eyes snap wider, adjusting to the unlit room, to find that I'm swathed in black fabric from chest to toes, with enough folded yardage to cover eight football pitches. Firstly, I never wear black. Ever. Secondly, where's my tutu and burlesque basque from last night – not to mention that God-awful T-shirt I was forced to wear? My hand reaches to ease my stiffened neck, only to discover that my tangle of blonde hair is also bound in fabric. My index finger traces the edge: it's tight, close-fitting and cuts into my cheeks and underneath my chin. Without moving my stiffened neck, I drag the woven fabric around and into my line of blurry vision.

I'm suddenly aware of the white moulded receptacle in which I'm lying: a roll-top bathtub! The elaborate gold taps and hand-held shower, positioned above my bare feet, catch my attention as I grapple to sit upright. As I gain a better view, my bare heel touches the metal plughole. What the hell?

I awkwardly glance left, to be greeted by a white ceramic toilet, a washbasin and, on the opposite wall, a humongous frosted shower screen. This bathroom is spotlessly clean, devoid of all belongings – simply a plush ceramic suite with a nifty black-and-white geometric tiling job. Thankfully, there is nothing and no one in here, but me. Though my budget room doesn't have an en-suite facility, and that's definitely not the teensy-weensy mirror in which I applied my make-up last night! In fact, where are my toiletries, make-up and hair brushes?

Where's my mobile? My handbag?

A wave of panic floods my veins; I've done some sorry-ass stuff in my life, but I didn't think this weekend would be added to the infamous list. If anything, I thought this weekend would be fairly tame; I was going to pace myself, act appropriately and go through the motions, as required of me. But no, it would seem I've managed to fall headlong into a situation, again! The bonus being, I don't appear to have the usual boozy hangover or even a thick head – interesting. Is this the end result when you start the night ordering from the top of the cocktail menu and work your way down the bar list? Wrapped in all this fabric, at least there was no chance of me being cold without a blanket.

I slowly twist my chin towards the panelled door, for fear of causing additional pain, and my gaze fixes upon the gold sliding lock: unfastened. Obviously, I didn't feel a sense of danger on entering the bathroom. Or falling asleep in the tub.

There's silence from the adjoining room – presuming there is an additional room – and no voices coming from outside the windows with their heavy blinds. Do I call for help? Or assume I'm on my tod?

Unceremoniously, I grab the edge of the bathtub, gingerly raising myself to a kneeling position, before feebly attempting to stand. I watch in horror as a fully shrouded nun emerges in the giant wall mirror before me, wimple and all.

'What the hell?' I gasp, my mind reeling at the vision. My

features might be staring back, but this apparition ... this isn't me! I've sinned for England – no convent would ever accept me!

Wrenching open the bathroom door, in the hope of finding reality – much like Dorothy discovering the land of Oz – I find an entirely different standard of accommodation to the budget deal I booked. Ignoring the tranquil lounge setting, in tasteful shades of muted moss-green, I view two women – either side of a ginormous four-poster bed. The mauve-haired woman is grimly clutching a duvet wrapped around her assumedly naked frame, whilst the younger redhead is barefoot and dressed as a sparkly flapper girl.

'Who the hell are you?' I demand, crossing the suite to stand at the bottom of their unkempt bed.

Both stare at me, open-mouthed, as we form a human triangle of bewilderment.

'And you are?' asks the Charleston dancer.

'I could ask the same of you,' demands the duvet-wrapped woman, before pointing accusingly at me. 'And why are you wearing my habit?'

Chapter Two

Koo

'Here's the big question – how did we get here?' I ask, buttering my slice of toast while the other two ladies sit opposite me picking at their cooked breakfasts.

I'm aware of the curious stares from other guests seated in the bustling breakfast room. We must be a sight to behold: a nun, a flapper girl and a blonde siren wearing a draped toga! Having regained my original hen-do outfit, I'd happily assisted Beth in tastefully draping Lulu in a bed sheet and persuading her 'no one will ever suspect'. She didn't wish to sport her original luminous-yellow tutu coupled with black fishnets in such a plush establishment – though in the circumstances, her slogan-emblazoned T-shirt declaring 'Looks like a beauty, drinks like a beast!' acts as a warning to others.

'I have no idea,' says Beth. 'Though surely the main question is, what's the rest of your hen party going to say?' She's looking perkier, having swallowed a couple of paracetamol provided by a kindly lady sharing our lift on the way down to breakfast. 'Let alone our fiancés. I've got a phone full of text messages I daren't answer for fear of the tongue-lashing I'll get. And if I reply only to the most patient and caring of my friends, who'll no doubt listen to me, the others will start stropping, thinking it's favouritism.'

'And mine?' adds Lulu, glancing around the busy room as if she might spot her wedding tribe seated across the way. Her hand instinctively reaches up to massage her stiff neck, which

I assume is still giving her gyp. 'You probably should reply to at least one, to let them know you're safe. Though who am I to talk? My mobile's safely stashed in my suitcase in my hotel room – because I never need it on a night out! The irony, hey?'

'Heaven knows where my phone is,' I add.

'I'm not even booked into this hotel,' adds Beth, gesturing with her knife towards the embossed ceramic salt cellar with its Royal Crescent crest. 'My party's booked into a B&B on a cheap-deal special weekend rate.'

'One of you must be – otherwise we wouldn't have a key card,' I say, knowing it's not me.

'Not me,' mouths Beth, before we glance at Lulu, finishing her flat mushroom.

'Err . . . eh, I'm staying at a budget, no-frills, room-only set-up costing twenty quid a night, called Christopher's . . . something or other. I assumed one of you was booked in here . . .' Her words fade as we shake our heads in unison. 'I'd best make the most of this breakfast then.'

Silence descends as we simultaneously munch and gather our thoughts. When did we meet up? Where are my belongings? How far is my original hotel from here? And are my hen party racing around the city searching for me?

'Have either of you got your handbag?' asks Beth, struggling to cut her crispy bacon. 'I've got my mobile, but that's only because I always push it inside my bra on nights out.'

'Nothing. I'm never without my make-up or a handbag – I feel naked,' says Lulu, biting into a whole pork sausage speared on the end of her fork and held aloft to bite.

'I have my purse, nothing else,' I say, trying to ignore Lulu's eating habits. Why she doesn't cut it up baffles me.

Our waitress delivers a jug of hot water to replenish our large teapot and we say 'thank you' in unison.

'I'm puzzled how we ended up together when we started the

evening in three different hen parties?' muses Beth, lifting the teapot lid and adding the boiling water to freshen the brew.

Finally, someone is on my wavelength!

'Forgive me for being upfront, but I've never met either of you ladies before, so I could do with establishing a few basics, so to speak.' I'm not wishing to break the pretence of friendship, having shared a bed, but needs must. Given my age and circumstances, waking up beside a stranger – especially a woman – isn't the norm for me.

'I agree. Maybe then we can piece a few details together,' says Lulu, through her mouthful of food, still waving the remnants of her speared pork sausage in the air.

I take the lead, hoping one of my breakfast companions will have a light-bulb moment.

'I'm Koo Bournebury, forty-seven years of age from Cheadle, in Cheshire. I have two grown-up sons, Felix and Felipe, and have been engaged to Judd for just over a year. This weekend was supposed to be my hen-do.'

The other two listen intently; Lulu's brow instantly furrows. Her gaze subtly lowers to my left hand, clocking my engagement ring – a canary-yellow diamond with additional sparkles set within the shoulders – before Beth picks up the metaphorical baton to introduce herself, thus denying Lulu the chance to linger on my bio.

'Beth Douglas, thirty-four years old, fiancée to Dale – we've been together for five years and engaged for four of those. Since leaving uni, I've worked as a museum archivist at Hever Castle – which I love with a passion. No children and one springer spaniel called Hugo. My hen-do too,' she says, quickly adding, 'Kent. I grew up in Kent.'

We turn towards Lulu, witnessing her hesitancy. Granted, she's wearing a bed sheet tacked together using the complimentary sewing kit found in the en suite – but still, she needs to speak up.

'And you, Lulu?' I prompt, having clocked her ringless left hand.

'Lulu James, a supermarket checkout gal from Kettering. Twenty-five, no children, no dog, no passion for my job, but I am pretty nifty on a till.'

'Hen-do?' asks Beth.

Lulu blushes, tilts her head slightly, before pursing her lips. 'Kind of. A hen party . . . but not mine. My cousin Kirsty's, in fact. Though I am the maid of honour who planned every infinitesimal detail on her behalf – for all the thanks it got me!'

'OK, two brides and a maid of honour – interesting,' I mutter, more to myself than the others.

'And neither of you remember losing your respective parties, or us meeting up?' asks Beth. 'Because . . . I don't,' she admits, her expectant expression switching between us. 'I remember starting the night with cocktails, we moved around from bar to bar, but then . . . nothing – I'm blank. I must have drunk far more than I normally would.'

I shake my head, and Lulu copies my action.

'How embarrassing,' sighs Lulu, her brown eyes glistening. 'I worked my ass off, planning and organising Our Kirsty's big weekend, and I'm not even on it!'

'Same here,' says Beth, with feeling. On seeing our interest she continues, 'I chose the world's worst maid of honour – she was utterly useless. Please don't judge me for admitting it, but I felt duty-bound to pick her, and I've paid the price ten-fold. She's a dear friend who I thought would be honoured to receive the title, and step up to the plate. Sadly, she didn't – though she wore her sparkly tiara with such pride.'

'Nah, they rarely do. Lifelong besties automatically selecting each other never works – they often fall at the first hurdle,' says Lulu, adding bitterly, 'it sounds like a dream job, but actually . . . it's the pits. The time constraints, the endless appointments, never-ending queries, constant demands – not to mention the problems caused by friends and family who RSVP, and then say they can't attend at the last minute. It's like taking on an unsalaried job for a year. Two years, if you're really unlucky! You need to pick carefully, otherwise it'll backfire on you.'

'Surely that depends on your bride-to-be?' I ask, swimming in unknown territory. I haven't got a maid of honour – or ever been elected as one.

Both ladies pull downcast expressions and shake their heads vehemently.

'I assume you were delighted with your own performance?' I ask Lulu, interested to hear more.

'Seriously? Do you see me seated amongst thirty females sharing a family resemblance, teenage memories, or hair of the dog?' asks Lulu, gesturing around the breakfast room with her knife.

'Nope,' I say, shaking my head, causing my wimple to chafe.

'Well then! I've totally ballsed up – on the final hurdle, rather than the first. But how?' rants Lulu.

Neighbouring guests are starting to glance disapprovingly in our direction, alerted by her shrill tone and choice of words.

'And that's what we need to figure out,' suggests Beth. 'Once we've made contact with our parties. They must be worried sick – wrong of me not to have answered before now,' she murmurs, pulling her mobile from her cleavage and busily tapping the screen.

'I hope mine haven't informed the police,' I add, knowing how security conscious my family are.

'I hope mine have; I'll be gutted if they haven't even noticed I'm missing,' says Lulu, before adding, 'though I've no way of contacting them.'

'You can borrow my phone, in a second,' offers Beth, glancing up whilst busily texting.

Lulu shakes her head. 'Totally useless unless you've got my contacts list too. I don't know a single phone number any more, not even my parents'.'

'Same here,' I add. I always suspected speed-dialling would be a slippery slope leading to this moment in my life.

'Nobody's?' questions Beth, swiping her screen closed before dropping the phone into her sequinned lap.

'Unless you count the elderly parents of my best friend from school, who still live next door,' sighs Lulu. 'Now, their number I definitely know!'

'Surely, they'll oblige with a quick nip round to your parents?' says Beth, before turning to me. 'And you, Koo. How about a quick message via social media to one son or the other – would that help you out?'

'Sure – if I was on social media. I'm not one for techno-stuff or Facebook postings. My lads take care of computers, phones and tablets for me.'

'I used to do Facebook but not any more,' says Lulu.

'Scuppered then!' sighs Beth.

'We are – you aren't,' declares Lulu sulkily, turning to me. 'I doubt you'll ever be stuck, wearing a rock that big!'

Cheeky mare! I ignore her remark, just as Beth's phone bleeps. I'm half expecting her to draw her mobile from her lap and begin reading the text, but no. She picks up her teacup and slowly begins to sip. We watch intently, witnessing her introspective pause. I'm not convinced there's much tea left, given the delicate size of the chinaware, but I wait until she puts down the empty cup under our steady gaze.

'What's up?' asks Lulu, obviously as curious as I am.

'Ah, well. That's the issue,' says Beth, cautiously. 'I'm not entirely sure that I want to read their replies – let alone try to explain myself.'

Beth

The smiley reception lady listens patiently, without interruption, as we huddle around her desk straight after breakfast. My petite stature makes it difficult for me to lean over the marble reception desk to stare at the booking details. Thankfully, Koo takes charge, probing her for answers.

'That's definitely my address, my credit card details and scrawly signature, so it's case closed. Upon our late-night arrival, it appears I booked the suite – for how many nights?' asks Koo, smiling at the uniformed lady, who appears to be non-judgemental at our plight and outlandish outfits. She reminds me of a highly polished member of cabin crew – a grounded one, if there is such a thing.

'Two nights, madam,' she swiftly replies.

'And may I ask the tariff?'

I want to plug my ears, but daren't. I rapidly assess the high-spec decor of our suite, our breakfast experience, and the luxurious location in which we find ourselves.

'A two-night stay totalling three thousand and two hundred pounds, madam – including breakfast,' comes her professional reply.

'Oh bugger!' mutters Lulu, drawing back from leaning over the reception desk.

'Ouch!' says Koo, bravely taking it on the chin.

'Holy moly,' slips from my lips, an expression rarely uttered by me, but fitting, in the presence of a nun.

The reception lady doesn't flinch at our reactions, nor at the resounding *bleep* coming from my cleavage.

'We'll sort it,' I add, patting Koo's arm sympathetically. 'Don't you worry.'

'Go Dutch, you mean?' asks Lulu, her peaches-and-cream complexion paling further, if that's possible.

'Yeah. Don't worry, Koo – between us, we've got this,' I reassure her, secretly relieved that I've mislaid my purse and cards so didn't drunkenly zap or tap that amount to my magnetic strip. Though I've foolishly done just that, many times before, on nights out, so I know exactly how Koo is feeling. And she's holding up well, in my opinion.

'Anyway,' says Lulu, sidestepping the booking shock, 'did we arrive together or separately?'

The reception lady scans her computer screen. 'Three breakfasts were ordered during check-in.'

'That answers that then,' mutters Lulu disparagingly.

I throw her a look; I don't get her attitude. If we're in this together, there shouldn't be any passing the buck! She might be somewhat younger than us – but grow up!

'And checkout tomorrow is at what time?' asks Koo, suddenly coming alive, requesting the essential details.

'Eleven o'clock,' replies the smiley lady. Her composure throughout has been impeccable; I can't imagine this establishment has welcomed many customers resplendent in fancy dress whilst questioning their own arrival time. Or is this kindly deference the perk of accompanying a nun?

'Perfect,' replies Koo.

'Right you are,' adds Lulu.

'Fine,' I say, wanting to convey complete acceptance, though I'd have little objection to it being sooner if it reduced our bill.

'Thank you for your help,' says Koo, before striding away from the reception area with more spring in her step than I could ever muster under such circumstances.

I hastily follow, with Lulu in hot pursuit, as my mobile chirps again.

'Koo, please don't panic. We'll get this sorted between the three of us,' I say, heading towards the lift.

Lulu is eagerly nodding but I'm not convinced that she's fully on board with easing Koo's dilemma.

'I'm not worried,' says Koo, pressing the call button. 'Marginally baffled that I can spend such an amount and not remember a bloody thing – now, that seriously pisses me off – but I'm not worried in the slightest.'

The lift arrives immediately, offering a welcome distraction. We enter, turn and stand apart, in a choreographed manner, waiting for the doors to close.

'Koo, it might take me a while on what I earn, but I'll pay you back every penny. My mum says I'm not a good saver, but I'm a great pay-you-backer!' announces Lulu proudly, between floors one and two.

I watch the brief exchange in the lift's mirror-lined interior.

'Thanks, but please don't worry yourself,' is Koo's only remark.

'Me too,' I add, afraid of being labelled a cheapskate based on Lulu's renewed vow.

'We need to figure out what we can each remember, and then attempt to contact our girlfriends,' suggests Lulu, as a resounding *ding* announces our arrival on the third floor. 'And you, lady – you need to answer those text messages. Otherwise we'll be needing an explanation.'

I suddenly feel awkward, shifting my stance and staring at the non-slip floor, only to mutter, 'It's complicated.' Or is that stating the obvious?

Lulu

I'm standing before the open window, my makeshift toga-dress rippling in the gentle breeze, overlooking the stunning view of the Georgian crescent and parkland stretching beyond. It's simply breathtaking. But, more importantly, it's being enjoyed by many people, supposedly tourists and locals alike, all strolling, playing games and enjoying the morning sunshine. Having spent my entire life in a market town, I didn't know city living could be so wholesome.

'Bath's a city, right?' I ask, over my shoulder, addressing the nun and the flapper girl.

They are each perched on one of the moss-green couches. Beth's on her phone, Koo looks deep in thought.

'I believe so,' answers Beth, without looking up, her thumbs working ten to the dozen.

I turn back around, absorbed in my musing. Somewhere out there, amongst the throng of streets and tourists, is a party of twenty-nine women heading towards the ultimate pamper experience at Bath's Thermal Spa for their ten o'clock time slot. If I run, literally tear-arse it down each street at full pelt, I could meet them, to complete the booking for thirty people. With a few well-chosen excuses, all will be forgotten ... but – and I mean this honestly, without malice or jealousy – I really can't be arsed. Could. Should, but won't. I'd prefer to stand here, overlooking a gorgeous landscape, taking in the beauty alongside my two new friends, rather than spend a single moment with ...

'Aren't either of you concerned about your parties checking out without you?' I ask, turning to address each, fearing to complete my internal monologue. 'It must be nearly time,' I add.

'Mmmm, it's not really my problem,' says Koo, checking her watch. 'There's no overnight stays for my ladies, more a series of events with various guest lists.'

'Possibly,' mutters Beth, engrossed in her mobile screen.

'Bath's hardly a huge place; surely, we could each locate and rejoin our party within the hour? I know where I'm supposed to be – after all, I made the booking.'

'And me,' says Beth.

'Likewise, I know the itinerary off by heart,' confesses Koo.

'Why aren't we, then?' I ask, turning my back on the glorious view, glancing from one woman to the other, across the expanse of luxurious carpet separating the couches. I can see the cogs churning behind their vacant expressions, much like mine, but no one speaks; we continue to stare, waiting for one another to answer.

Aeons pass before Koo says, 'Because I don't want to. I never wanted a crappy hen night. My family sent me on a guilt trip weeks ago, forcing me to agree to this weekend of activities organised through an events company. Then Saturday night arrives, with our laminated itinerary in hand, my girlfriends ply me with drink, shove me into a nun's outfit, before demanding I start having fun, bang on six o'clock, not a minute sooner, by lining up three cosmopolitan cocktails to be downed in under a minute. That's not my idea of fun!'

Beth is nodding her agreement frantically from the other couch, having finally looked up from her phone.

Koo adds, 'And it's cost me a bloody fortune, to add insult to injury!'

'Same here,' says Beth. 'I never asked for this. Tara, my supposed maid of honour, didn't even ask if I had a preference about a location, she simply booked the accommodation, collected and paid the deposits, and then did bugger all afterwards. I thought Bath was all Jane Austen and historical settings, which feeds into my love of history, so I booked the literary walking tour. My party weren't interested in listening to our guide, they just wanted to get hammered – hardly my ideal hen night! The Charleston dresses, for the evening, were my insistence. We all love The Great Gatsby – and I knew the girls wouldn't have donned Austen petticoats and bonnets.'

'Mine simply pleased themselves, under the guise of giving

me a bloody good send-off, when I know full well that . . .' Koo falters.

'Know what?' I ask, intrigued to hear all.

'They don't give a sod!'

'Of course they do!' I reply, without thinking, much like a chiming clock responding to the hour hand.

'Oh, please! There's no point saying otherwise. Given my age, it's all old hat to them – they've been there, done that, worn their hen party T-shirt, years ago – several have celebrated their silver wedding anniversaries already.'

'Mine are the same, Koo. Last night, my hens put more effort into getting sozzled than they ever did into attending any of the dates I organised for their bridesmaid fittings, make-up rehearsals or hair appointments – all of which I've paid for,' says Beth, a twinge of sadness cracking her voice. 'This here – relaxing and being together, as we are – would have been my idea of a hen weekend. But I simply wasn't given a choice.'

I get where they're coming from. I've seen similar responses from Our Kirsty's bridesmaids – for which I've picked up the slack, each time they've failed to meet the grade.

'Everyone's so keen to accept a role when initially asked, but very few are prepared to complete the tasks they're assigned, apart from me. The "wanna-be-involved" brigade was my secret name for Our Kirsty's bunch,' I say, having found common ground with my two companions.

'Apparently, I've been AWOL since half ten, or so their text messages say. They retraced their steps to the previous bar, thinking I'd got lost wandering off to join the queue for the ladies' toilet. They're pretty annoyed, and rightfully so, they must have been worried sick about me,' explains Beth, turning her screen to show us the numerous text messages.

'Which is to be expected,' I say, trying to be fair. 'But what did they hope for? If they didn't deliver a decent night out, but

got themselves trolleyed, without making any attempt to tailor
the night around what you like doing!'

'What's it to be, ladies? Shall we stay here, as we are, and
glean some enjoyment and escapism from this weekend? Or quit
this place, convey our sincere apologies, and meet up with our
original parties?' asks Koo. She glances between us, awaiting
confirmation.

'Stay,' insists Beth, without a moment's hesitation.

'Us three,' I say, gesturing between us. 'Though I'll need to
find my handbag.'

Koo's angelic face breaks into a beaming smile framed by her
wimple. With her mauve hair hidden, she looks quite serene.

'We'd best get organising ourselves and save them any more
unnecessary worry . . .' Koo roars with laughter. 'What are we
like – absconding from our own hen parties?'

'Not all of us!' I say, guiltily.

'Technically, you are, given that you've planned the lot!' says
Beth, joining Koo in raucous laughter.

'I suppose.' My words sound hollow, but deep down I know
it's a whole lot more complicated than that.

Chapter Three

Koo

Never before have I entered Marks and Sparks, the moment the store opens, dressed as a nun to purchase lacy underwear. The cashier's polite but quizzical expression tells me it isn't a regular occurrence – nor the toga queen and flapper girl accompanying me as we approach her counter.

'I'm not one for Marks' undies,' whispers Lulu, holding aloft the tiny hanger displaying her chosen knickers, before adding them to our undies pile. 'I'd much prefer . . .'

'Beggars can't be choosers,' snipes Beth, glancing around me to view Lulu. 'I'm grateful to have a fresh change, and for Koo's generosity.'

'I'm not complaining. I'm just saying – their designs aren't always to my taste,' retorts Lulu, lowering her voice as if the cashier might take offence at her opinion.

I smile at Beth's expression – agog, mid-gasp. Her features are so expressive; there's no hiding her thoughts when her face gives the game away.

'I'm grateful too, please know that, Koo. I'll pay back every penny,' adds Lulu.

'I know,' I say, opening my purse to retrieve my credit card. 'I'm sure undies are the least of our worries. We're each going to need a complete new rigout.'

'Koo, you can't possibly buy everything,' says Beth, as our purchases are swiftly zapped through the till.

'Are you dressing like that all weekend then?' I ask, knowing I can't wait to ditch this wimple, despite the unexpected delight of shocking the general public. All morning, I've wondered if a real wimple chafes as much?

'Not really, but it seems so frivolous, especially when my luggage is stashed somewhere else in the city,' says Beth. 'Wouldn't it be cheaper to collect our belongings?' she adds.

Lulu agrees with an eager nod, as our fresh undies are piled neatly and placed inside an M&S carrier bag.

'Sure. But it's all or nothing right now. I'll look weird changing into civvies to accompany you pair, if you remain dressed as you are,' I say, tapping my credit card on the card reader. 'How much of your wardrobe did you pack? Two outfits at the most?'

'Very true,' says Lulu, glancing at our current attire.

'What's it to be?' I ask Beth, taking the proffered receipt and bag from our cashier.

'Well, when you put it like that . . .' she says. 'Are you sure you're OK to stand us for this amount as a loan?'

'I'm certain.' I don't elaborate, it really isn't necessary.

It takes all of thirty minutes for us to select three simple but complete outfits from the extensive womenswear department on the floor below. It feels like a treat to be doing everyday stuff that other women – 'normal' women, as I call them – do. It certainly makes a change from my usual shopping routine and store appointments, when outfits are selected, delivered for approval and simply returned by my PA, if they aren't suitable. What my boys wouldn't have given to enjoy this level of freedom when they were little! Browsing an entire range, selecting off the peg, trying on and then deciding. I've few regrets about raising Felix and Felipe in my chosen manner, but the seductive convenience of private appointments is definitely one of them. It felt like saving time, when the reality was that it deprived my sons of an array of family experiences growing up. They had anything money could buy, yet missed out on the luxury of normality. Instantly, I feel guilty at recalling long-forgotten memories; if I had my time again, I'd do things so differently. Though despite our close bond, and now aged twenty-four and twenty-six, they wouldn't thank me for reminding them of my past mistakes.

I chase away my motherhood demons by pocketing my credit card before we nip into the changing rooms, where we swiftly disrobe. We depart the store transformed, as three stylish women, with our hen-do costumes stashed safely inside logoed carrier bags.

The morning sunshine highlights the surrounding Georgian architecture, the pale buttery stonework and elaborate decoration on every lintel and window ledge, adding a theatrical feel to our impromptu shopping spree.

'That feels much better,' I announce as we walk, three abreast, joining the throng of Sunday shoppers on Stall Street, albeit still wearing our party shoes to curb an additional expense. 'Nothing beats that new bra feeling!'

'I agree, though it's slightly hampered by carrying last night's undies through the streets,' says Lulu, visibly cringing. 'I can't imagine your Jane Austen got up to such frivolous behaviour on a Sunday morning.'

Beth and I cease walking to stare intently at her.

'I wrapped mine in a tissue and discreetly dropped them into the changing room bin,' says Beth.

'And me,' I add, as our lingering stares slowly descend towards Lulu's carrier bag.

'No one said!' exclaims Lulu, holding her carrier bag away from her side as if it doesn't belong to her.

'Remind me not to help you unpack your bags,' chides Beth.

'Cheers,' snipes Lulu, sulkily. 'That leaves me walking around a beautiful Roman spa city with a yucky memory attached to it. Can it get any worse?'

'You'll feel better once we've collected our belongings!' says Beth, looking around at the busy pedestrian walkway. 'Though I don't fancy the argument that might occur in the process.'

'Me neither,' I add.

'I'll be dead meat, that's for sure,' bemoans Lulu. 'Our Kirsty has been planning this weekend inside her head for years. But you pair . . . surely, you get to choose whether you stay or go?'

'You think?' sighs Beth, narkily. 'Hardly a weekend planned around my interests, was it? And now, I have to face the girls, explain my actions and hear their opinions, before attempting to wrangle my belongings from the B&B unscathed. I feel somewhat selfish, I must admit.'

'You don't have to face anyone. I'll collect your stuff,' I say, linking arms with Beth as a means of showing camaraderie and support. 'Lulu can collect mine, and you can collect hers – it'll avoid any unpleasantness or emotional scenes, and allows your friends to travel home feeling reassured that you're safe and sound.'

'Precisely!' says Lulu, peering around me at Beth, on my right side, who is schtum and open-mouthed.

'Come on, you know it makes sense, let's get a wiggle on – we've got a hen weekend to salvage,' I say, striding forward towards the Roman baths.

Beth

I feel awful. It's like being a child without pocket money queuing alongside your mates at the school tuck shop. You know they won't leave you out. You're dying for a Mars bar, and you'll definitely pay them back, but you still feel awkward accepting their generous offer.

'Relax, Beth,' says Koo. 'You've called the B&B, they're getting your things ready, and in thirty minutes, I'll nip over in a taxi to collect them. It might seem strange to you, but for the hotel reception staff it's just a routine request. I thought we agreed earlier that you and Lulu would do the same?' Koo is sipping her champagne, delivered courtesy of room service a mere ten minutes ago, on the pretext that we're still on our hen-dos, supposedly.

'We did,' confirms Lulu. She is stretched out on a chaise longue positioned before our spectacular view of the crescent below, and looking decidedly more comfortable sipping her bubbly than I feel. It appears my vow never to drink again lasted all of three and a half hours – thankfully, my hangover didn't make it past breakfast.

'It's just me, I'm such a stickler for doing the right thing in life. I feel as if we're taking advantage. After all, we know very little about . . .'

'Each other?' asks Koo.

'What more is there to know? We were each forced to attend a hen-do we'd rather not be at, so we escaped. Simple, it was fate,' explains Lulu, summarising in a nutshell.

'Yes, but we haven't even established how . . .' I gesture between us, squirming under their intent gaze, before continuing, '. . . all this came about. When and where did I meet you pair?'

'Does it matter? I'm grateful for small mercies,' announces Lulu, her nonchalant tone irking me, but not nearly as much as when she tips her glass in Koo's direction, as if complimenting our generous host.

'Actually, it does matter – to me anyway,' I say, sounding a little terse. I don't attempt to backtrack on my reaction but notice Koo's fleeting glance; she's heard my frustration.

'Lulu, you go first and tell us what you remember,' says Koo, offering me a reassuring smile, a subtle sign of forging an alliance. It's not meant as a put-down towards Lulu, but the age difference definitely shows.

'Our Kirsty's posse are on a tight budget,' explains Lulu, 'so

we downed two-for-one cocktails at Turtle Bay, before nipping
into Maccy D's for a quick bite to help line our stomachs. We
were supposed to be heading for a night of dancing at a club that
had been recommended earlier in the day, but we got sidetracked
by a stag-do playing body shots with tequila. The rest . . . well, I
don't remember. Though I recall being ticked off that our night
of dancing fell through – I really fancied a night strutting my
stuff on the dance floor. Lord knows where my original group
disappeared to, or when I bumped into you two – so yeah, that's
my hazy summary of last night.' Lulu finishes, sipping her drink
without a care in the world.

'See, we didn't do Turtle Bay,' says Koo. 'Nor MacDonald's,
because mine was organised as a private do within the hotel. My
party didn't need to leave the premises – everything we had was
pre-ordered, on tap and organised by the events company. The
hotel staff couldn't do enough for us.'

'A conference room or in-house restaurant?' asks Lulu,
glancing at Koo, though the relevance is baffling.

'Neither, to be fair. Anyway . . . unless you pair wandered in
and joined us, I can't see how we'd have crossed paths,' continues
Koo, ignoring Lulu slurping the dregs from her champagne flute.
'I didn't need to leave the building all evening.'

Both ladies wait for me to recite my remembered itinerary,
which I can hardly forget; I planned every aspect, thanks to Tara
not playing ball as my maid of honour.

'After Tara booked the hotel rooms, then bailed from her
duties, I organised the basics for a weekend away. I'd have pre-
ferred to cancel but we'd have lost our deposits if we pulled out,
so I had little choice. We started with the Austen walking tour,
followed by afternoon tea in a quaint coffee house, which was
nice but pricey. Then nipped back to the B&B for showers, plus
the full regalia of hair and make-up for a night on the town. We
did the full works: enjoying cocktails galore in a swish venue,

downing sickly-sweet shots in a neighbouring bar, visited a gin palace tucked along a quaint side street ... I do remember dancing till my feet ached and then carrying a tray of sambuca shots through a crowded bar, before someone had the bright idea of lighting them despite loud protests from the bar staff, and ... then it's a blank. I must have passed out.' My memory grinds to a halt as my two accomplices hang on my every word, patiently awaiting the lifting of my fog just like theirs. 'There were no body shots, no gate crashing hotel gatherings, and certainly no male strippers, though we were accompanied by an inflatable boy band with five identical expressions.'

'For someone who didn't want a hen-do, you sure made the most of it, Beth,' teases Lulu, pulling a comical expression in Koo's direction.

'What would you know?' I snap, frustrated by her less than funny remark in the circumstances.

'Hey, h-hold your horses, there's no need to jump down my throat,' stutters Lulu, clearly stunned by my response. 'We're all in the same boat, so to speak. We've all messed up – one way or another.'

I quickly rein in my irritation; Lulu might not be a bride but she's obviously witnessed the stress her cousin's been under.

'I'm just saying, you've no idea of the actual stress and pressure I've been under in recent weeks, or months even, and yet you make flippant remarks, as if ...' I stall, fiddling with my champagne flute, wishing I wasn't so honest, or snappy.

'Go on, Beth. We're listening, but first let me top up your bubbles,' says Koo, grabbing the champagne bottle from the ice bucket and crossing the lounge area to where I'm sitting curled against the arm of my couch.

'Here. Now you can begin,' she whispers, refilling my glass.

'Thank you.' I take a long sip before speaking. 'Our wedding is next Saturday, at two o'clock—'

'And mine,' interrupts Koo, a look of delight etched on her face. 'And Our Kirsty's.'

We eyeball each other in amazement.

'The twenty-sixth is a busy date – a nice coincidence though,' adds Koo.

'The last weekend of August is always a popular choice, or so Our Kirsty keeps telling me,' adds Lulu, holding her glass aloft for a top-up, which Koo obligingly does without hesitation, before asking, 'So, what's the issue?'

'Dale had his stag weekend a month ago, a typical boys-on-tour weekend away in Newcastle, filled with beer and banter – nothing outlandish. Whereas I put this weekend off for as long as I could because . . . well, I simply couldn't . . . I mean, I didn't want to . . . I just did.' I bail, ahead of my confession.

I crumble a little inside at the thought of revealing the truth. Because the minute I put my thoughts into words, it'll be out there, and I won't be able to erase what I've said aloud. I don't want to admit it, but needs must, because right now these women are assuming they know me. And they don't. I roll my lips together as if preventing the words from spilling forth.

'Out with it,' urges Koo, resettling herself on the opposite couch, glass in hand.

'I don't think I want this wedding.' There, I've said it aloud, after eighteen months of planning, admittedly not to the right people, but job done!

There is a stunned silence as I stare at their faces. Neither utters a word. Surely, they heard me? Please don't make me repeat it.

'Me too,' whispers Koo. 'I want to be married to Judd, but I don't want the wedding that's been planned. My family have taken over, and it's nothing like I imagined for us.'

'Nor me . . . well, Our Kirsty's,' mouths Lulu.

'Pardon?' I say, my head twisting in different directions as each woman speaks, to see two guilty faces staring back at me.

'Go on, Beth – we're listening,' urges Koo, gently. 'Our stories can wait.'

I take a deep breath. 'Sorry, for how this sounds, it's all jumbled inside my head. Initially, I thought it was nerves, something every bride goes through. I imagined it was normal to have doubts and wobbly moments at the prospect of committing yourself to one man for the rest of your days. But months ago, I realised the true reason . . .' I pause, again – knowing the next line needs to be said but will make me sound like a terrible person. 'Despite loving him dearly, I'm not sure if Dale is "the one" for me.'

Lulu

Did Beth say what I think she said? I stare at Koo, awaiting her reaction so I can gauge my own response.

'Full marks for your honesty, Beth. That takes some courage,' says Koo, gulping down her bubbles before continuing. 'I'm not too proud to admit that I'm dreading the idea of next Saturday too, for different reasons though. You've done the hardest part, Beth – admitting it. Lulu's right, maybe it's fate that has brought us together. I'm relieved, actually.'

Beth is now dumbstruck and staring too.

'Beth, are you OK?' I ask. She visibly shakes herself to revive her thoughts, and returns to the present moment. This is all pretty surreal.

'I thought I'd come clean but never expected that you . . .' she points at Koo, before continuing, 'are in the same boat. Seriously, I don't know whether to laugh or cry!'

'It's no laughing matter, but it's definitely the easier option,' Koo replies, raising her empty glass as if to perform a toast.

'I keep telling myself, I've simply got cold feet,' declares Beth, as if she's on a roll, now that she's begun to come clean.

I follow Koo's lead and nod sympathetically. It's not my place to judge, having never reached the bridal stage in the game of life. And judging from my own situation, I'm unlikely to.

'I agreed to this . . . well, not *this* precisely, but the hen-do thing, as I thought it would help to settle my doubts, maybe ignite something inside me, confirming I'm doing the right thing. Having a hen weekend felt like a rite of passage – so I was cajoled into it, at the beginning. It's been like a runaway train gathering speed. Everyone else got so excited at the prospect of a wedding and so invested in the details of our planning, I've been carried away in their rush of happiness . . . but forgotten my own.'

'And now?' asks Koo, fleetingly glancing in my direction, probably as a polite way of including me.

'I don't know how to stop the wedding train and jump off,' declares Beth, her brow furrowing deeply. 'Worse still, I'm not entirely sure if I want to get off! One minute I do, the next I don't. I honestly thought this weekend would squash my fears, banish my nerves, and I'd return home knowing I want to get married to Dale on Saturday – but that hasn't happened!'

'Does anyone else know?' I ask, feeling obliged to contribute something to justify my presence.

Beth shrugs.

'Have you actually said this to Dale?' asks Koo.

'No, but that doesn't mean he or others don't suspect. I mean right now, given my absence at my own hen-do – I think they'll realise something is wrong with the bride-to-be!'

'Likewise. Though I have a funny feeling it's not me my tribe will be missing, but hey!' mutters Koo, more to herself than us. 'Anyway, what do you want to do, Beth?'

She simply shrugs again.

'Uh-uh, shrugging is not an option, lady,' says Koo, reaching for the champagne bottle and pouring a round of refills.

'I want this ... them ... to simply disappear – *poof*, gone!' Beth's fingers wiggle, suggesting a magical vanishing.

'That's settled then. You don't want *this* and you didn't want Bath. And you, Lulu?' Koo turns an expectant expression in my direction.

'Me?' I'm stunned she's turned the spotlight on me after Beth's confession.

'Yes, you! You might not be a bride-to-be but you still get a vote,' urges Koo.

'I'd prefer to stay with you pair. I reckon my so-called tribe can survive another night without me. I printed out their itinerary multiple times, completed every imaginable detail, and prepaid every booking!'

I pretend not to notice their swift exchange of glances; whoever heard of a matron of honour who doesn't wish to honour her bride – especially having completed all the hard work? Yeah, exactly that!

'That's sorted then!' announces Beth, her breezy manner returning after the relief of her confession. 'Though I'm expected at work tomorrow.'

'Easy. Pull a sickie – you can call your boss in the morning,' offers Koo, waving a dismissive hand, as she tops up each glass.

'Do you not want to talk about it?' I ask, carefully trespassing into Beth's territory.

'Right now? Not really! But thanks for the offer, Lulu.'

'Best drink up then, because we need to reclaim our clobber and let your girlfriends get the hell out of here,' says Koo, slinging the empty bottle upside down in the ice bucket.

The centre stage spotlight remains on Beth; I have no wish to reclaim it, so I hastily gulp the remnants of my bubbles. This is not the weekend I had planned.

Our Kirsty is going to kill me.

Chapter Four

Koo

'Any chance you could wait for a return journey?' I ask the taxi driver, just after midday, as he draws up outside the address scribbled on my slip of paper in Beth's handwriting.

'Sure, but the meter will be running, lady,' he replies, half turning in his seat to answer over his shoulder. I note his aged hound-dog expression, his flat tone, and assume he's been doing this job for a lifetime.

'No worries, I'm fine with that. There'll be a tip for you,' I say, climbing out of the rear seats to stand before an aging box-like establishment. A private venture typical of most cityscapes, where a cheap bed and convenient transport links are given more thought than a much-needed face-lift to the drab exterior. It's not exactly hidden from view within this beautiful city, but understandably won't be appearing on any glossy postcards. Beth said the reception area looks swish, but beyond that it's all anaglypta and painted woodchip in the rooms.

Collecting each other's belongings was supposed to be a means of saving face and avoiding confrontation, but now, I'm nervous. I felt for Beth earlier, trying to be brave and honest about her reasons – I wanted to magic all her troubles away – but life's not like that, is it? I shove Beth's crumpled address into my pocket and proceed through the tinted glass doors into an enormous foyer and a never-ending reception desk, behind which stand male and female receptionists and a uniformed porter, complete with regulation smiles.

I've hardly had a chance to enter and cross the polished yet cracked tiles before I'm addressed.

'Good morning. How may I help you?' calls the lady, her polyester pussy-cat bow sitting high beneath her chin.

'Good morning,' I say, heading directly for her, hoping for a little understanding and compassion between females. 'I'm here to collect the belongings of Beth Douglas . . . she was staying in room . . .' I don't finish my sentence, as a flicker of something eclipses the young woman's expression.

'We've had instructions to stow her suitcase ready for collection. Your name, please?' Her voice is efficient, almost verging on robotic, suggesting her customer service training was conducted whilst employed in a larger, more commercial venture.

'Koo Bournebury.'

The young woman gives a fleeting nod before disappearing into a rear storage area and swiftly returning, trundling a maroon wheelie case.

'If housekeeping find anything else – we'll be in touch.'

I'm impressed; that was easy-peasy, almost regimental in its completion. I only hope Lulu is having a similar experience collecting my suitcases.

'Can I ask . . . are the party still here?' I ask, glancing towards an adjoining bar area.

'No. Ms Douglas' party checked out – you just missed them leaving.'

'All of them?'

She gives a brief nod, her lips pursed. She's keeping it professional, but I'm guessing she knows the full story.

'Did they leave a message for her?'

'Not here at the desk,' she says, straightening the worn cuff of her uniformed jacket. 'Will that be all?'

'The bill is accounted for, I presume?'

'Fully paid in advance, madam.'

'Well, there's nothing more – thank you for your help,' I say, taking hold of the suitcase's extended handle and exiting, hoping that my taxi driver is as good as his word.

Beth

The words had spilt from my lips before I realised and now, twenty minutes after my wobble, I wish I could retract them. How unkind of me to actually say it aloud. Dale deserves better than a reluctant fiancée, let alone a runaway bride-to-be! It's one thing to admit it to myself in the wee small hours, quite another to voice my misgivings to total strangers – as lovely as they are. I did spend an entire night sleeping beside Koo, but surely that doesn't count.

I briskly walk through the streets of Bath, mobile in hand, following the designated route shown on my app with my final destination pinpointed by a chequered flag. Lulu hadn't a clue where to direct me, but eventually located the postcode via a Google search when I offered her the use of my phone. She seemed terribly sheepish at first, when I said I'd happily collect her things, but instantly mellowed when Koo was supportive. I'm not expecting a plush hotel. She keeps mentioning the price of twenty quid a night – what can you buy for twenty quid nowadays? Even with exceptional planning and organising, I doubt Lulu's bagged that price on a competitive hotel website. We're in the centre of Bath; it's hardly a cheapskate place.

As I pass along Broad Street, certain bars and restaurants look familiar – clearly, I passed this way yesterday with my hens. Was it during our walking tour or the pub crawl? Either way, specific sights are jumping out at me like signposts reminding me of yesterday – hopefully, it'll only take one or two to jog my memory and fill in the blanks. At least I have my mobile, though I can't bear to reread the stream of text messages demanding 'where are you?' let alone answer them. Earlier, I sent a flurry of text messages outlining that I was perfectly safe and wanted my suitcase taken to reception, ready for collection by Koo. I haven't explained myself properly, though I possibly should. I might appear guarded, especially amongst lifelong friends, but I'm not sure they'll understand my predicament – they all seem head-over-heels in love with their partners. I've already browsed Facebook in case they've launched a 'Missing persons' post – thankfully, they haven't. As long as they don't call Dale; I owe him that much. I don't want him worrying about me. They promised not to in their texts – but still, given how angry they are with me for disappearing, I'm surprised they haven't taken this further.

This could be one occasion when talking to a stranger wins over sharing with loved ones. Koo and Lulu seem level headed, but you never truly know with first impressions. Only time will tell! Though Koo was so supportive earlier, encouraging me to say what was on my mind; she didn't seem to judge me or take the moral high ground by dishing out advice. Lulu looked lost for words, but then when you're younger, you don't imagine such things happening the week before your wedding – or rather, I didn't.

I stop just shy of reaching the chequered flag on my mobile screen. I stand before a doorway announcing 'St Christopher's Inn', but this can't possibly be right – because this is a back-packers' hostel. Surely, Lulu's party haven't stayed here for a hen party?

I'm stuck. I don't know what to do. Should I walk back to our new hotel and check the postcode with Lulu, or enter and enquire if they have her suitcase ready for collection? I opt for the latter; my walk has taken a fair amount of time, but it's given me a sense of space. I'd hate to have to retrace my steps – and it does seem likely that this establishment's room rate would fit the budget mentioned by Lulu.

I push open the glazed panelled door to find I'm actually entering a lively bar, with colourful murals on each wall and optics galore – ideal for a hen party weekend. Cutting through the groups of joyous revellers, I spy a tiny reception area in the corner, and a young man appears as if by magic.

'Can I help you?' he asks.

'I hope so. I've been sent to collect a suitcase belonging to Lulu James, but I'm not sure this is the right place,' I say, as drunken chanting and deafening applause fill the air, making it difficult to be heard.

'The hen party?' asks the guy, glancing towards the noisy crowd attempting to recreate a drunken rugby scrum in the middle of the bar.

'Yes, the hen party.' I'm relieved that he knows.

'It's upstairs, we received a call earlier and passed the message on to the group. The ladies are out at the minute, so they asked if I'd show you up to the room. Would you like to come this way?'

To say I'm shocked is an understatement. Lulu never claimed it was a conventional hotel, or even a regular B&B, but she certainly didn't say hostel!

I follow the young man, as he leads me through a Georgian building that's been revamped and modernised, with colourful murals adorning each corridor and stairwell, giving it a new lease of life.

'Have you worked here long?' I ask, scurrying to keep up with his leggy stride.

'For two years, on and off, when I haven't been away travelling. I suppose it helps that I've seen what's on offer in other countries, and this is pretty smart for the price.'

'But they're on a hen-do,' I mutter.

'If you want to be out and about – enjoying what the city has to offer – then we're the cheapest overnight stay in Bath,' he says proudly. 'The bar can get a little noisy at times, but we guarantee you a clean bed. The ladies booked the entire place, so have all the dorms.'

It makes sense, but it would never have entered my head.

'Here we are.' He opens the door wide, revealing a dormitory of wooden bunk beds, each with a little privacy curtain, and an array of suitcases and holdalls stashed around the room.

'Bunk beds?' I'm taken back to my school days and a summer excursion to Paris.

'We've got two more along the corridor. This dorm is usually female only, and the others are mixed. But as I said, the hen party booked all the beds for two nights.'

'They aren't checking out today?'

'No, Monday morning.'

I fall silent; Lulu hadn't mentioned that detail either. No wonder she wasn't fazed by Koo's suggestion of an extra day, or my need to call in sick.

'I'm told this is the one you're collecting,' he says, indicating the nearest wheelie case with a bright floral design. 'I'll carry it downstairs for you, if you wish.'

'Thank you. I assume they've packed her belongings.'

'I believe so. They were frantic last night and first thing this morning, but then the call came through explaining that she was safe. She is safe, isn't she?' he asks, lifting the case with ease.

'Oh yes, quite safe. She'd have come herself if she'd been sure it wouldn't lead to arguments. I assume the bride-to-be is upset?' I ask.

'She calmed down after we passed on the message, but these things happen. We see it all the time; travellers fall out one day and are best buddies again the next – it's part of life.'

We immediately retrace our steps towards the bar. My mind

is buzzing with questions for Lulu, so I don't attempt to fill the silence. He doesn't appear to be put out by my rudeness, and maintains his polite manners.

'There you go,' he says, plonking the case down on its wheels. 'Can you manage the door alright?'

'Thank you so much. Yes, I'll be fine.' I take hold of the suitcase handle and cut through the bar, heading for the sunshine. The task was easy enough, but I'm niggled that Lulu was a little ambiguous about the full details of the hostel – she could have said. She obviously thinks I'll judge her. I reach the door and stand aside to let a group of women file in. The odd one mutters 'thank you' on passing, but most of them don't even look at me; they're too busy chattering to one another. The last few stragglers enter and the final lady holds the door open, stepping backwards for me to exit as she spies the suitcase.

'Thank you,' I say, squeezing past her on to the street.

'Kirsty? Look!' she calls into the bar, then gestures towards me.

A swarm of eager faces turn towards me, following the woman's gesture, before they hastily gather at the open doorway and simultaneous pout in my direction, each looking me up and down, having noted the suitcase.

'Hi, I'm . . .' I begin, extending my hand towards the woman at the front of the group.

'I don't give a frig who you are! Where's Lulu?' demands the strident brunette, peering at me around the doorjamb, leaving my hand to hover in mid-air. I pause, stand tall and stare, eye to eye with a true Bridezilla, in skinny black jeans and a glittery T-shirt announcing 'Mrs Hammond'. The other hens huddle behind their bride, staring over her shoulders at me.

'Beth. Nice to meet you. Kirsty, isn't it?' I say, extending my free hand more purposefully, wishing I'd dare to say 'Our Kirsty'.

She flinches on hearing her name, but her twitching scowl doesn't falter. 'Well?'

'She's safe and well,' I say, conveying the basics but withdrawing my offered handshake.

'*Phuh!* I bet she bloody is! On her own then?' she asks.

'Yes. Apart from me and another woman.'

'And you are?'

'I'm a nobody.'

'Not a work colleague?'

'No.'

'A drinking pal from The Peacock?'

'Nope.'

'What – a complete bloody stranger?'

I see where this is going before Kirsty utters another word. 'Yep. That's me – a complete bloody stranger. She's asked me to collect her things and she'll be in touch.'

'Well, tell her, I know. Right? Make sure you tell her that. *I. Know.* If she thinks she can put a halt to my wedding, she's in for a surprise.' Kirsty swipes the wheelie case handle from my clutches, as if she's about to hold it hostage or declare ownership, before adding, 'My mum reckons she's . . .' Her scowling brow is so deeply furrowed it'll take a week of relaxing beauty facials to unknot it before her wedding ceremony next weekend.

'Excuse me, that doesn't belong to you! It's Lulu's!' I say, snatching the handle from her grasp. 'I've been sent on an errand. Lulu needs her things, and I'm prepared to collect them. Like I said, she'll be in touch . . . when she's ready.'

'And tell her . . . she's sacked!' bellows Kirsty, as the other hens giggle in an awkward huddle behind her.

'OK, I will do. Bye.' I turn and walk away.

There's no backwards glance, no wave goodbye, I simply stride up the street, trundling Lulu's suitcase behind me.

Lulu

I enter the lift and press the button for 'penthouse', something I've always dreamt of doing.

'Going up' announces a robotic voice, bouncing jauntily off the mirror-lined walls.

I can't deny it, I'm thrilled to be collecting Koo's belongings; I can't imagine Beth's B&B compares to this experience. This feels like a 'bucket list' moment in my tiny world. A far cry from the annoying bleep of a bar scanner and the never-ending conveyor belt of supermarket goodies. My stomach might be lunging and lurching, unsure of what I'll find when the lift doors slide open, but it can't be any more surprising than what I've already experienced today. Since opening my eyes this morning, despite the crick in my neck, I've had a wonderful day – and it's only half twelve. Admittedly, I felt a little awkward when Koo pushed a crisp twenty into my palm, to cover the taxi fare for this short journey, but this is unarguably a 'red letter day' – albeit unplanned – which I'll never forget. So, if it ends abruptly, in a matter of minutes, I won't be complaining. Even if the penthouse door is firmly slammed in my face and I'm rudely instructed to speak to the concierge at the front desk, I won't complain.

I've thoroughly enjoyed today's teeny-weeny brush with luxury. I thought Our Kirsty's hen weekend would be a hell of an endurance test, but this, well *this*, is turning out to be the greatest weekend adventure I've ever had. A sleepover in a luxury bathroom at The Royal Crescent hotel, an exquisite breakfast dressed in a toga, several glasses of proper bubbly, a complete new rig-out, and the company of two new friends – all before midday. No, I won't be complaining – this could be the best morning of my life!

Ding. The lift doors softly slide open, revealing a plush landing tastefully decorated in cream and gold, with an array of large potted palms on either side of the suite's door. Which isn't closed, but pinned open with a red fire extinguisher – wrong on so many levels – revealing a sumptuous suite inside, where a noisy party is in full flow. There are smartly dressed women clutching half-filled glasses, scattered in huddles and busily chatting, gesticulating wildly with their free hands. At a glance, I identify them as the sort of women who never do a regular big shop – they have staff to complete such tasks – but wander in mid-afternoon with our tiniest shopping basket slung over one arm, topping up on fresh salmon, breadsticks, a pot of hummus, and possibly those tiny bottles of yoghurt drink formulated to sustain the flora within your gut. The type who rarely speak but mainly snap at me, insinuating that I'm wasting their precious time, working at a snail's pace, or am simply beneath them in society's pecking order.

The noise they're creating in the suite is unbelievable, definitely drowning out any music that might be playing, not that I can hear anything in the background. I enter gingerly, aware that I'm not expected.

A team of uniformed waiting staff wander around topping up drinks from napkin-collared bottles. Other staff unwrap and replenish the food platters along the buffet table, a full spread laid out upon linen-covered tables like a posh wedding reception. No doubt everything is of the highest quality and ultimate freshness – there'll be nothing nearing its sell-by date here!

There must be upwards of fifty women attending. Who are all these people? Koo wasn't explicit about her hen-do numbers, or the fact that the party is still in full flow, of sorts, although without the lady in question. But I expected it to be smaller than Our Kirsty's bash, which was limited to thirty. I watch the carnival before me, half expecting an official photographer to be circulating amongst the Manolo Blahniks and Jimmy Choos. I might be a checkout girl from Kettering but I recognise serious money when I see it. Koo said her hen-do wasn't in the hotel restaurant or function suite – no, it's filling the penthouse suite! And given the on-point make-up, freshly coiffed hair and smart attire, these ladies didn't arrive last night! They are fresh, brand-new arrivals for what . . . a luncheon buffet? How posh is that? Picturing the size of Koo's engagement ring, her ability to meet a hefty hotel bill, and her command of our M&S shopping spree without breaking into a panic, and now this, I'm guessing there's more to our Koo than meets the eye. Koo? Koo Bournebury? Where have I heard that name before?

I wander in, sidestepping the group gatherings, noting every detail, assuming Koo will probably expect a full rundown once I return to our seemingly modest suite at The Royal Crescent.

Despite my utterances of 'excuse me' and 'whoops, sorry', not a single person acknowledges my presence. No one has noticed that a stranger has entered the party; they are too absorbed in their incessant talking, shrill screams and polite but tipsy laughter. I doubt they'll notice anything until tomorrow's hangover kicks in. What time did this crowd arrive? First thing this morning? Who dresses in full going-out regalia at this time of the day – unless you're going to Ascot, which I never have.

I pick my way through the medley of bodies, heading for the double doors on the far side of the suite's tastefully furnished lounge. Which is where, I assume, being the furthest away from the entrance, I will find the bedroom.

The sheer size of the bedroom, let alone its elaborate decor, the soft furnishings and fabrics, makes me grateful that Koo didn't collect my belongings. She would have been shocked at seeing what twenty quid a night can buy. I'm sure Beth must have stayed in similar surroundings once or twice in her younger days, but Koo – never. She's got that classy but laid-back vibe about her, because she can afford to have options in life. Whereas me, I can be generous, if I have it to give – but I've rarely got a surplus of anything to offer anyone.

The canopied bed is a pile of twisted sheets and duvet – clearly someone has taken full advantage of the unoccupied room. I've made my own bed every day since I was six – obviously, some people see that as somewhat beneath them.

I fling wide the ginormous wardrobe doors ... to find three Louis Vuitton suitcases, aligned like Russian dolls, stowed neatly beneath a full clothing rail. How many outfits does one woman need for a weekend away?

I heave the largest case on to the end of the bed. The swift zip action gives a satisfying noise as the case opens wide. I robotically empty each hanger – not caring to fold or roll each item but simply dumping and stashing until the clothes rail is empty. I've never seen so many designer labels in one room, and a satisfying flourish of the zip signals the end of the task. Gravity assists my attempt to lift the case from the bed, with an accompanying thud. Taking the two smaller cases from the wardrobe, I eagerly swipe loose items from every surface, be it a deluxe hairbrush, a tiny tube of lip gloss, or a fancy emery board. I feel like a burglar working a diamond heist; my hands are packing as quickly as possible, before anyone realises I've snuck in. I'm expecting to be unceremoniously frogmarched from this suite at any minute.

Within no time, I've retrieved every lotion and potion bottle from the plush en-suite bathroom – I've slept in smaller rooms for a fortnight's package holiday.

I let the bedroom door slam, accidentally on purpose, as I leave the room. I'm invisible – they probably assume I'm part of the hotel's housekeeping team – whilst struggling to drag the three designer cases as the tiny wheels keep catching in the thick pile of the luxury carpet. The groups of women have changed positions like a choreographed scene of musical statues and chairs – but still no one speaks to me or acknowledges that I'm present, let alone challenges me for leaving with more valuable designer clothing and personal possessions than I had upon entering. I squeeze past, sidestepping every obstacle, mainly women lounging decorously and sipping their drinks. So many beautifully posed people, it could almost be a photo shoot taken from a glossy mag, the sort I frequently pore over during my coffee break . . . glossy mags – that's it! Oh my God, Bournebury! Bournebury's chocolate! Koo Bournebury and her canary-yellow diamond. My oh my, I've slept in Koo Bournebury's hotel bathtub, and she's trusted me with an errand to collect her belongings! Wait till Beth hears about this!

By the time I reach the entrance doors to the suite, I'm narked beyond belief. How dare they? Supposed girlfriends, each taking advantage of Koo's generosity, and yet no one has the manners to ask after her well-being. Have they not noticed that she's absent from her own party? Or don't they care less, as long as she picks up the bill for their Dom Pérignon?

My mouth opens before I put my brain into gear.

'Bye then, ladies – nice seeing you all. I'll let Koo know you asked after her!' I yell, above the noisy chatter.

Several huddles turn and stare before returning to their conversation. The nearest couple cease chatting. 'Are you not part of the concierge entourage?' asks the younger one, flashing an exaggerated pout in my direction.

'Absolutely! For twenty quid an hour I'll run errands and tasks at breakneck speed all over town simply to keep you happy,' I jest.

The ladies exchange an eager glance, before the older one asks, 'Do you accept card payments?'

'Sadly not. Cash is more my style,' I say, wheeling the cases into the lobby area as they look me up and down, as if I'm dirt from the gutter.

They're no better than me, though their lip gloss alone probably cost more than my entire outfit. Sadly for them, I witness the bemused glances and self-important sniggers exchanged after my swift remark. I do the only revengeful thing I can muster; I grab the fire extinguisher, removing it as a door stop.

'This is dangerous! And certainly not the correct method of usage!' I shout. Then I pull the release pin and aim the foaming nozzle at two pairs of rather posh-looking stilettos before dumping the red canister beside them, only to disappear lugging three suitcases amidst their screams of dismay.

The suite door softly closes, while I hastily drag Koo's belongings across the lobby towards the lift; eager to depart. I really shouldn't have done that. Why can't I ever rise above certain situations and calmly walk away? I repeatedly jab at the lift's call button, as if that'll hasten its arrival. The resounding outcry of 'ruined shoes' is muted behind the suite's closed door, just metres away from where I stand, alone, loaded with baggage, awaiting a lift. Says it all really – the story of my life.

Chapter Five

Beth

Koo looks up from her relaxed position on the couch as Lulu and I return together, laden with suitcases. I feel somewhat dejected, despite a successful mission.

'How was it?' she asks, glancing between us.

'Easier than I was expecting, to be frank,' I say, suddenly aware that Lulu hadn't asked as much since meeting in reception and catching the lift together. Her silence seems somewhat dubious, now that I know about the hostel situation.

'Your party is in full swing – if that's what you're asking,' declares Lulu, thumping her cases down before retrieving an item from her pocket. 'Here's your mobile from the night stand – and I've got change from the taxi fare, Koo.'

'Lulu's bride is more concerned with being denied the opportunity to sack her, face to face, from the wedding party!' I say, kicking off my party stilettos and settling opposite Koo's couch. I watch her as she acknowledges the handful of cash, before eagerly tapping her mobile screen.

'Typical Kirsty, is all I can say. I've run around like a fool to bring her weekend to fruition,' complains Lulu, unzipping her case and rummaging about, before retrieving her own mobile and charger. 'Damn it, my handbag isn't here. I honestly thought one of the others might have picked it up by accident last night.'

'At least now we have what we need,' mutters Koo, gesturing towards my suitcase, which she's left standing by the en-suite door. 'Your belongings were ready and waiting, without harm or hassle, Beth.'

'I thought they might be. The girls had vented their initial anger in text messages so probably had little else to say.' I give a heavy sigh, knowing enraged friends are the least of my worries. 'They'd have hit the road, eager to get home, by the time you arrived.'

'So now what?' asks Lulu, plugging her phone charger into the wall socket and jabbing at her blank screen, hoping for signs of life. 'Has either of you heard from your other half?'

I shake my head. 'Nope. But it's only a matter of time.'

'Same here,' says Koo. 'Though I'm not expected home until tomorrow.'

'Nor me,' adds Lulu, over her shoulder, whilst rummaging in her suitcase.

'I suggest we contact our loved ones first then,' offers Koo, her index finger busily tapping. Like me, I guess she'll be using punctuation and fully spelled words, with an overdose of colourful emojis. 'Then we can settle, seeing as everyone knows where we are – safe and sound.'

It sounds like common sense, and yet . . . I can't see my conversation with Dale being as plain sailing as theirs. On second thoughts, my conversation with my mother might be worse. Dale will be patient and listen to what I say, hoping we can address the issue, whereas my mother will hit panic mode at the thought of not wearing her brand-new hat on Saturday.

'I would if I had some juice in this thing,' moans Lulu, waving her dead mobile.

'You might be grateful in the circumstances,' jests Koo, as her mobile begins to ping repeatedly. 'Oh, it looks like my sons are awake and texting, which is early for them. I'd prefer to call Judd first, then explain to my lads.'

I tune out as Koo begins to explain their usual weekend habits

of late nights and morning lie-ins before Sunday afternoon normality resumes. I've got bigger concerns of my own, now that
my hens have hit the road heading for home. I have no choice
but to call Dale and explain. The question is, how much do I
mention – full details or keep it brief?

'Hi Judd, yes . . . I'm fine, darling. I've opted for a little diver-
sion to my weekend plans. Safe and sound, yes. I just couldn't
hack being surrounded by the usual types, you know what I
mean.' Koo's conversation pulls me from my own dilemma. I
watch her body visibly relax as she cradles the mobile between
her shoulder and ear and a radiant smile brightens her features.

'Aww, how sweet,' sighs Lulu, kneeling beside her open suitcase and witnessing Koo's response. Lulu appears mesmerised
watching Koo, as if she's studying her every detail.

'I know,' I whisper, not wishing to disturb Koo's call. My heart
melts a little; I wish that were me.

'I'm going to freshen up,' says Lulu, jumping up and gesturing
towards the bathroom.

'Sure. I need to phone home too.' I watch Lulu saunter from
the lounge area, clutching a make-up bag. I must remember to
tell her the message sent by Our Kirsty. What was it? 'Tell her,
I know.' I should have mentioned it in the lift, but forgot to.
It can wait till she returns; Kirsty's message isn't my current
priority. Dale is.

I gingerly tap my screen, connecting with his number as his
smiling photo fills my display. I'd usually opt for FaceTime but
today, I'll settle for a call. A wave of guilt floods my veins; my
explanation about a delayed return home will be unexpected,
but the possibility of a delayed wedding is the last thing on earth
he'll imagine hearing. Here goes . . .

Ring, ring!

'Hellooo, wifey-to-be – how are you enjoying yourself?' Dale's
voice is bright and bubbly, as always. I can picture him in our

lounge, watching sport on the TV, the dog lying across his feet, sleeping.

I gulp. I simply can't do this ... not to a man who truly has the kindest heart I've ever encountered.

'I'm good, babe. You?' I say, cringing that the others might be listening, though Koo appears engrossed in her own call.

'Good, good. How was Saturday night? As saucy and as lewd as you were anticipating the girls to be?' he asks. I can hear his infectious laughter bubbling beneath his inquisitive tone.

'Not quite, but it was heading that way. Anyway, there's been a little change of plans regarding us travelling home together. I met up with a couple of girlfriends, literally bumped into them last night, and I haven't seen them in years so we're planning on staying for an extra night – as a trio. There's nothing to worry about, I'm quite safe. I've got my luggage, we're planning on sharing a room – so I have everything I need.' I cross my fingers, telling a tiny white lie, quickly adding, 'We're just having an extended weekend – nothing more.' I keep talking, for fear of hearing Dale's confused questioning; sensing his silent vibe reaching out to me, it feels safer and requires less dissembling. I finally draw breath and await a response.

'O ... K ... and the rest of your party?'

'They're heading back to Kent, as we speak.'

'What about work tomorrow, Beth?'

'Look, I never do this, you know that ... but I'll call in sick ...'

'Beth?' his tone is as surprised as I expected.

'I know. It seems bad, given it's the week of the wedding and we're off on a fortnight's honeymoon next week. But how often do I fill in for staff sickness? Other people do it all the time ... giving no end of stupid excuses – poorly cats, stomach bugs or ear infections. I never do.'

'So why start now? It sounds ridiculous ...'

'Dale, it'll be fine! I'll be home on Monday night, then work on Tuesday, as usual. I promise. Anyway, I'm officially off from Friday onwards – so what's one more day, hey?'

'I suppose, but is it worth it, Beth?'

'You worry too much,' I say nervously, through gritted teeth, knowing that I'm going against my own better judgement as well as his.

'If you're happy doing that ... just be careful that you don't create a situation at work if others find out – that wouldn't be a smart move, now would it?'

'*Phuh!*' I mutter, knowing he's absolutely right, so I don't need reminding. What the hell am I doing? Lying to Dale. Lying to bosses. Upsetting my friends and family. And for what? Some last-minute nerves in the face of commitment ... or is it more than that?

'Old school friends or ex-colleagues then?'

'Who?' I say, confused by his question.

There's a lengthy silence before Dale continues.

'Your old girlfriends?'

'Oh, them. Yeah, school friends – you wouldn't know them,' I quickly say, grateful that we grew up in different areas of the county despite being the same age. 'We go way back to our primary school days.' I continue the lie.

'Bloody hell, I'm surprised you recognised each other!'

He's got a point. I'm not that practised at lying, am I?

'They spotted my name on a venue list,' I continue, crossing my fingers, knowing this little gem might bite me on the ass sometime soon.

As I end the phone call my relief is immense; I'm crippled with guilt for disrespecting such a trusting heart. Apart from my obvious avoidance tactic, creating imaginary school friends, every other word and sentiment to Dale was genuine. How could it not be when coupled with such a kind, caring, loving man? I'd do anything within my power to prevent him feeling a minute's pain or upset caused by me. He doesn't deserve that – not now, not ever.

'Are you OK?' asks Koo, watching me thoughtfully, snuggled against the arm of her couch.

'Yeah.' My voice is small and weak. I feel awful.

'Well, that's my face reapplied. I can take on the world now!' announces Lulu, striding from the bathroom like a leggy cat-walk queen in Milan. I'm grateful for her interruption, as Koo obviously overheard – or listened in on – my phone call to Dale.

'Look at you, beautiful,' sings Koo, whipping about in her seat to view the newcomer.

I nod in appreciation of Lulu's make-up artistry; unable to speak as I recover from my call.

Lulu instantly twirls as she crosses the floor, causing her blonde hair to flare outwards before it cascades about her shoulders. She is stunning. I feel quite dumpy and insignificant when confronted with such an image of health and youth, but not from anything Lulu's doing, simply my own insecurities and self-doubt.

'Is everyone done and dusted with home?' asks Lulu, taking up her usual position on the chaise longue, befitting her artistic beauty.

'I am. Judd's fine with my arrangements, though my lads might be a different kettle of fish when they hear. And you, Beth?'

'All good,' I say, dredging a bright smile from somewhere deep within. I daren't meet Koo's gaze; she knows the truth.

'Perfect. I say we enjoy the remainder of our hen-dos, without tantrum or torment,' Koo says, gesturing towards the suite's telephone. 'A bottle of Bollinger Rosé ... pink champers to celebrate – girls only.'

'I second that,' quips Lulu, glancing at me, before snatching up the handset. 'Shall I?'

Koo gives a tiny nod.

I remain unmoved, watching. Lulu's pretty quick to oblige Koo, even quicker than she was earlier today, if I'm not mistaken.

'Is that what we're doing?' I ask, while Lulu busies herself with room service.

'I certainly am. I'm free from my bridal obligations to entertain others – I can settle and enjoy good company.'

I'm unsure if I feel the same way; my guilt is flowing thick and fast. I may have managed to rid myself of the hen night obligation, but I'm sure this won't be the end of the drama. My girlfriends will be furious, my fiancé unsettled by my actions, and my brain is already totally scrambled by the events of the last twelve hours. Absconding from my own hen-do might have seemed a good idea at the time, but it doesn't solve my problems; if anything, I've made them worse. Much worse.

'Ten minutes for bubbles and some nibbles!' announces Lulu, replacing the handset, excitedly glancing between us. 'Though there's no chocolate, I'm afraid!' she adds.

'Sorry?' I ask, confused by Lulu's final remark.

'Nothing,' giggles Lulu, as if I'm missing the joke.

'Just enough time for us to unpack and settle ourselves for an afternoon of girls being girls,' says Koo. Her expression is deadpan as she swings her legs from beneath her frame and wiggles her toes in the lush carpet, before standing tall.

'Bagsie not the bathtub for a second night!' hollers Lulu, with another giggle.

Lulu

Our celebratory bottle of champagne arrives in no time, courtesy of a uniformed concierge with a sleek buffet trolley and an ice bucket. Despite the suite's elaborate dining table and matching chairs, we opt to cop-a-squat on a nest of silk couch cushions encircling the coffee table, and leisurely pick from the silver buffet platters laid before us, amidst half-filled champagne flutes. My only disappointment was our food didn't arrive under domed silver cloches – which happens in all the best chick-flick films.

'What's the plan?' asks Beth, uncurling her legs to reposition herself whilst nibbling at the remains of the cress and rocket garnish.

'We can please ourselves, can't we?' says Koo, glancing between us and seeking confirmation.

'A weekend in Bath wasn't my idea,' replies Beth, nonchalantly.

'So, what was your choice of celebration, Beth?' asks Koo, leisurely sipping her bubbles, kneeling in an uncomfortable-looking yoga pose. I'd have pins and needles for sure if I followed her example, so I sit cross-legged, grazing the remnants of the buffet.

'I didn't get a choice. As soon as we'd set the wedding date, I busied myself with making countless lists and appointments. Whereas, my maid of honour focused her efforts on ordering inflatable willies, tacky card games and plastic wine glasses for the train journey. Tara assumed I'd be up for the traditional banshee chorus, then lost all interest once she'd collected the deposits and paid the B&B,' says Beth, nibbling on more salad garnish. 'I couldn't afford to change location so went with Tara's choice.'

'And you?' I ask Koo, intrigued to get a glimpse of how the other half live.

'No say, José! Though I packed my passport in case anyone decided to spring a last-minute surprise. Sadly, they didn't.'

'Except for picking up the tab?' I add, instantly flinching at the unexpected harshness of my comment. Why do I always state the obvious – can't I filter my response like a proper adult?

'Sadly, yes. The events company did ask for a ballpark figure regarding a budget ... and access to my address book – after which, away they went and did their thing by organsing a weekend of party events. You briefly attended the early bird cocktail reception, which followed the Saturday night function, but preceded the summer soirée – planned for the rooftop terrace – if I've memorised the weekend itinerary correctly.'

'Nice touch, if that floats your boat,' I add, unsure that such formal arrangements are my idea of a final fun-packed weekend with the girlies. 'Is that happening right now, even without you?'

'Probably. Those who RSVP'd will enjoy the customary meet and greet, and will happily mingle with whoever attends,' explains Koo, staring into her glass as she speaks. 'They'll each take home their goody bag full of gifts too.'

'Wow! How many friends did you invite?' I ask, besotted by her lifestyle.

'Mmmm, now there's a question,' sighs Koo, slowly sipping her bubbles.

I watch as both women drift off into their own worlds; their expressions fade to blank masks, their eyes devoid of life, like classical statues.

Great celebration this is turning out to be! I need to inject some pizzazz, otherwise this'll morph into another laborious evening much like Our Kirsty's hen-do. Another night of me jollying the troops along, though I hope I won't be separated from these two.

I jump up, dash over to the executive writing desk and grab the hotel's embossed letter-headed paper, which I'd spied earlier.

'Here, take this. Write down your hen-do wish list . . . anything and everything you desire,' I say, issuing each bride with a piece of paper and a pen. 'Let's see if I can turn this around for you two.' Instantly, both women perk up, as I plop on to the couch cushions, quietly watching yet eagerly awaiting their wishes.

Beth begins to smile, while Koo chews the end of her pen, pondering.

I mightn't have any qualifications, be a skilled worker, or

possess talents for much in this world, but my forte is organising. I'm definitely one of life's doers – I can pull a metaphorical rabbit from a top hat in order to deliver a fun time, if nothing else!

Suddenly Beth begins to scribble details, her hand swiftly moving across the page. Koo continues to think; her page remains unblemished. Her dreamy gaze meets mine.

'And you. What would your dream hen-do look like?' she asks.

I'm about to suggest that she's lost her marbles, but decide she's on the right track. Why not? I grab a sheet of paper – I don't need asking twice.

I join Beth, my hand scribbling details on to the page; Koo remains unmoved.

'Are you done?' I ask Koo, my hand aching from the frantic writing.

'Mmmm,' she hums, replacing her pen lid.

'Did you write anything?' I ask, unsure if her pen even touched the paper.

Koo doesn't answer.

'Sorted,' says Beth, sitting back, carefully folding her list in half and depositing her pen on the coffee table.

'I've got loads,' I say, flipping my page around to flash my wish list. 'Which seems wrong, since I'm not a bride. Beth, you go first.'

She glances at Koo, receives a warm smile, and clears her throat, before unfolding her paper.

'Mine is simple. I wanted a . . .'

Koo suddenly begins to write.

'Oy! No, you don't – your time is up. There's no cheating around here,' I blurt, interrupting Beth and pointing at Koo.

'But I didn't write what I wanted to write,' protests Koo, her bottom lip protruding in a comical fashion.

'Time's up, lady!' I waggle my index finger at her.

'Lulu, let her write what she wants. What are your hen parties missing, Koo?' asks Beth, a sympathetic look adorning her features.

'I'm missing a few things in life but . . . I really shouldn't complain,' says Koo, apologetically, before jotting a few details down.

I thought as much. Koo doesn't realise it, but I'm picking up little life clues about her – left, right and centre – she's being elusive with the full details, but I've got her sussed.

'Sorry, Beth, please continue, I rudely interrupted you,' is all I say.

'It's silly really, but . . . well, this!' Beth flips her paper on to the coffee table.

Koo and I automatically lean in and peer. There are a few words: time, peace and picnic. Besides that, what had appeared to be frantic handwriting was, in fact, a tiny pen sketch of a cottage.

'Remember, what I actually got was a city break, with clear instructions to pickle myself from the inside out on cheap plonk!' Beth's eyes glisten as she recalls the details. 'What I truly need is time and space, to figure out what I want to do.'

'Bless you, honey – everyone deserves clarity and time out, especially now,' pipes up Koo, holding her barely used paper close to her chest. 'You next, Lulu?'

'Are you sure?' I ask, slightly embarrassed by my lack of an engagement ring.

'I'm sure.'

I take a deep breath. 'I'll apologise now, before I offend anyone. But I'm only getting married once, so I need to make the most of my future hen weekend.' I clear my throat. 'I want to be indulged, be totally pampered, have an endless flow of bubbles. I want my hen-do to last longer than one night – more like a mini-break. I want it to be memorable, with no daft squabbling or jealousy between girlfriends, and I want new experiences thrown in.'

'You don't want much then?' mutters Beth, adding the finishing touches to her cottage drawing.

'Like I said, I'm only getting married once,' I remind her.

'Koo, what did you wish for?' asks Beth, suddenly looking up from her masterpiece.

Koo visibly squirms before answering the question. 'I simply put "friends" and "Florence". That's it . . . as I said, I shouldn't complain.'

'Oh shit, is that your phone ringing?' I gesture towards Beth's mobile as it vibrates upon the carpet's lush pile beside her silk cushion.

Beth leans forward, peers at her screen and grimaces. As if planned, Koo's mobile blares into life with a dated, tinny ringtone. Then, bang on cue, our faces turn in unison and stare in horror as my mobile, still charging, suddenly comes to life on the other side of the suite.

'Now what?' asks Beth.

'I suggest we answer,' says Koo, peeling herself from her cushion and tapping her illuminated screen. 'Hi, Felix, how's my baby?'

'Lulu?' mutters Beth, as if in need of help, showing me her caller display announcing 'My mum'.

'I've no other option,' I say, staring at my dad's photo, indicating caller ID. I accept the call, readying myself for a potential ear bashing. 'Hi, Dad.'

Beth

Annoyed and frustrated, I hastily end my call and slump backwards on the couch, observing my roommates contentedly chatting to their respective families. Koo is lying comfortably across the canopied bed and Lulu is leisurely curled up on her chaise longue before the picture window, which beautifully frames the afternoon sun.

It took all of five minutes for my mother to question my antics, absolve herself of responsibility for my behaviour, and ponder what her neighbours will say when they find out! Anyone would think I'd run off with the milkman, rather than staying for an extra night on my weekend away! I don't even live with my mother – I share a new-build terrace with Dale – so why her neighbours are so high on the priority list baffles me. My call hasn't ended on the best of terms.

Growing up, that was always the case; Mum was more concerned with what the outside world thought than with what was going on behind our front door. We weren't the only single-parent family in the street, but you'd think we were. Mum kept up a running commentary on what she believed the street thought of us. I doubt the neighbours cared about, or even noticed, the mother and daughter living at number 71. Let alone noted whether our groceries were in branded carrier bags or from discount stores, whether our whites were whiter than white on the clothes line, or whether we had garibaldi biscuits and Battenberg cake or boxes of broken biscuits as our weekly treat.

Lulu giggles and smiles throughout her conversation with her dad. Koo's conversation ebbs and flows, accompanied by numerous expressions, fluctuating between surprise and pure frustration.

Meanwhile, I sit simmering at the scolding I've just received from the one person I expected to show me some understanding. I don't need my mum's gloomy foreboding. I don't need reminding how close my wedding day is – I've been planning it for long enough, with daily reminders pinging at me from my phone's cute animated tracker. And the final line, prompting me to end our call abruptly, was her remark, 'Don't you disappoint him now!' What's that supposed to mean? I presume the 'he' is Dale, but it implies a lowly expectation of me – as if I'm in the habit of making wayward decisions. I can do without an emotional guilt trip, when all I'm doing is taking an extra day and night for myself. I deserve a little chill time. I've spent aeons pleasing others, attempting to accommodate all their needs and hopes for our wedding day. Which, yes, is in precisely seven days' time!

Flashbacks from my uni days flood my memory. Mum was eager to brag, tell everyone how proud she was when I became the first member of our family to enter higher education. But she failed to mention her late-night calls, snarkily asking, 'Why are you bothering with this?', 'What's the point in the long run?' or, the ultimate put-down, 'Beth, you don't need qualifications to be a wife and mother!' Every step of the way, she undermined my studies until I graduated and returned home with a first-class degree in History. And now, some twelve years later, having completed my post-graduate courses and secured a flourishing career at the castle, she still implies I'm a child who can't make a mature decision.

'Are you OK, Beth?' asks Koo, returning to the lounge area, having finished her call, and pushing her phone into her pocket.

'Fine, thanks,' I say, aiming for a breezy tone.

'Not good, hey?' she asks, settling on the opposite couch.

'I'm used to it. It's been the story of my life where my mother's concerned . . . I can venture into pastures new, dream of bigger and better things than I knew as a child, but if I dare to cross her boundary line . . . *boom*! She tries to put me in my place, as if I'm still a child who needs a damned good talking-to.'

Koo listens intently, as a burst of laughter from Lulu interrupts our chat. We both turn to observe her stretched out on the chaise, happily chatting away, twirling a strand of her blonde mane, without a care in the world.

'Why can't that be me?' I ask.

'It could be . . . if . . .' Koo hesitates, glancing back at me, before continuing. 'If you weren't weighed down with whatever it is you're burdened with.'

Ouch! I flinch as her words hit home.

'Is it that obvious?'

Koo repeatedly nods, before adding, 'Yep. You're no different to me – we're in the same place but for different reasons, I guess.'

'And Lulu?' I say, gesturing to our happy companion giggling on her phone.

'Ah, well, I suspect she has an entirely different set-up to ours.' Koo's eyebrows lift, emphasising her point. 'Probably a sticky situation, all the same.'

'Have I missed something?' I ask, unsure what Koo's suggesting.

'Mmmph, maybe. She's sure having a great chat – with her dad, did I hear her say?'

We sit in silence, watching Lulu happily chatting. In light of Koo's remark, Lulu morphs from a dutiful daughter taking a call from her father into a woman who seems incredibly flushed and giddy, in a matter of seconds.

'That's not her father, is it?' I whisper.

'I don't think so,' answers Koo.

Neither of us says another word, as we settle back on our respective couches. I assume, like me, Koo has one ear cocked in Lulu's direction. I can't make out the conversation, but her body language is speaking loud and clear.

'Any news?' calls Koo, as Lulu finally ends her call.

'News? Not bloody likely!' she retorts playfully, peeling herself off the chaise and crossing the lounge towards our couches. I'm sceptical of her answer, given her renewed energy and sunny disposition.

'Your conversation appeared less tense than either of ours,' I add, intrigued to hear her explanation. Right now, given the difficult call I've endured with my mother, I'd benefit from some encouraging words and a supportive hug from Dale to soothe my fraught nerves. Ironic, if nothing else.

'Really?' Her brightness instantly fades. 'Tough, was it?'

'You bet. My mother just insinuated that I'm up to no good,' I retort, scrutinising Lulu's manner as she flops down on the far end of my couch.

'My eldest son used the opportunity to apply a little more pressure to my guilt-ridden conscience,' adds Koo, sounding slightly dramatic.

'Guilt-ridden? Pull the other one, Koo. Surely you, out of the three of us, have the least to worry about?' says Lulu.

Suddenly, I'm at sea in this conversation. What's Lulu on about? Koo's frame sinks a little under the weight of her remark.

'If you haven't guessed, I've got you sussed. Did you think we wouldn't know?' Lulu remarks, accusingly.

Koo and Lulu lock eyes; their expressions aren't threatening, more a case of each challenging the other to speak. In the space of five minutes, the carefree vibe we've had all day has been replaced by a frosty chill, despite it being August.

'Know what?' I ask, baffled by the unexpected turn the conversation has taken.

'Go on, tell her,' urges Lulu, in a softer tone.

'Be my guest, since you appear to know so much,' mutters Koo, haughtily.

'Tell me what?' I sound like a confused parakeet repeating disjointed phrases.

Lulu hesitates, seemingly deflated – and embarrassed? – by Koo's response.

'Have you ever snaffled a bar of Chunky Nougat Nut, secretly scoffed an entire slab of Crunchy Bournebury Brittle, or made yourself ill consuming a family-sized bar of Marvellous Mint Moments?'

'Yeah, hasn't everybody?' I reply, glancing between the two, unsure where Lulu is going with this.

'Well, Koo here is a Bournebury ... as in the famous family of chocolatiers. Heiress, aren't you?'

'Shut up!' My words burst forth in a surprised but aggressive tone.

Lulu shakes her head, before lowering her gaze.

'Is that . . .? What she just said . . . is that true?' I ask, whipping around to view a silent, stone-faced Koo.

Koo gives the tiniest of nods. Blink, and I'd have missed her response.

My mouth drops wide; I'm speechless. Suddenly, things make sense. My stunned gaze takes in the sumptuous surroundings, as if truly seeing them for the first time: the luxury suite, canopied bed, the huge en suite, this seating area and chaise longue, the stunning view overlooking the crescent – it takes a certain kind of wealth to pop this on a credit card, without batting an eyelid. Not like my lifestyle, where spending sprees and budgets need to be planned beforehand. If I could afford to waste money, I'd have swiftly cancelled Tara's idea of a hen-do in Bath and not given two hoots about losing the group's B&B deposits, knowing I could repay their losses. In fact, their deposits wouldn't be necessary; I'd have picked up the entire tab.

'Feel better, now?' whispers Koo, without actually addressing Lulu.

'Not really, but—'

'But nothing,' interrupts Koo, arching her right eyebrow.

'You can hardly keep it a secret, can you? Your face is splashed across the glossy mags every other week – and that rock didn't come cheap, did it?' says Lulu, attempting to justify herself, while my brain continues to unscramble the information.

Both women remain silent, averting their gaze from each other. The atmosphere is uncomfortable in the wake of our earlier sincerity towards one another.

'Well, this is . . . t-turning out . . . to be a r-right w-weekend,' I stammer, unsure if I should add anything to the mix. 'Before the phone calls, we were getting along fine and now, well – this!'

Lulu comes to life, snapping out of her downcast state, looking around for our discarded wish lists. 'That's a point!' she says, collecting the sheets of paper lying amongst the buffet debris.

Koo's sparkle instantly returns, as if by magic. She reaches across the coffee table and snatches the papers from Lulu's clutches.

'In that case, let's make this happen for us three.' Koo jumps up, brandishing all three lists, despite hers being merely two words and not an actual list. 'No arguing, no objections, please. Beth can find space to decide what's happening regarding her commitment to Dale. I can figure out how I might rehash the current wedding planned by my family. And Lulu . . . well, you can enjoy a bloody good week of relaxation and rejuvenation. This is going to be a once-in-a-lifetime, girls-only escape from our current worries and dramas – proving dreams *can* come true during hen week!'

'Hen week? Koo, I'm due back at work come Tuesday morning,' I say, a tinge of panic edging into my voice.

'Me too, though I'd rather not go,' says Lulu, her playful expression reappearing, before she settles beside me.

Koo begins to pace the floor, her excitement growing with each step, as she reads the lists.

Lulu and I exchange a dubious expression.

'Come on, please!' squeals Koo, brandishing the lists.

I hesitate. It appears the sudden tension of the last few minutes has evaporated – all is forgiven. I want Lulu to answer first, despite her role as a maid of honour and not a bride. Boy, she'd be getting a dream hen-do, without the unwelcome nerves or cold feet.

'Seriously, we can do this, together! A week of pleasing ourselves, living our dream, and enjoying the basics of friendship.' Koo stops dead, turns to face us, before delivering her final invite. 'Come on, ladies . . . are you with me?'

'I am . . . but I need to locate my handbag first!' squeals Lulu, her arms flailing around like a teenager.

Chapter Six

Lulu

'Are you recognising anywhere?' asks Beth, clutching the creased map, supplied by the hotel's concierge.

'If you held it still, it might help,' I snap impatiently, attempting to reposition myself so I can at least see it clearly. 'And remember, I wasn't the only person out and about around Bath last night!'

'I'm totally useless – I'm lost. I have no idea how I got from there . . .' Koo prods the map, before waving her open hand above the colourful print, 'to anywhere, to be quite frank with you.'

'You must remember leaving your own party – for a breath of fresh air, a nip to the toilets, a quick request from the concierge?' asks Beth, looking at Koo in a bewildered manner.

'No, no and no. Why would I? I'd have phoned the concierge, and I can step out on to the roof terrace or use the perfectly good bathroom in my suite. I don't need to leave my penthouse for any of those things.'

'It was a humongous bathroom too,' I add, just for good measure.

'Why's it so unbelievable that I can't remember – but neither can you, and that's OK?' asks Koo, her frustrations getting the better of her.

Beth shrugs. 'Maybe because I feel ridiculously stupid being in the situation I'm in. With my head totally scrambled and relying on friends to walk me around a city I'm hardly recognising and having to admit to myself, as a supposedly sensible adult, that I can actually be that sloshed, and not remember a thing after the flaming sambucas! I'm embarrassed! OK?'

'At least you retained your belongings ... whereas I have no idea where my handbag is. It's got my house keys, my driving licence, my debit cards, some cash ...'

'And yet not your phone?' says Koo.

'No. Why would I take my phone out on a girls' night out? I've dropped three mobiles before now whilst tipsy, and smashed the screens. It's not as if I'll need to phone my girlfriends – not when I'm actually out with them – now is it?'

'Unless you get separated,' mutters Koo, to which Beth gives a wry smile before turning away.

'Ha, bloody ha, you're so funny. Head back then, I don't mind, I'll locate my handbag without your help. I'll walk the streets until something jogs my memory and then maybe I'll know where I left it. Otherwise I'll need to spend the evening on the phone cancelling my bank cards – and we know what a drag that is.'

'Don't be daft!' says Beth, looking worried. 'We're in this together. Now come on, let's stop the bickering and find our bearings. I've only recognised the bar selling the sambucas. Koo hasn't recognised anything, as of yet, but I'm sure she will. Is there anything that jumps out at you, Lulu?'

I spin around; the buttery-coloured masonry, the cobbled streets and the graceful archways aren't calling to me. 'It might help later in the evening, when the neon lights and signs are switched on – my brain must have logged something of my surroundings. A street name, a shop frontage, or a poster advertising a gig?'

'Can we grab a drink?' asks Koo. 'I feel we're acting like tourists, standing here aimlessly,' she says, pointing to the nearest pub, with its alfresco tables.

'Koo, what's the last time you remember being with your ladies?'

asks Beth, taking charge as soon as we have three G&Ts before us.

'Ten o'clockish, maybe a little after. I'm certain of that, because I was feeling ... wanted ... was hoping ...' she gives a huge sigh. 'I was bored stiff. There was no fun, no atmosphere, no jubilation – just business talk, networking jabber, and non-stop standard we-need-to-get-together corporate schmoozing!'

'And friends thought that was suitable for your hen-do?' Beth asks, indignantly. 'I remember snogging an inflatable boy band – which I'm bloody grateful for now, after hearing your rundown!'

We sip our drinks, enjoy the passing parade of tourists, despite Koo refusing to admit her own tourist status. All is calm, as we ponder our situation and chase away the frightening possibilities and scenarios which might have occurred, but thankfully didn't.

'How famous are you, really?' asks Beth, grimacing at her own curiosity.

'I'm not,' says Koo, without hesitation.

'You are!' I scream, shocked by her answer.

'Seriously, I'm not. Granted, my surname is, but me as a person – I'm not famous, Lulu. You might recognise my name from the glossy mags or even the red-top tabloids, when there's little news or gossip circulating about true celebs or the royals, in which case they'll pap a photo of me as a filler.'

'That's being famous,' I say, drooling over the idea.

Koo shakes her head. 'I'll give you an example. Beth, do you know who Aristotle Onassis was?'

'Yeah, I think so ... the shipping tycoon,' she says gingerly, as if unsure.

'Precisely. Do you know his daughter's name?'

Beth blows out her cheeks, '*Phuh!* Er, I'm thinking Christine – but I'm not one hundred per cent.'

'Exactly. It was actually Christina, but nearly right. And her daughter?'

'Nope. Definitely not,' says Beth.

'See, but if it mentioned Onassis beneath any paparazzi photo – would you link them to the shipping family?'

'Sure, there must only be one Onassis family in the public eye,' says Beth.

'But you couldn't pick his granddaughter out from a line-up, could you? No, or name her. And no doubt most people wouldn't be able to pick me from a line-up either, but my surname mentioned in any photo caption tells all ...' Koo glances at me before continuing, 'suggesting I'm famous. I'm not. Does that make sense?'

'Perfectly. And you're right. I know the Bournebury name – I've grown up with it, it feels familiar, as if it relates to me. You're right, I don't know your face from Adam's.'

'The brand feels familiar because we've marketed the products so aggressively – you've known our brand throughout your life, since childhood.'

'If you don't mind, I'll be sticking with my original thought, thanks. As you're the most famous person I've ever met – since I served Dot Cotton, from *EastEnders*, to a slab of cheddar on the deli counter at work.'

'Sweet Caroline' blasts from the pub's open doorway, accompanied by a crowd of joyous voices crooning.

I cease talking. Beth pauses, drink in hand, and Koo turns, eyes wide, suggesting a light-bulb moment.

'Oh my God, I remember singing this last night!' squeals Beth, excitedly grabbing at my shoulder.

'And me. I was swaying, holding on to other people and singing at the top of my lungs!' I say, eager to confirm and align my memory with hers.

'But where?' asks Koo, grabbing for the map.

'I now remember drinking from a paper cup!' announces Beth suddenly, closing her eyes as if reliving a vital moment. 'Other people had slung their arms over my shoulder and I was clutching on to a metal pole to stay upright and steady myself.'

'What?' I jest, as Beth's not making any sense, which clearly proves how drunk she was – we all must have been.

'Now where? My original hotel lies in that direction, yours was that way, and Beth's was way over on the other side of town – yet we ended up finding each other, so how?' says Koo, as we stand on a street watching the traffic fly by, deciding our next move.

'The big yellow party bus!' I scream, frantically pointing at the enormous double decker cornering the street and pulling in at the kerbside. 'Koo, that's nearly as big as your engagement rock!'

The lower deck's windows provide a clear view of a bar in full swing; swirls of white smoke collect at the windows, with flashing neon lights distorting the party-goers' features, as loud music seeps from within.

'Hey, ladies, we meet again – good to see you haven't lost each other, tonight!' hollers the doorman, dressed in security attire, holding the vertical grab bar at the vehicle's rear entrance. 'Have you recovered and returned for more happy times on the party bus?'

'You remember us?' I ask, dashing across to the bus entrance.

'Of course. I've got a great memory for faces. You seemed lost and slightly the worse for wear, if I may say. You'd misplaced your hen party crew and were lost. We don't ignore folk, you know – it's safer to invite you aboard than have you wandering around the city, alone, looking for your friends and family.'

'Wow, I'm impressed with your diligence,' says Koo, full of praise, above the noise of the singing and chanting coming from the lower deck.

'Safety comes first around here, plus it helps that we've got CCTV cameras fitted, in case we need to identify people,' he says, gesturing towards the two cameras positioned above his head.

'Though not recommended viewing for some, given how tipsy they actually get during a night out.'

'And you remember me being alone too?' asks Beth, appearing at my shoulder.

'Yep. Initially, you mentioned feeling sick and queuing for the toilets, only to find you'd been separated from your friends. And the other lady was sick of networking so nipped out seeking real party people – hey presto, you found our bus! Though you soon got chatting and left as a trio – the tutu girl, a Charleston lady, along with a nun – so my colleague and I assumed you'd found your lost buddies during our city party tour. People often do!'

'I was sick of networking?' asks Koo, to which he nods in confirmation.

'So, it was fate that brought us together!' I say, chuffed to have an answer but startled by the details.

'Where did we get off this bus?' asks Beth, butting in before I can ask about my missing handbag.

'Up the top end, just before The Royal Crescent,' he confirms, welcoming two gents on board over our shoulders. 'Our route takes an hour to circle back around, but you weren't anywhere to be seen. So, we figured you'd happily gone on your way.'

'That makes sense,' giggles Koo, as a sense of relief washes over us.

I feel quite choked to think complete strangers can watch out for your welfare when you're vulnerable in an unfamiliar city.

'You didn't happen to find a black slimline handbag, did you?' I quickly interject.

'I believe we had two left behind last night – I didn't see them, my colleague upstairs found them. Every weekend, we find lost property – it'll be stashed at HQ, so you'll need to identify its contents with the boss to retrieve it. I'll radio over if you like?' he says, removing his walkie-talkie from his breast clip. 'Bus calling Base, pick up!'

'Roger, Base here, how can we help?' comes a distorted voice.

'Was a slimline black handbag logged in lost property last night?' our saviour asks, shouting into the radio, as a roar of laughter is heard from the upper deck.

'Positive. Roger. Name and content details needed,' comes the crackly voice.

'Lulu James. My driving licence and bank cards are in there, along with a tiny purse filled with change and about fifty quid in notes.'

The details are swiftly relayed over the radio, and we wait with bated breath for the response.

'Roger. Positive ID regarding the slimline handbag, they can collect from HQ,' crackles the voice.

'Yesssss!' I shout, pumping my fist into the air.

'Are you ladies jumping aboard, as the driver needs to move to our next stop?' the doorman asks, gesturing for us to move along. 'Grab a drink from the bar, if you like, there's three more stops before HQ – I'll shout you when we get near.'

'Absolutely!' says Koo, clambering aboard and heading along the lower deck. 'I assume the bar is this way?'

Chapter Seven

Monday 21 August

Koo

As my back sinks into the pale calfskin seats, I exhale any lingering doubts about my choices, regarding the extended weekend, the chauffeured vehicle, or my travelling companions. They are both lovely women, though I remain unimpressed by Lulu's announcement yesterday, exposing my identity and heritage. I thought I'd have to endure an interrogation, justifying my existence and explaining every paparazzi shot in the glossy mags. Not that I wish to appear in them, but social platforms are fixated on the upcoming nuptials of a Bournebury. 'Riches to rags' is how they pitch it, with their incessant focus on Judd's job. Lulu's revelation certainly spares me from continuing the pretence about my wedding. Some would say I'm being ungrateful, that having a sumptuous celebrity wedding must be a dream, but not if it's your idea of a nightmare. Admitting who I am opens the usual can of worms, quickly followed by a stream of crazy questions, but all I can do is simply be me. They'll either like me or not.

'I love that "just cleaned" smell of leather,' says Beth, sitting beside me in the rear, awaiting our departure.

'You can buy it in an aerosol can, you know,' says Lulu, turning around from the front passenger seat to view us full face.

'Really?' I quip, unsure if she's pulling my leg.

'Oh yeah, we sell loads of it when it comes in as a "special buy" – though the smell only lasts for a day before you have to reapply it.'

'Like an air freshener then?' asks Beth.

'Yeah, similar, but you spray it on the actual seats,' explains Lulu.

'On leather seats?' I ask, unsure I'm keeping up with her product USP or the instructions for use.

'No, on fabric seats – but it gives you that new-leather smell,' says Lulu, as if the irony is lost on her.

I exchange a swift glance with Beth; her furrowed brow suggests we're on the same page when it comes to the need for such a product.

'Anyway, there was a stretch limo available but I thought a bit of class would be preferable when travelling such a long distance,' I say, hoping my choice befits their wish lists, despite neither one mentioning a hen-do vehicle.

'It's beautiful, very classy for the likes of me,' says Beth, admiring the interior trim of leather and polished wood. 'It's a . . .?'

'A Rolls-Royce Phantom,' I say quickly, realising she hadn't noticed the Spirit of Ecstasy emblem on the bonnet.

'Nice, very nice,' she adds, settling back as our uniformed chauffeur closes the boot, having loaded our luggage. 'We're splitting the cost, right?'

I don't answer. Instead, I lower the side window for my final view of The Royal Crescent. It had only taken a quick call to my PA last night and – without fuss or bother, despite the late hour – he'd promised to send a car to collect us straight after breakfast. With the prospect of a five-hour journey ahead of us, I had no intention of slumming it – travelling in style is one of life's highlights. I'd called Judd before breakfast, assuring him that I'd keep in touch on a daily basis. And as for the wedding, I'd figure that one out as soon as I could. My aim being to alleviate as much wedding stress or upset as possible, rehash a few wedding details, and tackle my father's wedding planner into submission. Though I doubt I'll win over the wonderful Electra, along with her habitual 'dharling' tag-phrase, as my father's paying her bill.

My boys are old enough, yet daft enough to cause mischief; they don't need their mother to be fussing over them whilst trying to straighten out her own head. Last night, I was a bag of nerves after speaking to Felix. Not that he's fazed by my absence – that's something he's accepted, having grown up witnessing the demands and constraints imposed upon me by the family business. He's surprised and annoyed at my spontaneity, which I admit, isn't like me. Felix will focus on his role within the marketing department while his younger brother, Felipe, oversees the production process. Though, bless him, his dear heart isn't in it.

Like others before them, my sons must deal with the pressure and personal sacrifice required to run a multinational company, learning how to balance the commitment, the conflict and constant demands of any successful enterprise against the search for individual happiness. I'm unsure if I should allow their futures to be so tightly bound to the family business as mine have proven to be. My father has always been a flamboyant, outrageous character, with a love for the limelight. He is as eager as ever to secure the interests of both my sons, just as he did with me.

My life has been filled with logical decisions, carefully constructed plans and projected forecasts, detailing my every move for years ahead, all signed and sealed with Papa's approval! Though he hasn't had the final say in some departments in recent years, much to his annoyance. Not that I'm gloating, or resent my strict upbringing, but my relationship with Judd has taken me by surprise as much as it has the family. I suppose when you're the current CEO, presiding over a successful fifth-generation family business, with global markets and worldwide product branding, you hardly expect your only child, your only daughter and heir, to fall in love and become engaged to a local dustman. I seriously thought Papa was about to have a coronary when we announced our intention to marry. And given that I haven't called it off in the ensuing six months, I suspect he'd probably opt for such a medical emergency in preference to what's planned for next Saturday. In spite of which, he'll save face by hosting a star-studded celebrity wedding for his only child. Informing my two sons had been the least of my worries – until I actually did so, and then they too joined my parents in passing judgement on my fiancé.

I don't see why they were so shocked by the announcement. Surely, they knew it was on the cards, seeing how happy Judd makes me? We hardly hid it, did we? Acting like lovesick teenagers half the time! That certainly wasn't the case in either of my previous long-term relationships, with Giles or Alberto, despite living together, having a baby with each and trying to be a family. Both relationships fizzled out within no time – and look how evenly matched we were supposed to be, sharing family heritage, business interests and social standing. *Phuh!* It counts for nothing, if love isn't part of the mix! Which is why the press pack were interested from the first hint of my engagement to Judd – they're expecting my previous relationship dramas to follow me all the way up the aisle. Now, that would be the money shot: wealthy chocolatier with his jilted heiress upon his arm!

Such a privileged life doesn't come without constraints, pressure or high expectations, which I suppose the likes of Lulu would never dream of. Earlier, I heard her attempting to joke about chocolate, but it's no laughing matter shouldering the burden of a family empire, all the time knowing you're next in line. I'm forty-seven and still working my apprenticeship on the board – awaiting the top job, so to speak. Not that I'm eager for it to come my way, given the implied demise of my father. I'm not ready.

I bet Lulu thinks my life is one big cocktail party, filled with posh frocks, handsome men and oodles of delicious chocolate. And as for her expression when she latched on to my engagement ring, despite trying to be subtle, she wasn't. I bet Beth's fiancé personally chose and paid for her engagement ring, whereas society expects me to wear a ring that's a symbol of our family wealth. Judd would have loved to choose a ring for me – something special, in the same way as Dale – a ring that no one else had previously worn, but no. Traditions within families such as ours means Judd was offered a selection of three family heirlooms from the bank's safe – my engagement ring was once my great-grandmother's precious keepsake. What I wouldn't give to be an ordinary bride, coping with the mundane worries of seating plans and pre-wedding nerves. Instead, I feel torn between what I truly want and what my family expect of me.

The thump of the driver's door closing brings me back to reality; our smart chauffeur settles himself, before announcing, 'If that's everything, madam.'

'Nothing else, thank you,' I say, as Beth and Lulu remain silent.

'We've an estimated arrival time of three o'clock, depending on the traffic,' he continues, starting the ignition and adjusting the air conditioning.

'Thank you. We'd welcome a brief stop for a comfort break partway,' I say, slowly raising the rear window, my head and heart having memorised a final snapshot of The Royal Crescent, complete with the waiting concierge.

Beth

Two hours ago, I'd performed my usual habit of saying, 'Bye, suite, thank you for the memories' – a daft routine but my quirky custom on leaving anywhere since my teenage years. I don't

suppose I'll remember every hotel room, rented flat or house
in which I've lived and stayed, but this particular weekend I
somehow doubt I'll ever forget. And now, seated in the back of
a vintage car alongside an actual heiress, I have every comfort
known to man – and yet, I've never been so uncomfortable in
my life. I daren't move for fear of my thigh making a squeaking
sound on the leather, or cross my legs for fear my shoe might
touch the interior and leave a black rubber mark – not to mention
the constant whirring within my brain of my nagging doubts.
Am I doing the right thing? Is it fair that I should be heading
up North when my home is down South? Is this the trouble
my mother was alluding to? And what will I say to Dale, later
tonight, when I don't arrive home in Kent? I'd already lied once
this morning when calling my boss. My 'I'm so sorry, but I'm not
feeling well' performance was instantly greeted with sympathy
and understanding – which made me burst out crying once I put
the phone down, much to Lulu's surprise.

'I don't get it. Why are you crying?' she'd asked, dashing to
my side, offering hugs and a concerned tilt of her head.

'Because I never do this. Ever. I don't tell lies. It goes against
my principles,' I'd snuffled through a handful of tissues.

'*Phuh!* I do it all the time. I'll tell you what will happen: your
boss will remark to a colleague that you're off sick, and your duties
will either be shared between the other workers or left for the day.
Someone will show kindness by saying, "Oh, poor thing, she's
rarely off ill," and another will sympathise, "It must be bad for her
to miss work," and then they'll all go about their work, not giving
you a second thought for the rest of the day – see, easy-peasy,' Lulu
had explained, meaning well but sounding slightly cynical.

I'd looked up at her from my ball of tissues.

'Don't look so worried, they'll be falling over themselves
to give you an excuse for this week, with the wedding on the
horizon,' she'd added, patting my back for further comfort.

A glance towards Koo for reassurance and I'd come face to face with a blank expression.

'Don't look at me, I've never called in sick in my life. I follow my diary appointments avidly, but if I need the day off I simply cross out a specific day. No questions asked, given the hours I usually work each week,' she'd said, giving a nonchalant shrug.

One advantage of being the boss' daughter, I suppose – though I didn't feel better, having heard their opinions. And now, having consumed two glasses of chilled bubbly en route to our hen week, my mood has sunk even lower, and I'm dreading calling in sick again tomorrow.

The lengthy silence inside the Rolls has provided a quiet opportunity for contemplation, but without music to distract me this journey seems endless. I imagine the slightly stuffy atmosphere is caused by the presence of a hired driver, standard practice and all that – though I haven't a clue. My first experience of a chauffeur-driven car was supposed to be my wedding day; not that we've booked a Rolls-Royce but a chauffeured Maserati, which is what Dale wanted.

'Have we had a response from the owner?' I ask, knowing Lulu has been tapping away on her phone screen since we left Bath on the M4, breezed up the M5, and now are somewhere along the M6. I've switched my phone off, for fear of being bombarded with additional text messages from my original hen party airing their views on my change of plans. I assume Lulu has bravely been answering hers.

'I'll check,' she calls from the front passenger seat, her fingernails clicking rapidly on her screen. Not that she volunteered to be the official correspondent for the party, but with Koo's phobia of technology and my bamboozled brain, Lulu thought it best to use her contact details. It was a gamble, for sure. Who surfs a holiday rental at ten o'clock on a Sunday evening, hoping to make a booking for the following day? No one. Unless you've the financial means with which to influence folk, should they need a little gentle but firm persuasion to meet your needs. Part of me was relieved that Koo and Lulu took control of the situation, but being the spare wheel alienates you from the situation, which never provides peace of mind. My biggest fear is we'll arrive at our destination to find the owners weren't truly prepared to cooperate at such short notice and, having paid the initial deposit, we're left without digs and with the prospect of spending the night in a plush chauffeur-driven car. Now, that would be embarrassing!

'We've got a reply!' calls Lulu, turning to face us, despite the restraint of the seat belt, to show us her phone screen as proof. After which she holds it flat, her gaze darting side to side as she scans the email. 'Jemima Campbell . . . bloody hell, she's based in Shetland!'

'What does she say?' asks Koo, coming alive.

'She's thanked us for the deposit payment and, despite it being short notice, she'll instruct her housekeeper, a local woman, to unlock and prepare the property for our arrival, from three o'clock today. She'd like us to transfer the outstanding payment as soon as possible, so that'll need to be while we're travelling then, Koo,' says Lulu, glancing up from her screen.

I cringe at the mere suggestion of more money being expended for my benefit. I promise I will pay back every single penny.

'Woo hoo, that's it, ladies, we have our dream cottage for one whole week,' sings Koo, jiggling her shoulders in delight.

'Though with nine bedrooms we'll have a choice of a different bed each night,' quips Lulu, smiling broadly.

'That's amazing, thank you, Koo,' I add, not wishing to state the obvious that a week's rental is far longer than we'll actually be needing. 'I can't believe that you're making our hen-do wish lists come true!'

Koo places a hand gently on my forearm before speaking. 'I can do with the thinking time and space for myself too, lovey.'

'I know, it's just . . . I'm not used to this sort of lifestyle. You have an idea, and instantly it happens – that alone seems magical. I have to plan and budget months in advance.'

Koo gives my arm a gentle squeeze before retracting her hand. I get that her family's mega rich, but still, she's got a humble nature, which makes it easier for the likes of me. I've yet to forget her expression yesterday when Lulu mentioned the glossy mags or the size of her engagement ring. I'd have kicked off big time if she'd outed me so crassly, though I doubt Lulu realises how it looked. Or sounded, for that matter.

Chapter Eight

Lulu

The second the car draws up before the quaint cottage, I'm out like a shot. I'm desperate – not to stretch my legs, as I took a short break at a service station only ninety minutes ago, but to make a call, in private. I didn't realise that Hawkshead was such a lengthy drive from Bath, but that's my ignorance and no reflection on the chauffeur's driving. For five long hours, I haven't dared to text back, for fear that either Koo or Beth might read over my shoulder from the rear seats.

'How gorgeous!' cries Beth, leaping from the rear seats to stand before the drystone wall surrounding our picturesque cottage.

It's exactly as pictured on the website – a quintessential country residence, with a white picket gate and cobbled pathway leading to the moss-green wooden door with an inset pane of antique bevelled glass. Large leaded windows balance the frontage, with the upper storey peering from beneath a traditional thatched roof with an abundance of wisteria cascading in a romantic fashion, adding a splash of lilac softening the rustic brickwork and tiny porchway. We are surrounded by a joyous cacophony of birdsong.

'I was impressed with the website images, but they hardly do it justice, do they?' says Koo, joining us at the gate. 'Though I bet that wisteria's a bugger to clip back, come autumn.'

Both Beth and I stare at her. What a strange remark. As if Koo does her own gardening; I can't imagine that Koo would ever need to foot a sturdy ladder, or struggle with a pair of secateurs.

As if reading our awkward silence, Koo unlatches the gate and enters. I notice Beth hesitates to follow, so I step forward. Standing on ceremony is all very polite but I want a little privacy, sooner rather than later. Beth falls into line, bringing up the rear of the party, as our chauffeur pops the boot release and busies himself with our luggage. I hear the gate latch give a natty little click as it slips smoothly back into position. Now, that's posh.

I'm unsure how some properties are classified as 'cottages', because this is larger than any house I've lived in. I honestly thought that cottages were supposed to be bijou and cramped, but with nine bedrooms this is anything but small. I spy the apex of a second thatched roof at the rear of the property, previously hidden from view.

'Koo, it feels like I'm dreaming,' calls Beth over my shoulder, as we walk up the cobbled pathway.

The front door swings wide as a spritely lady appears on the doorstep, complete with a neat pleated skirt, sensible brogues and a weathered but beaming smile. 'Hello! Welcome to Lakeside Cottage!' she announces, gesturing to an artistic name plaque beside the door. She steps back, inviting us into the hallway. 'I'm Josie – caretaker of the keys, so to speak.'

I feel the urge to remove my shoes, a habit I always do on entering other folks' homes, but I resist, as Koo doesn't remove hers but strides straight inside.

'Good afternoon, I'm Ms Bournebury,' Koo says, extending her hand in a formal manner, before adding, 'Ms James and Ms Douglas, respectively.'

It's not a gesture I've ever done on entering a property, so I don't follow suit. I'm hoping I don't appear rude or ungrateful.

'Hello,' I say, keeping it simple.

Beth does likewise, which instantly makes me feel comfortable.

Comparison and self-criticism have always been my downfall, whether at work or home; other people can make me feel inferior in an instant. Scanning items from the fruit and vegetable aisle at work usually provides at least one moment a week when a customer loudly exclaims, 'What, you've never tried it!' as I'm trying to be sociable whilst serving.

The hallway is a fair size, decorated in muted tones of mustard and gold, with a wide staircase directly in front and numerous panelled doors positioned on either side. I love properties with authentic metal doorknobs and picture rails – so different to the modern semi-detached with plasterboard walls in which I was raised.

Beth closes the latch on the front door as Josie points to the hall table on which an array of items are placed.

'There's a set of keys for you each, a housekeeping manual detailing everything you're likely to need – from instructions for electrical equipment to local bin collections – and a guest book, if you wish to sign, though not everybody does. A list of emergency numbers, including my own, is pinned inside the pantry door.'

We follow her gestures and nod in unison, confirming our understanding.

'If you'd like to come this way, I'll give you a quick tour before leaving you in peace.'

Josie briskly opens the first door, to the right of the entrance, leading us into an extended lounge, with an impressive open hearth, generous sofas and furnishings, and a gleam of beeswax on every wooden surface. It's clean, fresh and tastefully deco-rated, with an air of prestige suggesting affluent owners, if this is what they let as a holiday home. If I owned this property, I'd definitely be living here rather than having the likes of me passing through.

'Such spectacular views,' gasps Beth, entering the room and dashing straight to the nearest window.

The view looks out across a large lake with a backdrop of purple-headed mountains beyond. Their contours dip and curve against a clear sky. Rich greens, deep purples and an assortment of blues provide a landscape which seems to stretch as far as the eye can see.

'Stunning, isn't it? This room is a particular favourite of mine, with beautiful views, a roaring fire – not that you'll be needing one, but there's logs by the back door if you choose to light it – and a quiet atmosphere, as we haven't any neighbours on this side for another half-mile.'

'Sounds idyllic,' says Koo, joining Beth at the window sill to marvel at the aspect beyond.

It's beautiful, I can't deny it, but we've just spent several hours being driven through equally stunning landscapes. Did they not see all the green? Or not expect it to continue right to the door of our rental cottage?

'Anyhow, that's the main lounge. Across the hall, if we may . . .' instructs Josie, leading the way to the opposite door. 'The dining room is the other room at the front of the cottage – again lovely, should you care to entertain or invite others to join you.'

We swiftly exchange a glance, before Beth speaks. 'There's just us three . . . we aren't expecting guests.'

Josie looks surprised. 'No worries, but it accommodates sixteen, if needed.'

We all sidestep her tiny frame to peer inside at the massive oak dining suite and accompanying chairs, sixteen in total. Another *Homes and Gardens* photo shoot opportunity, if ever there was one. I can't imagine the noise if all the seats were filled; you'd have a job hearing each other over the clattering of the crockery and cutlery, let alone the chattering of the guests. And that would be before the wine had been replenished numerous times. Why would someone choose to rent out such a home, and not live here themselves?

Josie begins to close the door, signalling for us to shuffle backwards into the hallway. She indicates beneath the staircase in passing. 'A record player, which probably seems to be in a daft spot, but it's heard throughout the cottage if the volume is high. There's plenty of vinyl in the cupboard beneath,' she says, before opening the next door. 'Officially referred to as the Snug.' As if by magic, she reveals a modern room with low-slung, squishy couches, a low coffee table, abstract prints framed on each wall, and a plasma TV in the corner. 'There's a selection of board games, DVDs and novelty items under the coffee table in case it rains, or you fancy a quiet night in. You'll find the remote controls in the basket beneath the TV.'

We nod in unison; personally I can't imagine us playing Monopoly in the coming days, but you never know. Though finding a quiet place to have a private conversation, which is what I'm pretty much after right now, will be an advantage.

'Along here is the kitchen. Now, I'll warn you, on first sight many people flinch, but once you get used to an Aga there's no going back!' jests Josie, leading us beyond the staircase and into the final doorway. I freeze. Large farmhouse kitchen is all I see: red tiled floor, scrubbed central table, a split stable door at the rear, and the largest yellow Aga I've ever seen dominating the end wall.

'I'm used to them, I wouldn't trade mine for the world,' says Koo, lovingly.

'That's good, because I haven't a clue,' mutters Beth, out of the corner of her mouth.

It might appear rude but I'm losing interest in the guided tour at this point, I simply wish to make my phone call.

'Through there,' Josie gestures along a flagstoned corridor, 'is an assortment of rooms, including a utility, storage rooms and the old scullery – though it's not as gruesome or as bare as it sounds – you'll find lots of household paraphernalia stashed in there.' She swiftly pulls open one fridge door, of the large double-doored appliance, to reveal a selection of delicatessen foods, fruit juices and wine bottles stashed within. 'I've created your welcome hamper and popped some items in for chilling . . . the rest are in a wicker basket in the storage room – you can't miss it. It's all in with the rental price, so you aren't charged any extra if you consume any items. So, do you have any questions?'

'Er, no, all pretty straightforward so far,' says Koo, glancing around the kitchen and spying a nifty chrome coffee machine in the corner. 'The instruction manuals are by the front door, you said – I'm sure we'll figure out the necessary as we use it.'

'Access to the rear garden is through this door, or around the side of the cottage – parasols and sunloungers are in the brick outhouse, there's even a couple of bikes, if you wish to venture out and about, plus a coal bunker and log store, should you want a fire. If we go back through, I'll take you upstairs.' Josie leads the way.

Without a word, we follow. Given their expressions, I sense that the other two have reached my level of boredom. There's nothing Josie's shown us that we wouldn't or couldn't have discovered if she'd thrown the keys at us and allowed us to explore. But I suppose, given the extortionate price of the rental, which definitely reflects the size of the property, I suppose the owners feel a tour is necessary. I suppose this is what pampering feels like; they're giving Koo value for her money. I daren't think how long it'll take me to pay back my IOU. But it'll be worth it in the long run. I hope.

We trudge up the staircase, which is wider than any house I've lived in, to be greeted by a huge landing furnished with yet another couch and a large bookcase filled with hefty-looking volumes.

'There's a selection of rooms: doubles, twins and singles. You're welcome to use all the storage areas, bathrooms and cupboard space. Loft space too, if required,' says Josie, pointing at various doors. 'There's fresh towels, bath robes and toiletries in this linen cupboard here, bed sheets in the one over there.' Finally, she stops, draws breath and smiles. 'If there's nothing else, I'll leave you ladies to enjoy your stay. Should you need anything, and I mean anything, please just give me a call – I am literally a short walk away.'

'Thank you, Josie – we do appreciate your effort, especially as our booking was made at such short notice,' says Koo, speaking on our behalf.

'My pleasure, enjoy!' In a heartbeat, Josie is dashing down the creaky staircase, leaving us three adrift in the middle of the landing.

Again, no home I've ever lived in has had a 'middle of the landing', they've never been large enough – this one is an additional room between rooms.

'Find a bedroom of your choosing, ladies, and make yourselves at home. I'm sure our luggage will be arriving any minute . . . now,' says Koo.

As if signalled by Josie's swift exit, our uniformed chauffeur appears trudging two suitcases up the staircase. 'Ladies, your luggage.'

'Thank you,' I say gleefully, realising one of them is mine. I allow him to place it down on the carpet. My first task is choosing a decent room, not the master bedroom obviously, that belongs to Koo.

'I'd quite like a double, if that isn't being too greedy,' says Beth, looking embarrassed for stating her preference.

'I'm sure there must be plenty of doubles, with en suites too – take your pick,' says Koo, striding across the landing to open the nearest bedroom door and revealing a large airy room, with a huge canopied bed, before adding, 'the master suite, I presume.'

'Which is rightfully yours,' I say, hastily adding, 'if Beth doesn't mind.'

'Of course.'

'Are you sure?' asks Koo. 'I'm quite happy with something a little less of a boudoir.'

'I'm sure,' I say, moving to the furthest door, presumably a bedroom positioned at the front of the cottage. I find a large double, not quite the size of Koo's room, but just as beautifully decorated in pastel shades of pink. There are wardrobes lining the far wall alongside a full-sized door, which I assume leads to the en suite. 'This will suit me.'

'Are you sorted, Lulu?' calls Koo, dragging one of her suitcases into the master suite.

'Yep, I'll be happy as Larry in there,' I say, returning for my own suitcase, which isn't nearly as large as Koo's.

Beth appears on the other side of the landing. 'I'm opting for this one, the decor is very feminine,' she announces, gesturing through the open doorway of the other front bedroom, opposite mine.

'Great stuff! I'll just unpack and be with you ladies in a short while,' I say, hastily disappearing into my room, closing the door and leaning my back against it. Finally, a minute's peace.

My gaze falls upon the view from the window. Beyond the criss-cross diamond pattern of leaded glass lies a breathtaking landscape of rolling hills and sky. No telegraph poles, no vehicles, no building sites or cityscapes – simply nature, as far as the eye can see. I breathe in the picture-perfect serenity before me as if standing in the open air and feeling the sun on my face.

The solidity of the wooden door against my shoulder blades feels like a blessing. It's not that I'm not enjoying my time with these ladies, but I need to make a call. And then, I might know where this is heading. It's one thing to skive off work for a week, but quite another to have no idea what I'll be returning home to at the end of it. And despite what the two brides think, I also have big decisions to make regarding next Saturday.

I grab my mobile phone from my pocket and search my contacts, a few screen swipes, and then tap the name 'Dad'. Instantly, the image of my dad appears as the connection is made and the ringing begins. It is picked up in three rings. Thank God.

'Hi, Gareth,' I whisper, as my heart leaps into my throat in sheer excitement.

Beth

'It's ready, come and get it!' Koo's hollering travels up the staircase, bringing me back to the present.

'Dale, I've got to go, they're calling me,' I say to the FaceTime image filling my screen. 'As I said, I'll be in touch every day, even if it's just a quick call or a text. But I need this time to think, to focus on us and make sure that I'm not hurting either of us by going through with Saturday's plans.' I fall silent, waiting for him to speak.

He doesn't. Instead, Dale's expression flickers with emotion, his pale blue eyes appear lifeless, as if the light in them has been extinguished, and he swallows, hard.

'I'm so sorry, this is the last thing I wanted to do. I know you don't approve of me missing work, but needs must. I'll speak to you tomorrow. Love you.'

'Do you?' he says, as quick as a flash.

'Yes. You know I do.' With a wrench, my heart begins to ache at the thought he'd even ask.

'I don't get it then,' says Dale. 'I love you, you say you love me – what more is needed, Beth?'

'Dale, I . . .'

'No, seriously. I'll give you the time and space you're asking for. I will. But surely, we have everything we need right there, in those few words?' His gaze is pleading with me, like never before.

I can't believe I'm actually doing this to the kindest, sweetest man I know. 'I'll call you tomorrow. Bye,' is all I manage before tapping the screen and killing the app.

'Beth!' hollers Lulu.

'I'm coming!' I jump up from the delicate stool, positioned before the shabby-chic dressing table, grabbing my mobile and a pile of playful hen party goodies found stashed inside my suitcase.

I've spent the last hour unpacking my belongings, freshening up and mulling over my situation. I get that the rest of my tribe are unsettled by my behaviour, airing their annoyance, irritation and confusion in numerous erratic text messages, but I'm not prepared to go into detail with them. The only person I wish to speak to is Dale, and now I have, so the girls need to back off. I need headspace to figure out my thoughts and feelings – that's not going to happen anytime soon if they continue to bombard and cajole me into returning text messages. I'm emotionally drained, with an empty tank and a deadline looming in less than six days.

I gallop down the creaky staircase in a bouncy manner, as if unpacking my belongings has renewed my flagging energy levels. I enter the kitchen to find Koo and Lulu standing before the scrubbed table dishing grated cheese and baked beans on to crispy baked potatoes.

'I hope you're hungry,' says Koo, nudging the third plate towards me. 'I figured that everyone eats baked spuds, so help yourself – there's more in the Aga, if needed. I reckoned we'd probably go out for a bite to eat later, so this will tide us over.'

'Thank you,' I say, plopping my mobile and the handful of goodies down on the tabletop, before selecting a knife from the cutlery pile and digging in.

'What are those?' asks Lulu, piling a mountain of grated cheese on to her buttered spuds.

'A selection of hen party games, "dare" cards, scratch cards and lewd confetti that I purchased, convinced they were the backbone for any fun-filled weekend. I shared them amongst the girls on Saturday night, and I assume they must've popped them back into my suitcase when they were packing up my belongings. I don't intend to keep them.'

'Ooooo, interesting! Our Kirsty bought a questionnaire-type game to play on the train journey. Boy, did it cause bad feeling!' giggles Lulu.

I watch her ladling baked beans on to her plate. Where she's going to put all that, I'll never know – there's hardly anything of her.

'Why?' asks Koo, obviously intrigued, with an eager expression.

'It proved how few of her girlfriends actually know her that well. Remember, there were thirty in our party, and hardly anyone could answer a basic question about Our Kirsty. Makes you wonder what true friendship is built on sometimes,' mutters Lulu, collecting a knife and fork before stepping back from the table. 'Are we eating in here or at the posh table?'

Mm-hmm, doesn't it just? Thinking about the text messages I've received, some of my hens are clearly more bothered about wearing their bridesmaids' dresses come Saturday than my welfare.

'Dining room, methinks,' says Koo, ladling baked beans on to her cheesy potatoes. 'Lead the way, if you will, Lulu.'

She doesn't need asking twice, which is something I've noticed about Lulu. Me, on the other hand, I hang back a little, but that's the story of my life – allow others to go first, before following in their wake.

'I'll be through in a minute,' I say, as they leave the kitchen, adding to my serving, with every intention of clearing my plate, filled with gorgeous gooey beans and cheese.

Within seconds, I'm following in their footsteps and entering the dining room, my plate in one hand, while I attempt to balance my mobile and hen night goodies in the other. Koo is seated on the right, nearest the door, Lulu directly opposite, leaving the head of the table available for me. I don't wish to sit there, so I squeeze past Koo's chair and settle on her right-hand side.

'This looks delicious. I didn't realise how hungry I actually was until I smelt it – and now, my stomach is growling,' I say, arranging my belongings on the chair beside me.

Koo gives a little chuckle; Lulu manages a rapid nod whilst chewing.

'Anyway, let's hear the controversy then,' says Koo, as if they'd waited to continue the conversation while I was dishing up.

'Well, exactly that. Her very best friend didn't score any points, while I only got two wrong answers from a list of about thirty questions. The others were all pretty low. It was totally embarrassing, especially as Our Kirsty was running a points-based scoreboard for the weekend, with novelty gifts for the winner and runner up – though I wasn't about to complain, as it meant I got a head start.'

'You are family though,' I say, trying to make a fitting excuse for the others. 'I'm not entirely sure my ladies could have answered too many questions about me. We share plenty of memories, but I doubt they know much about certain aspects of my life.'

'Nor mine,' says Koo. 'In fact, correct that – mine wouldn't have scored any.'

'Given that some were too busy networking, I shouldn't think so. But surely, your other friends would have answered correctly?' asks Lulu, her knife and fork suspended, awaiting an answer.

Koo busies herself eating, as if she hasn't heard the question.

I glance between the pair. Lulu is waiting and the silence is lengthening, until Koo inhales deeply, puts down her fork and looks up. There's a definite manner in the raised angle of her chin, the way her shoulders ease back, and the supposedly casual way she purses her lips before finally answering.

'Well, no, actually, they couldn't. The simple reason is, I don't have such people in my life – my world, as you might say. I have my two sons and contact with their fathers, so my ex-partners. I have my divorced parents and for the last six months, I've had Judd, but other than that . . . no one. Nobody I would class as a best friend. I have family and acquaintances – no one sits in the middle ground.' On her final word, Koo immediately resumes eating.

Lulu glances rapidly in my direction. I'm not entirely sure she knows what to say in response. Neither do I, for that matter, but someone needs to speak.

'Thanks a bunch, lady. Given the unexpected weekend we've had together, I think I fill the brief. I might not be family, but I'm certainly not an acquaintance, seeing as I've accompanied you both through the streets of Bath wearing yesterday's undies. I can't say that about anyone else.'

Lulu laughs first, followed by Koo, who chokes and splutters on her food.

'And I trusted you enough to wrap me and pin me into a bed sheet toga and parade my sorry ass along those same streets. Surely that can't be classed as an acquaintance, can it?' protests Lulu.

'No. You're right. I certainly haven't shared a king-sized can-opied bed with another woman, either,' adds Koo, pointing her knife in my direction.

'There you go then, so please don't say there's no one in-between, because I bagsie that spot, alongside Lulu,' I say, giving Koo a warm smile of appreciation for everything she's done for us this weekend.

A sudden blush colours Koo's cheek and a glassy twinkle appears at the corner of her eye, before she lowers her head to focus on her dinner plate. I hate to think that she feels so alone, despite her good nature and generous manner. I can't imagine ever thinking there's no one in the middle ground between family and virtual strangers.

'Open them up then,' insists Koo, after a few minutes of silence, gesturing towards my pile of goodies. 'Let's have a look.'

'These?' I screw my face up at the tacky mementos.

'I thought such games were on your hen-do wish list!' jests Koo, eyeballing Lulu.

'Absolutely! Though I refuse to keep a scoreboard tally,' giggles Lulu, pulling my leg.

Whilst chewing, I grab the top packet of 'dare' cards and open the gaudy pink box, withdrawing the laminated playing cards, adorned with 'L' plate symbols and puckered hot lips, and slap them down on the table.

'Classy,' says Koo, shaking her head.

'They were only a fiver, so I can't complain,' I add, turning the pile over to show the suggested task.

'Anything good?' asks Lulu, craning her neck to read upside down.

'The usual. Blag a drink, kiss a stranger and perform a sexy dance – hardly daring, in the grand scheme of things,' I say, neatening the pile and passing them across the table to Lulu.

I'm not surprised by the 'dares', but in the cold light of day and stone-cold sober, they seem somewhat childish – and possibly, in the throes of my drunken Saturday night, somewhat tame.

'We've probably each done the most daring thing on our hen night by quitting it for better company,' adds Koo, finishing her meal and pushing her plate away.

'Is that what we've done?' I ask.

'I have,' she retorts. 'Or rather, I think I did. I wasn't enjoying myself – it was a drag, a bore and . . .' Koo looks at me, while Lulu busies herself flipping through the 'dare' cards, and softly whispers, as if not wishing to alert Lulu. 'I need to decide what I'm doing on Saturday.'

'Likewise,' I say, in a hushed tone.

Koo gives a double blink and a tiny nod, confirming she understands. Which feels strange – because for two women who are
worlds apart, maybe we do have something in common.

'Can we just ditch these corny cards?' asks Lulu, shuffling
the pack.

'Yes. If we're going to do as we wish this week!' I say.

'Mmm, and who said I wouldn't be heading out for a drunken
night amongst friends?' asks Koo, a minxy sparkle returning to
her eye.

Chapter Nine

Koo

I nip out from the kitchen's stable door, cradling a fresh coffee, in need of a breath of fresh air. I'm not used to being around people all of the time, so having the liberty to enjoy a wander in the garden while I sip my coffee is a touch of normality for me. Not that I do much gardening – I haven't the time – but I still admire and draw strength from its beauty.

From the doorstep, I cross a largish patio area complete with a built-in barbecue and an arrangement of flowering ceramic pots. I can't imagine it's easy keeping a rental property looking smart throughout each season, so large ornamental arrangements are obviously the answer; they provide a splash of cascading colour, softening the drystone walls and the slabs nudging up against the coal bunker and a sizeable outhouse. Josie did mention that the sunloungers and parasols were stowed inside, but I don't intend to settle longer than a quick coffee break. A flight of stone steps leads me to the upper terrace consisting of a huge expanse of lawn, which is in need of a quick cut – though, given our late booking, I wouldn't have expected otherwise. A couple of sturdy wooden benches are positioned on opposite sides of the lawn amidst borders of variegated shrubbery. A higgledy-piggledy path of aged stepping stones litters the turf, leading towards an attractive hedgerow of dark purple sculpted to form a central archway, alive with twittering birdsong. I opt for the bench positioned behind the outhouse, not that I wish to be hidden from view, but

I do wish to be hidden, just in case my emotions get the better of me. I'm not a crier by nature, but the sheer frustration of my situation throws me off kilter at the unlikeliest moment. And now is not my chosen moment.

A sense of déjà vu washes over me. It's like being back in boarding school, surrounded by new or older girls, when I was desperate to be back at home instead of returning to school after the holidays. My schoolgirl heart used to ache with the feelings of isolation, anxiety and renewed home-sickness that occurred at the beginning of each term. Made harder by knowing that I had a full day of timetabled lessons and extra-curricular activities to complete, plus attending mealtimes and study sessions, all with a chipper smile, before I could at last be alone and have a little cry in the shower as I got ready for bed. I might be thirty-two years older, with two grown-up sons, but despite being here of my own choosing, this moment feels exactly the same as back then. I've a history littered with fake friends and demanding family, coupled with a deep sense of loneliness. If I focus, I can keep the emotional floodwaters from crashing on to the beach until nearer bedtime. I can, and I will.

I sip my coffee, while focusing my gaze on the perfectly shaped archway in the towering hedgerow across from my seat. I've no idea of its botanical name, but it's beautiful nevertheless, as the unusual leaf colouring creates a statement of colour against the emerald lawn and variegated shrubbery. I bet its nurturing demands a decent set of green fingers and a barrowload of patience. Neither of which I possess, but still, the contrasting colour is attractive.

Contrasting colour – is that what we all crave in life? Something, or someone, to complement our natural tones by being similar but different enough to intrigue our curiosity? Is that what I've found in Judd? My 'bit of rough', as he lovingly calls himself. A giggle escapes me; my spirits are lifted by the very thought of him. I picture his clear blue eyes beneath a low, commanding brow, while his pale skin is stretched like a taut canvas from cheekbone to jawline. His gentle nature and unwavering resilience . . .

'Are you OK?' Beth interrupts my thoughts, appearing at the top of the stone steps.

'Yes, just taking a minute – you know how it is.' I lift my coffee mug as if proving my point.

'Do you mind?' she asks, gesturing towards the bench.

'Be my guest,' I lie, knowing an extra five minutes of peace would have done me the world of good. 'I was just admiring the colouring of the hedge.'

'Purple beech, I think. Though it could be a laurel of some sort,' says Beth, without hesitation in naming, or settling herself. There's a heartbeat of silence before she continues. 'I'm getting the gist of the situation, and thought I'd come and be upfront about my dilemma, as I think . . . there's a chance we're in the same boat.'

I nod. I've had the same thought.

'I've spoken to Dale about the wedding,' says Beth in one gushing breath, before inhaling deeply and sitting back, allowing her gaze to meet mine.

'And?'

'I thought it best to speak to you in private. Please don't think I'm going behind Lulu's back but she's young, free and single, so it makes a difference, doesn't it? She's in a different stage of life compared to ours.'

I like her honesty, and her empathy towards others, but I think she's heading in the wrong direction when it comes to our mutual friend. But that's Lulu's business to share, not mine to dig up.

'I spoke to Dale and explained the idea of this week away. I asked him for some space and he agreed, though the sadness in his eyes nearly killed me.'

'It was the right thing to do, Beth. I'm no different in some respects. I'm torn between my head and my heart,' I say, knowing she's waiting for an explanation, otherwise she might as well have stayed inside to ponder her own situation. 'My family wants what's right for me – actually, sod it, *I* want what's right for me! But their perception of Bournebury wedding plans didn't include me marrying a local man who used to empty our bins for a living, regardless of how much he loves me.'

'Is that what Judd does for a living?' asks Beth, without a hint of condescension.

'Yep. I can see there's a gulf of difference between my family background and his. But the bottom line is, this is the man I have chosen to marry, not the man I was expected to marry. Whenever we discuss wedding matters with my father, he's wanting to show off his wealth, his heritage and status at every turn – regardless of the compromises Judd and I have offered to make.' Beth listens intently, without a sign of interrupting, so I continue. 'The truth is, my parents simply wish I was marrying someone more to their liking . . . someone like my ex, Giles, or even Alberto at a push – but neither of them ever wanted to commit to getting married, a child was enough in their eyes. And look how quickly we separated after each boy was born – too interested in building their business empires and playing Casanova when they chose to. Whereas Judd . . . well, he's nothing of the sort.'

'So how does Saturday stand, at the minute?'

'The whole shebang is being planned and coordinated by my . . . no, correction, by *my father's* wedding planner, "Dharling" Electra. We'll be married at the local parish church, nestled beside my father's country house to which we'll be returning for the wedding breakfast, hosted within the grand dining room, followed by a second wedding reception held later that night in a marquee within the grounds. Despite my age, I wanted a traditional white wedding. As I'm an only child, my parents – they're long since divorced, by the way – feel they've waited long enough to throw a showstopper celebration, having witnessed and attended so many . . .' I pause, before adding, 'Despite not liking the groom or truly wishing for Judd to join the family.'

My voice fades at the mention of his name: Judd, with his simple pleasures, his warped sense of humour and endless patience.

'Wow, your whole face lit up at the very mention – you're very much in love, aren't you?'

I bite my lower lip and nod, before saying, 'We wanted a small, intimate church wedding. How he's shouldered the continual rebuffs from my parents and sons is beyond me – I'd have crumbled by now.'

'Really?'

'Oh yeah, it's been verging on cruel. Their comments, the knock-backs – uncalled-for and totally rude. His family would never treat me like that.'

Beth purses her mouth but remains silent. Oh, I get it, refraining from airing her point, so I'll say it instead.

'And that isn't just because they're hoping to benefit from our family wealth, or even playing mind games – they're genuine folk, simply welcoming me into their family. Judd's family can see what we have, whereas my lot are so focused on the family fortune – they're going to make a huge mistake . . . well, if I . . .' I cease talking, I can't verbalise my thoughts at this moment.

'Wouldn't it be wiser to call the wedding off, set a date in the near future, so all parties can get to know each other a little better? It'll clear the air, ready for a happy celebration,' she says, kindly.

'Hardly romantic, though, is it? It would feel like yet another budgeting decision or business contract, with a deadline and a conclusion. That's what I loved when Judd proposed – and it was him, it wasn't me pushing for a commitment. We took it slowly from the word go, but we couldn't help how we felt about each other. By the time we'd reached the six-month mark, we both knew "this is it" – that's why I accepted his proposal. It felt right for both of us, a Bournebury family pow-wow wasn't necessary, nor a lengthy discussion with a panel of board members nor a vote amongst shareholders. Just the basics of life: two people in love who wish to make a commitment to each other and their families. That's it, that's us.'

I slurp the last of my cooling coffee. As I lower my mug I notice Beth's furrowed brow.

'Sorry, but I'm confused – doesn't Saturday deliver exactly what you want then?' she whispers, apologetically. 'To be married to Judd.'

'Not quite. Back home, it's full steam ahead with all the prep and organising for this top-notch wedding day, with all the glitz and glamour that folk expect to see in the glossy magazines, and yet deep down I know that Saturday is going to signal the beginning of the end for us. The us I love and treasure, the unspoilt us that hasn't bought into Daddy's demands – unless I take drastic action now.'

'Make a stand, you mean?'

I nod. 'My heart aches at the very thought of doing so, but if we walk down that aisle on Saturday, I'll be playing into the hands of my father for the rest of my days, taking Judd with me. And Judd deserves better than that.'

Beth's mouth drops wide in shock. 'I hear what you're saying, Koo, but surely no father would wish for his daughter – his only child, did you say? – to feel like this as her nuptials approach,' she says, playing down her bewildered expression.

'How many times has your father been married?' I ask, sensing this is a better tack to take.

She shakes her head. 'I have no idea. I don't know who my father is . . . it's one of those situations where my mother won't discuss what happened in her younger days. It's just me and her; I've tried to push her for answers but without much luck.'

'Sorry to hear that, how typical of me to put my foot in it,' I say, reaching out to squeeze her forearm.

'No worries, but if he's a typical guy in life ... I'm guessing once, maybe twice ...' Beth hesitates.

Bless her for humouring me, despite her own painful experience.

'Precisely, a typical bloke. My father has been married six times. Six times! Of which three marriages and two divorces have occurred in the last decade.'

Beth respectfully waits a heartbeat, before answering. 'Maybe he's trying to prevent you following in his wake. He obviously knows the pain of failed relationships.'

'Ah, there's a difference ... he's made sure he's only ever married wealthy women, hoping their eyes weren't on his prize, as well as their own worth. That's his bargaining chip, so to speak – marry similar, so all's fair in love and war. Which is why the likes of Giles and Alberto came top of his son-in-law wish list. But not Judd.'

'And what do you think?'

'I think we have as much chance of happiness within a marriage as the next couple; no one can demand a happy-ever-after in these modern times. I know Judd, and every vow he utters will be honoured. He's no Casanova, no gigolo type, no wide boy on the make. If I were from the local housing estate, no one would be questioning our decision to get married, but because of ... well, because of our family wealth and connections, the world and his wife have certain expectations – and my father upholds them in his outrageous manner.' My final explanation is delivered more like a rant than I had intended, but my spirit is beginning to flag.

'So what's the problem? Get married on Saturday and show

each and every celebrity guest just how committed you are to each other – simple.'

Beth's missed my point, or I haven't explained myself well enough.

'Firstly, we need to make it to Saturday by sidestepping the underhanded tricks I fear may be heading our way in the coming days. Secondly, if we reach the twenty-sixth, how would you like to be one of only two people attending the ceremony who truly believe in our union? Every eye will be scrutinising and every tongue will be whispering about how long it'll last.'

'I see. When you put it like that . . . no – I wouldn't dream of entering into a marriage where everyone else is behaving in such a negative way towards my intended.'

I give Beth her due, she's listened and taken every word on board.

'Everyone expected Judd to have jumped ship by now, but he hasn't. I've gone through the motions of this wedding as far as I can stomach it, but I'm not about to stand by and watch them destroy the man I love.'

'Is that why you left your hens behind?'

'*Phuh!* They weren't my hens – as I said yesterday, each and every one was a businesswoman taken from my contacts list, attempting to feather her own nest by attending a freebie weekend at my expense. I imagine half of them, if not all, will have received a wedding invite too. The whole charade is fake, an illusion of a wedding celebration, with only the bridal couple truly believing in each other. That's not what I want.'

'No, it's not what any bride would wish for, Koo. A wedding should be a happy event – not a day filled with angst, bad feeling and unfortunate predictions.'

'Making this week of self-discovery vital in calming my mind, lifting my spirits and scaring away the demons.'

Beth's hand reaches for mine, giving it a tight and very welcome squeeze.

'You only need to shout, if there is anything I can do to make this week—'

'*Gareth! Noooooooo, Gareth!*'

There's a sudden hollering coming from inside the cottage. We both whip our heads around in surprise, but our view from the bench is blocked by the rear of the brick outhouse.

'What the hell! Quick!' I say, jumping to my feet, my empty coffee mug dangling from my fingers.

We scurry across the lawn, down the stone steps and inside the cottage, ready to assist an obviously distressed Lulu.

Lulu

I throw down my mobile in frustration, causing it to bounce off the sofa cushions in the snug. How dare he cut me off mid-sentence, when I've been calmly listening to him for so long. I didn't rant. I didn't question his actions. I simply listened, and yet the minute I . . .

The door bursts open as Koo and Beth charge in, their features etched with concern – and no doubt a million questions.

'Are you OK, sweetie?' asks Koo, edging nearer to me as I stand in the middle of the room with my head bowed, tears dripping from my chin and my fury clearly on display. 'Here, sit down.' Koo snakes an arm around my shoulders and guides me towards the sofa.

I obediently lower myself, my hand instinctively feeling along the cushion for my discarded phone.

'Can I get you anything?' asks Beth, lingering in the doorway. I shake my head, not daring to raise my gaze.

'Tea? Coffee? Maybe a cold drink – how about some juice?' I repeat my refusal, and she falls silent.

My head flops backwards, resting on the sofa's backrest, my

gaze stuck fast to the ceiling, as my tears divert their trail from my cheeks to leak from the corner of each eye. Why did this have to happen? Our second phone call had started off perfectly well, only to descend into emotional chaos. It's alright for these two women; bloody big rings on their fingers, and wedding dates arranged – the likes of me are still playing the waiting game.

'Here,' says Koo, snatching a tissue from the box on the coffee table and pushing it into my hand. 'Take a few deep breaths, and then we can talk.'

Talking is the last thing I want to do. Sobbing, wailing and redialling his number are my priority. Talking means admitting. Admitting means sharing. Sharing means others will know, and them knowing will ruin everything. Everything we've shared will be destroyed. There'll be no going back. No retracting the details. No solution to the problem. No future. No present. Just a remembered past to which I'll cling, reliving it as often as I wish, like a modern-day Miss Havisham, because it will be all I ever have.

Koo sits down beside me, Beth silhouetted in the doorway of the snug. I dab the crumpled tissue to my eyes and inhale deeply, as instructed, but neither action helps. Nothing will make me feel better until I've redialled his number and his voice is in my ear, saying what I need to hear him say. I don't want excuses, or for him to make me fake promises. I don't want negative talk or put-downs intended to hurt others – just the truth, which lies deep within. The truth he is denying but which we've both previously declared and have known for ages. For years, in fact.

'Are you sure you don't want a cuppa?' asks Beth.

My head shoots up from its position on the backrest, I'm irritated by her question, my gaze spins in her direction, and my voice is far angrier than I intend.

'No! I don't w-w-want your frigging t-t-tea, Beth. But if it makes you feel better, then off you p-p-pop and prepare some hot sweet tea – just leave mine on the side to go c-c-cold,' I stammer through angry tears.

'Well ... I ... ' Beth's mouth falls open.

'Hey now, there's no need for that, my lovely,' says Koo, taking my hand and rubbing it frantically. 'She's only trying to help.'

'Help? As if either of you can h-h-help me,' I wail, as renewed tears well up, and my vision blurs. I've lost him, that's it – we're finished.

'We could help, if you'd let us,' says Koo, continuing to rub the back of my hand.

They let me cry some more. Beth goes off to make herself a cuppa, while Koo ceases tenderly rubbing my hand and pulls me into a big mumsy hug.

'I don't know how much you heard,' I eventually say, pulling back from Koo's embrace to sit upright.

Koo glances at Beth, who is now perched on the edge of the opposite couch.

'Nothing really, just a name ... Gareth,' says Beth.

Koo doesn't respond, but simply waits.

'Enough, then,' I mutter, feeling calmer. 'Yeah, Gareth ... our call started off well, but it didn't go to plan; we ended up arguing, unlike our call earlier. It didn't help that I had to move from room to room as my phone signal kept dropping out. I had to redial several times. Anyway, he cut me off when it all went sour ... and yeah, I think I screamed his name as I threw my phone down.' I calmly recall the events as if they had happened to a third party.

'And Gareth is who?' asks Koo.

'Our Kirsty's fiancé.'

'So, he's had a go at you for leaving her hen-do early?' asks Beth, cradling her mug of tea.

'Not quite.'

'For causing her upset?' asks Koo.

'Sort of,' I mumble.

There's a heartbeat of silence before Koo speaks again. 'Lulu, who exactly is Gareth to you?'

I burst into tears before attempting to answer. 'He's my guy.'

I don't witness their reactions as I bury my head in my hands.

'I thought you said you were single . . .' Beth's voice is altered by confusion.

I don't answer or lift my head.

'You're seeing . . . Kirsty's groom?' asks Koo, tentatively. 'Does Kirsty know?'

I shake my head.

'Actually, that reminds me. She gave me a message the day I collected your suitcase . . .' says Beth, tailing off when my head shoots up. 'Sorry, I forgot, what with my own situation, the confusion about how we met up and . . .'

'What did she say?' I bleat, staring at her.

'Kirsty said, "tell her, I know" – it was just before she said you were sacked from the wedding,' recalls Beth, staring ahead as if reliving the moment in Our Kirsty's presence.

'Oh, so you remembered to tell me the "sacked" part but not the important bit, thanks a bunch, Beth!' I holler, attempting to calculate how many hours ago that was.

'Ladies, ladies, enough please!' demands Koo, getting to her feet as the situation threatens to escalate. 'The last thing we need is to be arguing amongst ourselves, we've got enough issues going on elsewhere in our lives.'

'She hasn't!' I snap narkily, pointing at Beth.

'What would you know?' spits Beth, her irritation clearly showing.

'Having cold feet is hardly an issue. Boo hoo, for your wedding nerves,' I rudely continue.

'Oy, cut it out, Lulu,' snaps Koo, her brow seriously furrowed with a stern glare.

'I forgot, that's all. I said I'm sorry,' mutters Beth, retreating into herself.

'*Mmmmph!*' is my only reply. I can't believe in the time we've spent together she actually forgot to mention the second, and most vital, part of the message. How dumb can you be?

'Not that I think you're deflecting your anger on to Beth, but seriously, Lulu – didn't you think this through?' asks Koo, sitting back down now the tension has passed.

I shrug; I don't know how to explain.

'Don't give me that. You're not a teenager,' replies Koo.

'It just happened.'

'Nothing just happens, Lulu,' says Beth, in a small wounded voice.

'Is it just physical, or is there an emotional connection too?' asks Koo.

'It's not just sex, if that's what you're suggesting!'

Koo gives me a nod, before speaking her mind. 'Well, you're in trouble, gal, because he's getting married on Saturday, and given the phone call you've just had, the likelihood is . . .'

'It's going ahead – he just hinted as much,' I whisper, crestfallen at the very thought.

'And you agreed to be their maid of honour?' asks Beth, her wounded tone remaining.

'Yep. Think what you will of me. I'm not proud of myself, but the heart wants what the heart wants,' I say.

Neither woman agrees with me. They both remain silent, absorbed in their own thoughts; possibly comparing my situation with their own wedding plans, after which they'll be judging my morals and behaviour.

If only Koo and Beth could see us together, see how well we get along, laughing all the time. Gareth's so relaxed when we're together – ours isn't some furtive, sordid or pointless fling. Oh no, not by a long shot.

My phone begins to ring. The smiling image of my dad fills the screen as we three stare at the offending object. I freeze, barely able to breathe.

'Talking to your dad might be a good thing,' says Koo, gesturing towards my screen.

'Actually, that's Gareth calling,' I say guiltily, before grabbing my phone, selecting a handful of fresh tissues and tapping the screen to accept his call. I automatically stand, preparing to take my business elsewhere, and notice both women exchanging a look, as if confirming a mutual opinion in silence.

Chapter Ten

Beth

'What are we even doing this for?' moans Lulu, as I forcefully link arms and drag her outside into the back garden, across the patio towards the built-in barbecue, where Koo is tending to a pile of smoking coals, armed with blackened tongs and my pile of hen party paraphernalia.

'Because, like it or not, we are on our hen party week!' I declare, offering Lulu a glass of chilled bubbles. Despite our earlier tiff, I've forgiven Lulu; I should have relayed Kirsty's message earlier.

'I'm not even a bride!' wails Lulu, stalling yards from the glowing barbecue grill and drystone wall, beyond which the most spectacular sunset of lilac and pink is forming behind the purple-headed mountains.

'This week you are, sweetie,' declares Koo, posting several 'dare' cards through the tiny slots on the grill plate and watching them incinerate on the hot coals beneath. 'Though I'm sure we've mislaid a pack of Beth's party cards – I thought you had more than this?'

'I just want to be his girlfriend,' wails Lulu, her misery reappearing.

'Ahh well, I do believe Gareth already has one of those, my darling,' says Koo, leaning forward and offering Lulu the spread of remaining scratch cards from which to select the next burnt offering.

I bite my lip; that sounded pretty harsh, despite the love and concern with which it was meant.

'Come on, lady – snap out of it! You're here now, and there's little we can do other than get into the swing,' I say, hoping I sound encouraging. I've pushed aside my own shock and revulsion at the thought of cheating. I grab the box of lewd confetti before sprinkling it across the glowing coals.

'Two more glasses of prosecco, the destruction of all the hen-do accessories, and then she won't care where she is,' whispers Koo, snapping the tongs in mid-air for effect. I agree, though there's no guaranteeing what kind of drunken fake-bride-to-be Lulu will make – one thing's for certain: she won't be sleeping in a bathtub tonight!

It takes a good twenty minutes of walking, passing numerous hiking groups and dog walkers, for us to reach the centre of Hawkshead village. Nestled between mountains and vast lakes, it's the prettiest village I've ever seen. Its parish church sits proudly on higher ground, surrounded by a mixture of Victorian stone buildings, numerous quaint tea rooms, and gift shops filled with ceramic bunnies and puddle ducks. The streets have that cosy feel, where pastel-painted buildings cast abstract shadows across their neighbours, and every frontage is connected by the zigzag of colourful bunting fluttering overhead. The pavements are empty as clusters of visitors walk along the quiet roads until a neat swerve or sidestep is necessary to allow an oncoming car through safely.

'The Queen's Head!' calls Koo, spying the pub she'd browsed earlier on the internet.

Our steps divert, heading towards the whitewashed frontage. A smattering of customers are nestled around tiny tables, busily chatting, until two ladies dressed in smart M&S casual attire, accompanied by a wimpled nun, approach.

'Evening,' calls Koo, lifting her hand as if to bless them, as we drift by and enter the pub.

'What the hell?', 'Is she for real?' and 'Hardly suitable!' are just three snippets we overhear as the door closes behind us.

I didn't think it necessary myself, but Koo reckoned wearing her habit would be a laugh, if nothing else. Though I suspect she might be playing it cool and lying low, for fear of a glossy magazine headline announcing the whereabouts of a runaway Bournebury!

We're standing in the centre of a noisy and busy bar area, traditional in every sense, with a red tiled floor, leaded glass windows and a low beamed ceiling. There are wooden bench seats edging each wall and oak tables positioned at regular intervals. Instantly, the noise ceases, as if the landlord has flicked a switch, muting every customer: complete silence.

'What's it to be?' I ask, grabbing two crisp notes from my purse and heading towards the bar.

A young woman, sporting short pigtails, eyes me warily from behind the hand pumps. I'm not about to make a show of myself by outstaring the other customers, be they regulars or tourists, who are pondering our entrance. Koo and Lulu smile uneasily, their gaze roving about the darkened interior and fixing on the nostalgic dog portraits and flickering candle bulbs lining the walls.

'A cocktail, for me,' says Lulu, pointing towards the only available table, situated at the rear of the bar.

'Me too,' says Koo, cutting a distinct figure as she navigates through the seated customers.

'We don't usually do cocktails, as such, but I can whip up a couple of mojitos,' offers the barmaid.

'Perfect. Three please,' I say, assuming that a wimpled nun isn't their usual clientele. 'Are we OK to sit in here? I don't wish to offend anyone.'

'Sure, as long as the nun can handle her drink,' quips the barmaid, grabbing three tall glasses and swiftly knocking each against the rum optic.

'Make those doubles, please,' I say, liking her humour.

'Sure. I'll bring them across, if you want?'

'Excellent. What's the damage?'

Within minutes, I'm joining the others at our table. Despite being empty-handed, my arrival is greeted by a cheer from Lulu; clearly the prosecco has reawakened her spirit.

'Don't panic, the drinks are coming. Mojitos whipped up courtesy of the bar staff, so no complaining,' I say, dropping several packets of nuts and crisps on to the table, unsure when we'll be grabbing a bite to eat.

'No worries, anything will hit the spot on an empty stomach,' says Lulu, a little louder than I'd expected, before adding, 'I want to hear some relationship details, so plonk yourself in the hot seat, Beth.'

I take my seat, and Lulu immediately starts the interrogation.

'Question one – where did you meet lover boy?' Lulu leans in, ready to swoon, just as the barmaid arrives carrying a tray laden with three very large glasses.

'Enjoy, ladies. Call when you need a top-up,' she says, depositing the cocktails.

We gratefully take a swig of our drinks before Lulu announces, 'Back to it, Beth – the details please?'

'We met at the cinema. Dale knocked my popcorn out of my hand as I was leaving the kiosk area heading for Screen Five. He was with a group of mates to see Stephen King's *It* – while I was early, and on my own, heading towards my third viewing of *The Greatest Showman*. My popcorn went flying. I nearly did too, but managed to steady myself – and that was it. I was embarrassed by the mess I'd made all over the red carpet. Dale was more concerned about me being OK, and offered to replace my popcorn. Which I refused, out of embarrassment, because by now an army of duty staff had come running with brushes and dustpans. Anyway, I scurried away to see my film, minus my usual treats, but when my screening was over and I was leaving, Dale was sitting alone on one of the foyer's sofas waiting for me. He called out, invited me to sit, and apologised for the umpteenth time.

'We ended up sharing a large bucket of fresh popcorn and two Diet Cokes before the cinema closed. That's it in a nutshell. After which, he asked for my number and walked me safely to my car. I figured if he could act so honourably after accidentally spilling popcorn he must have a good heart, so we went for a drink a few nights later. The rest, as they say, is history.' I stop talking and find both of them doe-eyed, heads inclined, sipping on their paper straws.

'Ah, why can't that happen to me?' sighs Lulu.

'Go on then, tell us how you met Gareth,' I say, happy to relinquish the hot seat.

Lulu has the decency to look embarrassed before speaking.

'Our Kirsty had a new bloke, though no one in the family had met him. My aunty kept dropping hints about this and that, you know how mums can be ... bragging to their sisters, especially the ones with single daughters. Anyway, there was a family bar-becue at their house, and we were all invited, and well, that was it ... I turned up and we just locked eyes.'

'What? In front of everyone?' asks Koo, plonking her glass down.

'Yep. There was no hiding it, no secretive meeting in the kitchen whilst grabbing a drink, no sneaky exchange over the paper plates or napkins. I walked into their garden and he was the first person I saw – and it was the same for him, he simply stared at me.' Lulu is beaming from ear to ear, hardly able to contain her excitement. Has she forgotten their earlier phone call?

'And this was when?' I ask, rattled that this bloke was taken when this occurred.

'Three years ago,' answers Lulu immediately.

'You've been having an affair for three years?' The accusation escapes my mouth before I put my brain in gear.

Lulu's expression instantly drops, and Koo grimaces.

'Sorry, that came out wrong. Very tactless of me.'

'No. Just this last year. We tiptoed around it for the first two years, denying our interest in each other, yet knowing we were lying to ourselves. I kept telling myself I was imagining it, especially when they got engaged. Every Christmas get-together, birthday bash or family celebration was a nightmare; neither of us wanting to admit what was happening,' she says.

I snatch up my mojito and take a sip, ensuring I remain silent.

'Didn't Kirsty suspect?' asks Koo, in a kindly manner.

Lulu chews her bottom lip, as if stalling, before shaking her head in answer.

'And the message earlier is the first indication that she knows?' I ask, realising the weight of my late delivery.

'Yep. There've been occasions when I thought she knew, but Gareth doubted it very much.'

'And you've actually discussed it?' I ask, instantly kicking myself for digging too deep into her private life. I can't help myself; I'm mystified that two people could carry on behind someone's back, knowing the consequences and hurt awaiting them. Whatever happened to the girl code?

'Selfish, I know, but yeah, we have.'

There's silence. One by one, we lift our drinks and take a sip, as if that will change the topic or lighten the atmosphere. I'm not liking Lulu's backstory. Maybe bad judgement doesn't make for a bad person? Unfortunate situations happen to good people, right?

'Sorry, but I have to ask ... how have you left things after tonight's final phone call?' I'm unsure if I'm being plain nosey, supportive of Lulu, or siding with Our Kirsty.

'He simply wanted to know that I was OK, hates to think of me being upset, especially given the way the second call ended. He's still going through with the wedding but . . .'

'But wishes to keep you tagging along, just for good measure?' suggests Koo, raising an eyebrow.

'No, but . . .'

'Lulu, that's so wrong. If he's choosing to turn up on Saturday then he's made a clear choice and needs to let you go, to get on with your life, while he and Kirsty focus on married life,' I say.

Koo simply stares, lost for words.

'And you need to let him go!' I add, for emphasis.

'It wasn't supposed to get complicated,' mutters Lulu, crest-fallen.

'It was always going to get complicated,' says Koo, finding her voice.

A tumbleweed moment occurs, as Koo and I exchange glances, before observing Lulu's thoughtful demeanour as she plays with her mojito glass.

'What about you, Koo?' asks Lulu, suddenly bright and breezy, as if flicking a switch, eager to conclude her interrogation.

'Us? Judd used to empty our bins every Friday morning. He was always cheery, always singing to himself, and we just got talking one day.'

Lulu's brow crumples.

'You just got talking to the local dustman? How? I'm not even up when ours do their rounds.'

'You're not up by ten o'clock?' asks Koo, glancing at me.

'Ours arrive early in the morning. I'd have no chance of a casual chat, if I were at home,' she corrects.

'So he knew you lived at that property then?' I ask, sussing out the details.

'Well, yeah. He knew, but he's no gold-digger – if that's what you're suggesting,' says Koo, hitting the nail on the head. 'It was me that asked him out for a drink.'

'No!' I gasp.

'No way!' shrieks Lulu, before covering her mouth with her hand, as the rest of the bar turn in our direction.

'Yep. I thought, why not? The worst he can say is "no thanks".'

'Koo, you're brave!' I blurt, knowing I could never pluck up the courage.

Koo smiles, adding, 'A gal's gotta do what a gal's gotta do!'

'My sentiments exactly,' says Lulu, cheerfully – much to my annoyance.

I'm not entirely sure how any woman can cheat on another, let alone with her cousin's beau.

Chapter Eleven

Koo

I tidy the kitchen while Beth attempts to put Lulu to bed at quarter to three in the morning. I'm knackered but there's no chance of sleep after the amount we've drunk, the revelations young Lulu has treated us to, and a greasy doner kebab currently repeating on me. I don't even like kebabs, so why I agreed I don't know. Obviously, drinking on an empty stomach is no longer my forte.

I check the rear kitchen door is securely locked, giving both the top and bottom a satisfying rattle to be sure.

'She's tucked in and sleeping like a baby,' says Beth, appearing from the hallway. 'Though it was a battle and a half getting her to remove her make-up – and I won't attempt to describe how she removed her clothing.'

'It's like putting a child to bed, isn't it? Constant babbling, appeasement, repeated promises of "in the morning", some tears and tantrums, alongside a half-remembered song or two.'

'That's exactly it. She'll probably have another cricked neck in the morning, and the mother of all hangovers,' says Beth, pulling out a chair. She plonks herself down at the scrubbed table, reaches for her phone and opens what looks like her Facebook app.

'And you?' I ask, flicking the switch on the kettle.

'Done in, to be fair. My head's a mess and I've broken a nail putting madam to bed.' She continues to stare at her phone but holds up her right hand, displaying her ring finger with a torn nail cropped at a strange angle.

'And your head?' I ask, grabbing two mugs from the cupboard.

'All over the shop.'

'Do you love him?' I ask, bluntly, without turning around to view her reaction.

'Yes.' Not a moment of hesitation in her answer or tone.

'So what are you not saying?' I ask, over my shoulder, whilst spooning coffee granules into our mugs. I don't turn around, on purpose; I want to hear her answer rather than witness it.

'What do you mean?' This time, there was a definite pause and rethink before she answered.

'I mean, if you love him, if the wedding is planned out as beautifully as you've dreamt of – I don't see what the problem is. You've built a life together, so why not enjoy it . . . together?' I turn around on the last word and come face to face with a worried bride.

There it is, what I've suspected all along . . . the opportunity to totally fess up when the right question is asked. Lulu's daft interrogation, placing Beth in the hot seat, has failed to produce an answer to the real question – not who, what, when and how, but why? The reality of my relationship is based on love. My love for Judd, his love for me. Even the family rift is based on love – airing opinions and concerns, ensuring I don't follow in my father's footsteps. Which I won't, as I'm not entirely sure my father has experienced love since my mother left him.

In Beth's silence, I've poured the boiling water, stirred the coffees and am walking across the kitchen, mugs in hand, when she answers.

'We probably will.'

I place her coffee in front of her, but she hardly sees it as her worried eyes are fixed upon mine, brimming with tears. Her thumbs remain glued to her phone screen, the blue glow of her Facebook app reflecting on to her jawline.

'Probably? Probably shouldn't come into it, Beth. And in the meantime, you're going to pretend that everything is hunky-dory until we leave here, and end up doing ... what? Walking down the aisle towards an untold disaster, all because you can't or won't open up to me? Someone who is prepared to listen to whatever needs to be said, and who might – I'm not saying definitely, but might – understand a little of what you're going through?' I settle myself opposite her, sip my hot coffee and wait. I don't have to wait for as long as I'd anticipated.

'I've lied,' she says, turning her phone over and placing it face down on the table.

'I'm sure Dale will forgive you.'

'Not to Dale, but to you guys.'

My ears prick up. Really?

'We have everything I've ever wanted in a relationship; a sense of togetherness, a frank and honest foundation. Our future plans match exactly. We both want a stable family life, a couple of children, and extended family – that's our happy-ever-after,' says Beth, the words tumbling out as if she's opened a floodgate.

'Sounds great, so where's the "but"?'

'But I keep thinking about my ex – Nick. There was a passion and excitement between us that I've never experienced with Dale,' confesses Beth, gulping at the end of her sentence. 'We'd met on a hen-do weekend, when I was there for my friend's celebration, and he was on his stag-do.'

'His stag-do?'

Beth nods, a guilty expression plastering her pallid features.

'Wow, now that's a twist I didn't see coming,' I whisper.

'Nick called his wedding off with six weeks to go.'

'And you and he were together after that?'

'Yep. From that very night. I was single at the time, so once he'd broken things off ... we moved in together. A small rental on the outskirts of town, you know the kind of thing, an apartment block, shared balcony and artificial plants in the lobby. It was my first home, my first serious relationship with a man, not a boy, and I was head over heels in love. I thought we had it all.'

'Until?'

'He went on his brother's stag weekend to Newcastle . . . Nick came home on the Sunday and moved out on the Tuesday. I was devastated.'

'Bloody hell, talk about karma,' I say, with a breathy sigh. 'Which explains Dale's concern when you didn't arrive home as scheduled.'

Beth gives a nod; guilty as charged.

'Dale knows what happened with Nick – we've been open with each other about our previous relationships,' she admits. 'And now, I keep thinking back to those days, my feelings for Nick . . . the life we were building together . . . what if?'

'But he left you for someone else?' I say, in a gentle manner, not wishing to sound brutal. 'And he originally left someone else for you.'

'Yep. He did. But what we had . . . what I felt for him was so much more . . . than I'm feeling right now.'

'So why pretend? Since Sunday morning, you've had the chance to tell it how it is. Are you in touch with this Nick guy?'

'That's the issue. I haven't heard from him in years, not since we split. Then, just three weeks ago, he sent me a friend request on Facebook. Nothing's happened – I haven't accepted it. It's stupid of me, but what if we were meant to be? What started as cold feet, worrying about my commitment to Dale, has intensified because of my feelings towards Nick,' says Beth.

'Phew! Big decisions, doll – to which only you have the answer,' I say, sounding unsupportive and generic with my answer. 'I guess you're as much in the wedding mire as the rest of us. At this rate, we'll all need counselling before this week is through.'

'That or a decent lawyer,' scoffs Beth. 'Can you be sued for emotional damage or even the cost of a wedding?' she asks, her eyes glistening as if unsure whether to laugh or cry about her confession. 'Sorry. I should have fessed up earlier.'

'Don't worry, I've got a contact list full of lawyers – in fact, one or two might have attended my hen-do.' I give a giggle, to lighten the load, but I can see the concern etched across Beth's brow. 'Are you seriously doubting what you have, in favour of a bloke-that-could-have-been?'

Beth nods. 'I need to know, otherwise I'll always be questioning myself. That's not fair to Dale.'

'Would it help if I suggest this Nick guy sounds like a non-starter?'

Her eyebrows lift in surprise. 'Thanks for the warning, maybe I need to find out for sure, Koo. Hiding my feelings has become a habit, and not a good one. I should have been a little more understanding about Lulu's situation – I'll apologise to her in the morning.'

We sip our coffees in silence, allowing the events and details of the night to slowly settle like sediment in a large lake. My one niggling question is, just how deep do still waters run? I've got a funny feeling that Beth is literally skimming the surface regarding her true feelings, rather than diving deep.

Lulu

The landing's wooden banister rail digs into my folded arms, on which I lean my forehead, attempting to hear every word they're saying in the kitchen. Despite Beth tucking me in nicely, I've had to get out of bed. My spinning head has hit the roller-coaster stage where my brain thinks I'm falling backwards, head first, down the big-dipper tracks, igniting another wave of nausea. Plus, I need water. Beth promised me a glass when she was putting me to bed, but she didn't deliver. And now, I know why.

I raise my head to stare through the carved spindles, down into the darkened abyss of the stairwell below. There's a sliver of mellow light escaping the kitchen door, which is partly ajar, hence the conversation drifting up from below.

Blah blah, Dale. Blah blah, Nick. Blah blah, stag-do.

Did Koo just ask who Nick was? I strain my ears to hear a little more, but Koo's muted tones don't carry as clearly as Beth's.

I'm not annoyed, as such, more disappointed that I've been so trusting and open about my difficult scenario, while Beth stayed schtum, yet hers is no better. Or is it because I'm just a maid of honour? I bet she'd have mentioned it if I'd been a bride-to-be too.

I shared loads during our mini pub crawl through the village: all about our first meeting, my struggles, my denial. *Phuh*, like that worked! And now I realise that, all this time, Beth has been avoiding the spotlight and hiding her true dilemma behind claims of cold feet.

I still haven't figured out what to do about Gareth. I can hardly turn up on Saturday afternoon, posh frock and all, to watch the guy I love marry someone else.

I can hear coffee mugs being washed up, chairs being repositioned. Finally, the kitchen door squeaks open, the sliver of mellow light stretches towards the front door; they're heading up to bed.

I swiftly return to my room, feebly jump into bed and fumble beneath my pillow for my phone. Despite our angry words earlier, I want to check the screen, one last time – hoping against hope there's a text message from Gareth. Perfectly timed, as usual, just before I fall asleep.

My illuminated screen is blank. Nothing.

I lie motionless on the bed, half covered by the duvet, in the balmy August night, and stare at the blank screen, wishing there was one final text, any message, containing a single goodnight kiss. Signalling all is forgiven and tomorrow is another day.

Chapter Twelve

Tuesday 22 August

Koo

After a quick food shop at the local Co-op, it takes all of ten minutes to drag three sunloungers from the brick outhouse and line them up on the patio. We stretch out in a neat formation, each sporting our undies, pretending we're in regular swimwear. Our relaxing home spa session on the sun-drenched patio – complete with Lulu's home-made avocado and honey face pack, sliced cucumber eye patches and a chilled bottle of vino – is my idea of heaven.

Our attire isn't quite beachwear, but who truly cares when there aren't any neighbours overlooking us? Although Beth seems slightly uptight and very self-conscious for a woman who has a cracking figure and should be flaunting it at her age; let's face it, a trim waist doesn't hang around for ever! Mine didn't – but I've had two children and spent a lifetime consuming chocolate. Lulu, on the other hand, is happy to bare all for the sake of ensuring no strappy tan lines. As I said, there are no neighbours, so who's to be offended?

'All we need is a butler to top up our drinks and bring us nibbles,' sighs Lulu, leisurely sipping her large glass of Pinot whilst happily blinded by her cucumber slices. Mine have inadvertently slipped from my eyes so many times that I can't be bothered to fish them out of my wine glass yet again, so I throw them aside into the shrubbery. I'll just have to do battle with the under-eye bags and wrinkles if they appear in the coming days.

'I think this is perfect, just what I wanted – a cottage, time to think, and some pampering. You wouldn't be sunbathing in your skimpies if we had serving staff on hand,' says Beth, speaking through a clenched mouth to preserve her face pack.

'Sure, I would. I hate to think what they must've witnessed during their hours on duty. I bet they wouldn't bat an eyelid at seeing me half naked. The mind boggles, but I believe discretion is the name of the game in these posh venues, especially where celebrity sorts hang out.'

There's been a snippy-snappy vibe between the two of them today. Beth doesn't have to say anything, but I'm hoping she's enlightened Lulu about her true situation back home. It would be wrong not to, when Lulu's been so open about her own difficulties. It can't be easy, admitting you're the other woman in any situation – let alone your own cousin's other woman.

'Where is it you're going on honeymoon, Koo?' asks Beth, clearly to change the subject.

'We're going on a trip across Europe – Judd hasn't travelled much, so we want to enjoy sharing the experience and making memories. But I'm not so sure, each time I think of it . . .' I skim over the details in an attempt to scale down the extravagance. 'And you?'

'We're not having a honeymoon. We're having time at home, instead,' Beth explains. 'We want to plough the money into the house. We've enjoyed several nice holidays since we've been together, so it made sense really.'

I make all the right noises in agreement, but part of me feels that's a shame. To start married life without a honeymoon feels like a big sacrifice.

'Was that your idea or Nick's?' asks Lulu.

Nick? A-ha, so Beth *has* spoken to Lulu about her ex. Good news.

'You mean Dale,' corrects Beth, earnestly.

'Do I? Sorry, Dale – was that his idea?' repeats Lulu, somewhat flustered.

'No. It was a joint decision.' Beth's tone is defensive.

No one speaks, though I can sense the tension. Despite not fully understanding the implications of what has just happened, I predict a situation is brewing.

The silence drags on, long after Beth's answer, allowing the conversation to drift into a social Bermuda Triangle.

'What made you say Nick, Lulu?' Beth abruptly pipes up, with a renewed breezy tone.

Her decision to reignite the conversation proves she's performed an internal dialogue before doing an 'eeny-meeny-macka-racka' choice, much like I do, before deciding whether to let the subject go or not.

'No reason,' says Lulu.

I glance to either side of my sunlounger and view a cucumber-blind woman on my left and my right.

Suddenly Beth sits up, snatches the discs from her eyes, and addresses Lulu with as much dignity as you can muster when sunbathing in a lacy bra and knickers.

'Were you listening to our conversation last night?' she demands.

'No.'

'You must have been, because I've only mentioned my ex, Nick, once in the entire time we've been together, and you weren't present. You were in bed!'

'If you must know ... I've noticed that your Facebook app frequently shows the details for the same guy, Nick Someone-or-other. I assumed there was a connection.'

'I browse lots of different people on social media, actually,' says Beth, her tone becoming less aggressive yet remaining spiky.

Lulu raises her head, lifts a cucumber slice and peers intently at a motionless Beth. 'Really?' She then shakes her head at me as I silently watch the proceedings, before returning to her original position and replacing her cucumber eye mask.

From my right, Beth does exactly the same, though her glance across at Lulu conveys more frustration. I'm not their mother, I can hardly interject, but I sense three days together might be resulting in a tetchy bout of cabin fever.

'Nick was part of my life long before I met Dale, but I haven't seen or spoken to him in a number of years. If you must know, he contacted me, not the other way around,' continues Beth, falling short of revealing the full details.

So, she's opted not to enlighten Lulu, which puts me in a pickle. What's the age-old saying? Two's company, three's a crowd – it appears it might well be.

Slowly, I drift into a relaxed state with the sun gently warming my skin. I can almost believe I'm lying on the top deck of a ginormous cruise liner, dreaming of the sumptuous food on offer at tonight's captain's table, when an unexpected shadow crosses my face. My eyelids lift. I'm expecting to spy a stray cloud overhead, blocking the sunshine, but I find a shady-looking bloke leaning over the drystone wall that surrounds the garden, snapping photographs of us with a bulky lens attachment.

'Oy, what do you think you're doing?' yells Lulu, her hands instinctively covering her exposed bits as she registers the shadow falling across the patio.

I don't need an answer, I know exactly what he's doing and can probably name the rag for which he's working. I jump up, darting towards the kitchen's open door, knowing full well he'll have got the shot he wanted before he made his schoolboy error. The cold floor tiles beneath my bare feet are a shock to my system but not the reason for my goosebumps. These cheeky bloody reporters ruin everything, all in the name of a big-money shot sold to the highest bidder. I can hear Lulu ranting at the top of her voice, giving him plenty of gossip fodder, as he attempts to justify his invasion of our privacy. A quick glance in the reflective surface of the hanging copper pans reminds me that my mush is plastered with a pale green gunk. My hair is pushed back from my face and secured with a pair of clean but twisted designer thongs and a couple of hairgrips. I'll die if I see this image, in full colour, splashed across the front page of the red-top tabloids tomorrow morning.

I peer around the edge of the doorway. Beth is on her feet, demanding he leaves immediately or she'll call the police. It's no good, she might as well save her breath. Nothing of the sort ever works with these guys. When you can sell a one-off image for thousands of pounds, these low-lifes are always going to find a way of making easy money, regardless of threats, or even calls for common decency. I try to grab Lulu's attention by beckoning her inside. She's a braver gal than me to stand with her hands covering her breasts while a photographer with a wide-angled lens is only a few feet away. She needs to come inside now, or risk being snapped and quoted in any write-up he sells.

'What the hell?' cries Beth, when she finally enters the cottage, her arms cradling a mish-mash of our belongings, hastily gathered up. She has clearly abandoned her mission of drilling for any hidden decency in the photographer.

'Tell me about it. I've had it all my life. All they want is to dish the dirt, nab a shot and flog it to a trashy paper.'

Lulu glides into the kitchen, her hands resolutely stuck to her bare breasts. I've got to hand it to her, she swans in like a beauty, standing tall, shoulders back, and proud of her figure, despite the dried clumps of avocado face mask clinging to the creases around her mouth.

'That bloody well told him!' she says, indignantly.

'Sadly, it probably hasn't. They've got thicker skins than

rhinos – he'll probably use your rant as a quote from "a close friend of Koo Bournebury", alongside the photo.'

'No way is that legit!' continues Lulu.

'Legit? They're rarely legit, Lulu. How do you think the glossies get the majority of their intrusive shots? The beach shots, the early morning jogging piccies, and worst still, those "out shopping" photos when you're dressed in your comfies and having a no-make-up day.'

'I imagined you invited them to your home, or your PA organised a studio session. Never did I think you'd be sunbathing with your norks out and *click-click* there's a guy hanging over the wall with his shutter going ten to the dozen. Though if my photo makes it inside one of the big sellers, my mum had better buy an issue. Do they tell you beforehand?'

My mouth falls wide. Does she not understand what I just said?

'How did he know where to find you?' asks Beth, looking panic stricken and ignoring Lulu's excitement.

'Exactly!' I say, switching my attention to common sense. 'It could have been phoned in by a member of the public, or he might have followed us from Bath, or perhaps the chauffeur dobbed us in for a quick backhander. Who knows? But now one pap knows – there's a chance there'll be others,' I say, wishing I had brighter predictions for the week.

'Well, we won't be giving any other photos. This is *our* week. A week in which we need to figure out the next chapter of our lives. I can do without the paparazzi hanging around and recording it for posterity, though I realise it isn't me they're hoping to glimpse,' says Beth, snapping out of her trauma mode. 'Though my boss won't be happy spotting me on the front page after I've called in sick again. A definite case of any publicity being bad publicity for me and my employment record.'

'And mine, though I doubt my boss would recognise me

without a till light flashing above my head,' says Lulu, with a wry smile. 'They follow your whereabouts and movements because you're rich and famous, Koo – I told you so. Clearly an entry on the Rich List, yes?' Lulu plonks herself down at the table to stare up at me, awaiting a response.

I give a shrug. There's hardly a right answer. Say 'yes' and I appear arrogant and bratty about wealth, say 'no' and I'll be a bare-faced liar. 'It must be a light news week, or else they sense I'll be creating my own drama at the weekend, so they intend to catalogue the run-up too.'

'They obviously think the Bourneburys are newsworthy, otherwise they wouldn't keep chasing you, would they?' says Beth, leaning against the countertop.

'How much is your family actually worth? Give us a ballpark figure then, in the region of what?' says Lulu, with a cheeky giggle.

'I haven't a clue. I know we have seventeen manufacturing sites across the world, with global exports to seventy-three countries, and our most popular bar sells nine million units a day! Other than that ... I have no exact figures,' I say, giving my standard answer.

'Bloody hell, Koo. You're quite a catch, gal!' sighs Lulu, staring up at me in a dreamy manner.

'Mmm, standing here looking like this ... I'm a belter. An absolute bloody stunner, standing in my underwear with dried avocado and honey flaking from my chops.' I gracefully gesture the length of my frame, from head to toe.

Beth snorts before she starts to giggle. I join her and, finally, Lulu sees the funny side of my remark.

'Seriously, I'm now worried about your safety,' declares Lulu, regaining control of herself. 'Shouldn't you be hiring bodyguards and minders?'

'Right now, you need to be more concerned for your own

safety,' I say, nodding towards her tightly held chest. 'Go and get some clothes on, and we'll discuss this matter later.'

Beth

I'm fuming as I pace back and forth across my bedroom. I'd had a difficult start to the day, having to phone work for the second morning to feign illness. I wasn't comfortable doing it – I shouldn't have allowed the situation to develop – and yet, I haven't jumped on a train heading home. Admittedly, I felt better once I'd called, received the obligatory wishes for a speedy recovery, and swiftly ended the call. Koo had made me a fresh brew immediately, sensing I needed sustenance after lying to my boss and colleagues, again. I'd even texted my mother, saying I was currently away for the week in Cumbria. Only to be reminded that I have a wedding on Saturday, as if I didn't know! I couldn't face calling her, for fear I'd hear the disappointment in her tone, her suspicion that her lifelong ambition of having a married daughter might be going down the drain.

My second conversation was with Dale. He'd called to ask how I was, and if I'd slept well? Our call lasted all of two minutes and nineteen seconds, upon hearing my answer. Bless him for asking, but what could I say?

This is not me, but then many of the things I've done in recent days simply aren't me. The sunbathing incident with the photographer was surreal, and Lulu's slip-up has topped my day off – and it's only two o'clock. Maybe it's the company I'm keeping? Or not.

I stop pacing the room and flop down on to my neatly made bed, disturbing the delicate satin cushions piled against the headboard, and stare at the enticing blue logo on my phone screen. I mustn't. Firstly, I've got plenty to figure out, without clouding my judgement. Secondly, it feels disloyal to Dale, though not as underhand as Lulu's situation – but all the same, secretive.

It's one thing for me to have shared it with Koo, but to hear Lulu accidentally mention Nick's name has ticked me right off! She's trespassing where she wasn't invited. If I'm being honest, Lulu wasn't invited because I don't want to admit that I'm not proud of my actions. It might sound like double standards, but my situation is not like hers. Being the archivist that I am, I've buried Nick away from the public gaze to be a teensy-weensy distraction on bad days, sad days – or any other day when my brain needs a little 'Nick-fix'. No different to an ancient Tudor vase catalogued in Hever Castle's collection and taken off display, expertly packaged, and stored in the vaults to hibernate; only for me to be sneaking a private peek whenever it suits.

I reach instinctively for my phone. If I allow my fingers to flirt with the screen, I might glimpse a recently uploaded photo, his latest check-in location, or whether his sister has had her baby yet. Not that I knew her that well, but all the same, I wish her well. I shouldn't care what Nick's doing. I shouldn't be interested in his life, but I am. And I am because he sent me a friend request, just three weeks ago. I retract my fingers, removing the temptation of tapping the screen; it's not as if we're friends, because I didn't accept his request. To view Nick's profile, I would have to find our mutual Facebook buddy, enter their profile, then scroll through their friends' library in search of Nick ... and bingo! Thanks to their lax security settings I can freely view Nick's page. His life. His friends. His photos. But we're not friends, as I didn't confirm his request. I can't imagine Nick's life is on pause; he was always one for adventure, daring days and passionate nights.

My fingers defy my good intentions by tapping the app, causing my screen to burst into life. A few additional taps, a quick swipe and I'm in my 'friends' section, purely to see if his invite is still there. And it is. A friend request alongside two oblong buttons: 'confirm' or 'remove'. And, most importantly, '3w' written in tiny grey text. A time stamp indicating three weeks, which represents my strength in the face of temptation, because despite my inner turmoil, I haven't tapped either button. I was initially shocked when the request came through, tempted to reconnect, casually catch up on news and update our situations, but wary of revisiting our history. Or rocking the boat. Might an instant rejection of his request have prevented my confusion? Could my feelings for Nick resurface, undermining my feelings and commitment to Dale?

I might be barking up the wrong tree, but it was Nick who sent the request. He found me. My index finger lingers over the two options. Do I do this, once and for all – confirm or remove – and to hell with the consequences?

'Beth!' hollers Lulu, from downstairs.

I'd like to think she's standing at the bottom of the staircase, but having witnessed her ear-splitting tirade against the photographer earlier, she could be resettled on a sunlounger. As much as I've warmed to her, her refusal to admit she was earwigging on my private conversation with Koo is a red flag for me.

'Beth!'

I glance at my screen. It's waited patiently for a reply, so a tiny while longer won't hurt. Will it? Though accepting might resolve my shoulda, woulda, coulda dilemma, and set me free from nagging doubts. Who knows, Nick might have changed his mind? My finger hovers over the screen, moving back and forth between the buttons.

'Beeeeeeth!'

Sod it, why not! You can't have enough friends in this world, can you?

I hastily tap the 'confirm' button, swiftly close the app, and jump up from my crumpled duvet, fearing that Lulu might bellow for a fourth time. I hate to sound catty but she really has got a mouth on her at times. I reach the bedroom door, check my room is tidyish, before stepping out on to the landing and finally answering.

'Yes, coming!' Though what I'm attending I have no idea, just as long as it stops Lulu's war cry.

'There you are. I wasn't sure if you were still showering,' she says, as I head down the staircase.

Little does she know her wailing has contributed to my acceptance of Nick's request. My face is deadpan as I reach the bottom step, waiting for her to speak.

'Koo wants to know if you're coming to explore the lake and enjoy the picnic on your wish list?' Lulu asks. 'She reckons that chap will be long gone, so we might as well enjoy ourselves with a late lunch.'

'Sure,' is all I can muster, my mind still distracted by my rash decision. Oh well, it's done now!

'Are you OK?' she asks, giving me a concerned look and a tilt of the head.

'I'm good. You?'

'Not really. My dad's just bellowed down the phone at me, demanding I stop playing silly games and return home immediately. No mention of the dreaded situation with Gareth, so I assume Our Kirsty hasn't spilt the beans. You OK?'

Now I know she's either digging or not listening, as she already asked me that, just two seconds ago.

'So-so.' I lead the way through to the kitchen, hoping to find Koo.

Chapter Thirteen

Lulu

'This way!' I call over my shoulder, traipsing across the luscious green pasture. I've no idea if we are trespassing, but I'll feign ignorance and apologise profusely if we're confronted by an angry farmer and his shotgun. There's no signpost to indicate this isn't a public right of way, so I continue. My bulky cargo of cushions and woollen blankets proclaims our intentions: lazing by the water, listening to the birdsong and watching the clouds pass by.

'How much further are we actually going?' shouts Koo, lugging a bag of provisions by one handle as Beth shares the weight and clutches the other.

'To the water's edge,' I reply, gesturing towards the lake's shoreline. 'Would you prefer to picnic in the middle of the stinging nettles?'

I don't wait for Koo's reply but stride on. My stomach is rumbling, and we've packed enough to feed an army – as long as the army enjoy deli-style nibbles in tiny pots and jars.

I can feel the vibe; I'm not stupid. Since I dropped a clanger this morning with Beth, she's been tetchy with me, despite my best efforts to smooth things over. She says she's OK, but clearly, she's not. *I'm* not OK, but I'm plodding on with the day. I've been yelled at by my dear dad, heard nothing from Gareth, and my mind is spinning at the thought of how much Our Kirsty really knows. I'm afraid to find out the precise details, or what everyone's doing in my absence, but the silence is killing me. If I'm sacked from the wedding, then I'm free to eat and drink all I like this week because there's no need to squeeze into that dress. I can save myself some dosh by cancelling the hair appointment, which I won't be needing, the nail appointment, which also won't be necessary, and the spray tan, which was optional, anyway. And if Gareth goes through with the wedding, like he said he's going to, I'll be comfort eating for England as my way of coping. We may have declared our undying love for each other, time and time again, but actions speak louder than words. And as hard as it will be to let him go, Beth's right – his wedding day marks the end of Gareth and me. I'll need to rebuild a life of my own, taking comfort in knowing that he may be married to my cousin but his heart truly lies with me.

I near the edge of the lake. It is vast, far bigger than I'd imagined from the roadway. It isn't boggy underfoot, but reeds and rushes cluster along the bank, creating a definite barrier to entering the water. Not that I intend to, open water swimming is not my thing – who knows what's lurking underneath the surface? I thwack away a couple of insects buzzing round my head; that's the other reason we shouldn't camp too close to the water's edge as we'll be bitten, stung and dive-bombed to death whilst trying to enjoy our food.

I hastily retreat from the water's edge before the other two can join me, throwing down the blankets and cushions to indicate my chosen spot. It's the best of both worlds – far enough away to avoid the pond life, yet close enough to enjoy the gentle rippling effect of the water.

'You can just see the thatched roof of the cottage from here,' says Beth, looking back across the fields in the direction we've trekked.

'Exactly, we could be anywhere, darling,' I say, adding a comedic tone and attempting to ease the tension. An all-out apology would probably do the trick but I'm avoiding the entire explain-thyself situation, if possible. Much like I am with Our Kirsty. 'Name the place and we're there.'

'Why would I choose to be anywhere but here? This was our choice, and Koo granted us our dream hen week,' says Beth, stating the obvious.

'I was only . . . never mind. Sit, sit, sit,' I say, not wishing to rattle Beth's cage any further. Though I'm sure she's implying, in her roundabout way, that I'm not grateful for Koo's generosity.

Beth grabs a plump cushion and throws it down on to the blanket before settling herself. Koo unpacks the food delights from the shopping bag and I grab the wine glasses from the cottage, each wrapped carefully inside a clean sock, ensuring no breakages. The way I keep putting my foot in it with Beth, I might as well stuff one sock in my mouth and be done. But I won't, because I know Koo chose a very nice dry white from the local supermarket this morning.

'Wow, what a glorious selection. I didn't hear you venture out to buy all this,' says Beth, scanning the nibbles spread out on the picnic blanket.

'You were in the shower, to be fair. We were there and back in no time, though Koo did act slightly unhinged as we strolled around the Co-op. She was grabbing food items like a contestant in a supermarket sweep challenge,' jests Lulu, waving her hand in Koo's direction.

'I miss food shopping. I rarely get the time to indulge myself browsing the aisles with a wonky-wheeled trolley. I miss squeezing the fruit and veg for freshness, checking the sell-by dates on the loaves, and spotting a bargain buy,' says Koo.

'Are you serious? It's the worst task of my week,' announces Beth, grimacing. 'I'd pay someone to do my food shopping.'

'You can, it's called a housekeeper,' says Koo, slightly bemused by the remark.

'We can hardly afford a mortgage, let alone a housekeeper just to do our weekly food shop,' retorts Beth, her voice faltering. 'Dale wouldn't be happy if I increased our outgoings with . . .' We watch as a bulbous tear spills over her lashes. 'Sorry, the very mention of him makes me feel so guilty. I've been teary, on and off, all day.'

My heart goes out to her, I can imagine it isn't easy contemplating whether to go ahead with the wedding on Saturday or not. Not that I'd swap places with her – I definitely wouldn't – but at least the ball is in her court and she gets to decide what's happening come Saturday. I don't. My life is in other people's hands, which is never a happy position to be in.

Beth dries her tears, then accepts a consoling hug from Koo, before we continue.

'Koo, will you say a few words while I pour the drinks?' I ask, still attempting to smooth troubled waters.

'I'd just like to say, here's a toast to good company, decent food and bloody good plonk . . . but I suppose you're expecting a bit more sophistication than that!' says Koo, handing out plates.

'I was, but if that sums up your mood, then I'm fine with it. Are you, Beth?'

'Yes. Why wouldn't I be?' says Beth, staring at me with yet another deadpan expression.

I sense she'd like to give me the full-on silent treatment. Bloody hell, I've got some sucking up to do.

'No reason,' I say, nonchalantly. I wish I'd apologised straight out and borne the brunt of explaining this morning. God help Dale or Nick if this is how she carries on at home.

'Cheers!' says Koo, clinking her glass against each of ours.

'Cheers,' we repeat in unison, though I notice Beth's glass doesn't quite touch mine during the toast, before we each take a swig.

'Oooo, nice,' sighs Koo, lowering herself down on to her cushion.

'Good choice,' says Beth, visibly relaxing with each sip and taking in the surrounding view.

'How come the mountains looked purple yesterday, yet today they're definitely green?' I ask, gesturing with my wine glass.

'A trick of the light perhaps?' answers Beth, her gaze following my hand. 'Though I don't understand how that actually works. Surely, I see what's in front of me?'

'Not necessarily,' adds Koo, looking beyond the nearby reeds and rushes. 'It depends on the surrounding influences.'

'Mmm, like seeing someone's true colours,' I mutter. I pick the cellophane from a platter of assorted cheese, before adding, 'How's your day been since our friend was spotted?'

'I'm having a glorious break from my wedding troubles. So far today, I've taken a call from each of my sons demanding my return home, then swiftly outlining how life will resume without the presence of my intended. I ask you, does nobody understand?' mutters Koo, looking as disheartened as she sounds.

'Anything from Judd?' asks Beth, opening a tub of black olives and stabbing several with a cocktail stick.

'He's fine. I couldn't ask for more. He's always supportive, always patient, and never has a bad word to say about my family, and yet . . . they never stop throwing insults at him.'

I glance at Beth, unsure how to respond. I'm about to say, 'Surely not!' but that hardly seems supportive in the circumstances.

'Surely not,' utters Beth, reaching out to stroke Koo's forearm, adding a little affection to the comment.

I expected more from Beth, somehow – I could have uttered the obvious. It seems to work, though, as Koo offers her a weak smile, before selecting slices of honey-roasted ham from a platter. A mere distraction, possibly?

'Come Saturday, all this will be behind you, Koo. You and Judd will be husband and wife – freed from all the stresses and strains, ready to enjoy married life,' I say, not allowing Beth to get a word in. 'You need to grin and bear whatever comes your way, knowing that after the arranged photo shoot, the red-carpet razzmatazz of your celebrity guests, and your father's costly publicity – ta-dah! You'll be married.'

'Do you seriously think so? Because I don't. Saturday will simply be the start of more tension, rather than resolving things with my family – not that my big day should be seen as the "solution" to anything. By taking sides, which they've pretty much already done, and playing mind games, my family have shown what they're capable of. I've no doubt the next round of plans will be hatched before I utter "I do". It feels so selfish of me to expect Judd to shoulder their contempt. Calling it all off would certainly be cruel at this late stage but maybe kinder towards Judd in the long run. A lifetime of prejudice and mistrust would destroy him. And me.'

'Didn't you consider jetting off by yourselves to get married somewhere else, Koo?' asks Beth. 'It might have saved you considerable stress and heartache,' she muses, continuing to stab olives.

'I didn't want a beach wedding or a city break wedding. I wanted the whole shebang, the traditional wedding in church, the private ceremony that other women are allowed to dream of and have as their wedding day. Not me, it seems. Thanks to my family heritage, I'm being put through this public spectacle for the sake of proving our family's worth and wealth to the world at large, while behind the scenes they openly criticise the casting of my leading man,' explains Koo, selecting more nibbles for her plate.

'Are you close to your father?' I ask, knowing how close I am to mine.

'Mmm, our relationship is strange; he loves me to bits but he would never say that – it's like he worships me, but from afar. I'm expected to know how he feels, without ever hearing it,' says Koo, pursing her mouth as if that was difficult to admit.

'That's a shame, my dad's openly affectionate with me, and I know he's proud of me. But then I'm a daddy's girl, so we gel anyway, if you get my drift,' I say, not wishing to rub her nose in it.

Simultaneously we glance at Beth, who hasn't offered a word.

'I don't know my biological father. He's never been part of my life, apart from the obvious. My mum refuses to talk about the details, so I have no idea who he is. I'd like to think he'd have taken an interest in me, but I suspect he doesn't know I exist. I get where you're coming from, Koo, because as much as my mum loves me, I feel there are always conditions I have to meet – not like other families I see.'

'Exactly. My parents' love isn't unconditional, either,' says Koo. 'You've hit the nail on the head. They want everything their way, denying me a voice in my own wedding. Ultimately, all they're doing is driving a wedge between me and them, not between me and Judd. Because this won't break us, you know? Oh no, this situation is simply going to make us stronger. My family clearly thought Judd would have broken off the engage-ment by now – making it unnecessary for Dharling Electra to implement the extravagant plans my father originally hatched for this society-cum-celebrity wedding.' Koo keeps her hands busy as her voice breaks with emotion.

'Hear, hear,' declares Beth, half-heartedly raising her glass as if giving a toast. Koo doesn't notice, and I'm not quick enough to join in with her gesture, before she continues. 'All the more reason for us to be grateful that fate brought us together, then . . . to support each other.'

I grab my glass as Beth takes a quick sip of wine.

'At first, I feared our drinks had been spiked that night, so it's been a relief to find out we each wandered away from our parties in a bid to escape our issues and our hens, admittedly under the influence of a tad too much booze,' I say, returning my glass to the bare patch of earth beside me, which I'm using as a coaster.

'I thought the same!' shrieks Beth, slightly aghast. 'You hear such stories, don't you?'

'Not a line I was expecting to hear today,' says Koo, glancing from me to Beth.

'It's the only explanation I could come up with, but now we know the truth about the party bus gathering us up. I'm good with it all – especially the end result!'

'Exactly. The very thought scares the life out of me – I'm glad we didn't mention it at the time,' says Beth, waving a speared olive in the air, as if that erases our suggestion.

Silence lingers as we pick and nibble at the delightful food platters laid out on the grass before us, lost in our own thoughts, surrounded by a stunning backdrop of mountains and all the natural beauty we could wish for.

Koo

'Whose bright idea was it to bring just one bottle of wine to a picnic?' I ask, cheekily holding the empty bottle upside down and waggling it around, sending the odd drip flying. 'A grand fail, methinks, ladies. Hardly a hostess with the mostest moment!'

'It was a joint effort, so we're equally to blame – it seemed adequate,' consoles Beth, shrugging, stretched out on the blanket and cushions.

'Now we're here, I could happily stay and open another,' adds Lulu, emptying the dregs of her wine glass. 'Shall I nip back and . . .?'

Bless her.

'Should hens ever refuse the suggestion of another round?' I jest, knowing I'll happily go myself – but if Lulu's offering, I won't argue.

'Keys?' asks Lulu, jumping up, spritelier than I could muster; my legs went numb with pins and needles some twenty minutes ago. I rummage around beneath the cushions, locating the cottage key, and deliver it to her outstretched hand.

'Anything in particular?' she asks, glancing between us.

'Yeah, wine!' says Beth, adding, 'And be quick!'

'Ten minutes there and back, I promise.' On cue, Lulu dashes off across the pasture, heading for our cottage.

'She's taking it seriously,' I suggest, as we sit giggling at her comedic stride. She's clearly determined to fulfil her mission.

'She better had, I'm dying for a refill,' remarks Beth, grimacing.

'Bad news?'

'You could say that, more a whirlwind of regret circling my mind.'

'I'm here to listen, if you want to unburden.'

Beth doesn't hesitate. 'I keep kicking myself. All I've ever wanted was to fall in love with a decent, honest guy, someone I could build a home, a family and a solid future with. I'm not bragging but that is exactly what I have with Dale. He's the nicest bloke you could wish to meet, Koo. Honest.'

'But?'

'I keep looking backwards, bypassing the Dale I now love, wondering about my past. It never does me any good. I'm asking myself if what I'm living now is a consequence, the end result, of other people's decisions and the impact they've had on my life? Have I happily settled for Dale only because Nick decided to let me go? That was his decision, not mine! But what if Nick hadn't made that choice, and we'd stayed together, because he was all I ever wanted, if that makes sense?' Her questions touch a nerve with me; I get where she's coming from.

'Well, that's his loss! Surely, you've made your choices from your own free will? No one is forcing you to fall in love with Dale, accept his marriage proposal and spend two years planning a wedding?' I ask, unsure if she wants questions or simply the space to voice her thoughts.

'Who knows?' utters Beth, looking off into the distance across the lake.

I can see the cogs whirring and the tears glistening in her eyes, as her emotions surface – so I wait. Whatever she's working through in this moment won't be interrupted by me, or by Lulu. Though a replenished glass of wine would ease the moment, rather than us both sitting here and staring past each other. I look beyond Beth's frozen frame to view an unspoilt landscape, a rippling lake, ginormous mountains thrusting upwards against a blue sky and billowing clouds – an idyllic skyline unchanged for millennia, against which I suddenly feel totally insignificant. How many people have pondered life's questions at this very shore? I'm a fleeting presence, probably an unmeasurable blip when compared to nature's timeline, humbly aware that this view will remain long after my demise.

Beth turns, abruptly ejecting me from my own quiet reflection.

'It's selfish of me, to be thinking solely of my own wants, but I'd like a shot at that ruby wedding anniversary; I want a marriage that ages and evolves as we explore life together. To still be in love, decades down the line.'

'And you sense there's a chance that future isn't with Dale?'

Beth bats her eyelids, as if a nod would be too revealing.

'I hate to remind you, but he loves you dearly – the fact that he's giving you space shows his level of respect. Would Nick have been so generous?' I ask, in a gentle tone.

'I need to do what I need to do, and make the best of the situation I'm in . . .'

'That sounds so wrong, Beth. Getting married on Saturday is no small step, my lovely. Dale will only want you there if the vows you are making are spoken from the heart – no half measures, no ifs, buts or maybes, but true honest commitment. You owe him that, if nothing else.'

'This week is going to be harder than I anticipated. I feel I've ruined everything by allowing my doubts to get the better of me. I've reopened old wounds and now my heart wishes to explore other possibilities. I thought the answer would simply appear, once I had space. My hen night pushed me over the edge, and now I'm here, still questioning my commitment to Dale. Maybe I should open the door to my past?'

'Have you contacted your ex?'

'I've just responded to his friend request on Facebook, if that's what you're asking. I'll know straight away, right?'

I purse my lips, undecided. Now what do I say?

'Won't I?' she asks, a quiver to her voice.

'Not necessarily, Beth. What happens if you open that can of worms? You might get much more than you bargained for,' I say, as her expression falls. 'I can't fill you with false hope – that would be wrong of me. I'm trusting you to be honest about my situation, and likewise, I must be honest with you about yours. And as tough as it'll be, we need to support Lulu with her predicament.'

I'm waiting for a response when Beth's demeanour suddenly changes. She unexpectedly sits up tall and stares fixedly over my shoulder, in the direction of the cottage.

'What the hell! What's up with Lulu?' she cries, pointing at the figure in the distance.

Lulu is rapidly approaching, a hessian bag knocking against her legs, running as if being chased by an angry bull.

'Quick! You n-n-need to h-h-hide, Koo. They're everywhere!' she pants, reaching us and doubling over like a marathon runner, with her hands on her knees. 'They're blocking the lane, parked on the grass verge and spilling all over the road.'

'Who are?' asks Beth, naively.

I needn't ask, I can guess.

'Press wagons, journalists, a bank of camera lenses along the garden wall . . . I was nearly crushed trying to squeeze past them. It's just like off the telly – they bombard you with questions.'

'They do, hoping you'll start answering,' I say, noting Beth's startled expression.

'Well, I didn't. Not one response. Despite their persistence, I kept walking until I reached the cottage door, went in and collected this.' Lulu pulls a bottle of chilled white wine from her hessian bag, which remains plump, as if padded out with packaging.

'Good girl! That's the spirit, we'll stay down here a little longer then,' I say in delight.

'Even better, when we do decide to return, I've brought this for you to wear.' Lulu pulls my nun's habit from the hessian bag. 'Genius or what?'

'That'll fool 'em, good and proper,' adds Beth, encouragingly.

'Bloody marvellous, my lovely! Now, get that bottle cracked open because Beth here needs a plan of action,' I say, hoping I'm not spilling her beans. But Lulu is part of our posse, after all.

Chapter Fourteen

Beth

I can hardly stifle my giggles when we eventually decide to return to the cottage after enjoying our second bottle of wine. The sight of two tipsy women trying to walk in a slow but straight line, either side of a fully costumed nun, is the last thing the press pack were expecting. Koo's appearance is enhanced by her graciously walking with her head bowed and her arms demurely folded across her body, ensuring her hands, plus sparkling engagement ring, are kept hidden inside the sleeves of her habit, like a winter muff.

The older generation sometimes complain that today's society has lost its manners and values, but never have I seen a boisterous media scrum instantly fall silent, as they do now, respectfully nodding in the nun's direction as we near, clearly not recognising her true identity. Koo plays her role to perfection, serenely acknowledging their response with a tiny nod and whispering 'Bless you' as she walks past. Though when we reach the cottage door, she goes a little over the top with the dramatics by turning, making the sign of the cross in the direction of the assembled press, before entering the cottage.

Lulu closes the door as we roar with laughter at our own antics, clutching each other between gasping for breath.

'That'll cause confusion, if nothing else,' I say, between bouts of laughter. 'I've never seen a crowd fall silent so quickly. I wonder if nuns always have that effect on people?'

'Or is it Koo's sheer beauty, swathed in raven black, that enthralled them? Your skin looks incredible in that wimple – like the stunning woman in the Scottish Widows advert, swathed in her black cape. Captivating.'

'I doubt it, Lulu. I bet half of them couldn't identify me in a line-up. They'll have been given instructions to snap "the woman with the purple hair". People see what they want to see, only rarely do they look a person in the face, let alone the eyes, so they fail to see what's standing in front of them. Having hidden my hair under this wimple, I've got away with it – I might scrap my entire wardrobe once I get home and only ever venture outside in this rig-out.' Koo's hands flutter up and down her body like a magician's assistant.

'The bonus being you don't have to do your hair in the morning, just your skin routine,' adds Lulu, kicking off her shoes and plodding towards the lounge with an armful of satin cushions.

'One thing's for certain, they'll be playing silly buggers for the rest of the day by ringing the bell and pounding on the door, so I'll bolt it good and proper!' Koo's right hand drifts to the ornate bolts at top and bottom, sliding each one firmly across.

'It'll make for an interesting front page tomorrow, with an unusual twist,' I say, heading towards the kitchen to empty our picnic bags.

'*Phuh!* I doubt it. I didn't see anyone snapping our photo – nuns are hardly interesting fodder for selling newspapers, Beth,' says Koo, slipping out of her costume. 'I'll hang this habit on the coat rack, in case of an emergency.'

I walk into the kitchen, plonk the bags down on the scrubbed table and begin emptying the picnic debris into the dustbin and stacking the dirty glasses in the dishwasher. A sense of calm descends on me, as if the mundane actions of everyday life – clearing up and tidying away – provide down time for my brain. In these few moments, my personal situation doesn't exist. Dale, Saturday's wedding, friend requests and exboyfriend Nick all disappear from my brain, to be replaced by disposing of empties, fishing for spent cutlery and folding hessian bags. For the first time in three days, I feel like me – the normal Beth, without a niggling problem, no stress or nerves about future commitments, as if I've just shrugged off a coat patched together from worries, much like Koo disrobing from her nun's habit. I can hear the other two pottering about, settling back into the cottage after our little excursion, but I'm not racing to join them. I need to retain this hard-won sense of myself if I'm to move forward with my decisions.

'Hey, look what we'd forgotten about,' announces Lulu, barging into the kitchen and interrupting my moment of calm, waving a hardback oblong-shaped book. 'The guest book. Josie pointed it out when we arrived and we've ignored it since.' She plonks herself down at the kitchen table and begins flipping through the pages.

I flick the switch on the kettle, hoping to maintain my current state of mind by making a round of hot drinks. I'll be polite, 'mmm' and 'ahh' in the right places, to satisfy Lulu, but I'm not interested in what past guests have written.

'Mr R Gubbins from Dorset has noted "great views" and "good value for money",' reads Lulu, flipping through the pages. 'Slightly saucy one here . . . a Miss Selina Fernsby from Chester has written "excellent mattress on the king size bed in the master suite – a decent bounce". Koo may be interested in that comment, if there isn't a mattress protector.'

'Nice touch,' I mutter, clearly not interested in strangers' opinions. I'm comfortable and feel safe – that's all I need from a holiday cottage.

'How sweet. Beth, listen to this . . .' says Lulu, her finger prodding the front page of the book, before reading aloud. 'Thank you for choosing Lakeside Cottage, Hawkshead for your holiday stay.'

'Lulu, can I just read it instead?' I ask, realising it'll be easier to give in than fight. I'm not trying to be awkward but it probably sounds that way.

'Sure,' she says, turning the book around so I can read.

Thank you for choosing Lakeside Cottage, Hawkshead for your holiday stay. We offer a blend of home comforts coupled with hospitality in an atmosphere of timeless elegance, within comfortable and stylish rooms and alongside unrivalled lakeside views of Cumbria.

We want you to enjoy every precious day of your stay so we pledge to you our service is guaranteed to meet your highest expectations. Should you require any additional help or information during your stay at Lakeside Cottage, please do not hesitate to contact our local host, Josie Adams (contact details are listed in the kitchen).

Please add notes or memories of your holiday to our guest book, as it provides a true history of the many and varied lives passing through this beautiful cottage.

Wishing you and yours the warmest of welcomes,
Mr and Mrs Campbell, Shetland

I read the short paragraphs over Lulu's shoulder, sensing she's attuned to my every breath.

'That's pretty special – they must be nice people for such warmth to radiate from the words on the page. Sometimes it can sound so corny or off, can't it?' I say, returning to the line of mugs.

'Are you adding an entry?'

'Nah,' I say over my shoulder as I add milk and stir each mug. 'I'm not one for such things.'

'Oh, I am. I leave my fingerprints in as many places as I can – ornamental statues, garden railings, overhanging tree branches, jolly Buddha bellies – I left a kiss at 84 Charing Cross Road once.'

I whip around on hearing her last remark. 'Sorry?'

'Oh yeah, we visited the empty shop during one of our weekends away – Gareth said it was the done thing, so I kissed the door frame. He did too.'

Words fail me, again. My puckered brow prompts Lulu to continue, without me asking her to explain.

'Some lady author, Helene . . . I forget her surname, used to write to a bookseller for years on end, ordering specific books to be packaged to America. Anyway . . . she loved that bookshop so asked people if they'd kiss it on passing, as a thank you for providing her with enjoyment and friendship.'

'You had weekends away?' I say, honing in on the point that's disgruntled me. I've totally overlooked the absurdity of her kissing a doorway.

'Yeah, every now and then we'd pick a location and have a couple of nights away together – travelling separately, of course,' says Lulu. 'We've spent long weekends in Manchester, York, Birmingham . . . before returning home, again separately.'

'And you've never been caught out?'

'Nope.'

I place her coffee mug on the table, before asking the biggy. 'Didn't you ever feel guilty for going behind Kirsty's back?'

'Yeah.' Her answer is immediate, no hesitation. 'I get that my actions make me sound like a shitty person but . . . love is love.'

I wait for her to elaborate, but she doesn't. I try again, treading carefully, as I don't want to offend or shame her, but behaviour like this blows my mind. I'm crippled with worry and I haven't done anything exceptionally bad, except keep a friend request hidden and view a media profile, now and then.

'Has Gareth ever said he's finishing with her?' I ask, cradling my coffee mug and leaning against the countertop.

'No. Never.'

My brain screams 'what?' but my mouth remains schtum. I don't believe what I'm hearing. Lulu's not stupid, she knows the score, and yet she's waded into this love triangle, without the lure of false promises or pretence, by the sound of things. Although I find her irritating at times, she seems a decent sort, yet hearing her express her feelings so plainly makes me wonder about her hold on reality.

'I get what you're thinking – that I'm some kind of home wrecker, or the jealous wicked witch who wants the ruby slippers – but I'm not. I simply fell in love.'

'Sadly, he was taken by another – the complication being she's not just another female, she's your cousin – and still you . . .' I don't know the end of my own sentence, so I fall silent.

Lulu gets my point.

'I'm not making excuses. What we've done is wrong,' she nods, 'totally wrong. I hate the fact it's happening within the family, but I'm not going to turn my back on loving him – not when he wants me, too.'

'Wants you, too? Oh, Lulu – how do you work that out? He could have left Kirsty at any time, if he solely wished to be with you.' My own situation seems a damned sight less fraught and complicated, listening to this tangled web.

'Look, you just don't get it, Beth. You have to see us together to appreciate the connection between us,' she says, justifying everything with that unbelievable line. 'It's just that he's in too deep with Our Kirsty to stop what's happening.'

'No! No, he isn't. Whether they are in debt as a couple, mortgaged to the hilt, got a baby on the way – or even, God forbid, three tiny children at this point – there is nothing that can justify what he is doing by . . . b-b-by . . .' I don't want to be lewd, but it's on the tip of my tongue, so I stammer on, 'living with her and seeing you, marrying her whilst dating you . . . and sleeping with you, I presume.'

Lulu nods.

While I pause for breath, Koo enters the kitchen. She looks

surprised at the topic being discussed.

My voice softens, as if speaking to a lovesick teenager. 'Lulu, you do know that he's sleeping with her too, don't you?'

Lulu bites her bottom lip and nods.

'And that doesn't bother you?' asks Koo, collecting her coffee mug.

'It bothers me but . . .'

'Whoa, no! Don't you go there, lady!' shrieks Koo.

I shift my stance, unable to believe what I am hearing from a grown woman. Lulu's making every excuse under the sun for this son of a bitch. Automatically, I check myself; I can't simply expect him to shoulder all the blame – remembering, it takes two to tango.

'You don't get it!' says Lulu, glancing between the pair of us now staring open-mouthed at her.

'You're too right, I don't. I wouldn't want another woman sharing dibs on my man. How about you, Beth?' asks Koo, taking the floor in the conversation.

I shake my head. I'd be mortified if I discovered Dale had another woman – and even more humiliated if she was a close family member.

'What did you think was going to happen once he got married, Lulu – you must have discussed that?' I ask, my empathy beginning to surface. She's obviously so confused she can't see what's wrong with her actions. 'You've got to end this now! You can't continue sneaking around come Christmas, birthdays – maybe christenings even – until you're found out. That would be totally shameful for all concerned, if that were to happen.'

'And innocent children would be brought into the mix,' adds Koo.

'I didn't think we'd get this far, to be honest. I thought somewhere along the way he would break it off with Our Kirsty, and they'd go their separate ways, but . . . he hasn't.'

'And now, it's nearly his wedding day – and what? You're waiting for another phone call telling you he's called off the wedding?' I ask, taking over from Koo, whose expression now matches mine.

Lulu puts down her cradled coffee mug, inspects her nails, before speaking.

'Viewing this from where you two are in life, I totally get how it looks. Totally trashy, cheap, possibly the stuff of daytime chat shows with wailing women onstage and lie detector tests. I can see that, but have you ever loved someone so much, and I mean with all your heart, that the very thought of not being with them for the rest of your life actually physically hurts? Like there's a pain right here.' Lulu taps her breastbone. 'As wrong as I know our circumstance to be, as hurt as Our Kirsty will be when this comes out – and I've got no doubts, the truth will come out, we can't hide this for ever – I don't want to walk away from this man. I'll wait for his decision, then decide my future. I might be relying on my good friends, strong women as you both are, to support me through the dark days.'

I watch Lulu's face melt into an expression of love that verges upon serene. She knows she will pay the ultimate price, she'll have to accept the fallout that is coming her way, regardless of his decision – because their affair will be common knowledge one day – and still, her depth of feeling keeps her going for another day. My God, love has a lot to answer for.

'I hope he's worth it, Lulu – that's all I can say,' adds Koo. Her tone is now mellow, matching mine. I suspect she too can't believe what she's heard or witnessed, over coffee.

Lulu shakes herself from her deep introspection, flashes us a genuine smile, which I can't help but return, before she speaks. 'Well, I'd best get on with writing a little something in this here guest book, and leave a few fingerprints behind, otherwise nobody will ever know that I've been here.'

She immediately busies herself with the pen secured inside
the cover of the guest book. Koo and I exchange a brief glance
over her bowed head.

Koo

'That was quite a speech she gave,' I say, when Beth joins me in
the garden to watch the sunset. The horizon is a wash of pale
apricot creeping between patches of baby blue, which is a slight
disappointment as I'd been hoping for a romantic lavender with
an undercurrent of pink.

'Wasn't it just! The details twanged a nerve or two with me, but
when she mentioned the part . . . the last part. I simply couldn't
argue with her, because isn't that what we're all chasing after and
searching for in life? That one special person, above all others.
I know I am. I have. I was,' says Beth, looking skywards and
admiring the view. Her right index finger swiftly flicks the outer
corner of her eye, preventing what I suspect is a tear from falling.

'What advice do you give in such a situation? It's obvious
she cares for him, yeah, even loves him deeply, but what kind of
bloke does that to two women?' I ask, unsure that I'm qualified
to give advice.

'Not the kind I want to spend a lifetime with, that's for certain.
Love is most definitely blind, isn't it?' utters Beth.

'Too right. Can you imagine the fallout that will occur when
the truth comes out? I think the aunty must be her dad's sister,
from what I've pieced together, otherwise Lulu's own mother
would have been on the hen weekend, wouldn't she?' I say,
applying the situation to my own family dynamics.

'Probably, but regardless of that, why did she accept the
role of maid of honour in the first place? Whether or not the
affair – let's call it out for what it is – has ended by this coming

Saturday, there is always going to be that secret lying dormant in the background, waiting to destroy the happiness of everyone involved,' says Beth, finally turning to face me. Her gaze is steady but there's a rawness around her eyes.

'I agree. Can you imagine finding out such a secret, five years into a marriage, by which time you've added a couple of children to the family, with holidays, happy memories and whatnot. Only to hear that for the couple of years leading up to your marriage there was a family affair going on behind your back. You wouldn't recover from such a secret, would you?'

'No point trying to salvage a marriage under those circumstances,' says Beth, shaking her head. 'It's strange, I never think that these situations happen to ordinary folk, do you? Such tangled webs are for the likes of footballers' wives, celebrity types and high society – but the likes of us, the ordinary ones, you never think of it. Well, I don't.'

I love that Beth speaks from the heart. I wait for her to realise what she's just said, knowing that I'll minimise her embarrassment when she tries to correct herself and back-pedal in an attempt to erase the stereotype she's just repeated. The moment passes and Beth continues to view the garden shrubbery and approaching sunset without a resounding penny dropping.

I don't know whether to laugh or cry that Beth includes me in her tribe of ordinary folk. It feels refreshing to be viewed simply as me, without the family label, the generations of branding, and my father's larger-than-life personality.

My phone's shrill ringtone ruins the moment, making Beth jump out of her skin.

'Sorry,' I mutter, snatching my mobile from my pocket to view the illuminated screen identifying the caller ID as Finch, Jaggers and Knightley. 'I wondered when I might receive this call. Excuse me, Beth – I'll go inside so as not to disturb your thoughts. Enjoy the sunset.' I hastily stand up, tap the screen to accept the call, and make my way inside.

'Hello, Koo Bournebury speaking,' I say, heading for my bedroom. I sense that I'll need to keep my guard up regardless of whether this call brings good or bad news.

'Ms Bournebury, Mr Jaggers here. I hope you are well and that I'm not disturbing you by calling at such an hour.' His voice is as deep and pompous as I remember, instantly igniting memories of my previous meeting with my father's legal team. I'd ugly-cried throughout the meeting, much to my father's horror. Mr Jaggers doesn't give me a chance to answer but continues in his authoritative manner. 'Your father has requested that—'

'Mr Jaggers, sorry to interrupt but—'

He then sternly interrupts me. 'Ms Bournebury, I've been asked to provide specific details, so please, allow me to continue addressing a matter of importance. Your father has requested that we draft and deliver a legal proposal ahead of your intended marriage this coming Saturday.'

Having secluded myself within my bedroom for privacy, I now wish I'd stayed alongside Beth in the garden. Better still, not taken the call.

I knew it! My father never discusses anything. Instead, he heads straight for his legal eagles when life throws up a situation. I should have seen this coming.

Mr Jaggers continues to explain as I pace back and forth, though his words blur within my fuddled brain, and my emotions add another row of bricks to the protective fortress I'm building around me. It takes ten minutes for the man to complete his legal spiel, providing the who, what, when, how and, most importantly, the why of my father's instructions.

'In a short while, you'll be receiving a copy of the said document. I advise you to read it carefully before signing and returning the necessary copies to my office. Such agreements are binding within the UK, and your family are trying to protect both yourself and your future prospects should an unfortunate situation arise.'

As if on cue, I hear the chime of the front door bell.

'Is that you?' I ask rudely, in my bewildered state. Before remembering that the press pack are still in situ and, for the umpteenth time, are probably chancing their hand by trying to make contact.

'Pardon?' says Mr Jaggers.

'The front door bell just sounded ... I wondered if ...' I dash to the nearest window, forgetting that my master suite faces the rear garden.

'Quite possibly ... my colleague and associate Knightley has been instructed to hand deliver the necessary document to yourself, preferably this evening, at Lakeside Cottage, Hawkshead. Your current residence, I do believe.' I assume my beloved sons have duly confirmed the address, when asked by their grandfather.

'Mr Jaggers, I am quite unprepared to receive such instruction on this, the actual week of my wedding. I don't think that my father has ...'

Rat-a-tat-tat.

'Koo!' calls Beth, knocking on my bedroom door. 'A letter for you.'

I silently open the door, my mobile at my ear, to be handed a large brown envelope on which my name is written in an elegant hand. 'Thank you,' I mouth to Beth.

She returns downstairs, hopefully to enjoy the tranquil garden and the beauty of the sunset.

Chapter Fifteen

Lulu

'I hope Koo's OK – she's been in her room for a fair while,' I say, settling at the kitchen table, dishing out the bundles of fish and chips I'd fetched from Main Street. On my return, it was nudging towards ten o'clock when I'd hollered up the staircase, but without reply.

'Despite your best intentions to cajole her into joining us, we need to respect her wishes. She'll come downstairs when she's hungry, and anyway, with the press pack camped outside, she's probably better off upstairs – they can't photograph her through the upper windows,' says Beth, nosing inside the pantry for salt and vinegar.

'They've got ladders, you know. I never realised how intrusive they are,' I mutter, opening my paper parcel. 'I'm feeling guilty for every glossy celeb mag I've ever purchased; it's people like me that are encouraging their behaviour.'

'I've lost count of how many times the cheeky sods have knocked on the door. The only reason I undid the bolts to accept that envelope was because I saw the guy, suited and booted, stepping out of his posh car – otherwise, nah,' explains Beth, carrying an assortment of salt and pepper shakers, bottles and pickle jars to the table.

I'd ventured out to the local chippy after borrowing a bike from the outhouse, managing to dodge the barrage of questions from our unwanted gathering. It has been years since I rode a bike – and never before dressed as a nun. It seemed the only safe option, but I averted my gaze when I passed the church on the hill, for fear of being judged. Firstly, for impersonating a nun, and secondly, for impersonating a nun fetching chips on a borrowed bike. Whatever people may think of me, I whole-heartedly refuse to apologise or be ashamed for loving others the way I do, because love is love. But still, some might judge my actions.

'Lulu?'

'Mmm . . .' I prod at my chips with a wooden fork, then realise Beth is staring at me, as if awaiting an answer. 'Sorry, I was away with the fairies,' I say, unsure what she's asked.

'I said, this week, it's full on, isn't it?' She wiggles her fork. 'Despite having no work meetings to attend, no wedding arrangements to oversee or errands to run in preparation – simply figuring out the situation with Dale has taken it out of me.'

'Mentally exhausting, in fact. I'm supposed to be in my prime, yet I could happily sleep for the week.'

'But you're coping – despite everything?' asks Beth, her steady gaze urging honesty.

'Kind of. My head is scrambled while I wait for an answer.'

'Wait?' A flicker of surprise alters her tone.

'Yep. As crazy as that sounds, I'm still waiting – even if I don't get a response until the actual morning of the wedding.'

Silence descends as we pick at our fish supper. I feel bad that I've ignored my faux pas from earlier.

'Firstly, I owe you an apology for the other night,' I admit. 'You helped me to bed, when I was very much the worse for wear, but I woke up soon after, desperate for some water. Which is why I was on the landing and overheard what you said about, well . . . what you mentioned to Koo. I get it, I'm not the same as you pair in the relationship stakes, but I do understand where you're coming from. The heart wants what the heart wants, right?'

Beth nods, still wiggling her fork whilst chewing.

'I am sorry,' I confess. 'I should have been upfront with you, and told you at breakfast that I'd heard, but . . . I didn't, as you know.'

'Thank you, I appreciate that. I felt awkward telling anyone, even Koo or yourself. I'm supposed to be living the dream, when the reality is so different. I knew once I'd said it, there would be no going back, but I should have been open with you both. It wasn't intentional, honest.'

'And have you?'

'Have I what?'

'Contacted him?'

Beth blushes profusely, before shaking her head. 'I've accepted his request, nothing more. It almost feels OK for me to be hurting, for me to be confused, but I don't want to hurt others. Dale doesn't deserve that. My mum can do without the additional worry. And I've no idea what Nick will think, after waiting weeks to get a response from me – he'll probably laugh his socks off.'

'You won't know until you message him. His intentions might be innocent – a friendly connection, a blast from the past, a long-time-no-see kind of friend request.'

'You're right, I won't . . . but I daren't send him a message. I know Nick, he's never done mutual friendship with women. He's made contact for a reason.'

'Saturday's cancelled, then?' I ask, seeing how her mind is working.

Beth bites her lip. 'Not necessarily.'

'Oh.' The word slips from my lips.

'I hear you, it's unfair.'

'Sorry, that isn't what I meant. From what I overheard, I thought you were set on seeing how the ground lies, and noting your feelings towards him after all these years. Which I think is very brave – but how does it resolve your situation with Dale? Won't you be adding more confusion to the pot?'

Beth's gaze is fixed on mine – pools of uncertainty and pain.

I daren't say another word, for fear of ruining the apology I've just made and requiring a second attempt.

'Probably. And that alone scares me like hell.'

'I felt like that when me and Gareth were at the avoiding each other stage, before we'd really spoken. We couldn't chat naturally. We daren't be alone in a room. I'd be so aware of where he was placed at any family gathering or lunch yet couldn't look or act as if he mattered in case it showed. As awkward as hell, until we finally admitted what we felt for each other, in private.'

Beth's brow furrows slightly.

'Crazy, isn't it? You grow up thinking the fairy tale happens to everyone at a certain age, when the reality is you fall in love at the most inopportune moment. In my case, with the guy I least expected, surrounded by a gaggle of family who haven't a clue what is going on right under their noses.'

'And now, you're left waiting to see what he actually does on Saturday?'

I nod. 'It makes me sound like second dibs, doesn't it? When, actually, choosing me would be the bravest thing in the world; the easiest would be going through with the wedding to Our Kirsty.'

'And if he does, what then?' asks Beth, her expression relaxing.

'As I said earlier, I'll pick up the pieces and carry on with my life.'

'Oh, Lulu.'

'Yep, that's my plan.'

'But what plan ever goes to plan, hey? This time last week, I was planning to attend my hen weekend – and look where that's got me!' says Beth, stabbing at her chips.

'How's this dream hen week turning out for you? Enjoying it?'

'I am. The cottage is beautiful. The company intriguing. I'm still as confused as I was but, yeah, this is exactly what I would have wanted if my girlfriends back home had taken the time to ask. You?'

'A bonus, to be fair – I'm hardly entitled. And Koo? What about her hen week?'

'This wasn't her choice, though,' says Beth. 'She wanted friends and Florence, didn't she?'

'Actually, she got one out of two wishes,' I jest.

'Yeah, but wouldn't it have been lovely to fully repay her generosity? Perhaps, one day – if we keep in touch – we'll be able to.'

'I do feel guilty for spoiling her fun, but I haven't got a passport, so there's no way I could have made her wish happen,' I say, peeling the batter from my fish.

'That's a point, I don't carry mine with me, either,' adds Beth, spearing more chips, eyeing Koo's untouched supper bundle. 'Should we call her again, just to be sure?'

I'm nearer the door, so I don't hesitate to go.

I take the staircase two at a time, despite the swathes of black material clinging to my ankles. I reach the landing and listen intently at Koo's bedroom door before knocking.

Rat-a-tat-tat.

'Koo, I've been out to the chippy to fetch supper if you're hungry . . .'

The door immediately swings wide, revealing a tear-stained figure clutching a pile of papers. Leaning against the doorjamb in the dim light, her slender frame looks half the size compared to this morning.

'Hi, sweetie, how are you doing?' I ask softly, unsure what's unfolded in her world.

'Not good, to be honest. Did I hear you mention chips?' she asks, not mentioning my outfit.

'You did, come and join us,' I say, not wishing to pry, but her puffy eyes and red nose give the game away.

'I need to eat something.' She exits the room, firmly closing the door behind her.

I gently wrap my arm about her shoulders and guide her to the top stair, where we descend in single file.

'What's with my nun's habit?' asks Koo, following in my wake.

'I borrowed it purely to avoid hassle from the media folk, along with a bike from the outhouse. The guy in the chippy didn't bat an eyelid – if anything, I think he gave me extra-large portions.'

'Life lesson noted.'

'Plus, you'll never guess what else I discovered stashed in the outhouse – a tandem!' I explain, heading for the kitchen.

'Never!' says Koo, with a snort. 'It would be worth a go just for the giggle.'

Beth

'Do you want me to pop it in the microwave for you?' I ask, as Koo settles before her chip supper.

Lulu stands behind Koo, giving me a wide-eyed expression and gesturing to the wodge of papers Koo has slapped down on the table. She confirms what I can already see: Koo's upset, very upset.

'No, thank you. I'm sure they'll be fine,' answers Koo, eagerly unwrapping her chips as if it were a pass-the-parcel party game from our childhood. My childhood, not necessarily hers – I keep making that error. What do I know of her world? Mine was filled with Co-op divi numbers, hand-me-downs and Findus Crispy Pancakes. I assume hers was filled with ponies, paid nannies and her father's numerous marriages. I made a similar error earlier, in the garden. Thankfully, she wasn't offended and didn't correct me – another sign of good manners and education.

Koo tucks into her supper. Lulu's watching me like a hawk, so I bite the bullet.

'Was it good news or bad?' I ask, not wishing to intrude but not wanting to appear unsupportive.

'Read for yourself.' Koo flicks the papers, scooting them across the table in my direction. 'See what you think. The phone call I received was perfectly timed.'

I stare at the paperwork; there seems rather a lot to have been crammed inside the envelope I took delivery of. I'm dubious about whether I should accept her invite to read through it. I might work in a castle but I'm hardly a clever clogs when it comes to official-looking paperwork. And this looks very official: a fancy black font upon buttermilk embossed paper. I gingerly take the pile of papers, straighten the edges – stalling for thinking time, really, but it makes sense to be efficient – before I start reading.

'My father's legal team, in case you were wondering,' says Koo, in an aside to Lulu, who is leaning forward in anticipation. 'I knew my father would do something underhand or pull a legal stunt to protect the family wealth – a leopard doesn't change its spots, does it?'

I read silently. The document's title shocks me, despite being written with the most beautiful and flourishing swirls of calligraphy, as if attempting to hide a blunt-force blow within a decorative piece of penmanship. I realise what I'm holding, and my eyes flicker upwards, meeting Koo's direct gaze over the edge of the page.

'Interesting, hey?' is her only comment.

I give a nod, which soon becomes a head shake as I scan the bold headings: *Between ... Background ... Now it is hereby agreed ...*

'I can't wait any longer! What is it?' asks Lulu.

'A pre-nup agreement,' I say, without lifting my gaze, though I can see Lulu's mouth drop wide open in my peripheral vision.

'No!' is her accompanying comment.

When I've finished with the first page, I place it face down on the table, only for Lulu to eagerly snatch it up.

Koo continues to pick at her supper, appearing as calm as you like, but I bet she's raging inside. What a world she inhabits, so different to mine! With each line I read, my heart goes out to her. The document and its accompanying appendices give a detailed rundown of her financial existence: property and land, company shares, legal bonds and hedge funds, even approximations for a substantial inheritance from her father. I don't read any further than the main three pages, I don't understand the legal jargon or need to know her personal business. I get the gist of the matter – her father doesn't believe this marriage will last. End of. I collect the papers and pass them across to Lulu, who is using her index finger to underscore each sentence as she reads. How can three women be so different, yet find themselves here together, united by circumstance?

'I don't know what to say, Koo. Other than I'd be majorly pissed off and offended if my parents imagined my intended to be a gold-digger, only after my family inheritance,' I say, grateful for my simple existence without such burdens. That document has allowed me to walk a few steps in Koo's party shoes, and it wasn't comfy or pleasurable.

'Is this legal?' asks Lulu, waving the page she's reading.

'Er, well, in the UK at the present time it isn't exactly legal, but it is a binding contract if signed by both parties,' explains Koo, between mouthfuls.

'Oh,' utters Lulu, returning to her task.

'And as you're about to find out . . . Judd has already signed it,' says Koo, offering a spoiler ahead of page three. 'That, in itself, opens a can of worms, because we discussed the idea of a pre-nup, and both of us said we were comfortable in the knowledge that we didn't need one.'

'Obviously, your father thinks otherwise,' I say, stating the bloody obvious. 'Is the legal team known to you?'

'Oh yes, I've known Mr Jaggers all my life. The team were instructed to file agreements with each of my exes regarding provisions for raising our sons, to ensure everything was shipshape and watertight on both occasions, before my waters even broke. Again, they were instructed without my prior knowledge, but in those instances everything has worked out for the best.'

'Did neither man take an interest?' I ask, unsure how these things work.

'No. Both are excellent fathers. And they were somewhat offended at first, but with all the "i"s dotted and the "t"s crossed it made things easier, so they arranged for their legal teams to speak with mine. Ours, actually.'

'They have legal teams too? Boy, what a world you live in.' I'm flabbergasted how the other half must live.

Koo shifts in her seat before answering. 'Felix's father is the CEO of Papercut Animations who create and produce—'

'Bloody Nora, Koo – everyone knows what they produce! Christmas Day isn't Christmas Day without watching their classic cartoons,' I blurt, interrupting her.

'And Felipe's dad is the CEO of Black Hole Studios who've just released . . .'

'The number one cinema smash hit of the year and likely to sweep the board at all the awards ceremonies,' I say, knowing both companies are massive. 'Their CEOs are major entrepreneurs, like global superstars . . .' I stop talking; Koo clearly knows their credentials.

Lulu is waving page three, and saying indignantly, 'Judd signed it. He's already signed it in your absence?'

'Yep, and check the date – it was weeks ago. Makes you question how my father got him to do that,' mutters Koo, removing the batter and flaking the entire fillet of fish before consuming it.

'This is so American,' adds Lulu, as if we didn't know. 'This . . . is an insult to your relationship, if you've already discussed it and agreed a pre-nup wasn't necessary.'

'I'm heartbroken to think my father would go behind my back and orchestrate an agreement with his legal team, at the same time as hosting a wedding extravaganza for Saturday.'

'Have you spoken to him?' I ask, not wishing to upset her further, before realising that my question fits both father and fiancé.

'No, but it totally sucks. It's like onstage and offstage antics.'

'Yeah, like private and public personas – I hate that,' says Lulu, folding the documents and placing them next to Koo's discarded chip wrappings.

In double-quick timing, both myself and Koo stare at Lulu as her remark hovers between us.

She blushes. 'Oh yeah, I just heard how that sounded – but my situation is slightly different, don't you think?'

'Not really. You have a private role with Gareth and a public role with Kirsty – I don't see much difference between that and what my father is attempting to conjure up for Saturday. Hey, let's witness and celebrate the big white wedding, but secretly, I don't trust the groom, knowing he'll rinse my daughter for all she's worth, so I'll either get rid of him before he reaches the altar or get the legal team on board beforehand!' comments Koo, putting her fork down and pushing the remnants of her supper to one side.

'I wouldn't like it, Koo, regardless of your father's good intentions,' I say, speaking frankly. I notice Lulu has fallen silent after realising she's guilty of double standards.

'It's like the media rabble out the front. Their news isn't worth the paper it's written on – well, neither is that,' says Koo, flicking the corner of her pre-nuptial agreement.

'Isn't that what they used to say about wrapping your chips in yesterday's newspapers?' offers Lulu, hesitantly.

'Exactly!' says Koo, her spirit returning.

'Are you signing it?' I ask, pushing my chair back and standing up, ready to leave the table.

'Am I bugger! And I wish Judd hadn't, either.'

'Good. Get it put away, because regardless of the late hour, we're supposed to be on a hen week, so we need a round of drinks and a romcom to lighten the mood,' I say, grabbing three wine glasses and a bottle of Pinot from the fridge.

Chapter Sixteen

Wednesday 23 August

Lulu

'Beth! Beth!' I whisper, in an urgent tone, pressing my mouth against her bedroom door for fear of waking Koo.

'Come in,' calls Beth in an expectant tone, as if she's hoping I'll deliver her a morning cuppa.

I'm not empty-handed, but this might ruin the start of her day. I enter, expecting to find a darkened room, curtains drawn and a swaddled hump snoozing in the bed. What I actually find is a bedroom bathed in brilliant sunlight, a well-made bed, and a busy woman sitting at the dressing table in a dressing gown with her phone in hand, jotting details on to a piece of paper.

'Morning, look at you being the early bird – I thought I was eager but . . .'

'Morning, Lulu. Did you say you haven't got your passport with you, or you haven't got a passport?'

'Errr?'

'Yesterday, you mentioned passports – I forget which you'd said.'

'I don't own one. Mine ran out ages ago, and I didn't renew it. The thought of all the form-filling and the faff put me off. Why?'

'What's that?' asks Beth, pointing to my hands.

'This, yeah, it's what I wanted to show you . . .' I unfold the newspaper and show her the headline: Heiress receives the Last Rites. Alongside it are a photo of me pushing the borrowed bike and a beautiful colour shot of Koo. Obviously, an official press release head shot, taken prior to our weekend. I'm grateful it's a photo of me on the outbound journey to the chippy and not one of me returning with three fish suppers tucked under my arm.

'Bloody hell!' mutters Beth, getting up to take the newspaper from me.

'I only nipped out for a breath of fresh air, but I spied this when I was walking past the newsagent's. I bought it and came straight back.' It isn't quite true, but she needn't know – I doubt she'll approve, even if I try to explain.

'I assume Koo hasn't seen it yet?'

'No. She's still sleeping, I think.'

Beth falls silent as she reads the opening paragraphs. I hadn't got any further than the opening two lines, sensing I'd better get back to the cottage as soon as possible.

'And the cheeky bastards continue to stage a vigil outside, despite thinking that she's dying?'

'I'd never have borrowed the habit if I thought they'd print something like this. Can you imagine what her father, sons and fiancé are going to think!'

'That she's lied. Or they'll know from experience what a load of tosh the press come up with – I'm sure there's been plenty of gossip or fake news printed over the years. Thank God the original photo of us sunbathing on the patio isn't being splashed around.'

'It is, in full colour, on page six! I hate to say it, but if you peer at the photo of me semi-naked, covering my boobs, there's an uncanny resemblance to the nun on the front page. We're in a national daily newspaper – it's mortifying! I'll never live this down if my boss sees this on sale at the supermarket kiosk.'

'You are going straight to hell if eagle-eyed readers spot the similarity – the press will be chasing you for a comment.'

'But how do we show Koo? I can't imagine she'll be happy.'

'I wouldn't recommend a "ta-dah!" moment, but the sooner the better, surely?'

'Come with me, please.'

'Are you serious?'

I give a nod. I might come across as slightly brazen and loud at times, but I know my limitations in life. And this is one of them.

'Can you wait just five minutes, while I finish this, and then we'll go together?'

'Sure. What's with the passport question?' I ask, as she darts back to her makeshift desk.

'I'm not sure, given that you don't hold a passport. I haven't got mine with me, but I know exactly where it is and can send home for it.'

'Koo's is in her luggage, apparently,' I say, recalling an earlier conversation, as Beth begins flipping through numerous open screens: flight times, hotel reservations and a view of a distinctive terracotta-red dome.

'Exactly. I was wondering if we could repay Koo's kindness and generosity towards us by nipping to Florence for a whistle-stop tour, but since you haven't got a—'

I don't allow her to finish the sentence before saying, 'Do it. Book it . . . you and Koo – I'm happy to go halves on the cost.'

Beth looks at me dubiously. 'I can't ask you to pay for half of a trip you're technically excluded from?'

'You can. Actually, I insist. It's my own fault for being an idiot about my passport, but seriously, it's the right thing to do – especially after what Koo's laid on for us this week. You work with artefacts every day, but hopefully it won't feel like a busman's holiday, more a treat to accompany her. Even more so, when she reads this morning's front page and finds out she's got an appointment with the Grimm Reaper. What time's the flight?'

'Tonight. There's spare seats on a flight from Newcastle airport, just after five o'clock.'

This feels right, so very right. 'Book it. But how are you going to get your passport?'

'I was thinking a motorbike courier – it might be costly, but it'll definitely get here if they meet us at the check-in.' Beth's features relax into a smile, instantly softening her appearance.

'You don't smile enough – do you know that?' I say, cautious of offending her.

'Do you think?' She gives a giggle, as if hiding her surprise at the remark.

'Yeah. I'm not saying you're uptight but, yeah, you're definitely uptight.'

'Thanks for that. Unfortunately, for my wedding week, when I should be relaxed and happy, I'm partway through an unplanned life crisis of unimaginable proportions – which might have something to do with it.'

'*Phuh!* Aren't we all!' I announce, flouncing over to the ottoman and settling myself for a short wait, as Beth swiftly begins a booking spree.

Beth

'Can you grab me a coffee while I read this article? I need to know exactly what I'm dying of,' jests Koo, spreading the offending paper across the kitchen table.

'Koo, please don't joke about it,' I snap, mortified that she's being so glib but relieved that she sees the funny side. A few minutes pass as I ready her coffee request.

'How rude! Have you read this? The cheeky gits have stated

that "the weight has dropped off her in recent months, much to the horror of her nearest and dearest" – show me a bride who doesn't lose a few inches before her big day!'

'Commenting on your physical appearance is a bit below the belt, isn't it?' says Lulu, camped opposite Koo at the table.

'Simply the norm, Lulu. They wouldn't dream of remarking on a man's physical appearance ... and this here too: "Ms Bournebury has recruited several carers to assist with her physical needs and well-being during this stressful time" – I ask you, where do they get such tosh? They're implying that I'm dying, you know!'

'What have you got?' asks Lulu, pandering to Koo's sense of humour.

'I haven't found it yet, but I'm bound to by the end of the article ... oh, here it is: "Ms Bournebury has recently been spotted sporting an eccentric hair colour in a brave attempt to brighten her days whilst undergoing chemo." So, they reckon I've got the Big C yet am carefree enough to be sunning myself alongside my half-naked, face-pack-loving carers.'

'They couldn't be more wrong,' I say, stirring the coffees, diverting my anger into physical movement with a teaspoon, before handing out the drinks. 'Here.'

'I suppose Saturday's wedding ceremony is my dying attempt to make an honest man of Judd before I pass.'

'Now seriously, Koo – stop it!' I demand, not liking to jest about such an awful topic.

'Tell them, not me,' retorts Koo, pointing towards the front door, indicating the media scrum. 'They make a killing by selling such trashy stories. Their minds and morals come straight from the gutter. Simply one of the reasons why my father is obsessed with micro-managing an extravagant Bournebury wedding, despite my choice of groom.'

'It all sounds so derogatory. Can you imagine someone who is genuinely ill and needs to arrange a wedding reading such remarks ... it could have a devastating effect, when kindness ought to be the order of the day,' says Lulu, accepting her coffee mug, along with my knowing glance.

'Have you finished reading, Koo?' I ask.

'Nearly, why?' Koo doesn't lift her head but ploughs on, taking in every unnecessary detail.

'We've got a surprise for you,' I announce, hoping she'll cut short her tabloid obsession.

'Mmm, such as?' she mutters, still not lifting her gaze from the newsprint.

'Koo. Stop reading, please,' Lulu admonishes her. 'Beth's got something lovely to tell you.'

'Firstly, you're not at death's door as predicted by the press, and so, as a result, we've decided to treat you to a speedy city break to ...' I hesitate, before delivering the final word. 'Florence!'

Koo's head snaps up, her attention well and truly diverted from this morning's newspaper.

'No!' she gasps, her hands flying to her mouth. 'Really?'

I excitedly glance towards Lulu, whose beaming smile is as wide and bright as my own.

'Yep, we're not joking. We wanted to treat you to a slice of your dream hen-do. Sorry that it can't be longer than a fleeting visit, but I promise we'll cram in as much as we can before catching our flight home.'

'I'm happy to keep shop here whilst you pair dash off ...'

'You're not joining us?' asks Koo, instantly shocked.

'I don't own a passport, but I'll be fine. Honest. I have everything I need here, and you'll be back before I've even missed you,' says Lulu, with a smile.

'If you're sure,' says Koo, the excitement growing behind her eyes.

'I've called Dale, explained where we're going and why, then asked him to dig my passport out of the desk drawer and hand it over to the courier I've booked. Bless him, he never fails me . . .'

My words linger, creating an awkward silence, which Koo feels obliged to fill.

'Ladies, I can't thank you enough for such a gesture. No one has ever . . .' Koo bursts into tears, like a child who's received a surprise puppy.

'Koo!' I put down my coffee mug and dash to her side, instinctively wrapping my arms about her quivering shoulders. 'Hey, hey, what's this?'

'We didn't mean to upset you, Koo,' says Lulu, a fraction of a second behind me. She reaches across the table to Koo, takes her hand and squeezes it affectionately.

'N-n-no one, apart from J-J-Judd ever thinks to arrange t-t-treats for me. I'm so grateful, ladies, you'll never know how much this means to me, especially after my hollow experience last Saturday night,' sniffs Koo, her face crumpling with emotion.

'Don't, please, you'll start me off,' I say, accepting her kind words but feeling myself in danger of blubbering.

'Honestly, I found myself in a room full of women I wouldn't give the time of day to, and yet they were supposed to be celebrating a milestone event in my life, so go figure.'

'Well, we're here now, and last Saturday night is long gone for all of us,' whispers Lulu.

'So where are we heading first, after we've checked into our hotel?' I ask, to shift Koo's mind to happier thoughts.

'I truly don't mind. All I want is to wake up in Florence and feel the sun on my face. That's enough.'

'Boy, you are easily pleased,' snorts Lulu.

I remain schtum, knowing that our budget is tiny, but I'm determined to make the most of it and repay this lovely lady, as a true friend would.

Chapter Seventeen

Koo

Our conversation naturally ebbs and flows until I reach the topic which needs to be addressed but which I'm determined will not become a bone of contention between us: the pre-nup signature.

'My darling, why didn't you say anything?' I ask, holding my mobile aloft to view Judd's forlorn expression.

His blue eyes have lost their sparkle and his face appears gaunt.

'Koo, I honestly don't care what restrictions or contractual details your father tries to impose – it's irrelevant, compared to what we have, isn't it?'

'So why sign the pre-nup?'

'Hobson's choice, really. Refuse to and it looks dodgy, so I thought why not? Sign and be done with it, get his lawyers off my back and give your father peace of mind ahead of the wedding, that's how I see it.'

'I'm not signing it.'

'Koo . . .'

'No, Judd, I'm not. All my life I've complied with his demands, keeping him sweet-tempered and on an even keel. I don't need a pre-nup, either. So I figure if you've signed, then he has what he needs, but I'm not completing the document.'

'It'll be null and void.'

'So be it! Dad got what he wanted, which was your willingness to sign, but he's not having mine.'

We both fall silent, which is not what I wanted. I'm desperate not to end the call on a bum note, but I won't entertain the idea of signing – it feels like a sodding omen.

'Are you OK?' I ask.

'I'm fine. I'm more concerned about you, being away from home, and for such a crucial week of your life,' he says, his thoughtful nature shining through.

'Apart from missing you and my lads, I can honestly say I've never been better, so don't worry, please – I'm with the nicest two ladies.' I spend a few minutes outlining how my surprise trip came about, the laughs we've had and the bond that is forming, in order to settle Judd's worries. My voice is overflowing with excitement as I recall the details. It's strange talking to Judd, allowing my childish excitement to spill over without restraint, knowing that he'll be taking pleasure from my joy, despite it lengthening my absence. I can be myself with Judd, revel in the sheer joy of the occasion, like a child at Christmas. With previous partners, I felt as if I had to act a certain way, retain an air of mystery, or simply live up to their expectations and maintain my decorum. When I was younger, I mistakenly accepted the restrictions placed upon me by both my son's fathers – which is ridiculous, when a loving relationship should be built on mutual respect and affection, not a slavish devotion to maintaining public perception as a power couple uniting ambitious global companies.

'Right, I need to pack, otherwise we'll be running to reach the departure gate on time. And no more worrying about ill health or last rites – it's simply the media pedalling their lies. Love you.'

'Love you too, Koo.'

I blow a goodbye kiss, which Judd duly catches mid-air. One tap of the screen and he's gone, hopefully feeling a little less forlorn than before.

I dash around the bedroom, from the wardrobe to the chest

of drawers, grabbing various items of clothing, without much care or attention, not that I have many outfits. I can't remember ever having girlfriends who made me feel this happy – correction, not happy, or content, but utterly delirious – by their thoughtful gesture. I simply wish to wake up with the sunlight blinding me, forcing me to stare at the dazzling red lining on the inside of my eyelids, demanding that I start the day. That's it. It's nothing grand, or ostentatious. I don't need champagne, or oysters, or sultry Florentine men serving strong coffee at breakfast – I simply want the joy of waking up in Florence. And to bottle that one moment as a memory.

As far back as I can remember, I have always treated others. At boarding school, with Battenberg slices squirrelled up our jumpers for late-night birthday treats. Or organising surprise drinks in the Student Uni bar. Or organising countless wedding gifts, christening pressies and anniversary milestones – just because I felt I ought to, not because I particularly wished to. One can't go through life ignoring the fun events, surely? Otherwise life is a miserable, repetitive 365-day cycle, with a blip every four years, in which we wake up, get up and dodge stuff, before retiring for the night.

I'm fortunate to have spare money to do something nice for someone else to brighten their day. Rarely is the gesture freely returned. Even when I had the boys, there was a barrage of excuses that 'You're bound to have everything, aren't you?', 'How many memory books and silver decorative rattles can one newborn use?' When the silent reality was clearly 'He's been born with a silver spoon in his mouth, from both sides of the family – how blessed!' I'd have loved to open tiny gifts decorated with blue ribbon, shared the excitement of friends eager to receive cuddles with my newborn, if they'd felt half the energy and excitement I'd shown towards their babies. I received very little from female friends – gifts, support or advice – suggesting people thought I had everything that life could bestow, so don't be greedy, Koo, and expect a lot, because you don't get everything you want in this life. And that's the bottom line, possibly the story of my life, which I have willingly accepted.

Take it from me, I am generous but I won't expect or allow you to treat me as kindly in return. A fault, I know, but my nature is fixed and unalterable at this stage of the game. I could have lowered my standards to match the lowly offerings of others, but I never did. But this … a lump returns to my throat as I begin stuffing items and toiletries into my smallest wheelie case, this is bloody marvellous – and to think I've only known these two beauties a matter of days! Whatever brought us three together on Saturday night, be it fate or fortune, I thank my lucky stars for the chance encounter. Maybe the universe was smiling down on me for once, and delivered what I truly needed: Beth and Lulu.

'Beth!' I holler, across the landing.

'Yes!'

'Is there anything in particular that you need me to pack?'

'Flat shoes, I suppose. Nothing else.'

That's fine with me. All I'll need for this glorious wake-up call will be a camisole and a smile.

'Beth!'

'What now!' she yells.

'Thank you – you've no idea how much this means to me!'

There's silence, and for a moment I'm unsure if she's heard my sentimental twaddle, until I turn around. Standing in the door frame are my two friends, their eyes glistening and their chins slightly wobbly.

'I think we do,' whispers Lulu.

'We've got you sussed, lady,' adds Beth, over Lulu's shoulder. 'Now, hurry up, our taxi will be here any minute.'

'Are you sure you'll be OK on your own?' I ask Lulu.

'Alone? What with your adoring crowd picketing the garden gate with their long lenses and Dictaphones! Somehow, I doubt I'll be bored. Anyway, you'll be back before I know it.'

'That's very true – and if someone would get a wiggle on, we could be on our way now rather than gassing and wasting precious time,' mutters Beth, ushering me from my own bedroom.

'I need to tidy it up, I can't leave it looking like a pigsty,' I moan, as Beth drags my wheelie case towards the door.

'Leave it, Koo! Who's going to see it? Now, come on, before Beth starts panicking!' screeches Lulu, stepping aside to make way.

I can't fault Beth's planning; our taxi duly arrives just as she bundles me from the cottage, and we haphazardly cut through the paparazzi crowding the front gate.

'Excuse me, have some respect, please – give her some space, that's all I ask!' hollers Beth, flapping her hands to free the route to our waiting car.

I instinctively lower my head, a habit I've always maintained. Smile at the press and they'll use the image to suggest you're looking smug and overly righteous. Glare or pout, showing your distrust and annoyance at being followed, and they'll ensure the write-up suggests you're a moody mare with a regrettable attitude problem. Falter and show the slightest hesitation, by being pleasant or cordial, and you'll be posing for photos for a month of Sundays. Lowering my head is the safest option – better still, if I was disguised under my nun's habit.

'My treat begins right now,' I announce, gratefully settling into the rear seat of the taxi.

'Good. I hope you enjoy it as a show of our appreciation for everything you've done in supporting us this week,' says Beth, securing her seat belt. 'Do you think Lulu will be OK on her own?'

'Lulu? Huh, she won't be alone for long, that's my prediction,' I say, with a cheesy grin.

'Koo, no – you're wrong. She's putting on a brave face and not admitting to her pain, but she's broken by what's happened to her this last week. Not that I'm shielding her from taking the blame – she's caused the situation ... well, part of it.'

'Brave face, my ass! Lulu's a right foxy minx – I'll tell you that for nothing. She'll do one of two things: she'll either be dashing off somewhere to meet old lover boy for one last tryst, or our beautiful cottage is going to be seeing a fair amount of action overnight. Now, place your bets and show me the colour of your money. I'm betting a purple note one of those spare rooms will need housekeeping by the time we arrive back.'

'She wouldn't,' gasps Beth.

'Wouldn't she?' I reply.

Beth stares at me open-mouthed. Bless her, she's obviously led a sheltered life, given that alarmed expression.

'Anyway, let's forget about Lulu's rendezvous and focus on our own. We leave Newcastle airport just gone five, have a brief stopover in Amsterdam for ninety minutes, before starting the second leg of our journey to Florence, arriving just after ten this evening. I'm sorry about the late arrival time, but seeing as your desire is to wake up in Florence, I assume it doesn't matter.'

'Absolutely, chick, after a taxi to the hotel, a quick shower and a drink in the downstairs bar, I'll be ready for my bed.'

'Exactly, we'll cram as much as we can into the one full day, before jetting back here to share our photos and stories with the "foxy minx", as you called her.'

I raise an eyebrow. Beth's not convinced, but time will tell.

'Though I hate to break it to you, we currently have an uninvited procession tailing us,' says Beth, gesturing out of the rear window.

I half turn in my seat to view the media cavalcade behind us.

'Ignore them, ladies, with the winding roads in this part of the world, there's no chance of them overtaking us or pulling alongside without endangering their own lives,' announces our male taxi driver, glancing into his rear-view mirror.

'Famous last words,' I say, not wishing to remind him of a certain tunnel in central Paris on another balmy August night.

Lulu

I give a final hearty wave from the doorstep as their departing taxi pulls away, with a trailing media scrum in tow, attempting to tailgate them for a clear back window shot. And Koo tries to tell me she's not famous!

I hastily close the front door, darting along the hallway towards the rear kitchen as if I'm participating in a solo challenge against a ticking clock. As thrilled as I am that Beth has made plans for Koo, enabling me to remain here at the cottage, I'm as nervous as a kitten, knowing I too have plans. Secret plans I wasn't brave enough to share with either of them, distracted by their frenzy of overnight packing. It was a conscious decision not to spill the beans; they'd have tried to talk me around, seeing how harmful it might be for everyone involved. Sadly, I can't help myself, I need this one final fling – a chance for us to be us – before events unfold come Saturday.

I dash through the kitchen and along to the scullery, in search of potatoes – not that Koo wished to buy them, but I'm glad I persuaded her at the Co-op. They are vital in making Gareth's all-time favourite dinner: cheesy mash pie. Hardly the most sophisticated meal, which is why Our Kirsty refuses to make it for him, but her refusal is my ammunition. Surely, she's heard of the old adage that the way to a man's heart is via his stomach? Not that comfort food is my forte when satisfying his needs, but if this is to be our last night together, I'm pulling out all the necessary stops, that's for sure!

I return to the main kitchen and begin frantically tidying surfaces, collecting cooking equipment, before eventually standing at the sink to peel enough spuds to feed a platoon. Fighting back the tears, my hands busy themselves. I recognise that everything about my actions, my plans and my expectations of him are off-the-scale wrong. I should be being gracious and walking away quietly, apologising profusely to Our Kirsty for causing her such heartache at this momentous time in her life. Yet here I am, elbow-deep in warm water, scraping potato skins in an attempt to make one final memory I can recall and hang on to for the rest of my life. I'm resigned to the fact.

I was relieved when the tabloid headlines and surprise trip to Florence distracted Koo and Beth's attention from my twitchy behaviour, though in time, they'll wake up to my true motivation.

I watch as the thin sliver of brown potato peel lifts to reveal a creamy white surface, unblemished by rot or unsightly eyes. Why can't life be blemish-free and perfect? I suppose it can be, if you meet the man first or stay well away if he's taken? I'll make the dish as perfect as I can, as cheesy and as golden brown as I can muster . . . I only hope Gareth accepts this morning's invite and manages to get here, so we can spend one final secret night together. After which, I'll let him go. For ever.

I fork the cheesy mashed potato into distinct fluffy peaks, enhancing the chance of a crispy golden topping during cooking. With a heavy heart, I put the finishing touches to my peace offering. I don't want this to be our ending. I'd give anything to keep repeating our discussion, but we can't keep retracing the circular nature of the conversation purely for my benefit. There comes a point of no return, when I'll need to accept I've lost him to Our Kirsty. It's me who is superfluous to their situation, me who skews their happy-couple relationship into a triangle. It's only right that it should be me who extricates herself from the tangled web. As the saying goes – last in, first out. Sadly, it means I have no right to demand anything of anyone.

Not daring to test my cooking skills with the Aga, I don the padded gloves, open the door of the fan oven, and carefully deposit my treasured pie – knowing the next fifty minutes will be the longest of my life. There's a ritual solemnity to the act, as if preparing a last supper, one final enjoyment, signifying the end. The big unknown, which I'm too much of a scaredy-cat to check, is whether Gareth is on his way, or not? Will I be spending the evening moping around whilst munching my way through an entire tray of cheesy mash pie and drowning my sorrows, in a beautiful picturesque cottage? I'll find out soon enough. I reach for the cooking timer and twist the dial, providing a countdown towards our last supper.

Without thought or additional feelings of guilt, I race from the kitchen and head upstairs in search of what will be, might be, our final room. I wouldn't trespass on Koo's privacy in the master suite, but likewise I don't want us sharing my room either, knowing I'll need to occupy it until Saturday, after he's left to begin another chapter of his life. My mindset has definitely switched; a few days ago, that thought didn't come easily, now it seems to be inevitable.

It feels as if I'm punishing myself as I sneak along the landing, peering in at each of the vacant bedrooms we hadn't viewed on our arrival. I can only guess at the lovers who have graced these eaves in search of love, comfort and privacy – though maybe such a large cottage is a little excessive for a weekend love nest. The twin rooms and single rooms aren't suitable for our needs, so I instantly close the doors and move on to the next offering. I want something romantic, for our final night together, something as pleasurable and memorable as the first time – which, despite the guilt we both felt, is a memory I'll always treasure. My cover story was a colleague's hen party in Liverpool, and Gareth invented a conference weekend in Brighton, while our reality had been a hot and steamy night spent in a Knightsbridge apartment, complete with a hot tub and cityscape views. We took a risk, chanced our luck, and found what we thought was comfort with each other. Who'd have thought we'd still be playing such games at this late stage? If our passion had fizzled out like a sparkler on Bonfire Night, I might have accepted our fate, but to get to this point, to experience this level of connection, and yet reach the same ending point, seems so cruel – to me, Gareth and Our Kirsty.

Finally, I find a large, high-ceilinged double room at the rear of the cottage, beautifully decorated in muted tones of cream and beige, with a hint of rose pink amongst the soft furnishings. This is it. The bedroom to host our final memory. I cast an eye across the ensemble of furniture, imagining an ice bucket and crystal glasses awaiting his arrival. Should I go the extra mile by scattering fresh rose petals across the bedspread, or might that seem a tad contrived?

Whilst running my bubble bath, I fight the urge to keep checking my phone and making sure he is en route. In this morning's conversation, as I walked along the main road into the village, he didn't actually agree to come, but he didn't say no, either. If he's to get from Kettering to Cumbria for our allotted rendezvous, he'll have needed to start driving hours ago. Between collecting my toiletries, undressing and submerging my bare shoulders beneath jasmine-infused bubbles, my index finger repeatedly hovers over my phone screen, itching to find his contact details, but I daren't connect for fear of hearing the truth. If he's on the motorway, heading north, then all well and good. But what depths of despair will I sink to if he stays at home, unmoved by my invitation?

I gulp back bitter-sweet tears. I can't help myself, even though I know I'm on a path to self-destruction. How I wish I wasn't doing this to me, to Gareth, or Our Kirsty.

Chapter Eighteen

Beth

We hotfoot it across the tarmac, dragging our hand luggage, and hurry towards the waiting aircraft. Observant ground staff steer passengers in rows 51 to 68 towards the rear of the aircraft, making sure we don't stray beneath the craft's giant undercarriage.

My haste might suggest our plane is about to leave without us, but no, we're simply part of that panicked 'I'm next to board' process; if I dawdle, my allotted seat 52B could disappear into thin air before I have time to buckle my flippy-clippy seat belt. I'm still hyperventilating and trying to calm my rapid heartbeat after completing the all-important mission of collecting my passport from the mighty expensive motorbike courier. I'll admit to experiencing a flutter of excitement at the handover; the man was a cross between the hunk from the Milk Tray advert, decked out entirely in black leathers with a crash helmet, and what I imagine a secret international drug smuggler would look like – not that I've ever dabbled in drugs, or have any desire to.

I'll assess the damage to my credit card another time; I haven't the inclination or the head space at the minute. I chose a career caring for museum artefacts and items that remain in situ for decades, ensuring a slow, gentle pace to my working day. Oh shit, I didn't call in sick this morning! Well, it's too late now; they'll probably assume the rest of the week is wiped out at this point.

'I can't believe how excited you are, Koo,' I jest, seeing her beaming smile as she eagerly follows the crowd queuing to ascend the rear boarding steps.

'Economy Class will be a first for me. I rarely take commercial flights, and I've never had to walk partway across a runway in order to board,' she remarks over her shoulder, as I attempt to keep up.

'Fill your boots then, Koo.' I scurry behind her. Here's me wishing I could afford First Class, while she's excited to be crammed into Economy. I'm praying that her knee caps aren't pushed up to her nostrils, and she has room enough to position her elbows at a natural angle.

When we reach the bottom of the boarding steps, Koo swiftly folds down the extendable handle on her wheelie case, with a sharp snap, before grabbing the tiny strap-handle.

'These are flimsy steps!' she announces, taking hold of the stair rail and giving it a hearty wobble. 'Are you sure about this?'

'Koo, stop it!' I urge, as two women further up the flight steps turn around in horror, feeling the rail shudder with Koo's force.

'I'm just saying.'

'I get it, it's all a learning curve,' I jest, climbing the steps behind her. Lord knows what she'll say when she arrives at seat 52A; it won't be the generous wide-berth armchair she's used to, that's for sure.

'Good evening and welcome to this Air-Italia flight – your seat is on the right-hand side of the aisle, madam,' says the flight attendant in her practised voice, with a matching wide smile, swiftly glancing at Koo's boarding card and gesturing us left upon entering the belly of the aircraft.

'Thank you,' says Koo, like an excited child eagerly following the crowd.

'Thank you,' I add, indicating we're together, to save the attendant repeating her instructions.

The plane's interior is two-tone navy and French blue, smart in appearance and colour coordinated to match the attendants' uniforms – which are stylish and practical, considering the number of passengers they meet, greet, and attend to when travel-sick.

The passengers' antics prevent us from moving smoothly along the aisle. Separated groups are finishing their conversations, narked parents are arguing over which child to sit beside in order to ensure a fuss-free flight, and couples are switching seats and attempting to hide the fact that he really wanted the window seat all along but was trying to be chivalrous. Added to the mix is the overhead storage drama confronting short people, plus those whose hand luggage doesn't fit into the standard lockers – all creating lots of 'excuse mes', 'thank yous' and a few terse swear words, providing Koo with a baptism of fire on this, the first leg of our flight.

The aircraft begins to taxi along the runway, readying its position for take-off.

'This is nice,' says Koo, fiddling with the buckle of her seat belt whilst simultaneously nosing around at our neighbours from her window seat.

I burst out laughing at her attempt to fit in.

'What?' she challenges me. 'It is.'

'You're telling me you wouldn't prefer to be up front in First Class being served champers? Yeah, pull the other one,' I whisper.

She gives me a smile before correcting me. 'They don't serve until the plane is airborne, *dharling* – as Dharling Electra would say.'

'I wouldn't know,' I protest, unsure if I'd be able to cope with the refinement and etiquette of such an experience.

My delicate nerves are requiring First Class but, sadly, my credit card just stretches to Economy. The only reason I'm so at ease with Koo is her humble manner. I watch as she continues to absorb every detail of our fellow passengers.

'I'll be treating us to prosecco once we're airborne,' I assure her, 'though don't be shocked by the plastic cork – the fizz tastes exactly the same.'

'Plastic cork?' mouths Koo, which makes me giggle.

'You've led such a shallow life,' I joke.

I switch my mobile to flight mode and spot numerous text messages and missed calls, all of which have arrived during the afternoon. Instantly, I feel sick. Given that it's Wednesday, I guess each message contains a question or demand, from a relative, the bridal boutique or a bridesmaid, wanting to know about collections, deliveries and possibly payments. I daren't reply to my mother's texts for fear of reigniting her wedding grief. The only person I've actually spoken to this week is Dale. Who's stuck to his word and given me the space I asked for, done me a favour in locating my passport, and is caring for my dog while I'm away! I'm unsure if his silence is unsettling, or typical of Dale. Do I want him to batten down the hatches until the storm passes, or fight for us with some dramatic act of chivalry that forces a definite decision about Saturday?

'Are you alright?' asks Koo, peering intently at me.

'Nah. Look . . .' I turn my phone, displaying the various messages. 'Everyone wants an immediate answer, and I've no idea what I'm supposed to say. Do I cancel the lot? Or string them along, letting them all think Saturday might actually happen?'

'*Is* the wedding happening?' she asks.

'Who knows!' My mood plummets like a Boeing 747 in a disaster movie. 'And now is not the time for me to decide . . . I just wanted . . .' My voice cracks in frustration.

I just wanted to give something back to Koo, to repay her generosity in giving me this week to myself, enabling me to contemplate my future, yet now I'm in the hot seat while others demand to know what's happening. And I'm the last person to be able to answer. I feel like crying, which would be an utter embarrassment, especially as the cabin crew are about to launch into their evacuation instructions, complete with toggle-pulling and whistle-blowing routine, to which I'm supposed to pay attention as if my life depended on it – as, indeed, it might. Though some would argue that my on-off wedding on Saturday might have bigger consequences for my life plan.

'Just watch the safety demo, and we'll discuss everything in a second,' whispers Koo, as the uniformed flight attendant flings her arms forward in parallel motion, before elegantly twisting her wrists like a synchronised swimmer to indicate various exit points.

I watch transfixed, purely to steady my mind. I've no doubt in the event of a true emergency I'll forget every word she's just said and will be racing for the exits like a raving maniac, following anyone who appears to know what they're doing, regardless of the light strip at floor level or the safety cards stashed in pocket pouches on the seatbacks. Finally, she performs the wraparound toggle manoeuvre, the top-up tube demo, and waggles the party cracker-sized torch – which I can barely see from four rows away, so Lord knows how it'll be spotted by the search and rescue team flying over the Mediterranean Sea. My impatience at her delay to wrap up this performance and jolly well sit herself down highlights my sourpuss mood. This is not what I'd hoped for on our ultra-brief mini-mini-break to Florence; I'll need to change my expression double quick, otherwise we'll be jetting home before my brow has unknotted.

'So what's the issue – the decision or the number of messages?' asks Koo, the second the attendant sits down.

Before I can answer, the increased thrust is felt in the small of our backs and the aircraft begins to take off – much like me being carried away by a swoosh of wedding plans.

'Both ...' I confess, 'but right now I feel harassed by the messages. I have no idea what to tell people. Do I let them think everything is okey-dokey but then drop a bombshell come Saturday morning? Or should I be totally upfront and honest, but run the risk of un-planning a wedding on Wednesday only to discover by Saturday that I wish ... I'd ...' My bottom lip wobbles at the very thought of my possible actions.

'Hey, hey, hey! There's to be none of this on our mini-mini-break, thank you very much. Now pass me your phone – I'll forward your messages to Dharling Electra, my wedding demon – sorry, planner – and she will have a field day answering all these little queries. But I'll stress she's to be non-committal and ambiguous when it comes to the exact details, which will give you a little extra time to decide what you're going to do. There. How does that sound?'

'Bloody marvellous, dharling!'

'Good. Look sharp and don't miss the drinks trolley while I tend to this little task.'

'Won't she be miffed at the extra work?'

'No way! Dharling Electra will be in her element! Seriously, the woman's as neurotic as they come, with a twisted obsession for organisation – the more plate-spinning tasks she has to contend with the better. Superb at her job, but an utter pain in the ass regarding detail,' explains Koo, alternating flicking through my messages with tapping on her own screen. 'She's like a stick insect on acid who annihilates her delicate features with bright lip liner and dresses entirely in black, like a quirky Tim Burton character.'

'And you trust her to plan your wedding?'

'Plan? It took her all of twenty-four hours to produce various mood and concept boards, spending thousands of my father's well-earned readies in record time.'

'Your father's?' The question slips out before I have a chance to put my brain into gear. 'Sorry, it's none of my business ... I just thought. Sorry.'

'No worries, I'm not offended. In my position, you rarely get much say when someone else is picking up the tab, so I've learnt not to argue, otherwise it ruins the entire experience – which is where my dilemma lies. My father will win in the end, so I might as well opt for peace while I can, as I won't win this battle. Paying the tab gives him bragging rights, which I've no doubt will be mentioned numerous times in his wedding speech.'

'Oh, Koo . . .' I don't really know what else to say.

'I'm used to it. People think money provides you with choices in life, but in some respects it holds you captive by imposing certain restraints – unless you're brave enough to throw in the towel and walk away from the entire family. Which few are, of course.'

I nod sympathetically; I can't imagine how frustrating it must be.

'I always hoped it would ease as I got older, had my boys, matured. And yet here I am, a few years away from fifty, and still I'm treated as a child when it suits my father. He always wants his own way. Maybe I *should* throw in the towel – make a stand for independence.'

Koo's mobile flashes a brief message.

'Ah-hah, you've made Dharling Electra's day. See, it's as easy as that – she'll attend to everyone's questions, stalling them for final answers.'

Funny how you think everyone else's glass is half full, or even brimming with luck and good fortune, until you see their side of the story. I might not have the greatest financial security but at least we hand-picked every detail of our wedding, without compromise or hefty persuasion from third parties.

We fall silent, until suddenly Koo begins to smirk and splutter, fighting to retain an impish grin.

'What's up with you?' I ask, unsure what's prompted her mood switch.

'I shouldn't complain . . . while my father was preoccupied with demanding a showstopper celebrity wedding, I insisted on buying my own gown. It was the only way to have exactly what I wanted. I certainly wouldn't be getting a Michael Cinco otherwise, would I?'

'A who?' I ask naively. I'm not up with designer labels or the current celebrity hotshots, but thankfully I don't have to feign interest or fashion knowledge in Koo's company. She takes me as I am.

'The gown designer Michael Cinco – I specifically chose one of his creations because I love his vision of femininity. Fingers crossed, the most gorgeous gown in a pale powder-blue will be winging its way from Dubai as we speak, to arrive on Friday—'

'You're not having white?' I interrupt rudely.

'Oh yeah, because virginal white would definitely suit me!' scoffs Koo, burying her head on my shoulder, in a fit of giggles, causing the man on the end of our end row to stare from behind his in-flight magazine.

I give the guy a 'sorry' look, before shoving Koo in the ribs to quieten her down.

'Costly, is it?' I ask, unsure what else to say.

'Perhaps, but it's my dream gown – which is some consolation,' Koo cackles loudly, as if delighted.

'Shh, will you? Anyway, here comes the drinks trolley, so shape up – otherwise she might refuse to serve us,' I say, as the uniformed attendant approaches our seats.

'She won't refuse us, we're on a mini-mini-break and need all the prosecco we can lay our hands on!'

The male passenger beside me rudely guffaws behind his magazine.

If only that were true. Sadly, I have a niggling feeling I'll be needing something much stronger before the night is out. I'm still in dire straits, unsure how to proceed with making the biggest decision of my life.

Chapter Nineteen

Lulu

I recognise the Audi engine before he's had time to draw along-side the garden gate. I wrench open the door and stand waiting on the step, dressed in my scanty lace camisole and bathed in a mellow light. Thankfully, the press pack disappeared chasing Koo's taxi; I'd never have been brazen enough to stand here oth-erwise. And there stands Gareth. Every fibre of my body yearns to race towards him across the cobbled pathway, to be swept up within a gigantic hug, but I also want to maintain my demeanour, waiting beneath the fragrant wisteria, savouring every last drop of this memory.

'Gareth!'

'Hi, Lulu.' His voice carries on the breath of a balmy night.

He slams the boot shut after retrieving his overnight case. I'm relieved that he's arrived, and grateful for a full overnight stay – unlike some previous occasions when our weekend break has been cut short by a catastrophe, forcing us to return home by separate routes to conceal our philandering. I'm mesmerised by his surly swagger, his broad shoulders and blond crew-cut – that's my Gareth. No one else's.

'I've missed you so much, Lulu.'

His frame fills my vision, his body stooping to wrap an arm around my waist, as his mouth lands forcibly upon mine. My hands instinctively reach up to his face, running my fingers along his slightly stubbled yet groomed jaw line, which is as welcoming to me as crisp cool sheets on a hot summer night. His holdall bumps against our outer thighs, as our entwined figures stumble backwards into the vacant cottage. Gareth aims a hefty but well-timed kick at the cottage door, which shuts with a resounding slam, before his holdall is dropped and I feel both his arms being wrapped seductively around my frame, pulling me in closer.

I'm not interested in giving him a guided tour, discussing the other two ladies, or even recalling our previous fraught and emotional conversations. I don't want to waste a moment. Tonight is ours. And only ours!

He rains kisses down upon my face and neck, as if refilling the empty void of recent days. This is what I've wanted. His energy, the passion and the temptation, all wrapped up inside one man-sized bundle. Finally, we can be alone together and enjoy every delicious moment, without interruption. Guilt-free, as lovers should be. I'll silently bear the social stigma, ignore the associated taboos and the derogatory name-calling, for one last night of sheer lust with this man. If this is the closure of our story, then we need to write a satisfactory ending I can treasure and unwrap when I need to relive this night. Surely, if we hadn't meant so much to each other, it would never have gone the distance? The fact that it has, suggests that our feelings run deep, despite muddying the waters for others. There will be no last-minute ultimatums from me, no crossroads, no moments of indecision – I'm resolved to accept my fate – what will be, will be. But tonight, he's mine.

'I've cooked your favourite,' I whisper, my lips gently brushing his as he showers me with affection.

'Cheesy mash pie?'

'Mmm, but first . . .' I flick my gaze upwards, towards the bedrooms, indicating my true intentions.

I feel his mouth widen into a smile, without him drawing back to answer me. He sweeps me up, my body cradled in his arms, and carries me effortlessly up the creaky staircase. I quickly indicate our double room at the rear of the cottage.

We tumble on to the double bed, a tangle of limbs feverishly revealing naked flesh, unceremoniously scattering the fresh rose petals I picked from the front garden – slightly cheesy, I know, but a symbol of our love.

'Gareth, do you want any food?' I whisper sleepily into the crook of his neck.

Our bodies remain entwined, like Rodin's lovers clinging to each other, sustaining our moment. We're both love-drunk on oxytocin and Moët, which probably isn't wise on an empty stomach.

'Sure, though I'll take a quick shower beforehand,' he says, rolling aside and releasing his grip on my naked frame, before leaving our rumpled bed.

I roll over on to my front, watching his naked form cross the dimly lit bedroom, stepping over our discarded clothing, tangled and abandoned, upon the carpet. I hear his footsteps pad across the landing, seeking the separate bathroom, then the abrupt yank of the pull cord. A burst of light darts across the landing before the door closes behind him. There's a comfort knowing he's here. But how will I live, breathe and function without him, if he goes through with the wedding?

I roll from beneath the crumpled duvet, grab my robe and swathe my nakedness in the skimpiest veil of satin, before hastily tying my belt and collecting our dirty glasses and empty champagne bottle. As I nip down the staircase, I hear the shower burst into life.

I focus on preparing his 'mid-time' snack, as I usually term it.

Within minutes, I've grabbed the oven mitts and dished up our usual: two large bowls of cheesy potato mash, accompanied with huge dollops of ketchup. Our comfort food, which I doubt I'll ever be able to stomach again, if tonight proves to be our last. I grab fresh glasses and lay the table in a slow, methodical manner. It feels like each movement is another painful step nearer to our fate, and possibly our final goodbye.

Koo

'Surely, you aren't suggesting we sit here for the entire ninety minutes?' says Beth, scanning the transit hall in Amsterdam, looking aghast at the rows of communal seating littered with families and their toppling piles of hand luggage.

'Not the both of us, if you'd prefer to wander,' I reply, making a beeline for my perfect seat, directly in front of the departures screen, with a clear view of the airport mall.

Beth's looking tetchy, which probably has more to do with her impending decision about Dale than my current position.

'Are you serious? Wouldn't you prefer to browse the shops?' asks Beth, following my lead.

'Not really. Browsing airport stores isn't my thing, but to sit with absolutely nothing to do but people watch – now, that's a real treat for me.' I instantly settle, staking my claim to the neighbouring seat and accompanying table.

'As if you haven't done enough of that already today! And you won't be offended if . . .?' Beth thumbs over her shoulder towards the enticing outlets.

'Absolutely not. I'll happily babysit your wheelie case while I give Judd another little call to hear any updates from my father's crowd. Though if you spy a bar of Toblerone on your travels, bring me one back. Preferably dark chocolate, but any will do.'

'Are you kidding me?'

'Nope. They might represent the competition, but I've got a fetish for their triangular chunks,' I jest, not ashamed to confess. 'But I rarely share, so please don't be offended when I refuse.'

'I've heard it all now. If you're sure . . .' Beth dumps her wheelie case down beside mine.

'I'm sure. Now let me find our flight number,' I say, peering up at the large plasma screen before me. 'I can trace its progress slowly up the screen.'

'Good luck, I couldn't bear it.'

'Such little respect shown towards the departures board. Travelling direct, I never get to do this, so it simply adds to the experience. It's no different to sitting on a direct flight but changing seat partway through.'

'If you say so! Don't expect a drinks trolley to come tootling through anytime soon!' says Beth, nipping off towards the souvenir stalls and perfume samples.

I peer at the list of departures, only to find the status of our connecting flight at virtually the bottom of the screen. It instantly refreshes as the top listing – a flight destined for Prague – disappears, enabling every flight to shuffle one line up on the screen. So satisfying, so orderly and methodical – I like it.

I settle back, grab my phone from my handbag and tap the screen, eager to speak to my darling.

'Judd, are you missing me still?'

'More than you'll ever know. And you?'

I drink in his voice, like a honeybee with nectar.

'Ditto, babe,' I say, sounding like a lovesick teenager.

'My best man tells me Electra's spitting feathers because she's organised the church rehearsal for Friday afternoon. She suggests you arrive back home first thing so we can walk through the bridal procession and practise our vows.'

'Ah, we don't need a rehearsal, do we?'

'It would be nice. I thought you were looking forward to the church service.'

'I am. I literally can't wait to say our vows . . . sadly, it's the rest of our wedding day I don't want.'

'Are you mad that I gave your father the satisfaction of seeing me sign the pre-nup?'

I gulp, wishing Judd hadn't asked. 'I'm not, I simply wish my father trusted you enough not to ask. Your willingness to sign is a credit to you.'

'Not a weak desire to please?'

'Judd, please – you're your own man, always have been, always will be.'

'Even if I can't stand up to my future father-in-law?'

'Judd – our marriage is between us, no one else. The rest of the family will need to accept us for who we are from Saturday onwards.'

'I hope so, Koo. Otherwise, your family can deliver a whole load of hassle, if they choose to.'

He's not wrong, but come hell or high water, my family will not be allowed to ruin what we have. Not now, not ever!

'Look, forget about this hassle, do whatever makes you happy, and return to your hen-do vibe ready for Florence. I have everything I need here, the groomsmen are joining me on Friday night at the hotel, and I'll see you on Saturday, at two o'clock.'

'I'll be with you bang on two.'

'Deal.'

'Deal. I'll be the one in the big dress carrying the flowers,' I jest, desperate to share details of my gown but not wanting to ruin the surprise.

'And I'll be the guy waiting, OK?'

'OK, love you.'

Instantly we snap back to our usual easy conversation, having navigated the minefield of family discussions.

After a round of kisses and wishes, I tap my screen and end the call, only to become aware of the noisy family pitched opposite my spot beneath the departures screen. Both parents are chastising the older child for spilling his drink. Meanwhile, their youngest is

busy pushing Wotsits up her nostrils and attempting to lick the
protruding bottom edge of the snacks with her extended tongue
whilst staring hard at me. It's not a sight I usually encounter in
First Class.

Chapter Twenty

Lulu

'Where are we going?' I squeal, consumed by excitement and tingling with nerves, as we dash hand in hand along the cobbled pathway, beneath the moonlight and out along the quiet lane.

'I passed a lake as I drove by – I wondered if we could find a secluded spot beside it and enjoy the night sky.'

It's nearing midnight so I doubt we'll meet other folks, but still, he's barefoot and bare-chested, clutching a fresh bottle of wine, and I'm in a tiny robe, with a blanket wrapped about my shoulders, cradling two glasses in my free hand. A full moon is traditional for lovers, but tonight the partially hidden face of this mid-cycle orb seems fitting for us.

'This way,' I say, dragging his outstretched arm. 'Yesterday, we had a picnic by the water's edge, though if I can find the same spot in the dark it'll be a miracle.'

It's a good job there are no neighbours overlooking the cottage, as they'd think we'd lost our minds.

We scamper along the lane, joyfully lost in a world of our own, as I attempt to find the cut-through leading from the road to the delightful pasture where we had enjoyed our alfresco lunch.

There's an eerie mist rolling low above the water line, the clumps of silver and grey bulrushes resonate with a haunting beauty, while nature beckons me nearer with each step. The earth is no longer baked and hard underfoot, like yesterday, but damp and cool beneath my bare instep.

'I think this might be it, though I'm not sure – the road seems closer to the water's edge here. We might have walked too far,' I say.

We gingerly traipse across the damp pasture, heading towards the shimmering water beyond the statuesque reeds. In the distance, the backdrop of rolling hills and rugged mountains appears to have shifted in grandeur, providing a boundary that encircles our secluded position and provides a velvety backdrop for the moon's reflection cast upon the lake.

'Look, a rowing boat,' says Gareth, diverting his stride towards a wooden jetty to which a tiny boat is tethered.

'We can't take it,' I say, nervous of wrongdoing.

'As long as we return it, we're not harming anyone,' says Gareth, crouching alongside to peer into the wooden boat. 'There are some oars too.' He quickly steps down into the hull, his body rocking from side to side as he adopts a wide stance and attempts to balance, without dropping the wine bottle. 'Here, take my hand, Lulu.'

My fingers wrap around his, as if clinging on for dear life. I don't like boats at the best of times, but here in the middle of the night, on open water and without mention of a lifejacket, my heart rate is sky-rocketing.

'Where do I sit?' I ask, unsure where to put my feet, as he assists me to step into the hull.

'Settle yourself at the stern. There might be some water sloshing around in the very bottom, but ignore that, and try to keep your position central. I'll sit here,' says Gareth, indicating the opposite bench, in the bow. 'Stash this wine bottle by your feet, if you can – the glasses too.'

I'm not sure I like this idea, but I'm not about to ruin our evening and ignite an argument – not when I'm on tenterhooks for fear of sullying this memory. I watch as Gareth settles himself, grabs both oars and slots them into the metal guides along the top edge of the boat.

'Can you grab the rope, Lulu?'

'Me?' I've never done anything like this in my life, so now I'm seated I'd prefer to stay that way.

'Reach across, you're quite safe ... simply unhook the rope from the post, and we'll be free to go.'

If only that were true. Free to roam wherever we wish, to disappear together for ever, without a care or a worry. But we aren't, there's Our Kirsty to consider.

Without moving along my bench, I attempt to stretch my arm as far as it'll reach, but without success, so I lift myself up slightly from the wooden seat, causing the boat to wobble unsteadily beneath us. My fingers work their way along the length of the tied rope, searching to unhook the secure loop from its post, while my breath snags in my throat. After a few tense moments, I drop the coiled loop and ease myself back into position.

'There, are you done?' asks Gareth, sitting tall, before pushing us away from the jetty's edge using an extended oar.

I'm trying to contain my anxiety as the expanse of water separating us from the bank of reeds and the safety of the jetty slowly grows. Gareth manoeuvres the oars in unison, allowing each to dip into the water, his arms and shoulders rhythmically drawing back and through with each stroke. There's no rush, no hurried pace, just a steady movement as our wooden boat mimics a graceful swan gliding upon the open water, leaving nothing but a gentle wake rippling behind us. How long does the disturbance last for? Or is it lost and forgotten – the calmness of the water's surface restored – within no time?

'I've never experienced such peace,' I say, surveying the land-scape and taking in the magic.

'Have you never been night fishing?'

'No, never. I can't believe how still the water is – there's hardly a breath of wind. I sense there are animals and wildlife

surrounding us, yet not a flicker of life, nor a splash, to indicate
there is anything here other than me and you.'

I melt as Gareth's smile broadens. That infectious grin spreads
from his lips, reaching his eyes, where it sadly dies, as it has done
for several months. There's nothing more to discuss, we've talked
all our talk, and deep down, I think I can accept what will happen
in the coming days. I think ...

'We'll stop here, shall we?' announces Gareth, retracting each
oar from the water and repositioning them inside the boat.

'Be careful, I don't want us to float off and go over the edge
of a weir, or something dangerous.'

'We're on a small lake, not Lake Windermere – we can't float
away anywhere, Lulu. Here, you grab the glasses while I pour
the wine, and we'll toast ourselves amidst all this beauty.'

I sit in silence, absorbing every moment of the moonlight,
while Gareth pours our wine as if we're starring in our own
poignant romcom scene upon a romantic lake. I trust him, he's
far more knowledgeable than I am, but still the idea of being
adrift far from the shoreline fills me with dread.

'Here's to us, Lulu. May we treasure the memories we've created and appreciate the time we've spent together.' Gareth gently
clinks his glass against mine.

I'm not conscious of my actions but follow his lead, with an
automatic gesture devoid of much thought or feeling, before
sipping the fruity claret.

I suddenly feel emotional, overwhelmed by a deep sense of
loss. As if my pain has risen to the surface and there's no way
of hiding or avoiding the reality I know has been inevitable for
months. This isn't what I was expecting; I truly believed I was
mentally more prepared than this. The details, the arrangements,
the commitment Gareth and Our Kirsty are forging together,
without any place for me ... but I'm not prepared to reach the
end of my journey with him. I've been existing within a parallel

universe, complete with my own Prince Charming, for so long; sometimes he disappears into Our Kirsty's world for a short while, but he always comes back to me. And my love. Love that I've freely given to the man I want to share my life with, though he's chosen to share his love with another, as well as with me. How pathetic am I, to have accepted such an arrangement? To have willingly played second best to another woman? Ridiculous, in every way.

'Can we lie together?' I ask awkwardly, as if our connection is fading since leaving the cottage, despite the surrounding magic. I don't mean like earlier but purely for comfort.

'Come here, babe,' says Gareth, lowering his body to lie on the rigid wooden boards in the bottom of the boat.

Clutching the sides to steady myself, I gingerly stand up, half crouched, which causes the boat to rock violently from side to side, before inching closer to his supine form. I lie between his thighs, along his torso, with my head resting on his chest, before dragging my blanket to cover us, to keep the dampness at bay.

'I can hear your heart beating,' I say, closing my eyes, finding comfort in the rhythm.

'Tell me if it stops,' he murmurs.

His words instantly bring a lump to my throat. I gulp, quashing my emotions, for fear of my true feelings spilling over and making me cry. I don't want him to waste a minute drying my tears or making false promises. The reality is, I won't be the woman who shares the highs and lows of these strong heartbeats. I won't be the woman who knows when he's sick, tired or troubled – and certainly not the one who'll hold his hand during the worst days of his life. All I can do is lie here, motionless, and memorise this beautiful sound, because after tomorrow morning I'll never have the chance again.

'You know you mean the world to me, don't you?'

'Mm-hmm,' I say, not daring to speak.

'Honest, you do. I never dreamt I'd feel this way whilst ...
but believe me when I say, I'm not proud of my behaviour, but I
couldn't ignore what we have. Our instant connection was like
nothing I've ever experienced before, Lulu, and ...'

He seems to be on a roll so I remain silent, absorbing every
word he utters; I'll need this memory on future nights, when
regret and sorrow threaten to overwhelm me.

'I hope that, one day, you can forgive me and we can settle on
a friendship. Not that it'll be easy for me, seeing you with others,
but that's the cross I alone will have to bear.'

'Gareth, please don't.'

'I don't want you to ever worry about anything ... least of
all if the shit hits the fan and ...'

'Our Kirsty knows about us – she told Beth last weekend.'

'Nah.' His reply is sharp and adamant.

I lift my chin to look up at the underneath of his jaw.

'Honest. That's the message she sent via Beth – except Beth
forgot to tell me until the other day. I have no other secrets in
life, Gareth. Believe me, she knows.'

Gareth shifts beneath my frame, propping himself awkwardly
against the wooden struts lining the rowing boat.

'So why hasn't she confronted us?'

I shrug. 'I've wondered that all week – I can't fathom it
out. Our Kirsty never shies away when she can be upfront.
She didn't have to kick me out of the wedding party for going
AWOL, yet she chose to. And so, assuming she does know,
why has she chosen to ignore the situation? It's as if she's
pretending it isn't happening.' Much like I'm doing regarding
Saturday's wedding.

'Because, deep down, she knows that me and her have settled ... compromised, because something vital is missing. On the
surface, everything looks rosy and bright, but we're stuck in a
rut, with no hope of getting out. Yet we're both accepting our lot,

instead of fighting for what we each could have with someone else, if we were only brave enough,' he concludes, regretfully.

I want to jump up, scream and shout at him, 'Gareth, just listen to yourself, for once!' but that would surely rock the boat big time. Plus, the subsequent ripples would be far-reaching and felt by many. So, I remain silent, pressing my lips together in a poor attempt to suppress the heart-wrenching sobs threatening to escape me. Why can't he see he's making such a mistake?

'Lulu?'

'Yeah.'

'It was supposed to be you, you know that, don't you? I would never have proposed as quickly as I did, if I'd realised that we shared such a mutual attraction.'

I don't answer, he knows that I know. I imagine his words lifting high above our entwined bodies and drifting skywards, floating towards the smattering of stars against the velvety night sky. With all my heart, I want to believe him, but I know I can't. Actions will forever speak louder than words. He's going to marry Our Kirsty and this – whatever it is we've found in each other – will end.

My gaze lifts skywards, taking in the stars, the dark night sky. On the periphery, as if elaborately framing my vision, are the sturdy mountains. Our presence here is but a brief moment in time. Our imminent pain is but a blink of an eye compared to the great legacies witnessed by this ancient landscape and the rugged mountains surrounding us. Even the moon, high above and smiling down at us, has seen our story repeated a thousand times before, enabling her to predict our tearful outcome.

I'm trying to be brave, to refrain from begging him to rethink, yet again. I'm holding it together, knowing that Gareth's words are the remnants of what we have – which ends in less than a few hours. My new life is waiting, ready to begin, the moment Gareth leaves the cottage in pursuit of the next chapter of his life.

I've promised to be kind to myself. I'll allow myself to cry a river of tears, wallow in the mire of the broken-hearted and, if needs be, absolve myself of guilt over any stupid behaviour I might indulge in alongside my all-consuming grief. However painful this episode of my life threatens to be, I need to pull on my big-girl pants and face a brand-new future.

Beth

'Ladies and gentlemen, welcome to Florence – the local time is 10.55 p.m. and the temperature is eighteen degrees. We hope you've enjoyed your flight with us and have a fabulous visit to Florence.'

Ping! The illuminated seat-belt light is switched off.

All hell breaks loose as passengers jump up, eager to claim their hand luggage from the overhead lockers and make a rapid exit from the aircraft. I sneak a peek at Koo, who is wide-eyed and mesmerised by all the activity. I can't believe she's still enthralled by the minutiae of this experience, absorbing every detail as folk jostle each other to grab their baggage.

'We'll wait a second,' I mouth to Koo.

'I have no intention of risking life or limb amongst this crowd, I wouldn't stand a chance,' she jests, watching the passing parade.

'You would,' I instinctively say.

'Seriously, Beth, I wouldn't. You and Lulu are made of sterner stuff than I am. You seem able to cope with the variety of people you meet each day and the situations you face. Whereas me, well, I meet the same kind of person, over and over again – same face, different suit or dress. We all behave in the same manner, strive for the same things. It appears we have more than enough in our world, and yet we continue to want more, whilst still longing for the simple things in life . . .'

'Are you OK?'

'What?' she asks, emerging abruptly from her trance-like monologue. 'Money – it creates more troubles than it's worth, doesn't it? If I were an ordinary woman getting married, there'd be no pre-nup worries, no issues for my sons to fight over, and my father might at least be attending my wedding for the right reasons.'

'Koo, plenty of women encounter struggles with their families accepting their new man.'

'Not like this, Beth. I realise you have your own worries about Saturday, but for all the fabulous finery that's being shipped towards my father's country estate right now, is it truly worth it? I bet these guys,' she gestures towards the other passengers, 'simply enjoyed their wedding days for the right reasons.'

We glance at the scrum of bodies passing like a wave along the narrow aisle before spilling out of the nearest exit, with a few muttering 'goodbye' or 'thank you' to the waiting cabin crew.

'Ah well, rich gal, it's not all doom and gloom, is it?' I quip, looking at my co-traveller dubiously. I'm afraid of offending her further.

Koo wrinkles her brow in puzzlement.

'I googled your dress designer in-flight – now, there's a gown that's worth any amount of wedding hassle. I could buy a small house with what it must have cost you.'

Koo bites her lip and giggles mischievously, before adding, 'I know. Naughty of me, but a girl needs to feel special on her big day.'

'I'd need to wear that dress for the rest of my life to justify the sheer cost – in fact, I'd probably need to be buried in it too – but it'll be one day's wear for you, missus.'

We laugh. I'm only teasing, but boy, how the other half live.

We fly through passport control, breathing a sigh of relief as we pass the crowd at the baggage carousel, and head out into the warm night air in search of transport.

'Hotel Duomo Firenze, please,' I instruct, as we climb into the rear seats of the first vacant taxi.

'Oh Beth, could you have booked any closer?'

'I know! It was a gamble based on price. I have no idea what the hotel is like, Koo, but the location is perfect. Fingers crossed, it'll be suitable – and if not, as long as we've got a couple of clean beds, we can cope.'

When we reach our hotel and check in, our twin room turns out to be modern, basic and nothing special to write home about – not when compared to our spectacular first shared room in Bath – but we have all we need at this late hour.

'Does this pass muster, Koo?' I say, settling on the tiny balcony.

Before us is the imposing view of the world-famous terracotta dome. Giotto's marble bell tower dominates the piazza below, where a steady stream of pedestrians continue to saunter.

'You can't miss it, can you?' I exclaim, awestruck.

'Hardly. It doesn't look real, in fact. Much like every other iconic view every tourist has on their bucket list ... St Peter's Basilica in Rome, Pisa and its leaning tower, and the Rialto bridge in Venice – we know them so well from photographs, don't we?'

'As long as you're happy. Our aim was to deliver your wish of waking up in Florence, nothing more – if we've bagged a room with a view to die for, that's a bonus,' I say, sipping my red wine. 'Ah, this is nice.'

'Delightful, and if this is it, I'm a happy girl – a beautiful view, a decent vino and good company – what more could I ask for?'

'Judd?' I suggest, cheekily.

'Eh, maybe, but it wouldn't be much of a hen-do if we invited the guys.'

'No, fair enough. But have you visited Florence with Judd?'

She shakes her head, vehemently. 'Never. The last time I was here, I was travelling alone for a business meeting, with other confectioners from around the world. It was when I realised how much Judd meant to me. That moment of realisation, straight out of the blue, when I first recognised my attachment and couldn't wait to return home simply to be with him.'

Koo's features mellow at the very thought of her fiancé, her voice softens, and she can't prevent the corner of her lip softly curling into a gentle smile. She is so in love.

Yet I am ... I'm actually jealous. I won't admit it aloud, or interrupt as Koo continues to talk, but seeing her reaction to Judd's name simply highlights my own difficulties. That should be my reaction, each time Dale is mentioned, but it isn't. I don't come alive. Or blossom. Or glow with such warmth. I can't actually believe this. It's the week of my wedding, an occasion I have dreamt of for many years, and instead of overflowing with love and excitement at the upcoming nuptials, I might as well be a million miles away from my wedding day. I'm visiting one of the most beautiful cities in the world, with an iconic view to my right and an heiress on my left, and I have never been more uptight and miserable in my life. What the hell is wrong with me?

In time, we slip into a comfortable silence, each sipping our wine and browsing our mobiles.

'Dharling Electra has sent a text for your attention – she's answered all the queries, and pretty much everyone has accepted her instructions to await further details. The only exception is your aunt, who has taken Electra's phone call to mean you've cancelled the wedding, so she wishes to return the seventy-six-pound gravy boat purchased as your wedding gift and get a refund.'

'I haven't decided anything yet! I can't be bothered to argue, tell her to do as she wishes,' I say, narked that family can focus on such trivial matters.

As we sit on our tiny balcony, watching the world go by,

sipping our vino, my fingers continue to flip and fly between screens. I'm not stalking him, simply scanning my social media, nonchalantly browsing and not consciously taking note of what's in front of me, but rather absent-mindedly going through the motions, as I have on many previous nights. I bet Nick's not browsing, phone in hand, wondering about me, during an important week of his life.

My finger taps the Facebook logo and the app bursts into life, revealing a wall of up-to-date posts and piccies. Nick is now my friend and I am now Nick's. Will making contact cast aside my doubts about my commitment to Dale? Or will my fear of missing out on a past love wreck my chances of future happiness? My brain acts like a mischievous imp, encouraged by the wine, taunting my fingers to tap the screen and bring Nick's profile page to life, to browse his photos, read his wall and message him – in a heartbeat, the deed is done.

Chapter Twenty-One

Thursday 24 August

Koo

I sleep the wrong way round in my single bed, with my upper body opposite our curtained balcony window. On waking, the sunlight is muted by the heavily layered voiles. I reach across, snagging a corner, before drawing the drapery aside, allowing the morning sun to flood our twin bedroom with golden light.

'Whoa!' moans Beth, pulling her blanket over her face. 'That's bright, Koo.'

'That's heaven on earth,' I mutter, closing my eyes and relishing the blood-red glow of the sunlight on the underside of my eyelids. I breathe in the moment, imprinting the memory for ever. 'It was a moment like this when I realised I couldn't live without him.'

'You knew, just like that?'

'Yes. For the first time in my life, I couldn't imagine living my life without Judd by my side, despite the cruel protests of my family. I'd rather suffer the inevitable difficulties with them than exist without him.' I answer Beth's question without opening my eyes, basking in the sunlight. 'I couldn't bear to lose either Judd or my family, so I thought I could manage whatever juggling was needed to have the best of both worlds. I'd never been prepared to do that before for anyone, not even the fathers of my boys.' Beth doesn't answer, and I wonder if I've been too honest too early in the day. 'And today, two days before my wedding, I'm relieved to say I feel exactly the same – with one important difference. I won't be compromising my love and affection for Judd in order to accommodate my family's prejudices.'

'Koo, that's wonderful … to have reached such clarity in identifying exactly what you need and want – and what you can bring to a relationship. You're right, you can't compromise on your happiness.'

'Or rather you shouldn't. Last time I was in Florence, I was prepared to compromise, to accommodate my family's needs and wants, but lying here, right now … nope. They can't have it all their own way! Call me selfish, overly protective, greedy even … I want what I want, with Judd. And no, I'm not prepared to compromise our relationship simply to please others in my life – blood relations or not. In two days, I get to marry the man I'm meant to be with – the one who sees me for me, the real woman, and with whom I can be my true self. For once in my life, I need to stand up for myself and show them that I'll fight for what's truly mine!'

'And you needed to wake up here for such enlightenment?'

'Nope. I already knew. I wanted to wake up here to bask in the realisation that I've made the right choice in life, and in two days' time I'm confirming that.'

'So you're definitely getting married on Saturday.'

'And you?' I ask, still basking in the warmth of the sunlight.

'I thought I knew when we moved into our first house together and reached that sweet spot of sharing our daily routines with each other. Not just the highlights of our week but the ordinary nitty-gritty chores – it was all exciting and new.'

'So what happened?' I ask, my eyes closed, not altering my position, reluctant to lose my mellow vibe.

'The treadmill of life, so to speak, where one step automatically follows another, without you realising that you need to pause, reflect and question if you're ready for the next step – if it's what you truly want. I was bowled over by the prospect of building a life together, and so I didn't put the brakes on, nor was I honest with Dale. I was scared to undermine the foundations of my new life, and overwhelmed by other people's expectations. My family were constantly pressuring me to take the next step when I was enjoying the stage I'd just entered. Right from the start, they were pushing for us to move in together, get engaged, plan the wedding – and I don't doubt they'll be constantly dropping hints about babies from Saturday onwards.'

'And when did this Nick guy re-enter your life?'

'Whenever I felt bogged down by the pressure, he'd creep into my thoughts ... and now he's popped up on my social media at the worst possible time. It felt nice to think he'd bothered to look me up.'

'As an escape route, or a distraction?'

'Maybe both. It made me question everything. Was I living with Dale just because I could, or because I wanted the life we were building?'

'Why didn't you reconnect with your ex straight away, then?'

'I was frightened. Getting in touch might reopen old wounds and pull the rug from under my feet.'

'Which it has!'

'I'm torn between what I actually have and the life I could have had with Nick,' admits Beth, in a low voice.

'Why's it taken you so long to answer his friend request, honey?'

'Ah ...'

My eyes snap open on hearing the tone of regret in her voice. 'What?'

'Oh, Koo, you'll never guess what I've done.'

I quickly sit up, getting a better view of my friend emerging from beneath her bedcovers.

She looks at me, shame-faced. 'I've been awake half the night messaging with him.'

I'm open-mouthed. 'Now that I wasn't expecting.'

Lulu

I've spent the entire morning hiding in the snug, dressed in my flimsy satin robe and wrapped in our blanket from last night, reliving every moment. My emotions ebb and flow, leaving scrunched-up bundles of damp tissue scattered everywhere – over the sofa cushions, the carpet and strewn across the coffee table – like precious relics from my romance. I wish the other two were here to rub my back, make me warm soothing drinks and remind me that I'm doing this for the best reasons: he isn't truly mine.

Having spent our final night drifting romantically on the lake, we'd caressed and held each other close until a new dawn broke. A day that didn't belong to us. A day that marked the end of our story and any hope of a future together. Gareth had rowed us back to the shoreline before securing the boat to the jetty, just as we'd found it. I was grateful for the time we'd stolen, without anyone being any the wiser.

I don't remember entering the cottage, making our way upstairs, or seeing Gareth's belongings strewn around the last bedroom we would ever share. All too soon, we were at the front door, silently clinging to each other with an emotional intensity that conveyed more than words ever could. Somehow I kept myself upright during the emotional intensity of our embrace, clutching his clothing with splayed fingertips as we slowly hugged, repeated misguided sentiments and made silent promises. Eventually, I had to release him, inching backwards until my fingertips became detached from his tender hold. I'll never know how I managed it, but I did.

We let go.

I'm still unsure how my legs kept me upright, how I kept my spine straight – only my eyes betrayed the full extent of my sorrow.

All the time, I was praying for him to change his mind, reject his plan to marry her, and choose me. Regardless of how last-minute his decision was, I would have been happy to accept a change of heart – call me love-drunk, lovesick, or looking through rose-tinted glasses. At the doorstep, the cobbled pathway, the garden gate ... at any moment he could have changed his mind – and I'd have accepted his plea ... closing the car boot, the driver's door ... the moment of silence before he turned the key in the ignition ... the stillness that remained in a quiet, empty lane.

I waited ... but nothing.

I stood, transfixed and traumatised, leaning against the door-jamb, foolishly waiting for my eruption of tears to subside. As if pretending our moment of separation hadn't occurred; still expecting his immediate return, some meaningful sign or a renewal of inner faith to brighten my day. I needed something to signify that I could survive this upset and move forward with my life. Alone, without Gareth.

And now, having lain here for hours, replaying every minute detail, over and over, until it is etched upon my brain, I want to replay it some more. But with a different ending. Try as I might, I don't recall our final words. Did he apologise? Say, 'Sorry we can't have longer, but I need to get back and prepare ...' As if I needed to hear that!

How I wish I owned a passport. I wouldn't have put myself through the emotional wringer for the sake of one last night together. It'll be hours before Koo and Beth return from Florence to support me through this final drama. I could text or phone them, but I'll only ruin their enjoyment. Best to be brave, stick it out, and keep busy by tidying our boudoir and erasing the evidence of last night—

My thoughts are rudely interrupted by a knock on the front door. I sit bolt upright, listening intently ... but nothing. My imagination is playing cruel tricks.

Knock, knock! Again.

Gareth's back!

Instantly, my world turns to sunshine and light at the very thought of him changing his mind. He's decided that what we have is more important than the life he's built with her.

'Gareth . . .' I'm eagerly trotting from the snug into the hallway when the face peering through the glass stops me in my tracks. Not Gareth. My heart plummets to the soles of my feet as my eager steps falter and my revived spirits are cruelly dashed on the hallway floor boards.

'Are you opening this door, or not?' demands Our Kirsty, her features distorted by anger and the bevelled glass.

'I'd prefer not, if I have a choice,' I mutter, appalled at the prospect of speaking to my cousin.

My fingers fumble with the door latch as my brain shifts into disaster mode. I can't look at her face, pressed against the glass pane. How has she found me?

'Hi,' I say, cordially, on opening the door and stepping backwards to let her in.

Our Kirsty simply strides past me, no pleasantries, her head and shoulders bobbing back and forth like a ruffled, angry chicken, or a demented hen, as she peers inside every doorway.

'Well?' she demands, squaring up to me in the hallway. 'Let's hear it!'

I'm spent. I have nothing to say, no explanation to give or argument to make. The last twenty-four hours have taken what was left of my spirit, and now I need peace and calm to recover. Much like your typical hell-raising hen weekend when the booze flows, the laughter spills out and every minute is jam-packed with fun. After which you need a few quiet days to process the mayhem, gather your thoughts and recover from such a crazy night. Not that I experienced that with Our Kirsty – but I might have, if I'd stuck around.

'Like that, is it? Cat's got your tongue, has she? I'll tell you what I know, then. I know that you and Gareth have been up to no good. I knew he was playing away behind my back at every opportunity he could nab. And you, you trollop! I thought you'd have enough respect for the family to keep your knickers on, but no, I should have guessed. The family's good-time girl is always up for some action – despite it being with my man!'

I say nothing. I hate to admit it but I can't argue with her summary so far. She's hurling derogatory phrases about – but who am I to complain? Whatever she throws at me, I'll take it on the chin. I can't justify the hurt I've caused her and her parents. If it's any consolation, I'm feeling it, too – every inch of the pain she wants me to suffer.

We stand eyeball to eyeball, her fiery expression burning with emotion. I suspect mine is empty, giving the only hint of my desperately unhappy state. All Our Kirsty sees before her is the other woman in her man's affections; I don't blame her.

'Have you nothing to say to me?' she screams, her shrill tone making me jump.

'Sorry. I never meant for it to happen, it just did . . .'

'Don't you dare say "it just did", because I don't believe you. You've skulked about for a year, hiding every possible sign of infidelity. You've both made me question my own sanity, suspect my closest friends, rocked the foundations of my family . . . while all the time you continued to see him.'

'I'm sorry.'

'Stop saying that! I don't want to hear it. I want this whole sordid affair to disappear, for you to vanish into thin air so I don't have to think of you ever again. You have no idea what you've put me through during what should have been one of the happiest times of my life.'

I shake my head. She's right, I truly have no idea what I was thinking.

'On the afternoon of my wedding dress fitting, he snuck off with you, knowing I was buzzing with excitement at having said yes to the dress!' Hot angry tears run down her cheeks as her arms flail about.

'No, that's not right ... I was with you and your mum in the bridal boutique. I was there,' I insist, knowing I've attended every appointment, each and every dress fitting, hair rehearsal or booking since the wedding date was set.

'I meant afterwards! You and he went AWOL in the evening and left me alone at home while you pair did whatever you got up to. I'll never forgive you, ever!'

I can't argue. I believe she's wrong, but without my diary to hand I have no idea. Not that I wrote down every detail – but some, yeah, some.

'And still you stand there without offering any explanation for why you hurt me in such a cruel manner. You're heartless, Lulu – totally devoid of anything other than selfishness and jealousy.'

'I'm not,' I whisper, barely audible to myself let alone her.

'What?'

'You heard. I'm not proud of my actions, or our behaviour, but I am not devoid of all feeling, Kirsty. You can't make me out to be the evil monster in this, who doesn't have any sense of the damage I've caused you. And am still causing you. I may be many things ... but I know what love feels like, Kirsty. I've experienced true love in all its heartache, and I admit that I've hurt you more than I can ever apologise for. But purely because I was desperate to hold on to the tiniest glimmer of hope that maybe, one day, the love I had found might be mine. Rather than yours.'

I'm expecting a reaction to my statement – a scream, a towering shout of rage or, worse still, she might actually slap me, which is never the answer. I brace myself ... but nothing. Our Kirsty's arms hang limply at her sides, she remains mute and her desperately sad gaze locks on to mine.

'Do you seriously love him?'

I can't lie. As painful as this is to admit. 'I do. I truly love him.'

'And yet, he's chosen me.' Her words knife me with unimaginable force.

I remain transfixed, waiting for the verbal blow to subside, but it doesn't. The pain lingers, adding to the earlier pain I experienced when we kissed goodbye, I saw his car driving away and peeled myself away from the doorjamb to hole up and cry inside the snug.

'And on Saturday, we will be getting married – with all the glamour and finery we have dreamt of surrounding ourselves with, including the smiling happy faces, celebrating alongside us . . . and you, Lulu, will be long gone from my life and will never darken my door again. I won't forgive you now, on Saturday, or any day in the future, do you hear me?'

I nod. I expected nothing more. I knew this day would come. I'll be on my own, attempting to cope, until my two friends arrive home.

'Don't you ever make contact with him or me again, do you hear me?' she screams. Her voice is gaining in confidence now that our initial confrontation has flared.

Any nerves my cousin might have had earlier dissipate, leaving me shaky and emotional – a scorned woman – in her wake. We're both physically, mentally and emotionally exhausted, only our erratic breath signals the remaining passion. There's nothing else to say, I don't wish to dissect the details or apportion blame – Gareth and I have both been weak and irresponsible. Though I can't blame Our Kirsty for ignoring his antics or trusting me as her kith and kin.

'Can I ask how you knew?' I say, unsure if this is taking liberties.

Her composure falters, as if I've asked the stupidest question ever.

'You really want to know? A legit tracking app downloaded on to his phone and hidden amongst his countless screen logos. It was simple enough to implement, once my suspicions were aroused, but I bided my time. I must admit, it took me a while to realise your routines and habits were coinciding with his. I'm surprised you were so foolish, seeing as half the time you were a matter of a few streets away. The tracker proved its worth again this morning. I'm no one's fool, I know what you've been up to all night – pity you're so brazen, isn't it?'

'I guess.' Or did I secretly want to get caught out, knowing the guilt I was harbouring?

'You took a risk when you decided to pull entire weekends away but even then, I knew his interest in you would wane, sooner or later ... because actions speak louder than words, remember that, Lulu. He doesn't wish to marry the likes of you, so he strung you along – well, that changes as of Saturday. I might appear to be down-trodden and misguided, but I still have my man. We can begin afresh as man and wife by putting this behind us. And you'll be long gone. To think I chose you as my maid of honour for the wedding party! My God, what a mistake that proved to be! You were supposed to be supporting me on the happiest day of my life, but all you were concerned about was concealing your pathetic infatuation with my man!'

The pain surges through my chest as her cruel insinuations land like punches. I have nothing more to say, nothing more to ask; I want complete silence until Koo and Beth arrive back home.

I could argue that I'd completed every task Kirsty required of me, organised a party of thirty women on the tightest of budgets, catered for every type of allergy, food phobia, and found us the cheapest digs in Bath – without enjoying the actual event whilst wracked with inner turmoil and frustration. Instead, I make my way unsteadily to the front door and fling it wide as her invitation to leave. There's nothing more to say, what's done is done, and so am I.

'Bye, Kirsty, I wish you both well.' I stand with one hand clutching the door latch, more for support than effect.

She baulks at the invitation to leave, glances around as if seeking something else to say, before adding, 'Everyone knows, so there's no point trying to save face. My parents, your father, my entire hen party know what's been going on. I hope you're satisfied.'

I drop my head, I've no fight left in me.

'Ha, too ashamed to defend yourself.' Our Kirsty pushes past me, striding out of this beautiful cottage which has witnessed my shame and humiliation – I might refrain from jotting that note in the fancy guest book.

From deep within a flicker of fire reignites, and my final justification issues forth.

'I'm not ashamed of loving him the way I have, you know! I'm only saddened to think that you're marrying a man with whom you've strived to create the perfect life – bought a house, saved for a traditional wedding and enjoyed every package holiday along the way – and yet neither one of you is happy with the other. You've either lost it or never felt the magic, and that ... that's what's missing ... which is why *we* happened!'

Our Kirsty's expression drops quicker than a sale price at New Year. Her complexion isn't looking great, despite having regular facials and expensive skin treatments for months so as not to be sporting such a sallow and waxy appearance two days before her big day. I daren't drop my gaze to inspect her fingernails as I suspect a similar catastrophe has occurred there too.

'You cheeky mare!' she utters, outraged.

I brace myself, in case she delivers me a slap as a final act, but she doesn't. She strides along the cobbled path and out through the garden gate, slamming it shut behind her with a resounding 'thud'.

I assume Our Kirsty doesn't want me to wave her off, so I go inside and calmly close the door behind me. Her fleeting visit has given me enough to think about. I need to attempt to make peace with myself whilst I await Beth and Koo's return.

If I can stay calm, collected and sit this out for a few more hours until help arrives, I'll have achieved something. An easier alternative is to be found at the bottom of a bottle – though previous occasions have taught me this is never a wise choice.

I plod down the hallway and return to the cosy quiet of the snug, the walls providing a safe environment in which to curl up and nurse my wounds. A swift glance at the wall clock suggests I have at least eight hours before the others arrive home. Maybe a little sleep, a quiet lie-down will do me the world of good, while the clock works on ticking the time away.

I crawl back on to the comfy sofa and settle beneath my blanket for a sleep. When I wake, a little of this heartache may have faded away. I may hate myself a little less.

Chapter Twenty-Two

Beth

The morning sunshine is strong upon our backs, softened only by a gentle breeze, as we leave the hotel and cross the busy street to saunter amongst the growing crowds around the Piazza del Duomo. Sadly, I feel ill, as a pang of guilt keeps rising in my throat like a badly digested piece of breakfast bacon; I can't believe I've tarnished the one desire Koo had. The smallest window of time in which to repay her kindness, yet I've effectively rained on her parade with my own selfish behaviour. How can I have been so stupid? This morning, I should have remained silent and allowed her to enjoy the experience of waking up in Florence, just as she'd written on her wish list. But no, my guilty conscience spilt the details of my messaging Nick. With our flight home this afternoon fast approaching, I'm determined to make up for encroaching on her precious waking moments this morning. How she refrained from giving me a lecture only serves to underline her generous personality and good manners.

Distracted by my mobile screen, I glance at Koo as she calmly walks alongside me. She seems to be unaffected by our earlier conversation, but I'm struggling as we near our guided tour, booked for eleven o'clock. With such a fleeting visit, I should be fully present in the moment, basking in the architectural delights that surround us: the white, green and pink marble, and the impressive decoration on every door panel and masonry lintel. My emotional equilibrium has crumbled after denying myself sleep like a lovesick teenager and spending several hours exchanging furtive messages with Nick under the bedcovers, catching up with his life. I thought a quick reread of our messaging would settle my nerves but it's making me cringe.

Nick: Long time no speak! How are things, B?

Me: Sorry about delay. I don't use social media much nowadays. Fine, fine, jogging along nicely. And you?

Nick: Same old, same old, you know me! Regretting past decisions when the hangover wears off ☺

Me: No change there then!?!?

Nick: Still at the castle?

Me: Yes, can't see that changing ATM. You?

Nick: Fell into antiques restoration – how unlikely was that? Travelling all over the place collecting/selling potential pieces. Worth it – pulls in the dosh.

I need to put my phone away and make sure Koo has the best time in Florence, but I can't tear myself away from our messages. Surely, they won't sound as suggestive as I remember?

Me: Single?

Nick: Sadly. No one special after you, B. You?

Me: It's complicated.

Nick: Always is, isn't it?

Me: We never were.

Nick: Ha. Till I ballsed up big time.

Me: You needed time to mature.

Nick: Done that – still no luck.

Me: Have you?

Nick: Sure. A fool to let you leave.

Me: Really? Sounds promising . . .

I can't bear to read any more, so I quickly close the screen and stuff my phone in my pocket. I'll focus on being in Florence, enjoy my time with Koo, and deal with Nick later. And Dale – I'll need to catch up with him, sooner rather than later.

'Are you looking forward to this tour?' asks Koo, fluttering a colourful paper fan she purchased in the hotel lobby before leaving.

'I am,' I assure her. 'I love historical artefacts, though it's been a while since I've indulged my love of the Renaissance. I've drifted in recent years, since working at the castle. And you?'

'I enjoy the experience of a tour but I rarely retain the information about each item on display. I like to mingle and mix with the other tourists, enjoying the vibe of simply being one of the crowd.'

'I'm starting to understand the attraction from your point of view,' I say, glad that our conversation is taking my mind off other matters. 'I love connecting with the past and forgetting the modern era.'

Koo gives me a double take, before remarking, 'You don't say.'

'Stop it! I didn't mean it like that,' I quip, the irony of my situation not lost on me.

'Come on, stop wittering and we can enjoy being tourists in this wonderful city,' says Koo, linking her arm in mine as we search for our allotted tour group beneath the bell tower. 'And you know what they say, "What happens on tour – stays on tour" – or something like that.'

'Mmm, that sounds so easy.' Sadly, I've got a feeling that accepting Nick's friend request may have been the first step towards opening Pandora's box.

Lulu

Despite falling fast asleep like a child at nap time, I'm not a happy bunny. Instead of a mellow slumber I experience a frantic nightmare with a freakish wedding disco, complete with garish coloured lights flashing on and off, a cheesy playlist of elderly aunts' favourite wedding jives blaring overhead, whilst I reluctantly lead the family conga from hell around a writhing dance floor. In my distorted dream, my relatives cling to the snaking conga line, clamouring to chase and chastise me for my poor behaviour towards Our Kirsty. My maid of honour gown fits perfectly, my make-up is on point, and my hair is perfectly coiffed – which feels like a bonus – but despite my best efforts to detach myself and join the orderly buffet queue, I am rudely ushered away by an accusing horde of disgruntled relatives. My subconscious appears to be trapped in a cycle of self-loathing; I'm locked in a conga formation, denied vital sustenance unless I choose to consume a large dish best served cold, courtesy of Our Kirsty. Though in comparison to Gareth, I'm getting away with murder. Our Kirsty has him chained to her ankle with a giant leg iron and partly hidden, gasping for breath and a pint of Guinness, amongst layers of floaty white tulle.

I wake up with a start, needing a second to remind myself where I am. The painful weight of reality crushes me – I'm alone, not at the wedding function from hell, which suddenly seems inviting.

Come Saturday, every wedding guest will hear a snippet from the rumour mill, tastefully mentioned between the canapés and the champagne toast. There's no chance of Our Kirsty under-playing her tale of woe or massaging the narrative – not when twenty-eight hens watched me go AWOL on her special weekend.

Even distant relatives on Gareth's side – many of whom

haven't previously met Our Kirsty, due to cancelled plans, long-distance living arrangements or clashing family commitments at Christmas – will hear the details of the sordid relationship between the bride's cousin and the groom.

'Hello?' calls a voice from the garden.

Gareth?

I sit up tall, like a demented meerkat, my heart pummelling in my chest, while my hands reach out and grab the arms of the couch for much-needed support. He's back! I can't believe it. He's changed his mind midway along the motorway and turned around to be with me. How romantic, how dramatic – how idiotic, when he only left a few hours ago! He must have inadvertently crossed paths with Our Kirsty, travelling in the opposite direction, which is definitely bad timing, however you look at it.

Within a heartbeat, I clamber to my feet and stumble from the cosy snug into the hallway ... to find a total stranger wandering in from the kitchen. The name I was about to bawl dissolves in my throat as the stranger, a man who is clearly not Gareth, stands before me, late-thirties, wearing nondescript jeans and a casual white shirt, looking somewhat perplexed. His blond hair and startling blue eyes are attributes befitting the boy band hysteria of twenty years ago but are now coupled with a mature masculine frame – which is blocking my escape route.

'Hi there, sorry to intrude ... I did knock the front door several times but there was no answer. Anyway, I could be in the wrong place but I'm looking for Beth Douglas,' he says apologetically, gesturing behind himself at his obvious point of entry, the kitchen door.

'And you are?' I rack my brains for her fiancé's name, but with my head this emotionally muddled there's no hope of coming up with a correct answer.

'Nick. Nick Kennedy. We're old friends from way back ...

when we were younger, and I was definitely stupid. Anyway, I've been driving for a fair while so I'm wondering if she's about . . .'

Nick? As in her ex? Is he serious? I assumed this was her fiancé . . . what *is* his name? Dan? Dave? No, Dale.

'Is she expecting you?' I ask, my question surprising even me.

'Sorry, and you are?'

'Lulu. I live here,' I announce, without putting my brain into gear properly.

'No Beth, then?'

'Not yet, but she should be returning in a few hours . . . if you want to wait. Sorry, but if you're her ex, then when did Beth contact you?'

He purses his lips before nodding distractedly, as if considering his answer, causing his fringe to flop across his eyes.

'We've been chatting for most of the night. She mentioned she was staying at Lakeside Cottage, Hawkshead . . . and I thought, why not drop by?'

'Right you are!' I chunter, surprised by Beth's actions and unsure of the correct etiquette on such occasions. 'Would you care for a drink?'

'Coffee? Please,' he says, eagerly.

'Suit yourself. I'll be topping up my alcohol content, after the morning I've had. If I may . . .' I gesture towards the kitchen door, hinting I need to squeeze past. What the hell has Beth been up to? Should I ask for ID to check he is who he says he is? Though given my newly acquired ability to find more in common with strangers than my own blood relatives, I might not bother.

'Yeah, sure.'

Nick steps aside before following me through to the kitchen. I busy myself by making his coffee and pouring myself an extra-large glass of wine. I know alcohol is not the answer to my situation but it'll go some way towards helping me survive the next few hours.

'Have you been here long?' he asks, settling at the table to fiddle with his car keys.

'Just a few days, though it feels like a lifetime, to be fair. Sugar?' I ask, changing the subject for a moment. I continue as soon as his bouncy fringe confirms yes. 'Anyway, Beth's been away visiting Florence with a mutual friend of ours for the last twenty-four hours, so I have no idea how your visit has come about, but hopefully you're willing to enlighten me. I imagine it involves her current predicament. Milk?'

Nick doesn't answer so I spin around from the countertop to see him rooted to the spot, frozen, wide-eyed and tight-lipped.

'Ah, right,' I say. 'I'm not the only one who's not up to speed with proceedings. How do I put this . . . tactfully?' I settle my back against the counter and ponder before continuing. 'She's arranged a special event for this coming weekend and was eager to get in touch with you beforehand, has she mentioned that?'

Nick slowly shakes his head, the motion causing his fringe to dance.

'I see. So you're here purely because she finally replied to your friend request, right?'

'Kind of. I'm heading home after a business trip. Beth contacted me last night, since when we've had a lengthy conversation via Messenger. She mentioned she was staying in these parts and I just happened to say it would be great to catch up when I was passing through, on my way home to Kent.'

'Perfect. Kill two birds with one stone,' I jest, stirring his drink and passing it across the table, wondering just how much I'm supposed to be sharing with this guy.

'Cheers. You could say that.'

'Where are you passing through from exactly?' I say, turning to top up my own refreshing tipple.

'Cardiff.'

'Cardiff?' I open the fridge, glancing across to check I'd heard him correctly. 'You're keen if you think this is en route?'

'Exactly. Am I busted or what?' says Nick, sheepishly. 'It sounds stupid but I thought, why not? It's been so long since we broke up – there's been plenty of water under the bridge. We got along great, had a good laugh, enjoyed quality times together, but it was me … I was too self-absorbed and immature to realise what a great gal I had. Back then, I thought life revolved around drinking games and going out with my mates, when I actually had a real belter of a girl to share my life with. I didn't see that at the time. No offence, but youth is wasted on the young, hey?'

'None taken, but yeah, I suppose. And now, you're single?'

'I've never settled down or found "the one", as you ladies say.'

'Uh, right.'

'And Beth? She said it's complicated, but she's still single – right?'

I gratefully take a long slow sip of my wine before answering him. 'Kind of complicated.'

Nick's gaze darts suspiciously quickly to meet mine.

I hastily reconfirm. 'Yeah, she's definitely still single at the minute.'

Chapter Twenty-Three

Koo

'Hi, Electra, how are things?' I say, scooting along the bell tower's narrow viewing platform away from our tour group in order to take the unexpected call.

'Wonderful, dharling. Your wedding is coming together perfectly – it'll be the event of the year, truly spectacular!'

I've heard such gushing enthusiasm every day since her contract was signed, I expect it to abruptly disappear come midnight on Sunday.

'Excellent news, is there anything else?'

'Not for yours ... but the other wedding,' she says, her fluid tone suddenly turning prickly.

I throw a fleeting glance towards Beth. She's been quiet all morning but is currently immersed in our rooftop tour, absorbing the guide's talk about the herringbone tiles of Brunelleschi's dome.

'OK. What can I help you with?' I say, not wishing to disturb Beth's current enjoyment.

'Her groom is refusing to collect his ushers' suits from the supplier. The florist is demanding confirmation regarding access to the church on Friday morning for decoration, and the cake designer wishes to speak to the bride regarding advised changes to the number of tiers required.'

'A little last-minute for the cake, isn't it?'

'Apparently, her mother has been in touch and is demanding the cake be reduced from five layers down to two – a refund won't be available at this late stage, as the baking process is complete.'

'That's fair. Anything else?'

'The aunt and her gravy jug – she rings on the hour, every hour, regardless of the hour – she is driving me crazy.'

'Can you collect the present from her and reimburse her for the cost, please. It isn't worth the fuss she's creating, or the upset she's trying to cause Beth. Tell the florist to contact the bride's mother – that'll keep them both busy. Instruct the cake lady to reduce the number of tiers, as the bill has been paid in full already – tell her Beth agrees. Arrange for the suit supplier to have the suits delivered to the groom's house. Anything else?'

'No, dharling, everything else is in hand.' Her voice has returned to her usual up-beat girly tone. 'My contract doesn't state two weddings, dharling – just one.'

'Good, good. Call me if anything else requires a decision.' I instantly end the call, returning my phone to my bag, for fear of unsettling Beth.

I'm no wiser as to what exactly she's said or done in relation to Nick, but I sense she's unnerved herself with their conversations on Messenger. I daren't ask too many question in case she topples over the emotional cliff edge. I'm anxious to avoid having to manage a drama during a plane flight. I'd much prefer to arrive back at the cottage before she spills the beans about her final decision or her conversations with ex-lover boy. Whatever her decision about Saturday, she needs to make it whilst on an even keel, not in the aftermath of high drama, which is bound to cause a desperate knee-jerk reaction. There aren't many occasions in life when I get to support true friends – but at least I can lessen some of the financial burden, which might otherwise break the camel's back.

'Isn't this magnificent?' says Beth, sidling up beside me from nowhere, pointing to the terracotta dome across the way. The backdrop is a higgledy-piggledy mosaic of white buildings and terracotta slate, creating the perfect cityscape.

'Stunning. Mind-boggling when you realise that it's a self-supporting structure – how does that work?' I jest, hoping she didn't spot me on the phone.

'Exactly. I'd become blasé about the impact of the Renaissance period but this ... this is ...'

'Enlightening?'

'Yes, that's funny, Koo.'

'I'm glad you laughed. I was going to compare it to a rebirth of art,' I add, knowing my humour is on point.

Beth gives a genuine and hearty laugh, convincing me that after a tetchy start to the morning her spirits have revived.

'Are you keeping an eye on the time? I hate that we need to leave this for our flight home,' she says, gesturing at the view, as other tourists start making their way down to ground level. 'Are you feeling fit to make a move?'

'I am – but I can't answer for my aching thighs, having climbed more than four hundred steps to reach this viewing gallery.'

'Ah well, let's hope our descent doesn't prove to be tougher than the original climb.'

If only that were true in matters of the heart, Beth – though I don't speak my thoughts aloud as I eagerly cajole her towards the stone steps.

Lulu

'Is Beth there?' I say agitatedly, the second Koo answers her phone. I've called Beth numerous times, but she's not picking up.

'Of course, why?'

'Put her on please, Koo,' I demand, knowing I shouldn't take my irritation out on her.

'Lulu, is anything wrong?' asks Koo, not following my request.

'Wrong? It's wrong alright. I've had a delivery for her, so I thought she'd like to know it's arrived safely,' I chunter, pacing the floor of the lounge and ignoring the pleasant view of the mountains in the distance.

'Delivery? Surely not! Electra's dealing with such things – there's obviously been—'

'Just put Beth on!' I rant, coming to the end of my tether.

'Hello?' comes Beth's tinny voice.

'Lulu here. Expecting something, are we?' I ask impatiently, not pausing for her to answer. 'Forgot to mention that I needed to be at home in case its arrival superseded your own?'

'Lulu – you've lost me,' says Beth.

'I'll give you a clue, he's blond, about six foot three, a maturing waistline and a definite boy band floppy fringe. Any idea as to who's arrived? And who, I might add, has bagsied one of the spare rooms because he's been up all night – messaging you, apparently – and after a long drive here via a route from Cardiff has decided that he's a bit peckish and so is currently scouting through the cupboards in search of food. Which I am not going to be cooking for him – as he is driving me batty with his constant questions about the adorable Beth Douglas!'

'Dale? Dale's arrived?' she asks, her tone edged in surprise.

'No, not bloody Dale – the other one!'

'Nooooooo!'

'Yes! Would you like to speak to him?'

The phone connection goes dead. Did she end the bloody call? I stare at the blank screen: nothing. I jab it with my finger and begin again.

'Hello, Beth?'

'No, it's Koo, Beth's gone. What's up?'

'Up? I'll tell you what's up, Koo. Beth's ex-lover, Nick, has dropped in for a little chat with the love of his life. He's got a million questions to ask her, and yet the only person here to answer them has no sodding answers. He is driving me crazy. Not a single answer can I give, because I have no idea what she's told him, how she's left things with Dale, or whether she wants me to break the news to Nick gently that she's pre-booked to get spliced on Saturday afternoon. Now do me a favour and put Beth on the phone.'

'Sorry, no can do. She's all emotional right now, there's no chance of her talking sense to him or you. We're at the airport, so just hold the fort and we'll be back before you know it – in just a few hours.'

'Koo, this isn't bloody funny!' I say.

'I don't think any one of us believes it is, sweet. Now, I have faith in you, you can do this for Beth. Make him a plate of food, or take him along to the pub for a meal – it'll fill a couple of hours – and then Beth can speak to him on her return. Bye.'

The connection goes dead. I stare at my blank screen, which appears to be my new habit when ending a call.

'She's getting married?' His voice makes me jump and turn. He's leaning against the doorjamb, his head lolling against the frame like a rag doll in need of stuffing. 'I knew she was engaged . . . but actually getting married!'

'Ah, right, so you heard. That wasn't supposed to happen!' I say, taking a seat on the sofa and fiddling with my mobile purely to buy time.

'This Saturday? That's two days away!'

I give a curt nod. It's not good news in any shape or form.

'But you said she's definitely still single . . .'

'Look, I know what I said, Nick. Beth is definitely engaged-single – if you want to use that term, OK? Come Saturday, she may or may not be single-single or definitely married! I know how it sounded, and what it implied, but the truth is, this has nothing to do with me, right. You and her, you and Beth, need to talk it through – fill in the gaps, so to speak. I have no idea how she avoided the conversation when you claim you talked . . . or messaged all night . . . but that's not my concern, either.'

He pulls his phone from his pocket and begins flipping through the screens.

'And I don't need to see the evidence of what's passed between you both, OK? Save it for Beth, she's at the airport so the countdown clock is ticking. Though I have a funny feeling it's been ticking since last Saturday night. Anyway, I need a drink, so excuse me.' I stand up to leave the lounge and fix myself a stiff drink. I've got my own world of disaster to be poring over while trying not to call my own ex-lover in a pathetic attempt to ease my heartache. I can do without nursing Beth's casualties, in preference to administering first aid to my own broken existence.

Nick moves from the doorway, allowing me to pass.

'Can I grab a glass of whatever you're having?'

Great! In my hour of need, I've gained a drinking buddy for the afternoon.

'What are these?' asks Nick, slouched on a couch in the snug, drink in hand, and pulling out a packet of pink cards from under a cushion.

'A daft hen party game I thought we'd barbecued along with all such mementos the other day,' I say, curled in the corner of the adjacent couch.

'See, stag-dos don't involve stuff like this . . . well, not the ones I've been on anyway.' Nick puts down his pint glass, half filled with wine, and opens the packet. '"Dare" cards, nice.'

'They're pretty tame actually, slightly ridiculous maybe, but when you're half cut on a hen-do, with a mixed group of women of all ages, I suppose they seem daring – probably are to your Great-Aunt Gertrude.'

I continue to sip my wine as Nick pops the cards from the

packet and begins to flip through them. His eyebrows jump errat-
ically as he reads and then flips each card to back of the pack.

'I wasn't expecting . . . well, here . . .' He shuffles the pile and
fans them out like a magician, before offering them to me. 'Pick
a card, any card, I won't hold you to it.'

'Are you bloody joking, mate?'

'Come on, we've got time to kill, you said yourself the game
wasn't played – so you're first up, now choose your card, lady.'

Is he joking or not? This could be dangerous. A swift glance
at Nick's insistent expression as he holds the cards out to me
suggests not. I've got him sussed, I sense he's not up to any funny
stuff behind Beth's back – not that I'd consider it, given my own
situation – but he's out of bounds, being Beth's ex. He's the kind
of guy whose supermarket basket includes vast quantities of milk,
cereal boxes, a multipack of Monster Munch and several Pot
Noodles. He knows what's right for an adult, knows how to act
grown-up, yet can't refuse the impish 'throwback' to teenage years.

'OK,' I say, but vow to myself I'm not stripping clothes from
anyone, regardless of the card's instructions. I lean forward
and study the fan of cards, praying I select an easy task, mild-
mannered and nothing daring. I tap my chosen card before gently
dragging it from the spread. I flip it over to read in private: *Get
a man to autograph your chest.*

'Ah, an easy one!' I declare, turning the card to face Nick.

He peers at the printed bubble writing. 'Fetch a pen, then,' he
urges, closing the spread and shuffling the pack.

'A felt-tip pen, more like – you're not ruining my skin with a
biro nib,' I protest, launching myself out of my squishy sofa, glass
in hand, and heading for the kitchen drawers, where everything
seems to be housed. 'Here,' I say, on returning, offering him the
red felt tip, before pulling my neckline a little to the right and
baring a minuscule amount of shoulder flesh. 'Right there will
do, thank you.'

Nick scribbles with a light touch before handing me back the felt tip. I can see the attraction in his smooth mild-mannered ways – for Beth, of course, not me. I can imagine, as a youngster, he was probably quite a chancer; even now there's a cheekiness to his personality – as if a hint or suggestion is hiding just below the surface of every sentence. I can imagine a younger Beth falling for his charms, but then suffering emotional carnage when his attentions turned elsewhere. It makes sense why she'd opt for Mr Reliable after heartache from Mr Chance-It.

'My turn to choose,' he says, as I offer him the spread of cards.

In the name of friendship, Beth, please make his selection a decent one and not one that will incite trouble and strife between us.

'Ha, ha, that's bloody hilarious!' he says, selecting a card and turning it around to show me: *Find a married couple and ask them for sexual advice.*

'Ironic, you might have to wait until Sunday and then take your pick of married couples,' I say, slugging back my wine to finish my glass. 'Another?'

'Sure, same again please,' says Nick, offering up his pint glass. 'And hurry up, it's your turn to select a card.'

Chapter Twenty-Four

Beth

'What am I supposed to say to him?' I wail, in an attempt at a hushed tone, looking sideways at my fellow passenger. My question interrupts the smiley flight attendant attempting to hold my attention whilst performing her lifejacket-toggle-pulling routine right next to my seat. She's frowned several times in my direction during her energetic performance but I'm not buying it, I want to openly chat with my friend. I feel like a pupil in the front row of class, talking under the teacher's nose; any minute now I'll be given a detention or have house points deducted. I'll take my punishment if the woman will just allow Koo to answer me – because if we're not allowed to speak then we shouldn't be seated together.

'Shh,' mouths Koo, glancing at the flight attendant, before gently patting my forearm. Enough, I get the message. I'll wait to have the mother of all meltdowns once I've read the safety card in the pocket in front of me. I grab the laminated card, wondering how many grubby fingers or sweaty palms have smeared their germs across it. I imagine the legion of determined germs, eager to be passed on to each new reader, and the image helps to focus my mind for a few seconds before I jam the card back into the elasticated pocket.

Finally, the attendant takes her seat, and I receive Koo's full attention as the aircraft prepares for take-off.

'Well?' I insist.

'It depends on the direction in which you took the messaging last night. Did you stay on the straight and narrow or did you stray from the path, so to speak? I can hardly advise you, Beth. You've wondered about him for years, and then to finally reconnect with him – you tell me, was it worth it? Does he sound like the same guy you knew back then? Or has the realisation kicked in that behind the simple friend request was a fully grown man with an agenda of his own?'

'Stop it! You're making it sound sordid, when it wasn't. We chatted, that's all.'

'Chatted enough for him to drive all the way to Hawkshead in search of our rental cottage – which, forgive me for saying, I don't think any of us even know the postcode for, and we've been living in it for the best part of a week!'

'I'll admit, that's incredibly scary – he was never very good at navigating, but to say he located us within . . .'

'Located you, sweetie, not us.'

'OK then, me . . . that quickly. Yes, slightly alarming – but with technology, these days, anything is possible.'

'Mmm, are you buckled up?'

'Yeah.' I lift my arms, showing her my flippy-clippy buckle as proof, before continuing. 'Anyway, what do I do if he's still there?'

Koo shrugs as the force of the aircraft is felt through our seats in the rear of the plane. We experience the thrust of lift-off, but pay it little attention; our focus is firmly on our conversation.

'That's hardly helpful, Koo.'

'Why would you imagine he won't be there? Poor Lulu's been dumped on, with the task of entertaining him for the entire afternoon. She's got a cottage full of drink, several pubs in her local vicinity and more than enough eateries within a stone's throw, and you think he might have gone home without seeing you?'

'Yes. No. I mean, I haven't a bloody clue. I didn't think he'd behave like this. I thought we might continue the conversation on Messenger, possibly tonight, and maybe I could ask a few more questions and establish a bit more about his life nowadays before ...'

'What? Asking his advice about walking down the aisle on Saturday with Dale? Because, given his rather swift reaction of driving all the way to Hawkshead, I've got a funny feeling I know his answer.'

'Ha bloody ha, you're too funny, Koo.'

'And you think otherwise, do you? You think ex-lover boy Nick is suddenly going to up sticks and dash off home after a cuppa and a slice of cake, when he hears that you're stuck in the middle of a wedding dilemma that's caused you to go AWOL for the best part of a week? I kid you not, hun – the guy that charges halfway across the country simply to pick up on a conversation with you in the flesh has more at stake than you are giving him credit for. I've news for you: firstly, that friend request was not a casual request. And secondly, he has been waiting and watching for your response to come through. And the night it did, he didn't waste a minute to chat on Messenger, did he?'

I slowly shake my head. 'And what about Dale?' I whisper, sinking lower in my seat, as if preparing to adopt the emergency brace position, ready to crash-land back into my life.

'I believe you've got more questions to answer than you think, Beth. Though now we're airborne and the seat-belt light has gone out, I do believe the drinks trolley is coming our way. Prosecco?'

Lulu

'As I was saying, we met on Sunday morning when I found myself waking up with the most awful crick in my neck after spending the night sleeping in a posh bathtub dressed as a nun. Now, tell me, have you ever started the day like that, Nick?' I finish explaining whilst pouring yet another round of drinks. I've lost all track of the time, my belly is rumbling, my head is starting to spin, and I can't believe that I only met the guy lying on the opposite sofa a matter of a few hours ago.

'And Beth?'

'She looked a knock-out in a silver Charleston dress, all shimmy and shine and sequins,' I say, gesturing at imaginary tassels hanging from a hemline.

'Having never met before? Complete strangers?'

'Never. I'm still convinced that fate brought us together on the Bath party bus. Koo generously footed the immediate bill, though we're paying her back. But hey, it's turned out for the best, hasn't it?'

'Seems to have, so far. Though we've been waiting a fair while, and it's not quite six o'clock. They aren't due back for another hour or so, what do you say to ordering a takeaway or grabbing something to eat?'

'I'd love to, I'm starving, but I want to be here when they arrive back. It's the least I can do after Beth's put herself out accompanying Koo to Florence – though she's hardly slumming it, is she? If you get my drift?'

'Completely. Maybe I could nip out and fetch something for us? The walk in the fresh air will do me good after the bellyful I've drunk.'

'Good idea. There's a chippy not far into the village, on the main road, decent portions and all that.'

'Sorted, then.'

I watch as Nick carefully peels himself from the couch cushions, steadies himself as he stands up, checks his pockets for cash and makes for the door, before asking, 'Is there a key?'

'You ask now, when you simply walked in earlier? Yeah right, everything's locked up tight and secure.'

He disappears from the snug. I rest my head on the arm of

the sofa and close my eyes; a little sleep will do me good while he's gone.

'Have you seen out the front?' Nick hollers, dashing back into the snug within seconds. 'There's camera crews and all sorts.'

'Shit! Really?' I rock myself up into a sitting position, then stand up a little drunkenly and barge past him into the hallway to see for myself. 'Oh great, the media crew are back just in time for Koo's return. How bloody annoying!'

'Lulu, who are these people?'

'Don't let them faze you – here, throw this on,' I say, grabbing the nun's habit from the coat hook. 'It might sound a bit freaky but it's really good fun. There's a bike out the back if you need it.'

I take full advantage of Nick running his errand to the local chippy to resume my little nap in the snug. Despite his reluctance to cover up in the habit, I know he'll be high on adrenaline when he returns from his adventure and bursting to tell his story. With his fringe pushed back beneath the wimple, I'm sure he'll pass the test and fool the press pack as easily as Koo and myself had.

I hear the back door open and noisily bang shut, prompting me to jump up from my half dozing state.

'Nick, is that you? Did you have fun fooling the reporters?'

There's no answer. His wimple must be too tight for him to hear properly, so I call again. 'Tell me you sang "Climb Every Mountain" at them or blessed them as you glided past.'

Nothing. Seriously, what's wrong with the man? The wimple's not so tight that it completely distorts your hearing. I stand up, feeling a little groggy, just as a man appears in the doorway of the snug. Instinctively, my heart leaps: Gareth! He's returned.

But no.

'Who are you?' asks the guy, getting his question in first.

I'm stunned into silence as I look him up and down from top to toe. Dark mid-length hair, deep olive complexion, low brow and broad, broad shoulders blocking my escape route from this tiny room. This is no man I've ever met before. I'd remember, for sure.

'Mr Campbell?' I say, tentatively – though why the cottage owner should spring to mind, let alone walk in unannounced when he has paying guests, is beyond my reasoning.

'Who?' the stranger retorts, looking baffled.

'Oh sorry, who are you, then?' I ask, similarly baffled.

I might still be dreaming, if it wasn't for the fact that my knees are turning to jelly at the realisation that I am cornered, with no source of assistance, despite a press pack being a hundred yards away.

'I'm Felipe, I was looking for my mother, Koo, but it appears she's . . .?'

'Not here,' I reply. 'She's flying back from Florence as we speak, but if you'd care to wait, I'm sure she'll make time to see you.' My words sound stilted under the pressure of his intense brooding stare.

I can see no likeness to Koo in his features. I'm getting a definite sense of irritation building on his part, either at my foolish jabbering or his mother's absence. Here's a man who rarely enters a supermarket, probably wouldn't know the shop floor layout for any item, and certainly has never owned a plastic loyalty card.

'Lulu. I'm Lulu, nice to meet you anyway, Philip.'

'Felipe, actually.'

'Well, if you'd like to take a seat, I can grab you a drink – a beer, a coffee, or maybe—'

'Jesus wept! How many funny looks do you get being dressed as a nun – and I've never been served so quickly in a chippy,' hollers a voice from the front door.

Felipe instantly turns in the doorway, craning his neck to view the new arrival. His mouth falls open and he blinks rapidly as I imagine the sight standing before him.

'That's Nick, Beth's ex – he's been to collect chips. Would you care to join us?'

'Look, I'm sorry. It must have seemed rude to burst in like that, but when I saw the press pack outside, my natural instinct was to put my guard up. Me and my older brother, it's all we've ever known,' explains Felipe.

We're standing awkwardly on opposite sides of the double bedroom. Mine and Gareth's boudoir, left untouched and untidy from our previous night's antics. Showing Felipe to a room would have been less embarrassing if he'd opted for a single bed – pity this is the only double remaining.

'Don't fret, there are bigger fish to fry around these parts, believe me,' I say, desperate to cover my embarrassment. I'm mortified that I didn't take it upon myself to straighten this room earlier in the day, and now, there's a witness to the disarray.

'And you're sure this isn't anyone's room? So what's with all this?' he asks, gesturing to the unmade bed, the dropped towels and, most embarrassingly, the array of scattered rose petals strewn by some half-wit across every inch of the carpet.

'Don't ask me, I don't pry into other people's bedroom habits – this might be reiki, meditation or some religious practice, for all I know,' I lie, attempting to kick the champagne cork under the bed rather than retrieve it. 'You're more than welcome to stay the night, I'm sure your mum will confirm that when she arrives. And you might as well have a double room, as no one's using this one.'

'Please tell me this wasn't my mother and her chap?'

'Oh no, no, no, no, no, no,' my words spill out faster than the champagne Gareth had poured for us amidst the passion.

'Thank God for that, I might be able to turn a blind eye to some things, but . . . urgh, no.'

'There's no love lost between you fellas?'

'No, in my opinion he's only after one thing. He's fooling no one by willingly signing the pre-nup agreement. He's just a con man. If Mum goes through with the wedding she's a fool for falling for his act.'

'She's very much in love,' I say, standing up for my friend.

'She's in love with love, nothing more.'

My cheeks are on fire, so I hastily busy myself by grabbing the corner edge of the bottom sheet before Felipe tries to help. If this continues, I may actually die of sheer embarrassment and be found by Koo and Beth stone dead in the middle of the mattress.

'Do you want to make a start with the petals?' I say, to distract him from the tangle of sheets as I start to strip the bed.

'Sure.' Felipe removes his jacket, slings it on to the nearest wicker chair, before stooping down to begin picking petals from the carpet. I watch as he fastidiously attempts to sweep them into his hands. Surely to God this is not happening? I've been muttering the same thought all the way through eating my chips, with Nick on one side and Felipe – or Philip, as I incorrectly called him, several times – on the other side.

'How long has the ex-lover been downstairs, then?' asks Felipe, standing tall to stretch his legs before resuming his task.

'The whole afternoon. We've had quite a laugh, actually, which is probably down to sharing a few too many drinks and a ridiculous card game.' I proceed to strip the remainder of the bedding, collect fresh linen from the stores, and remake the bed whilst giving him a full rundown of the tasks on the hen-do 'dare' cards from earlier. I cut out the mundane ones: 'down a pint', 'ask a female stranger for her phone number'. But I highlight the humorous ones I think will amuse him. In no time, Felipe finishes his task and empties the rose petals into the bin, before settling himself in the wicker chair to listen to my remaining anecdotes. I'm clearly on a roll; Felipe's belly laughs erupt as I recall our antics in the snug.

'I said to him, that's the worst one and I'm not doing it, you can't make me – it's as simple as that. So Nick said, "I'll go first." Well, it was like listening to a boar snare his goolies on a barbed wire fence – the noise was unbelievable,' I say, struggling not to laugh.

'He never? I dare you to do an impersonation,' says Felipe, highly amused.

'He sort of sounded like this: *honk, honk, honk!* I nearly died laughing.'

'Then what?'

'I had no choice but to give a true rendition of what he should have been aiming for. Not my finest hour, but still – I'll never see Nick again after this week, so what does it matter?'

'Go on then, let's hear it.'

I'll probably never see Felipe again either, once Koo leaves.

'Where's the harm . . .?'

Chapter Twenty-Five

Koo

'Hello, we're home!' I call, as we enter the rear kitchen.

We've survived a dash through the melee of reporters still stationed at the front of the property. I did my usual trick, head down and speed walk, dragging my wheelie case behind, bouncing over the cobblestones.

There's no reply to our announcement.

'Where's Lulu?' asks Beth, standing in the silent kitchen, before a blond male appears in the doorway. 'Nick?'

Ah, bang on cue, and still here – very much to Beth's surprise. I watch as she awkwardly steps forward, they embrace, and he attempts a routine cheek kiss that misses the spot.

'Koo, this is Nick K-Kennedy ... I-I've mentioned him,' she stammers, under his intense gaze.

'Nice to meet you, Nick,' I say, stepping forward to shake his hand.

My intention isn't to begin a conversation but to leave these two good people alone for a decent chat – and maybe a decision on Beth's part.

'Likewise ... er, Lulu mentioned the unusual set-up and how you all met. Koo, are you aware that your younger son turned up a while back? He's apparently staying the night too.'

'You're staying?' blurts Beth, her complexion turning ghostly white.

'Felipe's here ... and staying?'

'Yes and yes, he's upstairs with Lulu, looking for a suitable bedroom, I believe.'

'I'll leave you two to it. Shout when you pop the kettle on, would you, Beth?' I say, gesturing upstairs.

I leave Beth staring at her newcomer and nip up the staircase in search of my offspring. Deep down, I know he's here to dissuade me from marrying Judd, but I'm still happy to see him after nearly a week. Hopefully, if he's staying overnight, we'll have enough time to chat about the elephant in the room without things getting heated between us. I can reassure him of my feelings towards Judd – reinforced by our little trip to Florence. I have never been more committed to my Judd than I am right now. Putting aside the pre-nup upset, the family squabbles, I'm ready to get on with it – and I can't wait to wear my Michael Cinco gown on Saturday.

As I reach the top stair a sound drifts across the empty landing. Not from the direction of our occupied rooms but from one at the rear of the cottage – the bedrooms we'd originally rejected. It sounds like . . . no, it couldn't possibly be.

I nip along the corridor, half expecting to be retracing my steps in a heartbeat. Surely, those rooms are empty? But as I'm putting my hand out to open one of the bedroom doors, the moaning noise increases in volume.

I'm no prude, simply cautious. As a mother, I'm respectful that my son has his own private life, but no one said he'd brought a lady friend with him. I stop dead in my tracks, listen in horror, and am about to double-back in search of Lulu, to ask who is accompanying my son, when I hear her voice. Lulu's, that is.

'How's that?'

'Very interesting, if not a little concerning, but have it your own way,' comes Felipe's voice.

'Again?' says Lulu, before the groaning recommences.

My God, has the woman no shame? Now what do I do? I've no intention of standing here listening at the door like a chamber maid in a Sunday night TV drama, but there's no way on this earth I'll allow my son to become mixed up in Lulu's torrid love life, creating an emotional *ménage à quatre*. I'll admit, Lulu's been incredibly honest and open about her feelings for Gareth, but facts are facts; she's been 'the other woman' and played her cousin something rotten. I love the young woman, but she's not getting her claws into my son whilst on the rebound from Gareth.

I wrench open the door before I've put my brain in gear; I've no idea what I'll be confronted with.

'What in God's name is going on in here?' I say, pausing on the threshold and taking in the scene at a glance.

Lulu is standing on the far side of the double bed, blonde hair thrown back, and groaning incessantly. Felipe is sitting a short distance away in a wicker chair, laughing at her antics.

'Mother! When did you get back?' he cries, on spying me.

'Koo! Awkward!' announces Lulu, plumping the pillow she is clutching whilst performing whatever she is doing.

'Is either of you going to explain?' I say, ignoring both of them. A wave of relief washes over me – they're both fully dressed, thank God.

'I was re-enacting one of the tasks I had to perform this afternoon, when Nick and I were playing daft drinking games with the "dare" cards downstairs. Really embarrassing then, and even more so right now!' says Lulu, her cheeks tinged with embarrassment – but not as much as mine are. 'You saw the nature of the dares when we first arrived. The "fake an orgasm aloud in public" is no mean feat, I can tell you.'

'Mother, really?' says Felipe, standing up to greet me.

I finally move from the doorway, stepping forward to receive his gentle kiss on my cheek.

'Where's your car parked, Felipe?' I ask. I'm certain we didn't drive past his parked vehicle when we arrived at the cottage.

'Further along the lane – your adoring press pack were hogging the road when I arrived. Lord knows what they're here for!'

'Thankfully, they're dwindling in numbers. Anyway, how come this room looks . . . dishevelled?' I ask, noting the pile of dirty laundry and towels.

'Don't ask me. I'll be staying overnight and leaving in the morning, Mother,' announces Felipe. 'But first we need a chat.'

'Do we now? Please don't take the moral high ground with me, Felipe. My decision is made – it's you, your brother and my dear father who need to give your heads a wobble, as Lulu here might say. I'm not having any further upset this close to my big day. Lulu, if you wouldn't mind?' I nod towards the door, hoping she takes the hint. 'Beth might need your support downstairs.'

'Sure, of course,' says Lulu, darting round the bed, collecting the pile of laundry and swiftly departing, as requested.

'Thank you, Mother – that wasn't awkward at all, was it?' says Felipe, the second we're alone.

I raise my index finger to silence him. 'I've learnt enough in a week to last me a lifetime, so hold your tongue, please. She might look like a beauty but she definitely drinks like a beast, my boy, so beware!'

'Mother!'

Beth

'Hi, Nick, long t-t-time no s-s-see,' I nervously stutter, closing the door of the snug after Koo has dashed up the staircase in search of her son.

Nick doesn't answer; instead he slumps down on to a couch and purses his lips, awaiting my explanation. He's hardly aged since the last time I saw him; those cheeky blue eyes remain direct yet suggestive, while his trim physique has softened with age, but he's still fit. I can almost feel that door from the past opening, inch by inch, in his presence. Boy, I'll be in serious trouble if a surge of emotion clouds my judgement further.

'I assume you'd like me to explain?' I say, settling on the opposite couch.

'You had five hours on Messenger in which to mention … Dale, is it? But you chose to skirt around the truth, ducking and diving like a mallard on an open lake – could you not have mentioned the wedding?'

'I'm sorry. I wanted to, but … I'm caught between a rock and a hard place, Nick. I wanted our first interaction in years to be natural, chatty and up-beat, to reconnect and see what was going on with you. But at the same time, my head is scrambled when it comes to my fiancé … I've been trying to make sense of the loyalty and feelings I have towards him. Don't hate me, please.'

'I don't hate you. I just wish you'd said you're getting married, before I made a prat of myself turning up here, expecting you to be single, and … well, if I'm honest, willing to give me another crack of the whip … to pick up where we left off.' Nick falls silent and bites his bottom lip. 'Bloody hell, there it is … the reason I sent you the friend request in the first place. I acted like a prat, back then, let you go … and yeah, I've regretted it pretty much ever since. I know you took it badly – people mentioned it along the way – and that stopped me contacting you before now.'

We sit in silence and stare at each other. I'm lost for words. I knew the request wasn't as casual as I've tried to convince myself it could be. I bloody well knew it!

I quietly move around the kitchen, tidying each surface as I go. I'm not wasting time, rather giving myself time to think. Felipe and Koo have shut themselves away in the snug, discussing the pros and cons of her decision to go ahead with the wedding on

Saturday. I can't see her changing her mind, or agreeing to any sort of compromise – not after witnessing the strength of her conviction on waking this morning.

'Are you OK?' asks Lulu, quietly entering from the hallway.

'Not really. My head's like a shed bursting with the muddle of ideas and thoughts it can barely contain. No sooner does one solution appear to be the answer than another takes its place. Is Nick still up, or has he gone to bed?'

'He's watching TV in the lounge, but I've get a feeling he's waiting to speak to you. I can't imagine *Question Time* is that absorbing when your ex-girlfriend is hiding herself away in the kitchen.'

'No, I suppose not. But I don't know what to say to him. I'm torn between my past and present. Seeing him again has stirred up all sorts of emotions. Remembering what we once had together has clouded my judgement even more than last night's Messenger chat.'

'And what about Dale?'

I sigh heavily, exhausted by the sheer thought of Dale. The sense of guilt and shame that reignites each time I hear his name, overwhelms me. The man didn't ask for any of this, and yet he finds himself days away from a wedding-or-no-wedding situation.

'Not a peep from him today, but then he knew I'd be in Florence with Koo, so maybe he's being respectful – or perhaps he feels too little emotion to care.'

'Not necessarily. Some guys are never good at expressing their emotions, only you know what he's truly going through.'

Bless her for trying to pacify me, but it won't work; Dale loves me beyond belief, but maybe he's having doubts now too? We're each dealing with this the best way we can.

'Would it be wrong of me to draw up a pros and cons list?' I mutter, grasping at straws.

'Absolutely! It would be heartless and cruel to contemplate such a task – you'd go mad if a man suggested doing that, comparing two women,' snipes Lulu, pulling out a chair and plonking herself down at the table.

'You're right, sorry.' I empty the washing-up bowl and begin wiping the surrounding area with a damp cloth. 'There are three options: Dale, Nick or neither.'

I glance across, to see Lulu slowly nodding.

'I'm so frightened of making the wrong decision – I fear I might not be able to make any decision at all.'

'That's obvious,' Lulu snorts. 'You've turned yourself inside out since last Saturday,' she adds, attempting to be more sympathetic.

'In Florence with Koo, I stood looking out across the cityscape and my world seemed so easy, as if I was experiencing a moment of rebirth or enlightenment – the choice almost made – yet here I am . . . *poof!* . . . the moment gone, and back to square one.'

'What tipped it for you?'

'Knowing the regret I'll feel, whichever option I choose – I'm not sure I can live with it.' The lesser of the two regrets, I can live with.

Lulu nods, her lips pursed, as if holding back from speaking.

'And you? Have you spoken to Gareth?' I ask, conscious that she hasn't let on much since our return.

'He arrived the night you left . . . we . . . well, let's say no more – I think it's finally over and he's gone.' Her voice is soft and low, dripping with hurt.

'Oh, Lulu, I'm so sorry. You knew, though, didn't you, deep down?'

'Maybe. It still hurts like crazy, despite how strong I told myself to be, how I keep cajoling myself along whenever he flits through my thoughts . . . and definitely that shitty moment when Our Kirsty confronted me.' Her sad gaze meets mine, measuring the impact of her words.

'Nooooo,' I sigh, unable to fathom how that scene played out.

'Yep, she stood right there and told me what she knew, and exactly what she thought of me ... before going on her merry way, hurtling head first towards her ridiculous fake wedding, knowing the magic is totally missing.' A tear escapes her lashes and trickles the length of her cheek before she brushes it aside. 'It won't last. How can it?'

'And you?'

'I had a little cry, had a little sleep and had a bloody good drink with that ex-fella of yours, Nick. And now, I'm whacked and in need of my bed for another little cry, if the truth be told.' Lulu slowly stands up, pushing her chair beneath the table to tidy it away. 'Hopefully, this heavy lump in my chest will lighten a little tomorrow, or some day after that.'

'You'll be OK, Lulu – we're here for you. Things will get better, you know that.'

'Sure, I do know. If not before, then definitely when the gorgeous Felipe walked in unannounced, because for just one tiny moment, he brightened a dreadful day,' says Lulu, an impish grin briefly adorning the corner of her mouth. 'Anyway, I'm still standing, and there are more Felipes out there, so I need to pull myself together and get on with my life.'

'And you will, after a little TLC. Are you travelling home tomorrow, like Koo?' I ask, unsure if I plan to remain here alone.

'No. I think I may stay until at least Saturday, it'll give me time to lick my wounds and allow my armour to heal a tad before facing the troops. Goodnight, Beth – I'm glad you enjoyed Florence, but relieved you're both home, safe and sound.' She plants a kiss on her index finger and flicks it in my direction, sending an angel kiss winging its way to me.

'Night, night, sweet dreams.'

Chapter Twenty-Six

Friday 25 August

Lulu

All night, I lie awake staring at the ceiling. I daren't sleep for fear my dreams will lead me to my happy place, only to suffer the disappointment of my world crashing down the second I wake.

I've listened to every creak, groan and snore that's resonated through the cottage from late last night until now. I heard Koo and Felipe separate on the landing after their fraught conversation in the snug, before heading to their bedrooms after a quick embrace. I heard the muted tones of Nick's disappointment as Beth wished him a standard 'goodnight', followed by the sound of two closing doors. I even heard the padding of footsteps, tiptoeing across the landing, some thirty minutes later, so I'm hazarding a guess someone changed their mind. And now the dawn chorus has begun, and there's no chance in hell of sleep as the birds must be perched in the blooming wisteria nestled beneath my window.

I throw the duvet back, ready to face a brand-new day, our final day together. My decision has already been made for me, but others, namely Beth, need to make theirs. Koo will depart, heading home to her father's country estate to prepare for tomorrow's big day. I assume Felipe will accompany her. Mmm, pity that.

I grab a woollen blanket to wrap around my shoulders,

and pad towards the door. If I fetch a cuppa first, I can enjoy a leisurely shower before heading down for breakfast with the rest. On opening the door, I see Beth's rear view; she's fully dressed, hurrying back to her bedroom and softly closing the door behind her. So that's the trick, hey – spend all night with her ex, but nip back to her own room before the cottage awakes – though I'm hardly one to talk, after my recent antics. I quickly glance along the landing towards Nick's room: his door is firmly closed. Confused or not, let's see what decisions Beth makes today, shall we?

I plod down the staircase, heading for my morning cuppa. Nothing is going to upset me; I need to keep a clear head to cope with my own heartbreak and avoid mulling over the significance of today for Gareth. I suppose a phone call to my father, with an attempt at an explanation, is long overdue too. I have no idea how I'll begin, but no doubt the jumble of words will sort themselves into some sort of order. Somewhere in the mix my favourite plea of 'love is love' will probably slip out, making me cry. No doubt Our Kirsty will have got her version in first, but he still deserves to hear from me why I won't be walking down the aisle behind Our Kirsty tomorrow.

There's a peaceful serenity to the silent cottage . . . until I reach the kitchen, only to find it sounding like an engine room! As I open the door, I hear every electrical item whirring, rumbling or buzzing as Koo choreographs a breakfast routine involving additional gadgets, kettles and pans.

'Morning, Lulu, tea?' she calls, turning bacon on a grill pan with a fork.

Her mauve bed-hair looks deliciously tousled. I bet mine simply looks greasy – I probably look like hell after drinking so much yesterday.

'Morning, you're an early bird. Mmm, yes please, I'm dying for a cuppa,' I say, feeling guilty and plonking myself down at the table, already laid with cutlery and giant trivets, ready to receive the hot serving dishes.

'Today's my last day as a singleton, so I thought I'd celebrate with a wedding breakfast for the whole cottage, though I'm not entirely sure they'll thank me for waking them so early. I couldn't sleep. Did you sleep well?'

'Nope. I was awake all night.'

'So you'll have heard . . .?' Koo performs a tiptoe action with her fingers walking in mid-air as her eyebrows lift meaningfully.

'I did – and it wasn't me,' I say, defiantly.

'Good. Sorry, that sounds wrong, but you know what I mean . . . you don't want to be complicating matters at the minute – not after the situation with Gareth. Fleeting visit, was it?'

'Yes, overnight, and away first thing. Which was a good job, seeing as how Our Kirsty landed soon afterwards.'

'Noooooo!' mouths Koo, multitasking with oven, grill pan and Aga.

'Yesssssss, sadly. I stood my ground, answered her questions and took what she dished out. How could I not?'

'Fair play, I suppose – though maybe not from her point of view. And afterwards?'

'I cried like a child, but that was always going to happen, right?'

Koo nods, before pouring me a mug of tea and bringing it straight over, like a morning tonic.

'It was bound to, honey. Just like it hurt her when she stumbled on the truth, the realisation that she'd been cheated on by two people she cared about – and just like you'll feel if the same thing ever happens to you.'

I nod. How can I argue? I did wrong, I got caught, and now I'm paying the price.

'What – with the likes of . . .?' says Koo to Felipe, subtly pointing across the table at me with the end of her knife. 'I can't see it myself.'

'Hang on a minute, Koo – are you forgetting something?' I blurt. I've had my cage well and truly rattled during the course of Koo's impromptu wedding breakfast. 'I think you'll find I've got a little more between my ears than you're suggesting, even if I'm only a shop girl. If I remember correctly, your Judd is a dustman. And you've spent all week condemning the way your bloody family treats him. So, please give it a rest, knocking the likes of me!'

There's a deafening silence around the breakfast table, broken only by the tinkling of champagne flutes and the clink of cutlery. A monologue of seething resentment erupts inside my head. Who the bloody hell does she think she is? She's spent all week with me and Beth, yet has the audacity to patronise us in front of her son as being salt of the bloody earth types. Thankfully, my embarrassment is confined to the four of us, as Nick has chosen to sleep in late.

'Sorry, you've got a fair point, Lulu,' says Koo, glancing between me and Felipe. 'I reacted in haste to hearing you and my son . . . you've shown me such kindness and compassion this week. You and Beth have both stuck up for me, never once taken advantage – and I dearly hope you'll both remain good friends, long after this experience,' she adds, pleadingly.

'Of course we will,' Beth reassures her.

'Speak for yourself, lady,' I say, not so easily swayed. 'I'm going to need time to think about it. Because for all your bloody squillions of millions, I insist on mutual respect and genuine trust in my friendships, and I, for one, am not liking what I just heard you come out with. My little incident with Felipe yesterday was purely innocent, he can vouch for that, yet your reaction was sadly predictable – and deeply hurtful. I'll get back to you when I've had a little think about the situation. I can't stomach the likes of you looking down on the likes of me, you know!' I arch an eyebrow as I draw my speech to a close. That told her.

'Oh, Lulu,' giggles Beth, finishing her breakfast plate.

'I'm serious, Beth – this isn't a joking matter,' I say, standing up, pushing my chair under the table and placing my dirty crockery on the draining board. 'Thank you, that was delicious,' I add. No one can accuse me of forgetting my manners.

I leave the kitchen, feeling everyone's gaze on my back. I've got no intention of throwing a hissy fit about Koo's behaviour – I've got standards. But there's no fooling me; I know exactly what she thought last night when she walked into that bedroom.

I'm halfway up the staircase when she calls my name.

'Lulu!'

I turn, to find Koo standing on the bottom stair, clutching the banister as if supporting herself, and staring up at me. Her expression is one of acute embarrassment, her gaze sorrowful and her stance apologetic.

'You don't have to tell me what you thought, it was clear as soon as you entered the room, Koo. You opened that door last night expecting to see a right sordid carry-on. And what you found was an innocent bit of fun, with me re-enacting an earlier drinking game. The part that irks me the most is that your instinctive reaction told me you think I'm not good enough for your son, in exactly the same derogatory way that your father thinks Judd isn't worthy of your love and affection. And that's what riles me, Koo. Not the fact that you thought I was some slapper, putting it about, or that I had the morals of an alley cat. But that after a week of knowing me, living with me and being incredibly generous towards me, instinct took over and revealed what you really thought of me. You're no better than your father!' On that final note, I continue up the staircase towards my bedroom. I might as well take a shower and grab myself some alone time. It might help me process some of the events of the last twenty-four hours.

I flop down on my bed, cover my face with my folded arms and have a little cry. It's moments like this when my hand would normally reach for my phone, and the first person I'd call would be Gareth. From today onwards, I can't do that, and it feels massive. So I do the next-best thing: I console myself with thoughts of our final night, in the middle of the calm misty lake. I remember the moon and stars way above, shining down upon us as we lay, sipping Merlot and cuddling, stretched out upon the damp struts of that tiny rowing boat. What I wouldn't give to go back there for ten, twenty minutes of my life, to relive those special moments when the surrounding mountains witnessed our presence, adding our special night to the lengthy timeline of their existence.

Koo

I've been submerged in this bubble bath for thirty-two minutes and despite the calming vibes, the drawn blind, the numerous scented candles and a hot flannel folded across my eyes, I feel dreadful for implying Lulu was making a play for Felipe last night. She's heartbroken over Gareth, even I can see that. My slip-up during breakfast was an unforgivable faux pas.

And now, I'm hiding from Felipe, having endured the most hideous conversation, with him masquerading as the family representative. I find myself cringing at the thought of tomorrow's celebration at Bournebury Grange. I understand my family are being cautious; they're frightened for my future, and wary of Judd having a hidden agenda, but he hasn't. Not to mention the publicity caused by yet another failed marriage within the Bournebury dynasty – the press will have a field day. But tomorrow, love will be my priority. That all-encompassing love

I share with Judd. It's so much more important than money –
that's what my father has lost sight of.

I'll put on a brave face. Dharling Electra's team of hyper-
excited planners have carefully selected, invited and brought
together the crème de la crème to adorn the glossy mags, creating
the perfect images to accompany the wedding event of the year.
I can honestly say I don't have a true lifelong friendship or close
connection with any of them. My side of the church will be like
celebrity rent-a-crowd! Not that I'm complaining about my life.
Having enjoyed an existence filled with opportunity, fortune
and the best education that money could buy, I've been blessed
in this last week to find loyal friends, by accident. Sadly, they're
not attending the wedding, more's the pity.

Rat-a-tat-tat! My musings are interrupted by a knocking on
the door.

'Mother?'

'Yes, Felipe.'

'Grandfather wants a chat about tomorrow – he's asked you
to call him back.'

'Mmm, tell him I've made my mind up, I won't be signing
his pre-nup agreement. And that I'll be arriving at Bournebury
Grange by suppertime. There, can you relay that message for
me, Felipe?'

'Mother?'

'Please don't argue. I'm trying to relax a little and enjoy the
final few hours of my hen week,' I call through my bathroom
door.

'Any message for Felix?'

'Yes, you can tell him I'd quite like it if he'd make arrangements for a final drink with Judd before I arrive home – to build
a few bridges. I'd be saying the same to you too, Felipe, but
since you're here with me, you might make a brief call to Judd
before we leave.'

There's silence at my suggestion. He's a grown man, he can do as he wishes, but I won't be pandering to him after today – I have other responsibilities to concern myself with.

'What if Grandfather refuses to walk you down the aisle and give you away as planned?'

I sit up, turn around amongst a swathe of billowing bubbles, and address the closed door as if Felipe were standing inside.

'I doubt he'll miss that moment, but if that's the case, I shall walk down the aisle in the same manner I've completed many of life's journeys – alone and single-handed.'

I hear him give a soft guffaw. 'Even my own father suggests this wedding should be called off, you know,' comes his reply.

'Does he now? Well, you tell Alberto from me, as much as I was in love with him all those years ago – and, dear boy, we did truly love each other once – even he wasn't the marrying type who swept me off my feet. And now, having found a gem of a man, I'll be heading down the aisle at two o'clock tomorrow!'

'But, Mother, won't you just—'

'Felipe, you are ruining my bubble bath. Please!'

My tone is harsh but honest, much like my love for my family will be from now on.

Chapter Twenty-Seven

Beth

'It seems a little formal, but perhaps that's how things need to be, Nick,' I say, leading the way into the dining room shortly after helping clear away Koo's wedding breakfast.

'I'm happy to talk – as I proved last night.' He quickly settles in a chair, before raking a hand through his hair in a failed attempt to tame his unruly fringe.

I settle opposite, which instantly feels like a mistake, creating the impression that I'm interviewing him.

'On the subject of last night, I think they suspect I spent it in your room, getting up to no good. No one has said a word, but Koo and Lulu were up and about early, so they must have either seen or heard me returning to my room.'

'Who cares? It's not as if anything happened.'

I instantly blush. It wasn't my intention to disturb him after saying goodnight, but I was acutely aware that the clock was still ticking. I needed to talk to him privately, to stay in his company, so when the others announced it was time for bed, the obvious choice was to talk in his room. Some might call me foolish – being close to him certainly heightened the chances of my thoughts being jumbled and my common sense trampled if passion reared its head. Yet it felt as innocent as any all-night conversation whilst studying at uni – a single bed, a single chair and a communal kitchen not far away. I'm not entirely sure if that's a good sign or not!

'I was surprised when the dawn arrived ... I didn't mean to spend the night chatting with you.'

'And now you're regretting that too?'

I blush profusely.

'No! That's not what I'm saying! I'm surprised how easy our conversation has been, after so much time has passed.'

'Cheers, so what you're saying is I've lost my touch and my social skills are now my only attraction!' Nick gives a snort, pretending to be offended.

'Can we put that aside for now? It really does complicate the situation. Surely, you remember what happened to us, back then?'

'OK, placed over there for another time,' says Nick, sliding an imaginary pile of baggage along the table at arm's length.

I take a deep breath.

'You broke my heart, all those years ago,' I begin. 'I honestly didn't think I'd recover. I didn't know what to do with myself, how to cope, how to recreate the life I once had before I made you a part of it. I couldn't remember half the stuff I used to do each week, so how could I attempt to rebuild my life afterwards?' My voice cracks at hearing my own honest account. 'I spent days lying in bed, barely eating, not going out, not socialising, and praying that you'd come back to me after you'd had a fling or sown your wild oats.'

'I knew that at the time,' he says, with a grimace, 'which doesn't sound good, but I can't deny it.'

Interesting admission.

'But you never did contact me, never called, never dropped by – and certainly never showed up begging for forgiveness for the hurt, the pain you'd inflicted, and the tears I'd cried. I lost track of what you were doing, where you were going – there were some friends who always mentioned you, always gave me a mini update about your latest girl, your new hotshot job, and even the latest set of wheels you were parading around town in. I pretended not to care, or be interested, but the truth was I wanted to hear every infinitesimal detail – regardless of the additional pain it caused me.'

Nick lowers his gaze to stare at the polished wood of the dining table.

'Then Dale arrived. I wasn't really interested in getting to know any man in the way I'd got to know you. Looking back, I was particularly harsh, very offhand, and probably didn't give him the easiest time in getting to know me, because I honestly thought he might repeat what you'd done to me. Was that going to become my cycle, my inevitable story? Find a man, give it my all, fall in love . . . and *boom*! He'd drop me like a hot potato the second something more interesting came along.'

'I was a kid back then, Beth.'

'I agree. Everyone kept commenting that you needed time to mature. We were a good match, but maybe not at the right stage in our lives for it to have worked. Despite building a life with Dale, I've secretly clung to all those half-baked comments, hoping you'd return.'

'And I didn't . . . until I sent the friend request?'

'So, why did you?' I ask, hoping the truth isn't too brutal.

'Send the request?' Nick sighs, quickly looking around the room before continuing. 'I was interested in knowing where you were at, and what you were up to. I thought you'd answer straight away – but it didn't work out that way, did it?'

'I saw it the same day but it felt wrong to reply. I'll admit I checked and rechecked, numerous times, to see if the request had disappeared. I felt torn and guilty for wanting to accept it, when I had a stable relationship, a wedding on the horizon and everything I'd dreamt of having with you – but with a man who hadn't changed his mind and run out on me.'

'I never changed my mind, Beth. I was unhappy, it didn't feel right at the time – too much, too fast – and that was because I was so young, back then. Immature, as you called me yesterday.'

I sit back in my chair, as if withdrawing from the conversation. My mind is spinning in circles and I don't want our conversation to go down the same path. Who knows what I'm expecting him to do? Come up with the answers to solve my life-crisis! Am I expecting him to declare undying love, offer sincere regret for his actions, or suggest we can still have the happy-ever-after I dreamt of years ago?

'Now what?' Nick asks. 'I hate to remind you, but tomorrow is supposed to be your wedding day, and to the best of my knowledge you haven't given your fiancé or your family any indication of your decision. So, enlighten me, Beth.'

I watch his expression as he peers at me, second-guessing a decision I've yet to make. Good luck with that!

'I've no idea what I should do, Nick. Is it ever a good idea to return to a previous relationship? Should I marry Dale, knowing what we've been through this week? Or do I simply need time to myself, to figure out what I truly want and need from this world? Maybe if I'd done a little more navel gazing after you and I split up then I wouldn't be having this dilemma now.'

Lulu

'Hi, Dad, how are you?' I say, seeing his jovial expression filling the FaceTime screen. Nothing ever changes in his world; he's wearing his familiar M&S jumper with his white shirt collar poking over the neckline and his hair smoothed down, defying his Brylcreem.

'Bugger how I am, gal – it's you that's the centre of this here drama. What's happening?'

'Dad, I've messed up. Big time.'

'More than that I'd say, my little munchkin. Our Kirsty's telling folk that you've been going off with that bloke of hers. Is that true?'

There it is, point blank and upfront.

'Sadly, yes, Dad. I've behaved in a despicable way towards her and the rest of the family. I can't pretend I haven't, or cover up the hurt I've caused. I just wanted to make sure you heard it from me, and reassure you that I'm not about to tell you lies. I wouldn't want someone to do that to me, even if I haven't always been entirely honest with my own blood relations. I've been foolish, stupid and blinded by my own stupidity but, well, if it makes them feel any better, I'm paying the price right now. It's killing me, but I've brought it on myself.'

'You won't be attending the wedding tomorrow, then?'

'Not likely, Dad. It would be sodding cheeky after the week we've all just had.'

'And what about that posh frock you bought? It cost a small fortune . . .'

'It did, but that's no excuse to turn up dressed up to the nines. I'll donate it to a charity shop so someone can enjoy a decent night on the razz wearing it.'

My dad shakes his head slowly.

'You expected more from me – I've let you down, I'm truly sorry,' I say, feeling so ashamed.

From downstairs, I hear the front door slam.

'Hang on, Dad – I just need to check something.' I nip across to the bedroom window to see who has left. Nick reaches the garden gate, unlatches it under the watchful gaze of the remaining three photographers, then stands staring back at the cottage, as if fixing the image in his mind, before striding along the lane, towards his parked car. If Nick's gone, I hope Beth is alright.

'Hi, Dad, I'm back. Sorry about that interruption.'

'Are you staying away for good, or just a short while?'

'Another day or so, I think. I'll let the wedding weekend pass and make my way back come Sunday, if that's OK with you?'

'Of course it is, my gal. Now remember, it takes two to tango, so don't you go blaming yourself for everything. Just half the blame is truly your responsibility, nothing more.'

A lump clogs my throat. How can he be so loving as to hear my crimes and still want to protect me?

'Thank you, Dad – I needed to hear that. I'll be going now, but make sure you enjoy what you can of tomorrow's family get-together. And don't worry about me, I'll be safe and well here, with Beth.'

'Bye, my munchkin, call if you need anything.'

I tap the screen, ending the call, as a sense of relief washes over me.

Chapter Twenty-Eight

Beth

They find me sitting in the snug, curled against the arm of the couch, dabbing tissues at my hot angry tears.

'Hey, hey, hey, what's all this?' asks Koo, easing herself down beside me, putting her arm around me in a comforting hug.

'Done,' I sob, wiping my nose, before reaching for fresh tissues from the box.

'Done, as in Nick? Or done, as in wedding?' asks Lulu, standing in the doorway.

'Both. Yeah, both, I think. It's unfair on Dale for me to go through with Saturday simply because it's planned and paid for. He deserves more respect than that.'

'Can I ask what Nick said, for you to reach this decision?' asks Koo, withdrawing her arm to tidy my hair away from my wet cheeks.

'We were chatting in the dining room, he was saying why he'd sent the friend request, and I was listening ... you know, when you listen not just to the words but to what's truly being said—'

'And not said,' interjects Lulu.

'Exactly. And he was saying all the stuff I wanted to hear from him, the "I made a mistake, Beth", "I wasn't mature enough, Beth", "I wasn't happy in myself, Beth" and it struck me that not once did his reasoning mention me. He wasn't saying that *I* had made him unhappy, or unsettled, or made him feel unloved, but that everything was about *him*. I sat listening to his catalogue of reasons, expecting him to start mentioning me at some point . . . but nothing. He just fell silent.'

'And what did you say?' asks Lulu.

'Nothing. I just sat there looking at him, I didn't want to flag up what I was thinking. But I needed to ask him the burning question, to hear what he'd say. So I asked, did it ever cross your mind that I might have wanted to know these things at the time? I could have supported you in the way you were feeling, talked things through – surely, anything would have been better than going off on a stag-do and cheating the way you did?' I fall silent, wipe my tears away before continuing, 'He said that was his only way out. He knew I wouldn't accept him cheating, so he did, and then moved out on the back of it.'

'What a prick!' blurts Lulu, her eyes agog and mouth wide.

'Lulu!' Koo admonishes her. 'But yeah, hardly the wisest thing to admit.'

'But he's absolutely right. We finished that day, because of the cheating – he packed his bags and left within hours. And now, I know how little he thought of me, how deliberate his decisions were, back then, regarding us – there was no *us*, was there? Just Nick Kennedy, doing as he pleased, regardless of the hurt and pain it would cause me.'

'So why come back and make contact?' Koo asks.

'Well, listen to this . . . he reckons Tara, my so-called maid of honour, bumped into him in town a few weeks ago, and she told him I was engaged to be married. He knew wedding plans were on the horizon – just not how close they were.'

'So he lied earlier!' says Lulu, aghast.

'He thought he'd try his luck and bolster his ego,' mutters Koo, shaking her head. 'Sounds to me like game-playing – and like history repeating itself, given that he cancelled his own wedding.'

'How stupid am I? To have harboured such feelings for years, only to cause this . . .' I say, engulfed by a new wave of tears. 'I called him out on it straight away. He's still the chancer he's always been – the years haven't changed him one bit. That's when he got up and left the cottage. Why did I invite him back in to my life?'

'We've all done it, Beth. There, there – a good cry will help,' urges Lulu, stepping forward with fresh tissues from the box.

'And Dale?' asks Koo.

'Our relationship is a separate issue from the wedding, I realise that now.'

'Have you called him?' asks Lulu, tentatively.

'Not yet, but I will. I need to be entirely honest about what's been going on in my head, explain about my unresolved feelings towards Nick, which are now finally resolved, and explain my decision about the wedding. I simply can't go through with it, I just can't.'

'Then you need to listen to what he wants . . . this week has been tough for both of you, from differing angles. Now, I'll make you a cuppa, a couple of slices of toast if you need it, and when you're feeling calmer, you make that call,' says Koo, in her best motherly manner.

'I'll call my mum too,' I say, taking a deep breath. 'Tell her the wedding is off – though I won't be explaining every detail at this point.'

'If you need me to call Dharling Electra, I will. She and the team can make other calls – to family, wedding guests or suppliers – to save you the time,' says Koo, giving me a tight squeeze before standing up to make a brew.

'Or me,' adds Lulu. 'I'm free to call people.'

Koo

We linger in the cottage as Felipe loads his car with my luggage. It helps delay the moment when I'll need to say goodbye to my girls, offering a welcome distraction as he treks back and forth.

Thankfully, the paparazzi have dwindled to just three die-hard camera trolls, who lazily snap my son's progress.

'You've got everything you need, yes?' says Beth, scouting around the kitchen for any forgotten items.

'I've already checked. My suitcases, vanity case and belongings have already been loaded. I've just got a few loose items I might need at hand,' I say, showing her the bits and pieces I'm holding.

The rawness around Beth's eyes is proof she's been crying – hardly surprising, after the call she's just had with Dale.

'Have you got your pre-nup? You might fancy signing it on the way down,' suggests Lulu, spying the legal envelope.

'I have, but there's no fear of my signature gracing the dotted line. No siree!' I jest, waving the said item. 'I'll use it as a bargaining tool mid-journey, if Felipe begins one of his unnecessary lectures.'

'Don't play silly buggers while he's driving – you can do without having an accident,' warns Beth sternly, as we drift into the hallway. 'You want this wedding to go ahead tomorrow, so don't do anything to jeopardise it.'

The cottage door opens and Felipe interrupts our awkward small talk.

'Are you ready?' he asks, looking between us, as if unsure who he is accompanying.

'Come here, you pair,' I say, flinging my arms around them both and squeezing them tightly to me. 'I want to say the biggest thank you to you both for providing me with the only thing in this world I needed this week, and that was true friendship – something money can never buy, and which you pair of lovelies have generously shown me from the moment we met.' I finally release them from my clutches as we all fall silent. They'll never know how much they've given me this week.

'*Phuh!* We've done nothing at all. It's you who've been so

generous towards the two of us, picking up two waifs and strays on a Saturday night,' says Beth, wiping a tear from her eye.

'Now, stay in touch – don't become a stranger. Have the most spectacular wedding tomorrow, and ignore what the others think, just let Dharling Electra shoulder the full burden – it's what she's getting paid for,' jests Lulu, glancing at Felipe when mentioning the family conflict.

'And thank her for everything she's done on my behalf too . . . tell her I'll be in touch. I promise,' whispers Beth, looking decidedly guilty.

'No worries, honey. Dharling Electra loves a challenge, despite what she says. Anyway, Josie the housekeeper doesn't need the keys back until ten o'clock on Sunday, so you're both welcome to stay until then,' I say, knowing I'm leaving behind two women with heavy hearts and minds. 'You've got my contact details – though don't call me tomorrow, I'm a bit busy.'

'Mother, we need to mosey, if we're to avoid the worst of the traffic,' urges Felipe.

We three friends linger, not wishing to part.

'Yes, of course! Kiss, kiss to you both – and don't forget, if all else fails, smile and wave. And if that fails, simply don a nun's habit and do it anyway. On which note, can you pass me my habit please? I won't be leaving without it.'

Lulu grabs the swathe of black fabric, which I swiftly pull over the top of my clothes, adjusting the wimple in place and covering my distinctive mauve hair.

'What a way to exit,' mutters Lulu, as they gather at the door.

'Love and best wishes to you both – and to Judd,' says Beth, linking arms with Lulu.

I turn away from them as Felipe opens the door and escorts me outside.

Chapter Twenty-Nine

Saturday 26 August

Beth

'Leave me be, I can't do it!' cries Lulu, grumpily batting me away from her bedside.

'You can and you will – there's very little choice. The day is here, it's happening, whether you like it or not. You can hardly delete it from the calendar. So up you get, lady,' I order. 'We're in this together.'

I tug at her extended arm as she attempts to fight me off. She's stronger than me, so I grab the duvet and yank it off the bed in a swift action, exposing Lulu in her cotton PJs, an angry glare on her face.

'Don't give me that. We need to get ready, get a decent breakfast inside us, and then make a plan for the day. I don't want to be moping around the cottage come two o'clock. Today is supposed to be my wedding day and I intend to have some pleasant memories to look back on, to add to the fun we've had this week. So get up, now!' I dump her duvet across the room and leave in order to make a start on breakfast.

'You win! I'll be down in two minutes, but we're heading out for breakfast so don't bother putting the grill on,' hollers Lulu as I descend the staircase.

'Interesting. Where are we heading, then?'

'If I'm not allowed to wallow indoors then we'll just have to tackle the great outdoors!'

I'm sure that Hawkshead village has never witnessed two such unlikely cyclists gracing Main Street on a Saturday morning . . . on a tandem. We'd bickered over who should take control of the handlebars and who should sit behind, trusting the steering and road sense of her friend in front – much to the delight of the solitary press guy, still pitched outside the cottage. I won the front seat, though with Lulu's poor sense of balance causing a definite wobble, it was no small feat to steer the tandem along the lane towards the nearest café, in search of hot bacon baps.

'Are you having any regrets?' asks Lulu, as we perch on the nearest wall and munch our breakfast, overlooked by the local church, with the tandem propped beside us.

'Nope. I've done the right thing, probably went the wrong way about it, but even so – as long as Dale understands and can see a way of supporting me, I'll be OK. You?'

'Mmm, now there's a question. I'm gutted, I can't lie. I never imagined I'd be standing here on Gareth and Our Kirsty's wedding day, but here I am!' says Lulu, spreading her arms wide, before continuing to eat her bap. Pausing between each mouthful, she continues. 'I know what I know. I'm trying to be as realistic as I can be, but I have to accept that come two o'clock they'll be husband and wife. Today's their day!'

'Have you heard from anyone? Your aunty? Kirsty? Gareth?'

Lulu shakes her head. 'No, but honestly, what more is there to say?'

'It gets to that point, doesn't it? Me and Dale have reached the stage where we both understand what's happened, there's no point in assigning more blame, and so the conversation falls silent as we tiptoe through the debris of what's left of us.'

'Exactly. Are you ready?' asks Lulu, wiping her hands on the paper bag, before screwing it up and lobbing it into the litter bin.

'As ready as I'll ever be.' I dispose of my litter before grabbing the tandem and straddling the front seat. 'Any idea where we're heading?'

'The café owner reckons there's an easy cycle route up ahead, signposted and suitable for all abilities. I suggest we give it a go for an hour or so. I'd like to be back at the cottage by lunchtime.'

'Same here, not that I want to dwell on it, but today is supposed to be my wedding day!'

It takes a matter of minutes for us to reach the cycle route suggested by the café owner. After which, we leave behind the tiny village of Hawkshead and are surrounded by nothing but green meadows, ancient hedgerows and a wonderful blue sky overhead. There's something therapeutic about the rhythmical movement of my pedalling feet, the breeze on my face, and knowing that a new friend is right behind me – though if Lulu leans any wider as we take these bends, we'll end up coming a right cropper.

'How good does this feel to be out and about?' shouts Lulu, from the rear seat.

'Amazing. It's a shame we didn't explore more of the area in this last week, but we all had a lot on our minds – we probably stayed inside the cottage more than we should have,' I holler over my shoulder.

'If we ever return, for a weekend away – I'm going to suggest this to Koo – do you think Dale would be up for it?'

'Maybe, once we've decided what our future holds.' That wayward lump reappears in my throat, as I steady the handlebars, correcting another of Lulu's wobbles.

I know I've made the right choice but there's still a way to go before I'll regain the inner peace I once knew.

Chapter Thirty

Koo

Brilliant sunshine streams into the morning room as I sit centre stage on an elaborately carved but uncomfortable hard-backed chair, admiring the scene beyond the open French windows and terraced gardens: my wedding marquee.

Wrapped in a fluffy towelling robe, my freshly washed hair being teased into shape by a professional stylist, I quietly sip my glass of bubbles and watch an army of hired busybodies in maroon uniforms criss-cross the framed landscape created by the open terrace doors. I observe a plethora of bodies fetching and carrying armfuls of linen, manoeuvring storage boxes and trailing lengthy floral garlands across my father's immaculate lawn. Later, a dozen male peacocks will be encouraged to roam the grounds, adding vibrant colour and elegance to the proceedings – make of that what you will!

Dharling Electra darts neurotically back and forth, gesticulating like a possessed octopus and barking orders at any young person caught in her cross hairs. I've purposely steered clear of taking a cheeky peek while they prep the reception venue, as Electra wants me to experience the 'wow factor' once it's complete. Though what she'll do if I'm not impressed is anyone's guess. Surely, the clock will have run down to zero hours by then, and it'll be too late to make any changes?

I'm recognising various elements 'in the flesh', so to speak, chosen from Electra's extensive mood board, so I'm not expecting any surprise decisions she hasn't already run by me. I just hope the final vision doesn't appear identical to every other society wedding I've attended or Lulu's pored over in the glossy mags. Periodically, a faithful old gardener wanders into the frame, with knotted twine and secateurs, ready to snip or tether a stray dahlia or leaning delphinium, much to Electra's annoyance. The herbaceous borders are bursting with an explosion of vibrant colour, but not a single tendril must be out of place. I assume Electra has chastised both gardeners and Mother Nature for any wayward plants not adhering to her stipulated plan.

It looks like a monumental stage set in which every last detail has been conjured, colour-coordinated and crafted to within an inch of perfection, to provide a dream wedding day. I can't believe today has actually arrived. There have been so many family difficulties and private discussions behind closed doors, some of which involved me and Judd. I watch the arrangements slowly come together before my eyes, knowing that we'll soon sit down to eat as husband and wife, each with a wedding band adorning our left hand, and a welcome smile for the guests present.

But is this truly my dream wedding? Since arriving last night, I've seen the marquee's jigsaw flooring being laid, chandeliers being hung and polished, and a multitude of dining chairs being covered and decorated with humongous netted bows – and all for what? So that I can eat, drink and dance my way through the most important celebration of my life, having married the man of my dreams, whilst secretly knowing he's my father's worst nightmare. No amount of tulle tie-backs, exotic bouquets or fine smoked Scottish salmon will disguise, or eliminate, the underlying tensions and hostility. Unfurling before me is a wedding with a millionaire price tag yet with just tuppence worth of gentility.

Apart from the hum of the hair dryer there is deadly silence; no laughter, no giggles, no lively wedding chatter to engage with. I'm surrounded by serious-looking ladies, each concentrating solely on their specific task. My hair and make-up are being meticulously stage-managed, my bridal bouquet is being hand-tied by two florists seated in the far corner of the room, surrounded by oodles of raffia straw and strange exotic blooms, and there is a steady flow of incidental deliveries, including last-minute apologies or wedding cards, arriving in the morning room.

'Excuse me, would someone mind finding some music, or a radio?' I ask.

The nearest young woman – who is wearing a smart maroon uniform, identifying her as belonging to Electra's team – immediately ceases her assigned task of stacking cards, and dashes at breakneck speed from the morning room. I assume she's under strict instructions to 'provide whatever the bride asks for', which makes me cringe somewhat.

Returning to my father's house in preparation for the wedding never seemed like an issue, until now. I'm wondering if I've made the right choice. I'd imagined that my childhood memories would offer comfort, familiar surroundings to help me relax, and the reassurance of loved ones to erase any last-minute nerves.

But there's not a blood relation to be seen. My mother is staying in a posh hotel, and the handful of relatives on my father's side are in their bedrooms on the third floor. I'm alone, in a function room filled with acquaintances hired to perform a task, duty or service. Right now, every person attending me or drifting through the morning room will be duly assigned an invoice, payable within thirty days, for their services rendered. How is this any different to my hen-do weekend in Bath? I might as well be in any grand hotel suite, surrounded by strangers, being prepped and primped under the scrutiny of Dharling Electra, who is currently lapping the Grange at fifteen-minute intervals in pursuit of service providers.

I haven't seen my father all morning, despite making

arrangements for us to breakfast together at eight. I arrived on the dot to find a full English being served in the dining room, my father's morning paper neatly folded and awaiting his arrival, yet the head of the table was empty. And so, I breakfasted alone, managing a meagre helping of scrambled eggs on toast before my nerves, and nausea, got the better of me. I was hoping for sustenance and jovial company . . . but nothing. Yet isn't this what I'm used to? A lifetime spent making the most of what could have been a perfect situation and yet was always devoid of the magic ingredient, because it never felt authentic. Hasn't manufacturing chocolate taught this family anything? The sweetest cocoa bean only provides the magic when mixed with the best ingredients – skimp on quality or time, on love or commitment, and you'll ruin what could have been heaven. Which only reinforces why I'm marrying my Judd, with his simple outlook, his lust for life, and his uncomplicated and selfless altruism.

Judd wouldn't care if my nails weren't manicured, my hair wasn't coiffed or my chilled bubbles weren't Bollinger. Judd only cares that I'm happy, excited and eager to say my vows at two o'clock. He openly shirks materialistic perfection, whereas my father would kick up a fuss if this Bollinger were tepid, the marquee incorrectly positioned three feet to the right, or the crease in his pocket square not pristine enough. And there, in a nutshell, is the difference.

I hope Judd and his groomsmen are having a barrel of laughs in their hotel suite. Jovial moments, shared with his mates, which can't be bought or traded in sterling, yet will last a lifetime. I imagine him tucking into a fry-up with gusto, or swigging a nip of Dutch courage from a shared hip flask. I only hope that my two sons don't rain on his parade or pull some last-minute trick to undermine him.

Right now, if I snap my fingers and ask for this glass of fizz to be changed, a platoon of maroon soldiers will scurry forward to oblige, no questions asked, no objections, because nothing is too much trouble for one of Electra's brides. Or rather, money talks by silencing the voices of others.

The truth is, I feel like a hollow porcelain doll being prettified for public inspection – no different to the medley of museum artefacts Beth cares for each day at work – posed behind glass, awaiting her fate but looking untouchable and, I suspect, rarely fulfilling her purpose in life as a much-loved doll.

I steadily sip my bubbles as my head is firmly tugged this way and that, thanks to a beast of a barrel brush expertly wielded before an industrial-sized power nozzle. There's nothing wrong with the champagne's vintage or temperature, I'm simply underwhelmed and feeling flat, consuming wedding fizz but without experiencing the tumble of hysteria befitting the special occasion. I suppose a couple of bridesmaids would have added fun to the mix at this point, but *c'est la vie*. In fact, I had more laughs at The Royal Crescent, sharing a breakfast table alongside two strangers whilst dressed as a nun. Go figure!

I could pretend, and take delight in how different the atmosphere would be if Lulu or Beth were present at this precise moment. No chance of being melancholy if I were being prepped and primped in the back kitchen of Lakeside Cottage, with cosmetics and hair products strewn across the scrubbed kitchen table – we'd be having an absolute ball. Lulu's dirty laugh would fill the air, Beth's quiet composure would be keeping order, and I would definitely feel like an excited bride-to-be instead of a woman going through the motions, sipping yet more bubbles whilst watching a glorified tent being fitted with expensive wedding baubles.

Somewhere elsewhere sits a bride-to-be without this pomp and circumstance, possibly sipping a plain orange juice whilst her hair is being dried by a friend. I imagine she feels like the Queen of Sheba, knowing that her entire family are thrilled that she's marrying the man of her choice. A lump settles in my throat;

how I wish that was me. And that's the difference between the perception and the reality; my father has thrown a shedload of money at this wedding, purely to convince others that he's the proudest father alive, when the reality is very different. How does a father spend so much money to create an illusion whilst the legal eagles work tirelessly in the background?

'Dharling, sweetie,' comes Electra's dulcet tone, drowning out the hair dryer. Her willowy couture frame darts across my line of vision like a slinky edging its way down a staircase. 'Music will disrupt the serenity of this moment ... blare, blare, blare,' she shudders theatrically, 'triggering migraines and twitchy nerves. You are wanting to experience calm and tranquil thoughts before your gorgeous gown is unveiled in five minutes. Your hair, dharling, looks *mwah* – to die for!'

'Electra, any further news from Beth?' I ask quickly, before she departs in her neurotic high-energy manner.

'Yes, yes, dharling. I've made all the phone calls necessary and fielded responses,' she says, en route to her next task. She trails a painted fingernail along the length of her cheek, as if depicting a tear, and is gone in an instant.

Oh, bless her, it wasn't an easy decision to make yesterday.

So, no background music on my wedding day, just pleasant and tranquil thoughts enforced by Dharling Electra. Yet another thing to endure and ignore, like my father's absence, the legal team's unsigned pre-nup, the blind eye turned to my sons' steadfast reluctance to accept Judd. Ultimately, the only thing that truly matters, and is vital today, are the vows I repeat to Judd – making us man and wife. Everything else is simply wedding fluff – expensive bloody fluff, but necessary fluff, all the same. I knock back my bubbles, eyeing the ice bucket and contemplating another drink, when the double doors of the morning room dramatically burst open, admitting a small army pushing a hefty wooden white cabinet on casters. At the head of the parade is

Dharling Electra, grinning like a Cheshire cat, her statement lipstick freshly reapplied and harsh against her pale skin.

'Dharling Koo, I can't wait a minute longer. Can you hear that? Listen carefully.' She dramatically leans towards the large white box, cupping her ear.

I visibly cringe at her acting; is my father paying her by the word or the action?

'This exquisite Michael Cinco creation is whispering your name, dharling. She's impatient. She's demanding. Refusing to wait another moment for the big reveal. Dharling Koo, may I introduce you to the gown you were born to wear . . .'

Oh Lord, give me strength.

With a dramatic sweep of her arm, Electra signals for the box to be opened. Two uniformed ladies scurry backwards, peeling open the cabinet doors like butterfly wings, to reveal a mannequin adorned in my wedding gown. The sunlight captures the shimmering silver embroidery sparkling against a powder-blue backdrop as the exquisitely gathered layers of tulle around the waist defy gravity with each lift and fold, gracefully cascading downwards and creating a ginormous full skirt that accentuates and compliments the fitted bodice and feminine sweetheart neckline to perfection.

'That's mine?' is all I can manage.

The hair stylist drops her hair dryer, both florists gasp amidst their orchids and foliage sprays, and the army of helpers stare from me to the gown, and back again.

'Wow, that is some g-g-gown,' I stutter, as Electra removes the empty champagne flute from my grasp.

And there it is. My wedding gown, designed and created to fit my measurements without the need for me to even slip down to my undies and parade in a short walk. It's as beautiful as I imagined, but now it's before me, the reality hits home . . . I am getting married.

'Dharling, that is an understatement! This is a Michael Cinco creation!' says Electra, heading for the ice bucket and pouring me a second glass of bubbles. 'Here. Enjoy the view, dream your dreams, and we'll have you prepped, primped and presented in your fabulous gown in precisely one hour.'

Chapter Thirty-One

Lulu

I'm surprised the rowing boat is still tied to the jetty, exactly as we'd left it. I assume if you own a boat then you use a boat – especially on a Saturday like this, when the lake is calm and the sun is glorious. I gingerly climb into the tiny vessel, my thighs and calves tender from this morning's exertion, conscious that I'm alone and without a hand to steady me – or fish me out of the lake if I fall in. I check the oars are lying along the bottom, before reaching for the rope and lifting it off the stake, untethering the boat. A rocking action unsettles me as I mimic Gareth's stance from the other night and settle myself on the bench in the centre. I wrestle the oars into the holders on either side. I'm not expecting this to be easy – Gareth struggled, despite his muscle and brawn – though the thought of my palms on the oars, overlapping his ghostly prints, brings some comfort.

The movement feels cumbersome but I can control it, if my body moves as one with the oars, and before I know it I'm moving away from the wooden jetty, crossing the lake. I've no idea where I'm heading, no destination, just an undeniable need to be surrounded by water, enormous mountains and, above me, a clear blue heaven at which to look, or cry, or wail.

Within no time, I've plenty of waves between me and the distant jetty. I can't believe I'm here and Gareth is all the way down south, getting showered and dressed, preparing for a gold ring to be placed on the fourth finger of his left hand, and pretending nothing ever happened between us. And she, Our Kirsty, is doing exactly the same, speaking vows that will bind them to each other despite the troubled knowledge locked away within their hearts.

I stop rowing, remove the oars from the brackets and place them in the bottom of the boat for safe keeping. I simply wish to drift, not for long, not far from this spot, but I want to lie down, stare up at the blue sky above and dream of happier times. When my heart wasn't heavy, my body wasn't tired and my brain didn't ache with a string of regrets – all self-inflicted wounds, but still, I need a moment of peace as the clock draws near to two o'clock. The magic hour printed on the wedding invites, pinnacle of the day's running order, and the moment when everyone who loves and cares for them will be solemnly gathered in the Church of Saints Peter and Paul in Kettering. All but me.

I shuffle from the central bench and ease myself down on to the slatted boards in the bottom of the rowing boat, the oars resting alongside me. It probably looks like the weirdest of actions, but it's surprisingly comfortable as I stretch out full length, basking in the warmth of the sun. I close my eyes, shielding them from the glare, and relax into a trance-like state – my very own Ophelia moment. I'm seeking temporary peace, to get me through the next hour while events elsewhere unfold, ensuring a different tragedy.

I can see the wedding scene before me. The pale buttermilk masonry of the church's great tower, with fresh blooms adorning the end of each pew. Guests are sitting on the polished wood in their brightly coloured finery. Our Kirsty is looking radiant in her dream gown, chosen months ago, a flowing veil trailing behind her as she prepares to walk down the aisle on the red carpet, with four tiny bridesmaids tottering behind her swinging their flower baskets. And no maid of honour present to cajole or encourage them to walk in line and smile sweetly. I won't be assisting Our Kirsty in straightening her veil, or taking her bridal bouquet or providing a supportive word or smile as the nerves take hold at the church door. An unnecessary role, rendered null and void by my own self-destructive behaviour – erased from the bridal party and the photographs for ever.

At the altar steps stands the solitary figure of Gareth, looking smart in his navy-blue suit, possibly a buttonhole spray, and a nervous glow to his forehead. What I wouldn't give to be the woman walking along the aisle towards him, to have him turn and warmly smile at me, in relief and surprise.

Why did I pursue this? Surely, I always knew the ending to this story?

The sound of Gareth's murmured 'I will' fills my head. A heavy weight presses down on my chest, crushing me.

'Hello!' The voice repeats, as if muted, in my dream. 'Hello!'

I jump at the realisation that I must have dropped off to sleep whilst imagining the scene inside the church. I scramble to sit up. The boat must have drifted back towards the edge of the lake, as I don't appear to be far from the reeds and rushes that fringe the shoreline.

On the jetty stands a figure, a blond male, hollering and waving both arms.

I squint into the sunshine. No one I recognise – though I wish it were Gareth.

I reposition the oars and manoeuvre myself back towards the gesticulating figure.

'Hello, thank you for coming back in. Are you Lulu?' asks the man, as I near the wooden jetty.

'Who's asking?' I ask, conscious that I'm alone with a stranger.

'Dale, Beth's fiancé – I'd like a word, if I could,' he says, with a shy smile.

I notice his blond hair is neatly clipped. Beth's definitely got a type – his appearance is uncannily like Nick's, though minus the heavy floppy fringe.

'How did you know I was here?' I say, securing the rope to the jetty.

'A photographer outside the cottage pointed me in this direction.'

'He's the only one remaining now, thankfully – Beth was at the cottage when I left.'

'She didn't answer when I knocked, so I got chatting to the photographer.'

'She's definitely inside – she was upset earlier, when she called Koo's wedding planner to thank her personally. I'm sorry about the way things worked out. She's put herself through the wringer this week, trying to figure out what to do for the best,' I say, sorrowfully, taking in his hurt expression.

'She's not the only one . . .' Dale shuffles awkwardly, before continuing, 'Any chance we could head back? I'd like to speak to her.'

Koo

'My darling girl, look at you!' cries my father, entering the morning room, now cleared of all wedding prep and Electra's mini army of maroon uniforms.

He looks dapper in his tailored morning suit, with his spritely gait and a huge smile adorning his tired features.

'You're truly a sight to behold,' he exclaims.

'Thank you, and you too, Dad,' I say, coming away from the French windows to receive a welcome embrace. My gown weighs more than I imagined, so I tread carefully, lifting the front hemline. 'I can't quite believe this is happening.'

'This day has been a long time coming, that's for sure,' he whispers, before releasing me.

I recognise that fact, but I'm not about to apologise for finding love later in life, so I remain silent. In less than twenty minutes, I'll be married, and such lingering sentiments will be forgotten.

'Just a little something before we leave,' he says, opening his jacket and fumbling inside his inner pocket.

I ready myself, half expecting him to withdraw a token gift, a tiny box, a precious heirloom. I only have to see the corner of the envelope to know what's inside: the folded pre-nup.

'Now, you know it makes sense, Koo.'

My heart sinks. Dressed for the finest hour of my life, and he delivers this blow – knowing my guard is down, my emotions are high and my mind is elsewhere, dreaming of what's to follow.

I don't utter a word. I calmly watch as my dad removes the paperwork, unfolds and flattens the documents on the nearest side table, and withdraws a fountain pen from his breast pocket, before looking up at me.

I compose myself before I speak, because inside I'm raging.

'So, you asked Felipe for the document?' I say, watching him intently. I know that his answer and actions come from a place of love for his only child, but sadly, not respect.

'We all want the best for you, including your boys, Koo.' His mind is as sharp as a tack. His features have aged with the years but his piercing gaze has never changed.

'And this is what you want?'

'Yes, the one thing,' he whispers, his forefinger gently tapping the paperwork.

'The one thing?'

Dad gives a tiny nod, offering me the pen.

I inhale, which feels like the deepest and longest breath of my life. My mind is made up, I didn't think it would come to this, but it has – under duress it has.

'I can do that for you, if nothing more, Dad,' I say, taking the proffered pen and unscrewing the lid.

'That's my girl,' he says, as I add my signature on the dotted line and swiftly date it: 26 August.

'Happy?' I ask, returning his pen.

'Happy,' he confirms.

His smile brightens, and he offers me the crook of his arm, which I dutifully take, though my heart is breaking.

Chapter Thirty-Two

Beth

I hurriedly divert my route along Main Street, taking the steep steps that lead up to the Church of St Michael and All Angels. The narrow steps are uneven, aged with moss, with a galvanised pole cemented at intervals as a supporting handrail, polished smooth by the congregation's hands.

I'm not a religious sort but it seems the right place to be today, at this hour, contemplating what might have been.

The steps lead to a pathway that cuts through the old grave-yard, where large granite headstones tilt at strange angles, partly toppled, like the shoulders of a gathered crowd. I glance at intervals at the faded inscriptions, the words of devotion and various dates – each a moment in time that was once painful for the departed's nearest and dearest.

The decorative arched doorway is not gated, so I enter the stone porch, passing the tired notice boards and the boot rack below the glazed leaded window – hoping the main door is unlocked. I pause to read the framed invite pinned to the door, welcoming all who enter to give thanks as they wish and to enjoy the music, architecture and handicrafts within. Just what I need.

Inside, I find a cool interior, away from the heat of the day. I look up at the heavily beamed rafters, admire the intricate wrought-iron lighting, hanging down low above the standard rows of wooden pews – dominated by an arched window of stained glass above the dressed altar. At the rear of the church is an elaborate screen of carved wood, which provides a suitable divide for the ringing room and bell ropes. The screen is home to a beautiful clock with a classic face, its delicate hands conveniently nearing the top of the hour.

'How beautiful is this,' I mutter to myself, admiring the church interior, 'much larger than I was expecting from the outside.'

I turn left and begin a slow walk along the aisle, passing the large archways and pillars, heading towards the front pews. There's a deep sense of calm in the familiarity of the signs and symbols adorning every surface, which I know will resemble those in our own church, the one that was supposed to witness our marriage come two o'clock. I settle on the front pew and sit quietly. I'm all cried out, exhausted from a week of constant thoughts and so many discussions – snippets of which appear in a series of unwelcome flashbacks, culminating in my final conversation with Electra earlier.

I simply want to sit here, whiling the time away, not thinking about choices, or weddings, or the upset I've caused my family – and most of all Dale. Kind, considerate Dale who hasn't hurried my decision but has waited patiently until I understood the workings of my own heart. Until I knew the answers.

'Beth?'

I look up to find Dale standing before the altar steps, watching me intently. His neat appearance, his solid stance and unruffled manner are exactly the same as always, despite a week of turmoil.

'Hi, how long have you been standing there?' I ask, surprised by his presence.

'Long enough to have seen the sadness etched on your face. It's going to be OK, you know? Your friend's wedding planner has handled the cancellations on our behalf, so there wasn't anything left for me to do, except I wanted to know you were alright. Truly alright, that is.'

'In a strange sort of way, I am,' I say. 'I've angered lots of people, upset and hurt many others, but I had to be honest with myself – and you.'

Dale settles himself, further along the front pew, and listens intently.

'I feel like I'm lost. Somewhere between wanting what we have and leaving behind what I once had with Nick, before I met you. I'm not sure I ever found my feet properly, between the two relationships, and it's all come crashing down around my ears since we started making our wedding plans. I honestly couldn't tell you what I want right now – but then I couldn't tell you much about the previous Beth Douglas, either. It's as if the true me has gone AWOL, and will be back shortly with some answers.' I give a weak smile, but I'm not joking in the slightest.

Dale nods. 'I realise that, as difficult as the last week has been for us both, you thought it was kinder than simply going through with the ceremony, then afterwards discovering you didn't love me—'

'I do love you,' I interrupt. 'I know that much . . . but it's whether I should be marrying you at all. Or whether, in time, I should be marrying you.'

'I see. I'm taking from that, there is a possibility that, in time, we can put things right?'

'Yes, perhaps, but first I need to sort myself out.'

Dale nods again, as if accepting my terms. I feel so guilty, he doesn't deserve such betrayal.

'We'd have been married by now,' I say, sounding brighter than I feel.

'Yep, probably be having photographs with family on the church lawn, the vicar tutting about confetti on the gravestones, and guests grumbling about what food will be served at the main reception.'

Sitting here in the calm surroundings of the church, I quite like that idea; the upheaval and planning not so much, but the security of marriage. Maybe one day.

'What's the rest of the day looking like for you?' asks Dale, as the rear doors open.

We turn in unison at the sound of a visitor bursting into the church.

'Beth!' calls Nick, striding down the aisle, a determined expression etched upon his face.

'Nick!' I say, in utter surprise. 'I thought you left yesterday!'

'Bloody great! The ex turns up,' mutters Dale. 'Just what we needed.'

'You can hold your tongue, mate! She isn't your missus yet, you know!' retorts Nick, squaring his shoulders as he nears us.

My gaze switches from one to the other, in panic.

'Pipe down, and remember where you are!' Dale retorts, irked by Nick's presence. 'Have some decorum, if nothing else. And as for my so-called "missus" – I wouldn't lower her status or insult her intelligence by referring to her in such an offensive way. No wonder she kicked you to the kerb at the first chance she got!'

'Actually, it was me that left her all those years ago, not the other way around!' corrects Nick, a smug grin on his face.

'Regretted it ever since, have you? And now, you've come back to see what you can wreck in the wake of her wedding day, given that your own fell through?' says Dale, with an air of disgust.

Nick's jaw drops.

'Come on, Beth – we need to talk,' says Dale, offering me his hand.

'How did I know he was going to reappear at that precise moment?' I say.

We're striding away from the church door, following the pathway through the graveyard, having left Nick standing speechless inside.

'Reappear? When did you last see him?' asks Dale, his tone becoming stern and his gentle manner threatening to dissolve.

'He turned up the other day when I was in Florence with Koo. Lulu spent the afternoon entertaining him with drinking games and a pack of cards whilst we travelled back and . . .'

'And you forgot to mention that?'

'No. I . . . didn't feel I needed to, Dale.'

'Didn't feel you needed to? Are you serious, Beth? I'm at home, waiting for your decision, yet you're up here gallivanting with an ex-lover?'

'Gallivanting? How dare you, Dale?' I stand stock-still in sheer temper, allowing him to walk on without me.

'Are you waiting for him?' asks Dale, turning around to view my shocked stance.

'No. But I'm certainly not accompanying you after such a suggestion.'

'So nothing happened between the pair of you when you were under the same roof?' asks Dale, retracing his steps and looking at me suspiciously.

Today has been tough enough. I don't answer him but continue to look him square in the face – Dale either trusts me or he doesn't!

'Boy oh boy, I'm hearing it all today, hey?' mutters Dale, turning on his heels and marching along the sloping driveway, avoiding the steep steps down to Main Street.

It's clear we're on very different paths.

'Beth!' hollers Nick, from the church steps. 'Wait!'

I don't wait for Nick to catch me up. Instead I take my original route, descending the stone steps and heading back towards the cottage.

I walk quickly, without shame or worry. If they wish to follow me, so be it; Nick knows where he stands after yesterday's discussion, as does Dale.

I won't refuse them entry. But I need to set my boundaries, focus on my own needs, and allow others to choose what's right for them.

I'm not demanding anything from anyone, apart from a little understanding, nothing more.

Chapter Thirty-Three

Koo

We stand in the arched doorway of St Mary's Church, awaiting the signal from the vicar to step forward and begin our slow march down the aisle. The church organ is playing a delicate introit, my bouquet of orchids smells divine and the bells are ringing. Dharling Electra quickly fluffs up my veil, repositions my elbows to make sure they're not sticking out, and pushes my bouquet lower, making sure I hold it in a natural line in front of my body, while the official photographer and his crew dance around us. An array of guests, with wide smiles and elegantly dressed in their finery, fill the wooden pews visible from the doorway, yet I don't recognise anyone. No special friend from boarding school, no partner in crime from my drinking days, no trusted girlfriend winking at me in encouragement. Just me, on the arm of my father, waiting patiently for a sign. Not that I need one after what just happened in the morning room, before our short drive to the church in the Rolls-Royce.

I imagined I would be standing here, with minutes to go, my thoughts in a whirl, worrying about Felix and Felipe standing near the altar, smartly dressed as groomsmen, my Judd twitching with nerves and pulling at his collar as he waits for me to arrive, or even my mum, her face half hidden beneath a wide-brimmed hat, poised and politely smiling at a sea of guests. But I'm not. I'm thinking solely of me. And what I want. What I need from this day forward. I've surprised myself by signing the pre-nup in the way I did, but I know it's my last offering to my father. The ultimate compromise, one step too far. I'm done.

The vicar beckons us forward, and with a last smile towards my father, I begin to walk. Dharling Electra falls in behind and the photographer moves aside, allowing my father to guide me into church. All eyes turn as the guests stand to greet us.

I see Judd's broad frame; he is waiting for me at the altar, with his best man duly beside him. I know my groom is as true as the day is long, so I can breathe easy on that score. With each step, I smile politely, a gentle nod now and then, acknowledging the presence of the hundred or so guests attending our wedding day. I beam as I see how many of Judd's family fill the pews behind him, relishing the genuine smiles they return from their hearts. That's what I want: genuine. No underlying concerns, no need to sign on the dotted line, no misgivings or financial restrictions overshadowing our day. Our lives. Our marriage. I simply want genuine.

We arrive at the altar, I blow my father a kiss from beneath my veil, and he steps aside, leaving me to stand beside Judd, who gives me a nervous but loving smile. And there it is, amidst all the materialistic debris threatening to blight our lives, that one moment shines through.

I know what I need to do, for us.

Dharling Electra steps forward to receive my bouquet, but I hold back. I see her brilliant smile falter for a second, before she twigs – I'm not handing it over.

I swiftly turn to Judd, his features unchanged, as I lean closer and whisper, 'Let's leave, now . . . just you and me.'

His brow furrows, his gaze widens in surprise – he asks no questions, I assume none are needed. And with the tiniest nod, he takes my hand and we turn around and we run – or at least, I do the best I can wearing a stunning Michael Cinco gown.

I don't hear the gasps, or my name being called, as we head

down the aisle, through the arched doorway and out into the
August sunshine, with my breath catching in my chest, my bouquet waving wildly at my side and my husband-to-be clutching
my ringless hand.

'Where now?' gasps Judd, his expression bewildered but the
light in his eyes as expressive as mine.

'I know just the place, but we'll need your car loaded with
the honeymoon luggage.'

Lulu

'Hi, Beth, did Dale find you?' I call from the snug, on hearing
the front door slam shut and footsteps plod along the hallway.

She hurries past the open doorway with no reply.

'Beth!' I quickly stand up from where I'm lounging on the
sofa, only to hear the door go a second time and witness Dale,
whom I met earlier, following in her wake.

Oh shit, this doesn't look good.

I linger in the middle of the snug, unsure what to do, expecting
to hear an argument erupt in the kitchen ... but no, the front
door sounds for a third time. Nick strides into the snug and
simply stares at me.

'And what the hell am I supposed to do now – sit it out and
wait, or simply piss off?'

'I thought you got the message loud and clear yesterday?' I
ask, stunned by his arrival.

'Maybe. But it appears I've already been replaced by him – the
current lover boy, I take it!'

'Yep, well, as current as you can get after you messed up yesterday ... a leopard never changes its spots, does it?'

Nick's eyebrows lift. 'Well, well, so girls do talk. So you know
she spent Thursday night in my room too?'

'Mm-hmm, just talking, I believe. I saw her return to her room the next morning, fully clothed. I can vouch for that much.'

'My money says you might have to, Lulu. Any drinks going?'

'Sure, plenty, but the booze is stashed in the kitchen, though please feel free to help yourself while they have their discussion. I'll have a large one, if you're brave enough.' I saunter back to my cosy sofa and sit down; there's no point standing when I can enjoy the comfort of stretching out.

'And you, any news? Or is it all done and dusted?' he asks, tapping his watch.

'*Phuh!* A two o'clock wedding will be signed, sealed and surely consummated by now. Well, it would have been if I'd been the bride,' I jest, not caring how trampy that actually sounds, given my mood today.

'No doubt about it, gal.'

Suddenly an eruption of voices is heard from the kitchen.

'Are you going to stand there, pretending you've got a chance with her, or run away from the situation, as you so honourably did yesterday?' I ask, grimacing at the noise level.

'I've messed up, again, so I'm going to go,' says Nick, gesturing towards the door.

'Too right you did! But you see, Dale didn't – so decide for yourself,' I jest, cringing at my own suggestion.

Nick gets up and leaves the snug, without a word. I'm listening for the sound of the front door slamming behind him, when I hear him say, 'She's in the snug, mate.'

'Hello?'

I hear his voice and it doesn't seem real.

'Gareth?' I stand up and dash towards the door just as he arrives and pushes it open from the other side. 'Oh Christ, it *is* you!'

'Yes, it's me, Lulu. I didn't go through with it, I couldn't. I simply couldn't,' says Gareth, before my mouth silences him with a passionate kiss.

Koo

'I've got no idea if they'll have locked the cottage door, but they're in for the shock of their lives if they haven't,' I whisper, as we sneak up the cobbled pathway, hand in hand. 'This is the delightful retreat that's been my new home for the best part of a week.'

'And the lone photographer, how long has he been camped there for?'

'I'm unsure, you know me, I rarely look at their faces in passing,' I reply, as the picket gate gives a satisfying click behind us.

'Now, I'm betting they're in the snug or the kitchen, so we can sneak in and surprise them.' I'm getting the giggles at the very thought of throwing my wedding bouquet in Beth's direction.

It's been four hours since we went AWOL, proving it was a brilliant idea to have loaded our honeymoon suitcases into Judd's car before the ceremony – perfect for a swift dash from Cheshire to Cumbria.

'Hold your fire, just one minute, Koo – tradition, I believe on your wedding night, despite us not being married,' jests Judd, his arm snaking around my back, pulling me in close and sweeping me, my bridal bouquet and Michael Cinco gown up into his arms, before striding across the threshold of the cottage.

I squeal in delight as he places me back on to my feet, planting a kiss on my forehead.

Simultaneously, two doorways burst open as four surprised faces peer into the hallway in alarm.

'We're home, but without wedding rings!' I yell, throwing my bridal bouquet into the air.

Chapter Thirty-Four

Sunday 27 August

Lulu

'Can I remind you all that Josie arrives at ten o'clock, so can you have your bags packed and decisions made by five minutes to the hour, please?' announces Koo, leaning across the breakfast table at which six hung-over adults are slowly consuming breakfast and downing their morning coffee.

'I didn't expect you to be so refreshed and alert the morning after the night before, Koo,' I say, in reply, wishing she'd lower the volume a tad. 'It's like our first morning in Bath. She was bright and bubbly, I had a crick in my neck and you had a banging headache, right, Beth?'

'Yep, exactly that, though we had bigger fish to fry, trying to locate our belongings and work out who had paid for the hotel suite,' explains Beth, before quickly adding, 'which we haven't forgotten, Koo – we just need time to organise it after the intense week we've had.'

Koo smiles politely, unconcerned amongst friends. Last night, she explained that she couldn't give any more to her family; how their high-end expectations and their controlling ways had culminated in that final forced signature, giving her father the peace of mind he wanted. But she refused to give him the fake wedding and accompanying publicity he craved.

'And the plans after ten o'clock?' asks Gareth, giving me a casual nudge.

'I'll be heading back to Kettering, to meet up with my dad and catch up on the news from yesterday,' I say, feeling slightly awkward in the presence of Our Kirsty's absent groom.

'The headlines will be the news that the groom didn't show yesterday but mysteriously went AWOL on the morning of his own wedding. I'm sure your father will have heard all the details – he was probably in church, expecting me to arrive before the bridal party,' explains Gareth, his cheeks colouring at the very mention.

'Wow! Is that what happened at two o'clock in Kettering?' asks Koo, clearly shocked by the details.

'Sadly, yes. I'm not proud of my actions, but I couldn't see it through and I'd left it too late to start a discussion. I'll face the music today and apologise.'

'To all the guests or just the bride?' prompts Dale, from the far end of the kitchen table.

'Whoever needs to hear an apology,' says Gareth, unreservedly.

'And you, Beth?' I ask, quickly wishing to change the topic of conversation.

'I'm off work for the next few weeks, as we'd planned a honeymoon at home, so I'm heading back to Bath for a few days. I thought a quiet break before returning to the same old, same old might do me some good. It wasn't a city I wanted to visit previously, but it could act as no-man's-land for a short break . . . help me to straighten out my head a little. I might even visit the Party Bus for a memorable "night-out" experience.'

'Sounds good,' says Dale. 'I'll drive you down later, if you want, drop you off, if you've booked a hotel.'

'Thank you, I'd appreciate it. It'll give us a chance to talk on the journey.'

'Dare I ask what happened to Nick?' asks Koo, draining her coffee mug, openly avoiding eye contact with Dale.

Beth glances at Dale, before explaining. 'He knew the score on Friday, but thought he'd chance his luck for a second time, turning up at the church. After which he left for a second time. I'm not sure if that officially ends things for him, or whether he expects me to fall at his feet, begging for his time and attention. I won't be doing either ... I need time to work things out on my own, and decide for myself, without pressure or constraints.'

'Too true,' I mutter, hoping Dale heeds her request.

'And you pair, the happily unmarried – what are your plans?' asks Beth, becoming instantly doe-eyed.

'We are jetting off on our honeymoon today – a ten-day trip to Florence!' announces Koo, beaming with excitement.

'Are you serious?' I shriek.

'But you've only just come back,' hollers Beth, looking to Judd for confirmation.

'Yep, she's right. A full ten days of waking up in Florence – that's all my wife-to-be wants. How can I say no?' jests Judd, wrapping his arm around Koo's slender shoulders.

'Unbelievable,' I gush, not sure whether I admire her for her simplicity or am dumbfounded.

'Our mini-mini-break was all I wanted with a girlfriend ... but this is all I'll need with my husband-to-be,' she says coyly. 'Anyway, we'd best make a move if we're going to catch our flight.'

'Can I remind you that some people haven't written in the guest book yet,' I holler over the noise of six kitchen chairs being hurriedly vacated as people prepare to clear their rooms of luggage and belongings ahead of Josie's arrival.

*　　*　　*

'I hate goodbyes,' I moan, hugging Koo on the doorstep, bracing myself for her departure.

'It's not goodbye, but simply bye for now. You'll see me in a couple of weeks – and I'll want to know how long that bridal bouquet of mine lasted in water.'

'Yes, thank you for that. I honestly thought Beth would be like a whippet out of a trap – I still can't believe I caught it.' I release Koo from our hug and wipe a tear from my eye.

'Using your elbows as lethal weapons proved helpful,' jests Beth, stepping in from the sidelines to give Koo a parting hug.

The three fellas stand on the path, making polite small talk, waiting until we're ready to leave.

'I see the solo pap guy has left,' I say, gesturing towards the garden wall.

'Nothing else to see, is there?' says Beth. 'The interesting stuff with the nuns and bikes was earlier in the week. He's probably gone home to his family for a quiet weekend before stalking a different celebrity next week.'

'I'm not a celebrity, thank you very much!' states Koo, indignantly.

'That's the first time I've seen you get huffy in a week, Koo. The term "celebrity" not your bag, hey?' I say, taken aback by her reaction.

'No way. I try to earn my corn each week, unlike some of those in the glossies. Come on now, we need to leave, otherwise we'll be cutting it fine,' says Koo, sending us each an angel kiss from the tips of her fingers.

Judd peels away from the men after they've exchanged parting handshakes. Beth and I stand on the doorstep as the happy couple make their way along the cobbled path towards their waiting car, which has already been loaded with their honeymoon cases – and a stunning gown to be delivered back to her home address.

'Koo!' hollers Beth from the doorstep, making our honeymooners turn around mid-step. 'Make sure you turn left when you board the plane – I'd hate you to fall into the habit of turning right and missing your luxury.'

Epilogue

Sunday 1 October

Beth

The bridal bouquet lifts high into the air against a backdrop of brilliant blue sky. The bell-shaped petals of lily of the valley tumble amidst an array of emerald foliage, with white satin ribbons fluttering behind, slowly descending towards a sea of outstretched hands – ringless and hopeful – waiting to snatch, grasp and claim this wedding honour as theirs.

A gathering of older relatives and some married friends observe from the sidelines as a group of ten wedding guests – mainly women, with a smattering of men – jostle shoulder to shoulder, hands frantically waving, whilst their undignified scrambling celebrates this age-old tradition.

Despite the designer labels, six-inch heels and perfectly coiffed hair, there are no boundaries – socially, ethically or morally – which can't be breached within this huddle. Each guest is willing the bouquet to divert from its current course, making its way into their outstretched hands. Dreaming that today will be their lucky day, filled with promises of joyful nuptials and a lifetime of happy-ever-after.

It's every woman or man for themselves.

Like a rugby lineout, we jump in unison, reaching for the prize. Though I feel it's pointless; I truly believe that whatever is intended for you won't pass you by!

'I didn't stand a chance, did I?' I whisper to Lulu.

We're standing in a small huddle, watching the proceedings beneath the great stone tower of St Mary's Church.

'You're not ruthless enough, Beth. Though you'll enjoy throwing the bouquet yourself come June,' replies Lulu, eagerly.

'Too true. I'll happily retire from my singleton days and willingly accept my new marital status,' I vow, knowing my journey to blushing bride could have occurred before now, if it wasn't for my honesty.

'How are things with you and Dale?' asks Lulu, with genuine warmth for a friend, glancing at my fiancé who is chatting with her partner, Gareth.

'All good. I've had to face up to the difficulties I encountered before I cancelled our previous wedding, and it hasn't been easy. But I was lost amongst the tulle and the taffeta and the arrangements for the hen party – blinded by the enormity of the commitment. Nick Kennedy amounted to a mere distraction I could have done without. He's simply a chancer in life, nothing more – I can see that now. I needed to explore all the possibilities before finding my way. I'm still as embarrassed as hell for cancelling, and my mother certainly hasn't forgiven me for bringing shame on the family, but still – we're in a stronger position as a couple, starting married life with no secrets and no regrets. My bosses at the castle were understanding but certainly haven't forgiven me for calling in sick, or forgetting to be in touch, though maybe I lost my head that week with all the pressure. And you?'

Lulu's expression instantly melts. 'Never better, Beth. Honestly, we're so happy. It's been difficult explaining things to the family. But Our Kirsty seems to be coping remarkably well, which has helped others accept what happened.'

'That's good to hear.' I glance across to our newly married couple, posing beside their wedding car, preparing to lead the way to their wedding reception. Koo looks radiant in her stunning blue gown. 'Look how proud Judd is of his bride!'

'Idyllic, isn't it? He's certainly come through and proved his love for Koo. Though we're privileged to be included in the wedding party at such an intimate wedding,' says Lulu, glancing around at the other guests. 'And today, Koo has the wedding that she truly wanted.'

'Apparently, Judd's refused to give up his role with the council, so Koo's happily supporting his choice. Her father's still as disgruntled as ever with her for skipping out on the previous wedding, but her sons are coming around to the idea . . . slowly. And, the signed pre-nup makes for an interesting talking point, framed and displayed on their dining room wall!'

'And she's wearing her gorgeous Michael Cinco wedding gown – which is truly stunning,' adds Lulu.

'On that note, I can cheekily tell you, in strictest confidence, that Koo's allowing me to borrow it for our Seychelles beach wedding next June,' I say, bursting with excitement.

'How wonderful! I bet she'll willingly give you Dharling Electra's contact number too, if you wish – but I doubt you'd want it.'

'No thanks, I'll pass – she sounds like a nightmare. Talking of which, did you see this?' I delve into my handbag, producing a folded page from a glossy mag. 'As you know, I never buy the glossies, but with so many of the press pack camped outside the cottage I couldn't resist. And look what I found!' I offer Lulu the folded page and watch as her face lights up in delight at the image before her: a radiant bride being carried over the threshold of a picturesque cottage, with an ancient wisteria in full bloom creating a natural frame around the happy couple.

'Aww, what a gorgeous shot – we'll have to book another weekend away, once you return from the Seychelles.'

'I'll hold you to that, Lulu – and this time we'll insist on dividing the bill rather than one generous lady picking up the whole tab and refusing our contribution.'

'Maybe, but you know what Koo's like when it comes to her dear friends.'

I nod, and give her arm an affectionate squeeze, before carefully tucking the photo back in my bag. A beautiful reminder of a momentous week and our summer dreams at the Lakeside Cottage.

Acknowledgements

Thank you to my editors, Nicola Caws, Kate Byrne, Celine Kelly and everyone at Headline Publishing Group for believing in my storytelling and granting me the opportunity to become part of your team.

To David Headley and the crew at DHH Literary Agency – thank you for the unwavering support. Having a 'dream team' supporting my career was always the goal – you guys make it the reality!

Thank you to my fellow authors/friends within the Romantic Novelists' Association – you continue to support and encourage me every step of the way. I'll never forget the delightful drive from the Midlands to Penrith, in Cumbria, on a Friday evening to attend my first RNA summer conference after a day at school – the scenic route towards great company!

A daily 'thank you' to The London Writers' Salon at www.writershour.com and the thousands of writers from around the world whom I sit alongside in silence and write numerous times each day. We may not be together, but something magical occurs at each session!

A heartfelt 'thank you' to a naughty little rabbit in a blue coat with brass buttons – who led me to the delightful villages of Near Sawrey and Hawkshead, inspiring a new series of books!

A reluctant 'thank you' to Wordsworth – I honestly thought I'd left 'Extract from The Prelude' behind in a previous career but I couldn't ignore the young scholar of Hawkshead Grammar School whilst mesmerised by the beauty of the lakes.

A five-star 'thank you' to The Sun Boutique and Lounge Hotel and The Queens Head, Main Street, Hawkshead, Cumbria, for welcoming a weary but excited author on her travels – where I found good people, excellent food and a beautiful four-poster bed!

A shout-out to all the 'hens' reading this book, may your weekend of celebration be filled with love, laughter and loyal company, because girls really do just want to have fun!

Unconditional thanks to my family and closest friends, for always loving and supporting my adventures – wherever they take me. Fond memories of my paternal grandmother, Dorothy – whose garnet ring was included in the story.

And finally, thank you to my wonderful readers. You continue to thrill me each day with your fabulous reviews and supportive emails. I'm truly humbled that you invest precious time from your busy lives in reading my books. Without you guys, my characters, stories and happy-ever-afters would simply be daydreams.

Don't miss another feel-good read
from Erin Green, coming soon!

CHRISTMAS WISHES
AT THE LAKESIDE COTTAGE

REVIEW

Sunny stays at the Shetland hotel

The perfect place for fresh starts, friendship and changing your life!

a Shetland Christmas carol

Curl up this Christmas with the new feel-good read for the holiday season from Erin Green!

Available now from

REVIEW

from Shetland, with love

**An uplifting novel about how friendship
can blossom in the most unexpected places . . .**

Available now from

from Shetland, with love at Christmas

Spend the holiday season in glorious Lerwick!

Available now from

REVIEW

New Beginnings at Rose Cottage

Don't miss this perfect feel-good read of friendship and fresh starts from Erin Green, guaranteed to make you smile!

Available now from

REVIEW

Taking a Chance on Love

The perfect feel-good, romantic and uplifting read –
another book from Erin Green sure to warm your heart.

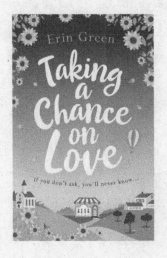

Available now from